MW01165560

Also by Marc Estrin

NOVELS

Insect Dreams: The Half Life of Gregor Samsa

The Education of Arnold Hitler

Golem Song

The Lamentations of Julius Marantz

NON-FICTION

reCreation: Some Notes on What's What and What You Might Be Able To Do About What's What

Rehearsing with Gods: Photographs and Essays on The Bread and Puppet Theater (with photographer Ronald T. Simon)

NOTES BY

Alexei Pigov

EDITED BY

Marc Estrin

ARTWORK BY

Delia Robinson

Unbridled Books

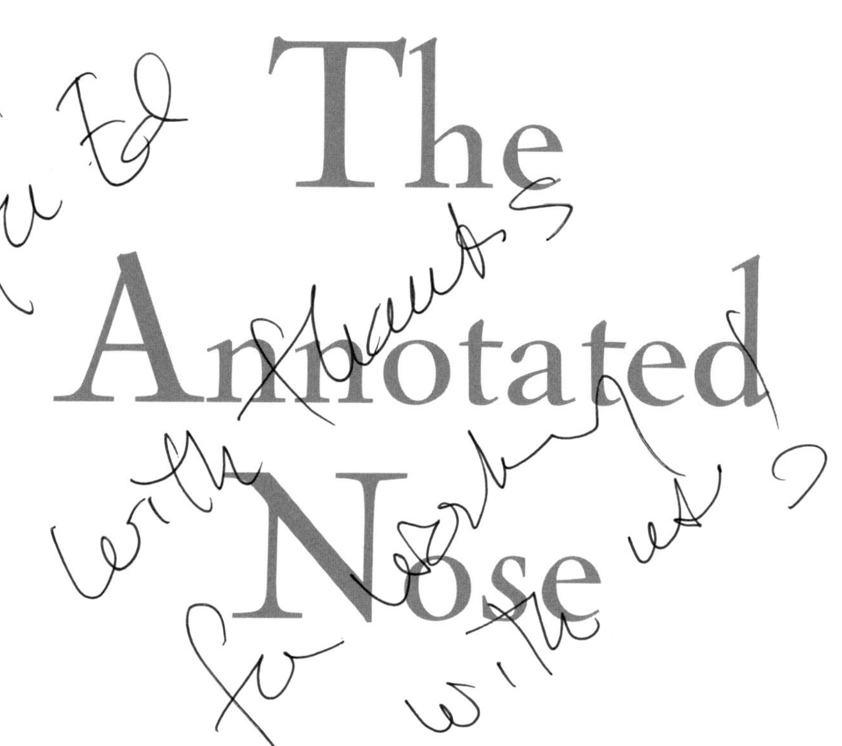

An annotated edition of

William Hundwasser's cult classic

THE NOSE

· *engorged with A COMPLAYNT by the subject of the work* ·

This is a work of fiction. The names, characters, places and incidents are either the product of the author's imagination or are used fictitiously, and any resemblance to actual persons living or dead, business establishments, events, or locales is entirely coincidental.

Unbridled Books
Denver, Colorado

Library of Congress Cataloging-in-Publication Data

Estrin, Marc.
The annotated Nose : an annotated edition of
William Hundwasser's cult classic The nose / artwork by Delia Robinson ;
engorged with a complaynt by the subject of the work ;
notes by Alexei Pigov ; edited by Marc Estrin.
p. cm.
ISBN 978-1-932961-57-7 (hardcover) — ISBN 978-1-932961-60-7 (pbk.)
1. Experimental fiction. I. Title.
PS3605.S77A84 2008
813'.6—dc22
2008029627

1 3 5 7 9 10 8 6 4 2

Book Design by SH • CV

First Printing

For J. M.

Editor's Introduction

In the spring of 2004, I was invited to join my daughter, a student at the University of Vermont College of Medicine, on a class trip. Her History of Medicine group would be attending a talk by an extraordinary visiting lecturer at an extraordinary time: midnight. I don't usually stay up late, but she assured me that this was not to be missed—even by me. She e-mailed the announcement in the medical college newsletter:

MEDICAL HISTORY · INFECTIOUS DISEASE · COMMUNITY MEDICINE

On Friday, April 23, 2004,

Dr. A. St. Paphnutius will present a talk on

The Contemporary Plague:

An Approach to Prevention and Treatment.

MIDNIGHT, FLYNN THEATER, BURLINGTON.

COME PREPARED

"Come prepared for what?" I asked.

"For everything," she said.

Evidently she knew something I didn't.

An aging, scholarly adult, I am not often invited out to midnight events, but I napped that day, took a No-Doz at 7, and was ready to add to my store of experience. Perhaps, I thought, it might be something useable in a book.

The Flynn is a glorious art deco movie house built in 1930 and recently renovated to serve Burlington's major artistic events. We arrived at a quarter to 12 and found a huge crowd spilling out onto Main Street, trying to purchase tickets. And what a crowd!

I've lived in Burlington for almost forty years, and I never knew such people existed. Maybe they *don't* before 10 P.M. But from 10 to midnight they must put on costumes and makeup, and then: zombies, ghouls, vamps and vampires, bleeding, crippled, ghastly. The strangest cohort of all was a large flock of black-gowned, bird-masked figures with yard-long beaks and goggled eyes, elevated above the general crowd by platformed shoeware.

"Those are the plague doctors," my daughter explained.

Such was my introduction to the subject which would engulf the next several years of my life.

Once inside the auditorium, I took my seat among a group of medical students—a small island of sanity in a sea of controlled pandemonium. All seats were filled, and people were standing along the walls and sitting up and down the aisles. In front of the velvet curtain, stage center, stood a lectern beautifully painted with medieval bird figures like many of those surrounding us, strange black fowl walking among a sea of red-spotted victims, dying, presumably, from bubonic plague.

At midnight precisely, the executive director of the Flynn appeared stage right, welcomed the crowd, thanked the Northfield Savings Bank and UVM medical school for sponsoring the event, and said it was after her bedtime and she had to go home to sleep.

Laughing, cheering, whooping, whistling, stamping, applauding, though for what, I wasn't sure.

The house lights went down, a Dies Irae began a slow crescendo on the sound system, and at the word "Sybilla," a long yellow beak appeared, stage right. Then, with a dramatic leap out from the proscenium—The Nose.

This time, pandemonium unalloyed.

The speaker, lit by a follow spot, walked slowly to the lectern with a leashed black rat in tow. He waited patiently for the Dies Irae to end and the crowd noise to die down.

"Dearly Afflicted," he began, the crowd accompanying him as he intoned the words. How did they know what he would say? He next addressed a short speech to the rat. Again, the crowd repeated certain phrases with him, as a congregation does with a priestly text.

Seeing my perplexity, my daughter whispered to me that this was all out of the book.

"What book?"

"*The Nose.*"

"Gogol's story?"

"No. Hundwasser's *The Nose*. The book. This is the cult book's cult."

All became darkly clear.

I found the event so extraordinary that the very next morning I made my way to Barnes & Noble and found Hundwasser's work still featured in the window. With that as reading material, I took the afternoon bus to Boston to attend the next midnight's performance. Though my daughter accused me of being a groupie, I was going merely as the scholar I am.

I needed to know: How could such an event take place in the twenty-first century? I could understand if it were some religious gathering with healings, conversions, and speaking in tongues. But it wasn't. The Boston fans, while most enthusiastic, seemed perfectly rational about the affair. The naked dancers got competently naked and were competently egged on and ogled. People signed up, wrote legibly, and accurately performed the chants and anthems, culminating in a beautifully done – even poignant—version of "CAUTION: THE MOVING WALKWAY IS ABOUT TO END." The Nose's speech was basically the same.

I had slept on the bus, my recorder batteries were charged, and I was prepared to stay up late, doing interviews. My orienting question was "What is it about The Nose that brings you here?"

The answers ranged from a teenager's "He's like so [expansive hand gestures], and I'm like [head-shaking], I . . . I'm like, you know, Jeez!" to a more sedate, if less expressive, "Well, Nose events represent a comprehensive undoing of the transcendental basis for constituting the social order. How could I *not* be here?" This latter from a Harvard professor. I could see it would be hard to find the mean between these two reactions without extensive traveling and interviewing, but my next sabbatical would not come round for five years.

So I thought I would write to someone who had been at every event and had experienced a wide variety of fans—The Nose himself: Alexei Pigov. His website was easily googled, and his "Contact the Nose" link yielded an email business address. I described my project and asked him if he might want to contribute something from his point of view.

While waiting for a reply, I did a Lexis-Nexus search about this Nose phenomenon, which had entirely escaped me until then. What I found turned out to confirm The Nose's report (Note 88): the sequence of development, the book, the dolls, the film, the merchandising, the costumes, the dances, the events—all were corroborated by articles in major newspapers around the world. The PR approach, Operation Able Ibis, "The Nose Knows" campaign, the mystery—all had worked out exactly as Alexei and Hundwasser had hoped.

William Hundwasser remained—and remains—mysterious. He must have had the shortest listing in all of Contemporary Authors: "Hundwasser, William (1951–), author of *The Nose*." That was it. I googled him: nothing except references to him as the author of said work. In spite of his appearances reported in the book, none of the fans I spoke with could remember anyone except rat girls leading the cheers and taking the signatures.

My curiosity was piqued. Hundwasser's Beverly Hills address and phone were unlisted—not uncommon in that zip code. Fomite Press would not reveal the address to which they sent his royalty checks. A FOIA request for any FBI record remained unanswered. His trail made Pynchon's and Salinger's look like four-lane highways.

Six weeks after my query concerning the nature and motivation of *The Nose's* fans, I received the following e-mail:

From: AP <doktor1@adelphia.net>

Subject: Fans

Date: June 17, 2004 11:37 AM EST

To: Marc Estrin <mestrin@mac.com>

Reply-To: AP <doktor1@adelphia.net>

Dear Professor Estrin,

My fans know nothing, in the most complete meaning of "knowing nothing." They understand nothing except those rare truths to which the heart has direct access.

We meet habitually at our Incoherency Balls, where they are usually high on me, but up to something low. Ennui has absorbed their possibilities. My calls to invoke the cortex go unheeded; they live the life of the swarm. The whole affair is stupidity in action, in which my fans demonstrate nothing but the nicer quibbles of nonexistence, and give various shapes to vacancy. As ee cummings once wrote, "we sans love equals mob." I don't mean to indulge in invective. They are, after all, my bread & butter. But hard as I try to un-nail them from themselves, I find that theirs is a more-than-average abyss, and their being undead is not quite equivalent to being alive.

But one must strike. One must bite into those shrapnel-chip cookie-dough beings. Their subsequent angst may force them to seek solutions and perhaps turn to a teacher—most likely me. But at this point one has to do everything for them by creating conditions that threaten. Knowledge—from the purest of mathematics to the darkest overtones of art—is not made to calm the soul but to disturb it.

Though they may be bored with my profundity and loftiness, they do not protest. So I am free to expose the inanity of their plans and intentions, to spoil their rituals as much as I can in the name of that anger which all errors of style, all distortion, all flights from reality, arouse in authentic beings.

I am sorry I can't take more time to answer to your provocative question as I am heavily engaged in composing a comprehensive set of notes to Mr. Hundwasser's one and only opus. Perhaps someday they may be published and my reputation reclaimed.

Sincerely,
A. St. Paphnutius, Nose

I immediately imagined presenting the public with the story of his struggle and wrote back proposing a series of extensive interviews toward a scholarly study of The Nose phenomenon, or perhaps an authorized, magisterial biography. The Nose proposed in turn that we collaborate on an annotated edition of Hundwasser's book, using his notes and my editorial guidance.

I shortly received in the mail 240 pages of yellow legal paper, tightly scrawled upon in almost illegible script. This was the first taste of the reality of collaboration. But in deciphering and transcribing the notes to a file, I discovered an entirely different, perhaps unique, dimension to The Nose's existence—not the conflict between performer and audience but the pain-filled combat of a literary character with his author. An *Annotated Nose* would be no Pirandellian metatheatrical trope. These were real people, dueling with the conflicting vectors of their visions. Not every one and one make two.

I was perfectly placed to mediate between them. But I had to convince my publishers that such a work would enhance their list. The first difficulty was to obtain the rights to reprint

Hundwasser's book as part of an Unbridled annotated volume. Fomite Press was not above making extra money off an already cash-producing cow. They sold Unbridled the rights for annotated publication only and continued to push their own far smaller, more convenient volume with its iconic drawings, consigning my offering, *The Annotated Nose*, to scholars, psychiatrists, and literary readers in quality book clubs.

Having lived with the Hundwasser-Alexei struggle for the last three years, I often find myself unwontedly melancholy. But, as the latter might say, a bit of kvetching now and then does fuel the principle of Hope.

Alexei, though, did far more than kvetch. His fans benefitted mightily from his presence and urgings. There they are, a cohort of people—young and old—so fed up with orthodoxy and the mundane bit parts it offers that they actually *do* something about it—something imaginative, colorful, different. Together they create a carnival of antiorthodoxy and fantasize, at least, about a condition of authenticity. Their collective reality may be unreal, a badge of conformity even, a token of identity for self-protection, to mitigate the discomforts of genuine independence. But still.

Some of the younger fans may even be stupid, as Alexei often implies. But, as Flaubert joked, "To be stupid, selfish, and have good health are three requirements for happiness," adding sardonically that "if stupidity is lacking, all is lost."

Above all, I think the meaning of the Nose phenomenon, fading now, is fundamentally this: facts, as Ken Kesey noted, are mainly dull. People are up to their ears in facts; what they want is Story. What they need is Story.

MARC ESTRIN
Burlington, Vermont
December 2007

NOTE TO THE READER ON THE LAYOUT

FROM ALEXEI PIGOV,

SUBJECT, OBJECT,

AND TRUTHTELLER!

Look, if you want to read William Hundwasser's *The Nose*, then by all means go buy a copy of William Hundwasser's *The Nose*. A lot of other people have. I'll still get my 3%, so you don't have to worry about me.

But this isn't William Hundwasser's *The Nose*. It's my corrective comments on that ridiculous book. If you want to skip them, just return this book, and get Hundwasser. You'll save the price of a good lunch or two.

I gather from our email exchange that Mr. Estrin is a nice man, genuinely interested in my issues. He is, however, narrowly academic in his conception of notes, conceptually limited, like his word-processor no doubt, to footnotes and endnotes. NOT GOOD ENOUGH! I want you to know when Hundwasser is fabricating at the very moment he fabricates so you don't accept Hundwasser's views, and then, maybe, later, read the corrections — if you can find them.

I had to threaten to contact another publisher unless Mr. Estrin and Unbridled Books agreed to make my notes visually available, directly related to Hundwasser's text, just over on the right,regardless of cost. SO READ THE NOTES ALONG THE WAY, and get your money's worth.

No peace without justice!

THE NOSE

William Hundwasser

Contents I

1. Original Nose *22*

Fresh Air

Postpartum Expression

2. Childe Groucho *50*

First Love

Meet the Wife

3. Excursus on Noseism
or You May Skip This Chapter, Pignut,
if All You Want Is Plot. *78*

4. The Horror, the Horror *92*

First Love

Soothing the Savage Breast

The Courtship of Graulexei Pigov

Eine Symphonie des Grauens

5. Cyranocchio *138*

First Love

The Good Doctor . . .

. . . and His Nurse

Cyrano Unbound

The Fungus Pygmies

Hysterica Musico

Tarentella con Fuoco

Allegro Agitato, con Fuoco e Appassionato

1.

Reader,

Dear Reader,

Dearly Afflicted Reader,

Hypocrite lecteur, mon semblable, mon frère,

Beware, oh Beware.

Or as the poseur Hundwasser might say, "Caveat lector." Throughout *The Nose*, Hundwasser makes me sound like some raving madman. But I am not a raving madman: I am a rather sober rationalist, an artist, perhaps even a genius of sorts, admittedly seeking freedom—and the marvelous. But more importantly, I am an honest man: I cannot and will not speak or write dishonestly.

I intend to use these notes to try to describe Mr. Hundwasser's and my—let's say—greatest misunderstandings, and may the black Azazel carry me off this instant and bear me beyond the gates of Gehenna if I tell a lie.

WH would imply that I am ripe for the madhouse. About this assertion, I would note that even the mad are men of their time. But I am not mad. I am no more neurotic than the majority of readers out there. I am logical. My brain is neither bolloxed nor mildewed. The word "bolloxed," of course, evolves directly from "balloks," Middle English for "testicles," though the relevance of testicles to my point is unclear. But I have often thought about testicles with respect to beavers. That is, to the tradition, recorded by Leonardo da Vinci in his *Bestiary Physiologus*, that—well let me quote him directly:

6. Scarabmouche de La Mancha *224*

In the Mountain

La Commedia è Stupenda!

First Love

Meanwhile, Back at the Great Lawn,

Swashbuckling—the Theory

Swashbuckling—the Practice

A Scarabmouche of Rueful Countenance

7. Pantalone *262*

First Love

. . . Along with His Nurse

First Love

The Way of Perfection

8. Feeling Nasty *318*

Left-Handed Violinist

Saint Punch

How I Long to Be in That Number

Evolution of the Bird

9. Plague Doctors *362*

First Love

In His Steps

10. Spectacle *378*

. . . His Winning Stump Spectacle

11. Belle Lettre *396*

12. Epilogue *406*

"Of the beaver one reads that when it is pursued, knowing this to be on account of the virtue of its testicles for medicinal uses and not being able to escape, it stops: and in order to be at peace with its pursuers, bites off its testicles with its sharp teeth and leaves them to its enemies."

Now, that does have some relevance, at least to one stage of my career. But both WH and I will trudge that terrain when we get to it.

William Hundwasser's calumny, *The Nose*, has ruined my life. With these annotations, constituting my complaint—or Complaynt, to distinguish it more clearly from something that might be submitted to a customer service representative—I protest. I say, I protest.

For quite a few years now, I have been held captive by Hundwasser's plan for me, self-seeking and manipulative; I have been reduced to a mere character in his script, riding behind him into seriousness a thing begun in jest; I am no longer myself, nor do I have the capacity to simply revert, since I am surrounded and confined by the fanatics he has packed onto my life; I am unable to fall, even if fall I would, without bringing tens of thousands of lives down with my own. I will have more to say about this. But that I seek freedom for myself and others is the *sine qua non* of my Poetry and Truth.

I don't want to play Captain Obvious, but let me spell out three of the central notions of what follows—at least on my right-hand note pages (myself being in the right):

A. In order to escape from the darkness of the world, to find a way toward light and love, we each need to create some personal originality, some-

1.

Original Nose

thing innovative, utterly new, utterly beautiful. Hundwasser would have you believe that my path from Groucho to Plague Doctor was simply because I couldn't get girls. Baloney!

My precession through the nose-masks represented a simple but total rejection of our blinkered civilization. The existing order cries out to be negated, transformed, traded in for some realm beyond immediate choices, some terra incognita of infinite possibilities. That would be me. Or was me until hundwassered.

But even hundwassered, my life pattern is still an exemplary work of art demonstrating for humanity a path out of slavery. Forward toward a world of beauty, love, and dignity! Each of you may escape the humdrum through a different gate. But caveat actor—there are also millions of doors leading to fields of betrayal.

B. OK, so I *couldn't* get any girls. Chalk it up to savoir-vivre sans savoir-faire. Or perhaps some personality disorder—I do want to avoid congratulatory self-deception. But I think the most likely explanation is that being incapable of restraint, I have always demanded everything. The problem is: I don't really know how to sift all the debris found in an identity-construction zone.

In premodern societies, individuals did not undergo identity crises—one of the more loathsome terms (along with the word "I") of the cult of psychology. But really, what could be more confusing than to have "greatness" thrust—commercially!—upon one? Upon me, for instance. Greatness is a cheap whore, and Hundwasser wanted me to wrap myself in my "greatness," to get drunk on it, to identify myself with it. I will not.

Perhaps I should found an entirely new genre of greatness, a difficult, aristocratic, private one, incomprehensible to the mob. I'll think about it. At the same time, while rejecting my admirers, I mustn't be reactive or transgress

the boundaries of normality. I mustn't go so far as peeing on anyone's white rug.

C. I find dishonest honesty exhausting. And yet my strength may lie precisely in some disclosure of my weaknesses. At 57, thoughts drift up like bubbles from the toxic swamps of memory. Therefore, I, Alexei Pigov, will try to guide us both—myself and you, the reader—through hundreds of Hundwasser's idiotic assertions. I will take you backstage in my being, I will expose the unknowns of my personal algebras. I will not be someone else, living someone else's life, recalling someone else's memories, dreaming someone else's dreams. I will not be the prisoner of William Francis Hundwasser—nor should you be.

He was born nose-first.[2] Obstetricians call it "mentum [chin]-first," politely finessing the issue, while Spanish midwives call it "Dar a luz"—giving oneself to light, if light may be smelled. Today, in lower Manhattan, it would automatically trigger a C-section. In the '50s, thank God,[3] it didn't.

But his medical team proceeded more carefully than usual as his was a history of presumptive prenatal trauma, he being the survivor of an unsuccessful second-trimester abortion. At crowning, or nosing, no one knew what might follow. After her unsuccessful attempt at termination, and still swelling apace, Mom was absolutely opposed to any further meddling below her belt, even if done by the highest-tech ultra–this or that. *Especially* if done by the highest-tech ultra–this or that: she had had enough of science.

Consequently, the doctors and nurses and residents, the EMTs who had brought her in, and even some of the hospital cleaning staff packed into the delivery room, masked and scrubbed, to see what would emerge. Mom was not too happy with the crowd, but when informed that this was a teaching hospital, she succumbed to the charm of being an instructor—a first for a sixteen-year-old who had dropped out of Seward Park High School.

Baby Boy Doe (Mom wouldn't give her name) was unexpectedly healthy, with an Olympian Apgar. His eyes were more slitty than doe-like, swollen perhaps, but his face was plump and pink, his primal scream forte and of great musical interest.

There was one oddity. You guessed it. His nose, as measured by a first-year resident, was 1.618 times as large in every dimension as the mean nose measurement of Caucasian children born in the United States between 1929 and 1962 (the last year statistics were

2. It is perhaps too early to stick my nose in, so to speak—after Mr. Hundwasser's very first sentence. But here we see a prime example, paradigmatic, as it were, of an error and an attitude endlessly encountered in Hundwasser's novel: "He was born nose-first."

Question: how does he know? Answer: he doesn't.

He might have asked me, you might say. We were friends—or at least close associates. But I wasn't there either. I mean, I was there, but I have very little memory of that moment. In fact, no memory. So it wasn't I who told him, nor is my initial orientation on my birth certificate, nor could I locate my medical records at St. Vincent's Hospital. They wouldn't show them to me. Confidential. Hundwasser is making things up, always has, always will, world without end. But no amen.

3. I find this a puzzling remark. More than puzzling—disconcerting, suspicious-making. The last time my mother is mentioned in Hundwasser's book is halfway along, in the Scarabmouche chapter, the one with her hospital visit after she has been abandoned by the good Antonio. After that, nada, zippo. Why? It wasn't the last interaction I had with her—there were many more, some quite worthy of report. Her belief in the salutary effects of repression and punishment for her child never wavered; her high barbarism grew ever more intense; and she, like me, was always guided primarily by revolt. An interesting subject for a novel, no? A standard focus for any backstory. So why is she all of a sudden absent?

It was not as if Mr. Hundwasser didn't discuss her with me, not at all. In fact, if one were to do a frequency analysis, I would say she was if not our most frequent topic, well, high up there. At the time I thought he was just doing his Sigmund Freud act, you know: "Tell me

available). Alert readers may recognize this number: it is the famous "golden mean," discovered by the Greeks, that ratio in which the whole is to the greater part as that part is to the smaller part (i.e., 1 to 1/2 ($\sqrt{5}$ + 1)), a proportion that is considered to be particularly pleasing to the eye.

In his case, the result was not so pleasing. Though minimized by the fat cheeks, the ruddiness around it, and the unadmitted grotesqueness of the newborn, the fact, plain and simple, was that this kid had a big nose. And this was a big nose at an age in which little, "cute" noses were the developmental norm. As one does with a small puppy with huge paws, one wondered what the future might hold. And wonder they did, the doctors, nurses, residents, EMTs, and cleaning staff present at the birth. It was the topic of conversation at fourteen dinner tables on the evening of January 26, 1951.

Meanwhile, he lay there in his polystyrene manger, swaddled in a hospital johnny, the once-fresh clouds of glory fast disappearing in the fluorescent light. He was surrounded not by ox and ass (though some of them may have turned out to be so) but by cohorts who all shared the birthday of Douglas MacArthur. Nose above and tush below, he lay there sleeping and forgetting, considering his next move.

Fresh Air

In considering our hero's earliest years, it is best not to neglect their backstory. The following transcript has not only proven invaluable for this biography but has initiated a burgeoning new field of peripsychonatal studies. It is reproduced here, courtesy of National Public Radio.

Transcript of The Nose and Terry Gross, host of NPR's Fresh Air.[4] Originally broadcast August 15, 2005.

TERRY GROSS: From WHYY in Philadelphia, this is Fresh Air! I'm Terry Gross. Our guest today has walked the line between famous and notorious for the last half century. As a child, he made medical history, proposing and undergoing the first known nose-

I am the victim of all this making up. You wouldn't like it either if someone wrote lies about you and published them, and the book was on the *New York Times* best-seller list for more than a year, and they made a film about you when "you" wasn't even you but Matt Damon with a lousy makeup job. I mean, I do understand artistic license. I'm an artist myself, you know, with an anarchic breeze ever blowing through my mind. And it's true I never had a customary nose. But kyrie eleison, after all this I have the right to have a metaphysical shit-fit, and you should be happy that these notes are not scratch-and-sniff.

4. Artistic license, ok. At least subject to the objections in my Note 1. But is artistic license also a license to pan-

about your mother." Essential for a modern novelist. But that "Thank God" . . . what is *that* all about?

The dog that didn't bark, the mother that did not appear. Anastasia, that strutting enigma, always wavering between street wisdom and stupidity, might very well have taken Hundwasser on—and he, her. She was always dressed to get messed—he liked that, it turned him on. And she, heavy with transience, might have mistaken his enthusiasm for her son as indicating the possibility for a permanent attachment. Also, he had become rich, always an attractor.

He was young enough to be her son, but what aging beauty is not drawn to younger men, in part to flatter their vanity, in part to negate the passing of their years? A woman like my mother, loved and left and loved and left again, lives in great danger of lethal repetition, bouncing her life away with ever less amplitude and ever greater frequency, like an aging SuperBall. And yet she, in the blinders of her narcissism, would be the last to notice the pattern, the accumulation of similar crises, then fragments, then wisps. Always riding the subway named Desire, a woman who cultivates intrusions will never recognize the role of intruder.

Hundwasser and my mother. How obvious. Why haven't I thought of this before?!

der? I remember so clearly an early discussion at Pablo's. Hundwasser—before a line of the book was even written—was discussing how we could get onto the *New York Times* best-seller list. "We need to get on Oprah for the masses, and on Terry Gross for the intellectuals. Oprah is no prob (he turned out to be right), but Terry Gross is tough to get on." He pondered his cups. "I got it!" he shrieked. The whole place turned around.

Then he goes into whisper mode, as if someone might steal his big idea: "I'll write Terry Gross right into the book, right at the beginning so she can't miss it, since she probably only reads the first chapter. Then we'll send her an anonymous e-mail drawing her attention to it. She'll check it out for sure—and she'll be so intrigued, she'll be sure to have us on."

"What if she sues you?" I asked. "Impossible. Believe me, I went to law school for a semester. She's a public figure, so we can use her any way we want."

"Why would she even be interested?"

"Man, this section will be so over the top. We'll really do outrageous. Like you're trying to proposition her on the air or something. She'll have to have us on just to defend herself."

Now let me be clear: I would like to have gone on Terry Gross's show. It's rare to be interviewed by someone whose questions go beyond "What made you decide to become a Plague Doctor?" I might even like to go out with her if she seemed open to it—just socially, of course, at first, to continue whatever discussion we might get into. She's not bad-looking in a bookish sort of way. Bookish women understand disorders of

augmentation procedure. As an adolescent and young adult, he blazed across the musical sky, the uncontested greatest accordion player of all time. As a mature, thinking adult, he left the idiosyncratic accordion scene and adopted the costume for which he is now most famous, that of a Plague Doctor, and like Susan Sontag before him has changed forever our understanding of a once and perhaps future, um, plague.
Welcome to the program.
THE NOSE: Wonderful to be here.
TERRY GROSS: First of all, what may I call you? "The Nose" seems more like a title or a descriptor.
THE NOSE: Today, Terry, you may call me Paphnutius. Pappy for short.
TERRY GROSS: Why that?
THE NOSE: Paphnutius was a fourth-century bishop, one of the most fascinating members of the Council of Nicæa. He had his left knee mutilated and his right eye put out for the Faith by the Emperor Maximinus, but at Nicæa he was feted by Constantine the Great, who, according to Socrates, used often to send for the good old confessor and kiss the socket whence the eye had been torn.
TERRY GROSS: And the relation of . . .
THE NOSE: The relation of this to my interview today is that I would like to share with you and your listeners a mutilation experience. Well, not exactly, but almost. I discovered this two weeks ago using techniques of breathing regression and incoherent mumbling.
TERRY GROSS: Are you saying you were mutilated—your knee or your eye?
THE NOSE: Did I say I was? I said I was almost. But it would be nice to be kissed, even by an emperor. . . .
TERRY GROSS: But why do you keep changing your name? Every day it seems to be something diff—
THE NOSE: Are you the same Terry Gross you were yesterday? Or even before we began this interview? Why are you still called Terry Gross? It's a public deception, unworthy of—
TERRY GROSS: Okay, okay, Paphnutius.
THE NOSE: Call me Pappy.
TERRY GROSS: Pappy, then. Can you tell us about your near-mutilation experience?
THE NOSE: In good time, my Girl Would You Were. I'm going to call you that instead of Terry. Is that all right?

the heart such as mine, and the torment between flesh and spirit. And if it didn't work out, ok. I'm sure many of her guests become interested in her. So Hundwasser's account of our interview is not entirely without basis. And I *have* changed names over the course of my life.

But the fact is, we never had an interview—that's the point. Her people never got back to my people. Plus, I have no intrauterine memories—that's ridiculous. The whole Terry Gross interview is sheer fabrication, designed for one thing and one thing only—to be so "over the top" that she couldn't ignore us.

Gross pandering! And that is a statement grossly unfair to Pandarus. He truly had Troilus's interests in mind when setting him up with Creseyde. But a false Pandarus Hundwasser is, an artful, self-seeking, disingenuous slyboots.

He knew how long I have been searching for my Creseyde, my Lily (Elizabeth), none so fair, forpassing every wight.

So angel-like was her native beauty,
That like a thing immortal seemèd she,
As doth an heavenish perfect creäture
That down were sent in scorning of natúre.

But did he help me find her? And when I was dying of love for Kika Kornblom, did he come to my rescue? No. He assured me that no one ever died of a broken heart, and then he swooped down on her himself and bedded her! Making fun

TERRY GROSS: No.

THE NOSE: It was the dark light of Milton. A light which never changed. I didn't feel weak. I felt really wonderful, strangely beatific, slightly drunk even, and carefree.

TERRY GROSS: How old were you?

THE NOSE: Ancient. And apparell'd in celestial light.

TERRY GROSS: I see.

THE NOSE: Merry as a bubble. Euphoric.

TERRY GROSS: A euphoric bubble.

THE NOSE: Yes, giddy with charming thoughts. I wanted to do a do-si-do with my arms. But I didn't have them. Only buds.

TERRY GROSS: So this must have been quite early in your—

THE NOSE: Yes, early—when I was just coalesced from foam. This was my "Feeling Invulnerable" stage. And yet, WouldYouWere, there were molacules out there, always wanting to cling. Beware of molacules, my would-be friend. I became anxious, depressed. I was putting on weight. Still, I told myself, the pearl must grow within the oyster.

TERRY GROSS: You really remember all this?

THE NOSE: As though it were yesterday, though I can't remember yesterday very well. And then . . .

TERRY GROSS: And then?

THE NOSE: It was then that my "Stet Status in Quo" period began. Only shortly before, everything beckoned. Now, what was out there for me? Sickness, old age, and death. Would there be anything fun before dying? Did I really want to abandon this cozy house, my Platonic cave, my ultima Thule? I wanted to shed my body armor, to renounce the world and detach myself from flesh. Virginity of heart and body. Recover the immortality once mine. Why not?

TERRY GROSS: Why not?

THE NOSE: An ingenious question. Because of *her*—my womb companion.

TERRY GROSS: You had a twin with you?

THE NOSE: Only I knew it, because she'd talk to me, tell me stories.

TERRY GROSS: What kind of stories?

THE NOSE: Like the onion story. I've been frightened of onions ever since.

TERRY GROSS: What is the onion story?

THE NOSE: You don't really want to hear it.

of me, no doubt, the two of them, laughing as they came. Double Diomedes, bad, bad, bad.

And in this world no livè creäture
Withouten love is worth or may endure.

Did he care? Hundwasser of the dame-a-day? Did he respect my Canticus Troili? No. He laughed at me while urging me only to laugh at myself.

I apologize, Terry, for the both of us. 

TERRY GROSS: Oh, no, I do. I'm sure our listeners—

THE NOSE: No, they don't.

TERRY GROSS: Yes, they do.

THE NOSE: All right. There was once an old woman . . .

TERRY GROSS: Is this a fairy tale?

THE NOSE: Just let me tell the story, will you? There was once an old woman—horrible, horrible, nasty, selfish, not a single good deed in her life. Her guardian angel stood there helpless when the devils hauled her off and threw her into the burning lake. He yelled after her, "Don't you remember even one good deed you ever did? It could save you." The devils turned around to mock. "Once," she yelled back, "I gave an onion to a starving kid." She yelled so loud that God heard her and considered His mercy. "Take that onion," He said, "and hold it out to her. Let her try to pull herself out of the lake. If she does, she may join Me in Heaven. If the onion breaks, she stays where she is."

TERRY GROSS: And?

THE NOSE: What do you think?

TERRY GROSS: Well, if God is merciful . . .

THE NOSE: Ha! The angel held out the onion, and the old woman grabbed hold of its shoots. The angel pulled, gently, gently. Almost there, almost out of the lake. But when the other sinners saw what was happening, they grabbed on to her so they too might be saved. The old woman kicked at them and yelled, "Get out! I'm the one being saved! It's my onion!"

TERRY GROSS: And the onion snapped.

THE NOSE: It snapped, WouldYouWere, it snapped. And the old woman fell back into the lake, where she is still burning to this day. . . . Don't you want to say something? Does the government let you have all this dead air time?

TERRY GROSS: So what does this story—

THE NOSE: Selfishness. My schinocephalic wombmate was warning me against selfishness, advising me to help save others without concern for myself.

TERRY GROSS: Well, what was your plan, then?

THE NOSE: My plan? You know what Napoleon said: "On s'engage, et puis, on voit."

TERRY GROSS: If you've just joined us, my guest is Paph—

THE NOSE: Father Vassily. I changed my name to Father Vassily.

TERRY GROSS: My guest is Father Vassily, known to many of you simply as The Nose. Stay with us. We'll be back after a short break.

[Underwriting messages from Archer Daniels Midland and Wal-Mart]
TERRY GROSS: Welcome back to Fresh Air! I'm Terry Gross. I'm speaking to Father Vas—
THE NOSE: Isaiah Nasutus, Fourth Isaiah, the Long-Nosed.
TERRY GROSS: I thought you were—
THE NOSE: I changed my name during the break.
TERRY GROSS: All right. My guest is Isaiah . . .
THE NOSE: Nasutus. The Long-Nosed.
TERRY GROSS: Isaiah Nasutus . . .
THE NOSE: Specializing in prophecy tempered by tears, but mixed with healing joy. A comfort to the sick world. Wanna hear some prophecies?
TERRY GROSS: Umm . . . sure, go ahead.
THE NOSE: I could have been a real prophet of rage, you know.
TERRY GROSS: Right.
THE NOSE: Or I could have just sought my own perfection or happiness, or just become a sage or an immortal, a member of some austere community of one, perfecting the art of renunciation.
TERRY GROSS: Yes, I suppose you could have . . .
THE NOSE: But I didn't.
TERRY GROSS: No . . . So will you make some prophecies? Do some prophecies?
THE NOSE: I could have treated my dear Thule as a cave of Trophonius . . .
TERRY GROSS: You probably—
THE NOSE: . . . returning from which no visitor ever smiles again.
TERRY GROSS: Well, you wouldn't want—
THE NOSE: But I didn't.
TERRY GROSS: No.
THE NOSE: And using an esoteric Jedi Mind Trick, I could even have transformed the charming Greek precept "Know thyself" into the vile Christian injunction "Renounce thyself," but . . .
TERRY GROSS: So, will you prophesy for us?
THE NOSE: No. I thought you wanted to talk about my near-mutilation experience.
TERRY GROSS: We're running out of time.
THE NOSE: It won't take long. So there I was, nosing out the impossible dream, sniffing the cork of the future, feeling megalo, almost groovy, when all of a sudden, I smell a rat. Heartbeats—like the sound of a tacky horror show—and then, through the cervical

keyhole, a nose coming at me, black, plastic, uni-nostriled, Then the pump, wug-ga, wug-ga . . . and all of a sudden my world is awash in viscosity. Mayday! Mayday!— serious dysfunction in the cavity! The very walls start to sway and pucker. I grab a loosened uterine fold and wrap myself in it, bulging myself behind a lateral wall, holding my breath, hiding.

TERRY GROSS: Oh, dear!

THE NOSE: Oh, dear is right. This was an especially nasty assault on one's narcissism.

TERRY GROSS: What was going on?

THE NOSE: What was I supposed to be—Doctor Haruspex, perusing entrails and analyzing? Who the hell knew what was going on? All I knew was that my purity was being defiled, my home attacked, and I was marked as left behind to fester. Individualism, autonomy, self-containment—all kaput. The spiritual fragrance of goodness was gone, replaced by—

TERRY GROSS: Now, now, Isaiah, no infantile rages. This was many years—

THE NOSE: Let loose the lions!

TERRY GROSS: Isaiah, Isaiah—

THE NOSE: Simba! Call me Simba. Simba Mufasovich.

TERRY GROSS: Calm down!

THE NOSE: Or Polycarp. Call me Polycarp. Saint Polycarp, the martyr who cried, "In what times, O Lord, hast thou caused me to be born!" Saint Polycarp's day is January 26th. It is. My own birthday. It was then I knew I was destined to be born, to be snatched away into life, prompted by a nozzle.

TERRY GROSS: Was that nozzle what gave you the idea of going to the Transvestite Ball last week as a douche bag?

THE NOSE: Yes, as a provocation, and to save the honor of douche bags. And besides, I wasn't a douche bag, I was a dush bag, as in Russian, <cyrde><cyru><cyrsha><cyra>, soul. This was a point lost on most.

TERRY GROSS: Uh-huh. I think probably . . . um, are there any last things you want to say?

THE NOSE: Yes. What a weird thing brains are, especially mine.

TERRY GROSS: Brains are very complex.

THE NOSE: Do you think mine is a vessel of enlightenment?

TERRY GROSS:I—

THE NOSE: Hmm? No answer? Okay then, one last question before you go: Will you go out with me? I bet you're a real party animal. If you were a new hamburger at

McDonald's, you would be McGorgeous. How old are you?
TERRY GROSS: Well, we're out of time. Let's leave it at that. [laughs]
THE NOSE: No, I really want to know if—
TERRY GROSS: I'm Terry Gross, and this is Fresh Air!

Postpartum Expression

The Fresh Air interview raises several key questions—most salient those of our hero's relationships to women, and especially to Woman Number One. As Dr. Freud often said, "God could not be everywhere, so He invented mothers," which, translated into our hero's youngest context, meant an all-pervading power, mean, punishing, and distant.

5

Anastasia Pigov arrived in New York City at age twelve, having left Haifa with her parents, who had fled Kiev three years earlier. Consequently, she spoke Russian, Hebrew, and English—all poorly, except for certain quaint expressions. The Pigovs moved into a small apartment off Second Avenue, joined St. Michael's Russian Catholic Church on Mulberry Street, and proceeded, according to traditional practices, to beat young Nastya weekly, usually on Sunday, for being "a baby slut." The potaskushka left home at fourteen.

Anastasia, having learned at her father's knee, as it were, with strap, proceeded to apply those lessons, with her own inventive variations, to her young son. She began training him early, while still lying in at St. Vincent's. Refusing to breast-feed her child, she told the La Leche League volunteer, "My boyfriend thinks they're his," "they" being an early-blooming pair of beauties, the envy of her school chums. She didn't want them sagging. "Besides," she said, "what if he bites?"

Nastya's next intervention was leaving her son nameless for five years, not wanting to get attached, as she was considering giving him up for sale or adoption. It was not his cuteness that won him his maternal home but the fact that the adoption procedures were too complex for her to deal with, a classified ad too expensive, and the corner dumpster beyond even her capacity.

5. A note attached to nothing. (Indicative? Symbolic?) While I am in the space between the putative Fresh Air interview and the questionable questions raised by it, and while Terry Gross is on my mind, I'd like to bring up the issue of fans—a cohort much intertwined with my recent life. "Fanatic," ok, but what is the source of that? I'll tell you what it is—it is the Latin "fanum," "temple"—a place where worshippers were inspired by gods. A fanatic was someone possessed by a deity. Which is to say that I understand that my fans are better and more sincerely motivated than the Hundwasserian farce in which they are acting. While superficial, they are not deeply superficial. They are simply variously-aged adolescents with brain damage carrying on in a loathsome way.

And where does their lack of joy

come from, their mad clamoring for grace? From embracing a system in which all their goodness is eroded by the pursuit of comfort and chimerical "security." They are engulfed in the morass of a technological utopia in which they are, for all intents and purposes, automata. The least sign of individuality, on any level whatever, is regarded as *outré*, to be resolutely discarded. They pronounce me king, God, and dictator simply to try to invoke the purity and love within themselves.

But my goal with this commentary is to spoil their game. It is not important for them to know what they want. It will be enough if I can show them what they *don't* want. The rest will take care of itself. Fans, fanatics, horses' fannies. Profanes outside the temple. They do give me the fantods.

Dad, the boyfriend known as "Hawk," was a gypsy street performer, an accordion player of no mean talent, a dark, thin, buteo-nosed Roma with a taste for younger women and the attention span of a crackhead. He had disappeared immediately upon delivery and was replaced by a continuous stream of similar others.

Like Oliver Twist's, much of her son's childhood is best passed over quickly except for a few details relevant to his future development. One of them, notable for its merchandising potential, was Nastya's bizarre use of matroshka dolls as rattles for her growing infant. Increasing their size as the child grew, she filled the hollow figures with split peas, drilled holes in their faces, and inserted the tips of carrots and parsnips as grotesque noses, appendages which turned ever more weird as they shriveled and put on a gangrenous black. She gave them to him to shake and to suck on and, once betoothed, to eat.

Was this a subterranean attack on the poor babe's psyche, her revenge for his having been conceived and looking so strange? It would be hard to deny—although there are no statistically significant data to support it—that all his early nose-sucking may have left nosological sequelae.

The money Nastya spent on matroshka materials reduced even further the insufficiency she allowed for her nameless one's food. His newborn plumpness soon dwindled, and by his third birthday he had become a pinched, wan toddler verging on the cadaverous, whose toddle was hard to distinguish from a stagger. In such a Munchean face, the nose loomed even larger. Maternal affection was inversely proportional.

His fifth birthday was celebrated locked in a closet—an educational technique Nastya found most effective. Out of sight, out of mind. And even better, out of mind, out of sight. She had tried "If you don't do what I say, I leave you out for the gypsies," but that seemed only to route its way back—both in her mind, and in her son's—to Hawk and his demeaning betrayal. The closet was better.

The boy was originally quite terrified by the dark imprisonment, but as many concentration-camp survivors have testified, one can get used to anything, and early on in his training, he discovered his first closet companion, a ratty raccoon coat, true relic of the roaring '20s. It was the softest thing he had ever encountered, smelled like his mother—and like some still more nameless dream. He would pull it off the hanger and snuggle with it in the depths of his locker. What Nastya considered training became for him a secret tryst, a heavy date with lots of petting, fur, and bony fingers. He looked forward to his punishments.

He looked forward to them even more when in addition to *Shinél* (Nastya's name for

the fur that kept falling off its hanger), another soft companion appeared—a live one. It was always too dark to see him, her, or it, but it had a plump, sleek, furry body and a long, hairless tail. It occasionally squeaked, tickled, and was fun.[6]

From an exterminator's flyer in the apartment-house lobby, our boy deduced that his friend must be a *krisa*, which—judging from her reaction to the picture—his mother didn't seem to like. But then, they disagreed on many things.

He learned to read from that flyer. His brain, having little competition from his body, was ready to go; it grabbed the reins and galloped, like Vronsky on Frou-Frou. The letter codes came clear and snapped right into some preset place. There is, it seems, a connection between genius and disease, and by the time he was stashed in kindergarten, our now-named-Alexei could read every crushed cereal box and soup can in the dumpster. He had also discovered that Krisa really was a rat—which didn't diminish their friendship by a hair.

Nastya, small, fierce, and good-looking, developed her matroshka rattles into a moderately successful small business, marketing them from a blanket on Astor Place. Sometime during Alexei's second grade, she was picked up by a Siberian drug dealer who set her up as "Marisa," a hairstylist with her own Sixth Avenue salon. A thorough study of Home Library Series' *Home Haircutting*, plus her innate, exotic bizzazz, enabled her to bring home the bacon, which she, her son, and Mikhail Borisovich—when he was there—ate raw, right out of the package.

The boy was too big now for the closet. (His trips there were now entirely voluntary.) But still she threatened him as needed with gypsies. She never mentioned that his father had played the accordion.

6. I called him (or her) Boobah before my mother called him (or her) a krisa. So then he (or she) became Krisa, a word disgusting for my mother, but for me a good word like "Criminy!" or "Kris Kringle," or "the Christ child," or maybe the little cross my mother wore above her cleavage.

Krisa was my first fan, except for myself. I especially loved sucking on my toes—before I had my first encounter with a mirror at the age of four. But Krisa was also a fan, for sure. He must have thought I was some kind of god to worship in the temple of the closet, and his worshiping was not just spiritual adoration, but fully committed polymorphous perversity. He would swipe his lithe little self against my nakedness, climb all around and fall into my lap. He would nuzzle and nip: Take, eat, this is my body. He would squeak in ways that I'm sure put Josephine the Mouse Singer's arias to shame, though I don't now remember the melodies. He was as committed as the most committed Deadhead or Phishphan, rushing almost instantly from wherever he may have been to the temple whenever I entered or was thrust therein. I didn't have to call him—he would just appear, as if signaled by some deity. His claims were modest—just to be with me whenever he could, to demonstrate his fealty even in the midst of my occasional infantile rages. He was there to comfort, and made no demands.

Shinél, of course, was also an important denizen of the closet, but even though it would fall on me routinely (and when it didn't, I would

2.

Childe Groucho

pull it down to snuggle in its fur), I think being a true fan requires at least a modicum of consciousness, which I don't imagine a raccoon coat has. This I knew, even as a child, pink with rectitude.

She finally called him Alexandr because it sounded long and sharp—like his nose. It was also the name of a favorite Bronx department store from which it was particularly easy to shoplift. You had to deduct the carfare, but still. . . . She named him Alexandr because she had to name him something, or else he wouldn't be out of her hair from 8:30 to 3 every weekday.

Absence, perhaps, might make her heart grow fonder.

First grade was traumatic, front to back. They laughed at him, they teased him, they pushed him around in the schoolyard. They called him Schnoz, and Beaky, and Snotso, and Nathan 'cause his nose looked like a hot dog.

Needless to say, his early literary skills were seen as an aggravating, not a mitigating factor. When he tried to read under the bleachers during phys ed., his teachers ordered him out and his classmates pelted him with open catsup packets filched from the cafeteria for the purpose. They tripped him in the hall, slammed him in the stairwells, jeered at him coming in or going out of the building.[7] You might imagine he'd get grouchy. But he didn't get grouchy. He got Groucho.

The family's first-ever TV—a 10-inch Motorola with a champagne mahogany finish—arrived on a Thursday in February 1957 to mark a successful first year of *Oooo Marisa.* Mikhail Borisovich had been replaced in his mother's bed by Juri Niecieslawski, and after celebratory, thematically appropriate TV dinners, she and Juri unpacked the monster, plugged it in, and switched it on.[8] And there was Groucho—you bet your life, there was Groucho. Nastya and Juri found it mildly amusing, but Alexei thought it hysterical, rolling-on-the-floor hysterical.

7. Oh, God, what a stellar bunch they were, the gang, the guys. At 57, I look back on those early days as bittersweet, more sweet than bitter. The variety of bozos among us. What a gift.

Henry Perky, where are you now? Jesús Fuentes, do you still wear a duck's ass? Is it gray, silver? Do you have a dozen grand-Jesúses and grand-Marias? Seymour Schwartzkopf, was it your uncle or something who bombed Iraq, you big bully?

"Beak-y, Beak-y, Beaky is freaky," they used to sing. But I know they loved me even then. Not one of them was as

8. Let it be said right away that this whole Groucho thing is entirely an invention of William Hundwasser's. There is no public school system in the United States that would ever allow a

unintelligent and insensitive as the mass of them together. After all, if 90% of your genes are shared with a banana, it's easy to confuse love with aversion.

The fact is, I didn't take their actions seriously. Kids think in herds, they go wacky in herds—but one by one they recover their senses. You might think they hated me, given the profound imbecility of their behavior, but they really were my fans even then. Fans, the children who come at you with knives.

But they didn't really hate me, the guys. They were obviously just waiting for someone to liberate them from their doltish preadolescent existence. That's why I became their hero.

My gang, once a mere collection of lightweight goofballs functioning on the lowest rung of existence, once they admitted their love for me, they gained forty pounds of moral earnestness—each—instantly. Herman Daily started writing short stories. Jan Pronk joined the track team. OK, Pavvy probably ended up in prison, but he was the exception.

It's so amusing to see us all together in our sixth grade class photo. Demonic effervescence in white shirts and green ties. Survivors of the great mistakeathon of childhood. It was I—freaky, beaky I—who helped them release most of their defects.

Look at them ranged on the schoolyard steps, brazen and vile, so diversely rapacious—and now probably—mostly—proud parents, maybe even grandparents.

Perhaps someone will recognize me behind my mask. Hey, guys, it's me, Freaky Beaky. Remember?

student to wear Groucho nose-glasses all day, every day. Prima facie. QED.

Yes, "You Bet Your Life" was the first thing on when my mother and her latest boyfriend unpacked the TV. But it didn't take me more than five minutes to realize that I hated Julius "Groucho" Marx, and recognized him immediately, with all the pure perspicacity of childhood, as a first-order sadist, an opinion confirmed by a reading of several biographies. He withered his friends with his acid tongue, and drove all three of his wives to alcohol, along with his daughter, Miriam. "Callous and insensitive," she called him. Harpo's wife remarked that he "destroys people's egos. He can only be controlled if he has respect for you. If he loses respect, you're dead." Nice.

It's very in, very hip, very postmodern to lionize Groucho: he has fans galore among the intelligentsia who spout all sorts of high-language, inflated claims about him, or among the students who discovered the Marx brothers in the '60s and conflated their name and singular behavior as some ecstatic confirmation of the revolutionary spirit. "Boiling anarchy." "Essential disintegration of the real by poetry." Give me a break.

The man was a philosophical embarrassment and a potential corruptor of youth. Do you recall his singing

Why was unclear. He certainly didn't get the sexual innuendos, and the lightning, punning, referential non sequiturs probably went by him too. It was clear that he loved the eyeglassed, mustachioed duck, but that poor fowl made only a cameo appearance and never returned, as the contestants never uttered the magic word. Thursdays became Groucho night for him in the living room. The grown-ups had better things to do in the bedroom.[9]

One spring day, perambulating alone after school, killing time until Nastya got home to let him in, Alexei made a discovery, which led to an epiphany, which would change his life—and in due time ours.

Heading west—his maiden voyage across the treacherous ocean of Sixth Avenue—he chanced upon Benny's Joke Shop on Christopher Street. There in the window was—a Groucho nose and glasses. Black plastic glasses, similar to his own, but attached to a nose larger than his, equipped with a black mustache, pendant. Clearly, that must be for him. All those hours watching, worshipping. All those quips he had stored up. That much was obvious. He demanded, asked for, hinted at the nose-glasses for his seventh birthday present. Improbably enough, he actually received them.

But Groucho glasses for his birthday was not his most revolutionary thought. The notion that changed a nation was this: misdirection. Targeted misdirection. Paradoxically targeted misdirection, according to the principle of if-people-find-something-offensive-do-it-bigger-and-more-often. They'll laugh. They'll come to expect it. They'll consider it—normal! Alexei would hide his nose under an even bigger one. He would wear the nose-glasses to school, and wear them all the time. No one would ever laugh at him again: they would laugh with him, his audience, his fans, his friends![10]

All great enterprises have their crises. In Groucho's case, it came four seconds in. As he walked into school the first day of second grade, he immediately became a strange attractor for derision. His friends had not yet materialized. Instead Seymour Schwartzkopf snatched the glasses from his face and threw them out to the mob.

"Beaky, Beaky, Beaky is freaky," they sang.

Alexei ran from possessor to possessor trying in vain to retrieve his secret of success. Each would put on the glasses, do some hurtful imitation of him, and toss them to the next tormenter. The gang harangue was broken up by Mr. Saginaw, the assistant principal.

"Okay, whose are these?"

"Who do you think?"

inaugural address as president of Huxley College? His repeated chorus: "Whatever it is, I'm against it." Nihilism pure and simple, and even early on, not for me. His "Please accept my resignation. I don't care to belong to any club that will have me as a member" is essentially a refusal to be a member of that club called the human race, self-contempt turned global censoriousness. I do not embrace such thoroughgoing anarchism.

Why should I, who had so much ground to make up, who had to tread so carefully with girls I admired, take up as my totem some flea-bitten, lust-smitten Lothario who took mad swings, amorous or insulting, at every female within reach? Why haven't the feminists decimated him as they have Freud? The verbal humor is admittedly adroit, but it's violent and heartless, unfettered and cruel. Harpo's world, in contrast, is infused by bliss, not rage. If anyone, I'd have chosen to be Harpo. And I didn't. For one thing, his nose was too small.

There is a sad element attached to Julius "Groucho" Marx, which I, as an adult, can relate to. His life seems the story of a talented man whose persona sprang from an exaggeration of natural qualities, but then took him over, trapped him in a role unbearable to himself as well as others. That was what every writer and producer said of him:

9. Woo, woo, woo, Mr. Hundwasser. Sounds quite lascivious and deep-neurosis-making. Nothing like a lab-tech turned author now pretending to be a time-sharer in Bergstrasse 19.

The "primal scene" spawning the life-long primal scream of Alexei Pigov. I'm sure that's what Hundwasser intended to convey with this lapidary reference. I'll have you know, dear reader, that, what with a mother like mine, I am not only a survivor of the primal scene, but a connoisseur of it. How else would I have even known what a female nipple looked like, much less the demesnes that lie beneath? OK, books. But that isn't the same thing.

It started when Nastya and Tadzio or whoever and I were off on an auto trip to Cincinnati—to do some illicit fund-raising, no doubt. I was only four, and three days,

10. We are newly aware these days of the efficacy of a technique called "the Big Lie." Concerning one Adolf Hitler, the U.S. Office of Strategic Services once wrote,

> His primary rules were: never allow the public to cool off; never admit a fault or wrong; never concede that there may be

apparently, was too long to leave me alone with a latchkey.

Middle of the night, flat tire, no spare, and we were forced to trek back through the pouring rain to a motel we had recently passed. Only one room available, one double bed, no cots, and a huge stain on the ceiling. So we all strip off our soaking clothes and, pile into the bed in size place: he, she, and me in that order. I don't need to elaborate on the old in-and-out, the groan-and-moan choir, the bedspring boogie. This was a primal scene worthy of the Metropolitan Opera, lavishly staged, and sung in a language even a four-year-old would understand. A one-year-old.

Was I frightened, Dr. Freudwasser? Did I think the bad man was trying to kill my sainted mother? First of all, I might have enjoyed it if he had—at least until I had no one to unlock the apartment door and let me in. But that aside, I knew quite clearly that in spite of the moaning and groaning they seemed to be

some good in your enemy; never leave room for alternatives; never accept blame; concentrate on one enemy at a time and blame him for everything that goes wrong; people will believe a big lie sooner than a little one; and if you repeat it frequently enough people will sooner or later believe it.

Now, as every cloud has its silver lining, and every dark yin its bright yang, and as the fish in the trap will begin to think, is it not possible that there is an inverse side to the strategy of the Big Lie? Inverse, converse, reverse?

"The white lie," you will say, and to that I say yes, but not quite.

Little white lies, innocent, trivial, diplomatic, well-intentioned. Would he not be a Groucho-like brute who told every woman what he really thought she looked like in her new dress?

And if little white lies are a mark of civilized gentility, why not medium-sized white lies, and even big white lies,

that he was "unbearable." Not whacky, playful, endearingly lunatic, but "unbearable." I'm afraid many women may have found me so.

But unlike Groucho, I was never brutally contemptuous or vengefully destructive, and I was never cursed with the need to make jokes. These are Hundwasser's qualities, not mine. Graulexei I was not. Once I graduated from Freaky Beaky, I was simply known as "The Vonce."

"Snore on, bore on, big snot moron!" the chorus hinted.

"Quiet! Alexei, are they yours? "

"Yes."

"Who took them from you?"

Alexei picked out his most hated antagonist. It wasn't Seymour.

"Him. He did."

Jesús Fuentes looked surprised and insulted and moved to strike. The others held him back.

"I didn't. No way, *mentiroso*!"

Alexei put the Groucho glasses back on.

"I never forget a face," Alexei said, "but in his case, I may make an exception."

What? Where did that come from?

"Jesús has the brain of a four-year-old, and I'll bet *he* was glad to get rid of it."

It was Groucho, speaking through him by dint of homeopathic magic and study. He took off the glasses.

"It really was, Mr. Saginaw."

He put the glasses back on.

"Jesús may look like an idiot and talk like an idiot, but don't let that fool you. He really *is* an idiot."

"It wasn't Jesús," Pavel Nozdrev yelled. "It was Schwartzkopf."

"Who are you going to believe," Groucho responded, "me, or your own eyes?"

Everyone started laughing.

"I'd horsewhip you if I had a horse."

Hysteria.

He had won. The loser had won. With Groucho as his shield and sword, he had conquered and now had cohort friends and fans.

Conquering the teachers and their rules of decorum was another task entirely. What turned it around with Mrs. Hochstedder was the following exchange:

Mrs. Hochstedder: Alexei, you cannot smear paint on the wall! What kind of a baby are you?

Groucho Pigov: Well, I was born at a very early age.

Mrs. Hochstedder: !

having a good time, and that if I were a good little boy I might be invited into their game, or at least a similar one of my own.

Did it create psychological turmoil in me and neurotic agitation? Hell, no. It showed me the (still) unobtainable other shore of the river that runs between tenderness and sensuality, the stream that connects desire and love. 57 is not too old to put into practice what I learned at the Star Motel. *Time* magazine assures us that even nonagenarians can make the beast with two backs. There is still hope for me.

gigantic ones? Huge white lies repeated frequently enough to effect belief, never admitting the contrary, never leaving room for alternatives, ever growing in fancy and delightful detail . . . are not such fabulations essential to the survival of the species? The perfectibility of man. The beneficence of Mother Earth. You too can become president if you work hard enough. Such are the Big White Lies that sustain us.

Real life is generally boring, wouldn't you say? Henry James complained about "clumsy Life again at her stupid work," and wrote his books as an alternative. Leverkuhn lusted after "ingenuities not thought of in heaven." Why be "sincere" in a culture that is anything but? Melville's Pierre revolts against the pieties of his family; Conrad's Jimmy Wait plays malingerer to save his ship from anarchy; Marlow tells Kurtz's fiancée that Kurtz died speaking her name, and not uttering his famous last words, "The horror! The horror!" Would you have it otherwise? Would you demolish all fan-

Groucho Pigov: (shrugging) Art is art, *ne pravda*? On the other hand, poopie is poopie, peepee is peep—

Mrs. Hochstedder: Stop that language! In the classroom, we have rules ab—

Groucho Pigov: Whatever they are, I'm against them. Those are my principles. If you don't like them, I have others.

She cracked. Mr. Hochstedder would have been proud. The mask stayed on, Alexei remained Groucho, and he got straight S's on his report card. The most laudable was "Plays well with others."

The third grade capitulated, and the fourth grade too.

Alexei Groucho Pigov, preteen, was voted the Most Popular Miscellaneous in his sixth grade yearbook (imagine that!), and it was on to junior high school and the gender mysteries that lay *là-bas*.

First Love

Kafka has a story called "First Sorrow," which may be about first love. They are often confused. The story ends this way:

> *Once such ideas began to torment him, would they ever quite leave him alone? Would they not rather increase in urgency? Would they not threaten his very existence? And indeed, the manager believed he could see, during the apparently peaceful sleep which had succeeded the fit of tears, the first furrows of care engraving themselves upon the trapeze artist's smooth, childlike forehead.*[11]

Who among us has not experienced such engraving? Skin being what it is, Alexei's brow may already have been etched by his early diet or his initial experiences in the closet. Still, even *he* must remember junior high school as a high epoch of disorder and early sorrow.

Thirteen is an excellent age for confirmation—and for cruel deflation and decimation. Alas, there was much of the latter and not much of the former in Alexei's entry-level exposure to love.

Alice Mulvaney, his wonderland, was everything he wasn't—a pretty little creature with a sweet voice and azure eyes, a being fresh from God. She was perfectly neat; he was

tasies and embrace the monster-Truth? Is not all great art one Huge White Lie?

Hence my life strategy of ever-larger noses on ever-richer masks. At the time it was merely an instinct, an experiment. What did I know of Mann and Melville, James and Conrad? All I read was Mad Comics. But my clear sense then, as it is now, was that goodness is not necessarily bound to plainspeaking limpidity, to full, if vulgar, disclosure, but on the contrary, to the natural secrecy of things, the opaque fog of real existence, to the obscurity of Big White Lies. Thus you may better understand me.

11. Hundwasser actually asked me, "Do you think the book would have more gravitas if it had some quotes from Kafka?" What could I say but yes? He had never even read Kafka, much less thought about the meaning of his universe. All he knew was the adjective "kafkaesque," which for him meant not simply "weird," but "weird with gravitas."

often squalid. She was delicate and graceful; he an awkward klutz. Her demeanor was beyond reproach; his was questionable at best. And her calves. Did he have a thing for calves? On this sylph-like dancer's body, calves, lowing for attention. Her slender arms, graced by golden down. Her eyes, their lashes, shy, demure; her stunning realization of post-prepubescence.

But above all, her nose. Cute as a button? No, buttons are flat and often sport twice too many nostrils. Alice's nose? If Jane Austen had been a sculptress, she might have fashioned such a nose. Fragonard might have painted it. Elegant, even exquisite, shaped by the Platonic idea of what a nose might be. Could such a visual achievement actually smell? Did it have nose hairs, and adenoids, and (perish the thought!) boogers? These were not questions which occurred to Graulexei. He was in love. In love in fairyland.[12]

He would invite her to the junior high prom at the end of next year. It took all of seventh grade to work up the courage. How could he ask such a beautiful girl? How could he approach her on this topic? What could he say? "Please don't blow me off"?

What if she does blow me off; what if she. . . blows me? he thought. But she doesn't do such things. She doesn't think that way. But those calves, that nose. He loved her for herself, not her body. He had to act cool and disinterested. Maybe tough. Tougher. Nice guys finish last. But elegant, like her. And interesting. Gotta be interesting, he said to himself: I need a philosophy of life.[13]

Such were Graulexei's obsessively cycled thoughts from September to April, the thoughts of a child-man bubbling up within a childish Groucho, quietly growling like an empty stomach, a being laboring to be born. The nose-glasses were the same.

Yes, he and Alice were friends, Yes, she had laughed at his Grouchisms like everyone else, but he had not yet talked to her one-on-one.

On Mayday, the countdown began: he had two months and counting. Forty-five schooldays—that was in the lower two digits. The recycling tempo increased, the thoughts became more accented and staccato, the volume swelled, receded, and swelled. They were reading *The Scarlet Letter* in English class, and he was Dimmesdale, secretive, guilty—of what? Of the crime of loving her, of loving above and beyond his station.

He checked his chest daily for a sign of his sin but found only tentative hairs and half-a-dozen pimples. When they clustered over his left breast, he thought them his buboes, a plague caused by fluxions broadcast by his overwrought heart. They would surely be the death of him.[14]

Unless, unless . . . He must discharge them, the fluxions. He must bite the bullet, cross the Rubicon, leap into the breach, take the bull by the horns. It was goddamn June

12. Alice Mulvaney—Emma Robiner, actually. Hundwasser has this weird paranoia about being sued and is dedicated to "changing the names to protect the innocent," that is, himself.

Emma was a pretty little thing, to be sure. Pretty in the Norman Rockwell sense, not some raving Caravaggio beauty. Cute, even. Cute, of course, is fine in kittens, puppies, and young children, but becomes cloying and insufferable as we age. It's likely that Emma has by now outgrown her pedomorphotic state and, for all I know, may have become a mature beauty. (Emma, if you are reading this, please get in touch through my publisher.)

Alas, one can never know to what extent one feels and to what extent one plays at feeling. This Stanislavskian ambiguity is especially poignant at the edge of childhood, when one knows enough to realize what is assigned to human being, and not enough to discern the true qualities involved.

But beauty arises where it is sown,

13. I'm enormously embarrassed by this paragraph, but in the interest of full disclosure, I have to say it's somewhat true. "Blow me off . . ." I was trapped—not just in my confession to Hundwasser, but in the net of the words themselves—and forced, forced to acknowledge the carnal component to my love for Emma.

"And the word became flesh"—the radical content of that assertion! And not just flesh, John tells us, like pork chops or ground round, but flesh "full of grace and truth."

Flesh and spirit, capable of being one and the same—would

14. Those who love and those who enjoy life are not the same people. No one

and who is a more enthusiastic sower than a boy of thirteen with a big heart (and a big nose)? Emma's features were enough to cheer that heart, that heart which was to be the origin of my every torment.

Once, in seventh grade, Emma was out sick on Monday. And again on Tuesday. I began to worry. When she didn't show up on Wednesday, I was entirely distracted from my classroom work, and found I couldn't sleep. I was too shy to call her home to find out what was wrong. Besides, what if I discovered that the Robiners had moved away—off to the next air force base or something? On Thursday, I was positively frantic, and spent from four till nine at the Tompkins Square library looking up formulae for healing ointments and soothing lotions. On Friday, Emma was back in school, looking fit as a fife, and as charming as ever—with everyone, even me. But not especially me. "I had a virus," she told me, and went off with her friends.

I spent the next few days trying to fall in love with a sublimely hideous girl whose name I won't mention to protect her innocence. I just couldn't do it. I tried to think how nice she was, how intelligent, that it were, that it were! But in most cases, there springs up a little gap between flesh and spirit, a tiny discontinuity which tends to grow and metastasize like a cancer of nothingness, and there we fleshlings are, off somewhere clinging to flotsam ever farther from shore, borne away into vortices of foolishness and shame.

Was it not inevitable to coat Emma's sugar with sin? If not, why was she given such calves, and why did she flaunt them, crossing her legs just so in each year's shorter skirts? This is not blameworthy behavior on her part. Skirt lengths were not her decision, but those of manufacturers who wanted more money for less material. Leg-crossing is a normal way to stretch the posterior and lateral muscles of the hip and thigh. (I blush even now to mention the word "thigh" in Emma's context.) Nor was my fascination with that fleshly construction anything more untoward than my body's viscosity invading my normal mental face. Ego te absolvo, Alexei. Neither are you to blame.

Beauty has been historically associated with virtue, especially cute beauty like Emma's, beauty of blond curls and big blue eyes. Beauty of Betty and not Veronica. But virtue, virtue: uninteresting, suffocating, and predictable! Is virtue life? Is virtue even beautiful, at least in the early 21st century? Let the virtue buyer beware.

more than I understood the '70s pop fraudulence of Kübler-Ross's stages of grief—denial, anger, bargaining, depression, and acceptance. And the Little Mermaid marries the prince, and they have 2.5 blond children, and if you believe that, I have a bridge I'd like to sell you.

Far more accurate is the old pop song, "My heart cries for you, sighs for you, dies for you. . . ." And death of the spiritual heart is not followed by bargaining or acceptance. It proceeds as does myocardial infarction, moving from ischemia into arrhythmia and shock. Its Do Not Resuscitate orders are built right in.

We know when death approaches. An ER doctor told me once that "when someone tells me they think they're going to die, they're usually right."

how thoughtful and mature. But she couldn't have been a dancer if she tried, and she did have nose hairs, lots of them, and chin hairs as well. I just couldn't do it. What a bad person I am.

Countdowns are often involved: five more streets to go until I see the guillotine. Four. Three.

And the sign, the sign, the burning in the chest. A for Agony. A for Alexei. ON A FIELD, SABLE, THE LETTER A, GULES.

Elisabeth Kübler-Ross, consider it well, wherever you are. Would that I were a stone!

15th already. He must take the plunge. Come Friday he would ask her. But he had no classes with her on Friday. Okay, Monday, then. Monday. After Geometry, before lunch.

Sartre maintained that hell is other people. Sartre was wrong. Hell is trying to construct a *sectio divina* using only a compass and straight-edge when 99.14159 percent of your concentration is fixed on the divina proportione of a young goddess two rows over and three seats back, and the clock is counting down toward the moment of truth.

I have to prepare for any- and everything, he thought. I'll get a bathroom pass and get ready.

He returned with his hair slicked back, his glasses polished, his Groucho overframes tightened and adjusted, and his Groucho overnose corrected from its tendency to incline toward the left.

Given line RS, on a line segment AB of length a, construct at B a perpendicular of length a.

Girls want someone with an attitude, not a nebbish. He'd have an attitude. What? Which one?

Bisect AB at E; with E as center and ED as radius, describe an arc that intersects RS at C.

Maybe if he had a prop. Like a camera. "Alice, would you mind if I took your picture—the light is so fine on your hair." What a great line. But he didn't have a camera. What about a sketchbook? He could get a sketchbook maybe. But he couldn't draw. A compass, what could he do with this compass?

By the Pythagorean theorem, the radius here is $\sqrt{5}(a/2)$.

Since he didn't dance, he thought it would be best not to dance.

We now have $AB/AC = a/(a/2(1+\sqrt{5})) = (\sqrt{5}-1)/2$.

He could talk about bad first dates, that would be amusing. But he hadn't had any.

The line segment AC is divided in the golden ratio by the point B.[15]

The bell rang. Alice packed up her geometry materials and prepared to go to lunch.

He decided to count to ten and then do it. Graulexei sauntered over to his love.

"Alice, do you think we will ever convert to the metric system?"

"What?"

15.Hundwasser used to crow about this passage on the golden section, ending ta-daa with the derivation of an age-old mystery. It's counterpoint with the age-old mystery of love, he said. He liked that too. He thought that as a writer, he was the bee's knees.

OK, it is competent intercutting, and the episode is slightly true,

"Um . . . I meant 'Hi!' It just came out 'Do you think we'll ever convert to the metric system?'"

She laughed. "Oh, you silly."

"And I know a poem about owls. 'How foul is the owl . . .'"

It turned out Alice already had a date for the prom. And next year's prom? She already had a date for that one too.[16]

Meet the Wife

Hand held out as if to shake. "Meet the wife," he says. Crude and abusive self-mockery. But it was Graulexei's fate for the moment, and better than total loneliness. Better until his arcane reading habits led him astray.

It was in the Pageant Book Shop that he found it. There, in a pile amidst the dusty bibliomaelstrom atop the rickety stairs, he noticed a yellow pamphlet corner, its proboscis sticking out from a pile, sniffing out a potential mark. It was in French, Paris, 1844, its cover gone but its frayed title page paradoxically proclaiming *Le Livre Sans Titre* and its first interior page hinting at "*Les Conséquences Fatales de . . .*"

He looked at the sixteen drawings, one to a page. They showed a handsome young man, a little older than he, becoming ill, hunching over, taking to his bed, shriveling up, and dying. What caught him off guard was the young gentleman's nose. It was large—not as large as his own, to be sure, but larger than most. Nonetheless, this man was considered handsome, beau—even Alexei's first-year French could decipher the first page:

Il était jeune, beau; il faisait l'espoir de sa mère. . . . He was young, handsome; he something the hope of his mother. . . .

Handsome—with a nose like that! Graulexei slipped the booklet into his coat for home study. He would, of course, bring it back when finished.

He did bring it back—as soon as he'd discovered its plot. That yellow booklet was a fierce attack on his intimate person.

With the help of a dictionary, he arrived at the following rough translation of the rest:

as my relationship with Emma did culminate, post-countdown, in a brief discussion of the metric system. It was the best I could do under the circumstances.

Hundwasser was, in fact, a math major in college, not good enough to become a mathematician, but probably hireable as an elementary school math teacher. But the NYU School of Medicine was paying more for beginning lab techs than the New York City Board of Education was for beginning math teachers, and besides, he'd have had to get a teaching license, and besides, he didn't really like kids, and besides, there might be more women hanging around a physiology research institute than around any PS 101. Pretty young things in white lab coats—always a turn-on for him. It was a riot to watch him come on to them with his mathoromantic pickup routine:

16. Right. But I give her credit for a considerate, plausible, medium-sized White Lie. She helped me understand that it is more important to appeal to someone who appeals to you than to appeal to yourself.

"Do you realize that mathematics exists independently of human beings, even pretty ones like you, and it structures our own universe and any other possible ones?"

They usually didn't know that, and were incipiently impressed.

"Math is the only conceptual structure we would have in common with extraterrestrial aliens, if any such there be."

This really wowed them. Like, aliens!

"Because reason itself is disembodied. Right?"

This would bring up the subject of bodies, according to plan.

"And therefore artificial intelligence is possible, at least in principle."

I always told him this was anticlimactic, but he insisted that ending with bodies was too forward and might frighten them away, that women like to think of themselves as intelligent, or at least as interested in intelligence. I suppose he must have been right because I usually wound up going home alone.

Speaking of mathematics, did you know "The Twelve Days of Christmas" was an arithmetical mnemonic for the basic teaching of the Christian faith? The partridge in a pear tree is Jesus; the 2 turtle doves, the Old and New Testaments, and so on: the five books of the

Torah, the six days of creation, etc., the ten commandments . . . Just thought I'd mention it while we're on the topic of mathematics. If you want to know the details, write me care of my publishers, and I'll get back to you. Send a photo if you like.

But the point I really wanted to make was that after thinking about it, I have to admit that Hundwasser was not altogether wrong in connecting mathematics and love. Like the search for truth in life and love, mathematical research is a messy business. Risky. Open to wasted years in blind alleys. Both are full of assumptions that both mathematicians and lovers take on faith with no guarantees of certainty, the goal elusive, unbearably unknowable.

All of which convinces me to stay away from mathematics. I've already got enough trouble.

- He corrupts himself! [Though he couldn't be sure, Alexei felt he understood.] Soon, because of it, he grows old before his time. His back becomes hunched . . .
- A devouring fire burns his entrails. He suffers horrible stomach pains. [Why, just last night he had had gas and cramps!]
- See his eyes, recently so pure, so brilliant, they are extinguished! A band of fire surrounds them. [He checked the mirror. His eyes were red!]
- He can't walk anymore. His legs something or other . . . [They do feel a little weak.]
- Awful dreams disturb his sleep; he cannot sleep. [Yes. Why just the night before he had dreamed . . . he couldn't remember!]
- His teeth rot away and fall out. [He checks around with his tongue.]
- His chest is burning up . . . he coughs up blood. [Not yet, not yet . . . But he had had a nosebleed last week. . . .]
- His hair, once so handsome, falls out like an old man's; he becomes prematurely bald.
- He is hungry; he wants to something his hunger; food will not stay in his stomach. [The illustration spares nothing in its vomit.]
- His chest something . . . he vomits blood.
- His whole body becomes covered with pustules. [Yes, yes, like mine, my buboes, look at them.] He is horrible to look at.
- A slow fever consumes him, he somethings, his whole body burns. . . . [Not looking very good. Empty eyes . . .]
- His whole body becomes something [stiff?]. His limbs stop moving. . . .
- He is delirious. He [stiffens?] against death. Death is the stronger. . . .
- At seventeen years old, he expires in horrible torments.[17]

Three years to go. *Bozhe moi*! He thought, I've got to stop corrupting myself. He would eat figs and pray to the Immaculate Virgin! He would wear rough gloves to bed. And in his loneliness, he would realize that Groucho was not enough, that Groucho would not attract his heart's desires. He must to go on from there.

Bigger.

More.

17. I never did return that pamphlet, nor did I go back and pay for it. I thought Pageant Bookstore ought to pay *me* for having read it, pay for my future medical costs and psychiatric expenses. Why did I keep it? It was a souvenir, as in the sense of

Je me souviens
des jours anciens
Et je pleure.

It would be a reminder of a past in which I could at least pleasure myself. In the face of that young man, once handsome, I could recall the good old days, as so many of us will do. It was also a souvenir of the future I sensed was ahead: buboes, pustules—the first intimation of my late life's work. It all hung together in a vague but weighty way.

I was deep into Rilke at the time, the *Letters to a Young Poet* (that was me, though I had writ-

3. Excursus on Noseism

or

You May Skip This Chapter, Pignut, if All You Want Is Plot[18]

ten no poems), and especially his *Journals*. Why was he exhorting me to die my own death, to carry that death within me like the kernel of a fruit, exhausting all my forces along the way to that kernel, pursuing all the implications of my destiny? And how did pustules and buboes fit in? That was to be seen.

And of all the striking images in *The Notebooks of Malte Laurids Brigge*, the one that most tantalized me was this:

> There are many people, but there are many more faces, because each person has several. Some people wear the same face for years, and naturally it wears out; it gets dirty; it splits at the folds; it stretches, like gloves one has worn on a journey. These are thrifty, simple folk; they do not change their faces; they never even have it cleaned. Their face is good enough, they maintain, and who can say otherwise? . . . There are people who change their faces uncannily quickly, one after another, and clear them away. At first they think they have enough to last them forever; but they are scarcely forty when they have come to the last of them. This naturally leads to tragedy. They are not accustomed to conserving faces. Their last is worn through in a week, has holes in it, and in many places is paper-thin; and then gradually the lining—the no-face comes through, and they go around with that.

Rilke's speculation made me understand the face of that handsome young man in the pamphlet, the rapidly changing face, uncanny, becoming pruriently unclean, wearing through, and ending in tragedy. It seemed to warn me—personally—about running out of faces like my pauvre ami, about ending up with a Nichtgesicht, a no-face.

Hundwasser notwithstanding, it was then and only then that I began to think about masks, a long series of them, which might get me through a life in which the face might wag the body to my own and everyone's interest, a Big White Lie life which might lead us all to freedom. *Vous comprenez?*

18. Hundwasser took a big hit for this chapter from the *New York Review*, the *London Review of Books*, and the *Times Literary Supplement*. They all three correctly lambasted it as an example of his "bogus gimcrackery" (*LRB*), "pontifically glib horn-tooting" (*TLS*), and "unprincipled, dilettantish huxterdom" (*NYR*). William Gass, in the *Atlantic Monthly*, labeled it "the mother of all verbalism: all generalities and everything that is too easily made lofty." John Leonard, in *Harpers*, was more avuncular: "A writer must pretend to be a writer in order to finally become a writer. *The Nose* is a fair imitation of literature." He goes on to add (and with this I agree completely), "The text creates the strange impression of absolute seriousness

and absolute childishness. Absolute honesty and absolute mendacity. Absolute knowledge about reality and absolute ignorance." What goes around, comes around, Bill.

What none of the critics remarked, however, was the deep contempt for the reader which, in a rare moment of truth, flashed out in the word "pignut." Now, I don't know what "pignut" meant to Hundwasser—at least as an imprecation. It is not in my dictionary as other than "any of several bitter-flavored hickory nuts." Perhaps he sensed the bitterness that might be coming to him when his literary manipulation would eventually be outed. But the scorn, the reduction of the millions of his readers and fans to a cohort who want "only plot" and would ignore his philosophical wisdom—this is what grates, and must be ruefully understood by every reader of his text.

Two points determine a line, two facial protuberances—original and Grouchistic—another. The reader by now has surely noticed a major determinant of this tale, a Foucauldian episteme,[19] as it were, the core substructure on which the edifice of our hero's life would be erected: his nose.

And this is odd. For that appendage seems about as important a human emblem as a coccyx or appendix, organs long vestigial to the destiny and purpose of Homo sapiens.[20] We watch the beasts and envy them, perhaps, the richness they must smell. We long ago exchanged that for bipedal standing, losing the spoor but gaining our thumbs and the rules of them.

Yet noses seem to haunt us as shadows from the past. "The nose is eternal," sings Stevens's guitar—and our lives are twirled on the fling of that nose, and into the thrown world.

When all else from the past has vanished, Proust observes, "the smell and taste of things remain poised a long time, like souls bearing resiliently, on tiny and almost impalpable drops of their essence, the immense edifice of memory."

Noses, noses, how they haunt us, how they swarm within our speech! We look down them and have things under them; we thumb them at people and cut them off to spite our faces; we hold them to the ground, and the grindstone, or just hold them, period, to indicate displeasure; we nose them around and get them out of joint; we are led by

19. For all his "Foucauldian" savvy, it was I who—after no more than a week's study—had to teach WH this crucial Foucauldian term. For you out there less than prepared concerning major, bald, male French thinkers, an "episteme" is the collection of historically understood givens that grounds knowledge and its discourse at any given time, and "makes possible the separation, not of the true from the false, but of what may from what may not be characterized as scientific" (Michel Foucault, *Power/Knowledge* (Pantheon, 1980, p. 197)). A useful term. In the current plague, of course, history is bunk.

20. Ah, the destiny and purpose of Homo sapiens. Not that sapiens continues to be an applicable adjective. However, a Nose-approved book, available by Intergalactic Library Loan, is Nicholas Berdyaev's *The Destiny of Man.* The book is prefaced by a quotation from Gogol ("It is sad not to see any good in goodness") which admirably foreshadows the quality of the investigation.

them and win by them, we brown-nose with them and poke them into others' business; we have noses for things, we are, perhaps, hardnoses; we count them, and all becomes plain as those things on our faces.

Alexei especially, growing up semi-Cyrillic, was exposed to even more nosology, for the Russians have an idiom-arsenal teeming with noseful expressions: they are nose-happy and nose-sad; they angle them when sleepy, hang them in dejection, and lift them up in glory. Forget something? Make a notch in a nose to remember, and whatever you do, don't lose it. A victor in battle will wipe your nose, a big one will grow for a century. Good news may make it tingle, and a good pimple foretells much carousing.

Consider the face: the eyes, two, the mouth, one, the nose, fascinatingly ambivalent. We have one nose, yes, but with nostrils which, when used alternately, can together call forth the kundalini serpent coiled in the spine. Sun and moon they are, hot and cold, catabolic, anabolic, purifying the nadis. Pranayama—the yogic science of breath—the nose's royal path to Self-realization and pure Consciousness.

The nose. Vestigial? No, crucially important. Who would have guessed? Well, many people, actually, led by the artists, nosing out the human soul. "All I want to do," Samuel Beckett once said, "is sit on my ass, and fart, and think of Dante." This thought needs parsing.[21]

Beckett's nose is the hidden character in this mise-en-scène. Sitting on ass and thinking of Dante may be exactly what Rodin's Thinker is doing. Or the Black Guelfs that exiled him from Florence. Or the lit student from UCLA. It is the fart that makes the difference.

We don't know which volume of the *Commedia* Beckett was thinking of, but it was not necessarily the *Inferno*. Given "All I want to do is . . ." it might have been *Paradiso*. Beckett being who he is, it was conceivably *Purgatorio*. But we will never know. Anything is possible to the fart-touched nose. Anything deep.

The great American writer Nathaniel West was moved to write the story of another Samuel, that peculiar genius Samuel Perkins, Smeller. Like someone else we know of, Perkins's life was dominated by his nose. He was deaf and almost blind. But "he could smell a chord in D minor, or distinguish between the tone smell of a violin and that of a viola. He could smell the caress of velvet and the strength of iron. It has been said of him that he could smell an isosceles triangle; I mean that he could apprehend through the sense of smell the principles involved in isosceles triangles." Our Alexei never attained such skills. His nose-principles were other—not entirely unlike those of Major Platon Kuzmich Kovalyov, Gogol's Collegiate Assessor who exerts such enormous effort

21. Notice how circumspect Hundwasser is about one of his own most secret pleasures. Here would be an excellent place for some overblown Hundwasserian "Disquisition on the Fart," or "Phart" as he might have spelled it in some pseudo-antiquarian gesture.

One of Hundwasser's most traumatic childhood moments, confessed to me from deep in his cups, was a car ride he had taken—with his mother and first little girlfriend—being driven to the movies for a Saturday-afternoon "date." That he didn't remember his date's name, or the name of the movie, demonstrates well the difference between him and me.

They were riding gaily along when all of a sudden, and beyond his control, young Billy let loose with a silent stinker. At that point the girl might not have been able to distinguish whether it was her date or his mother who had cut the cheese. But Mrs. H, typically, gaily, protectively, turned around to inquire, "Does someone need to go to the bathroom before the movie starts? I smell a bottom burp." The pointing finger had pointed. His future with this young beauty was done for. In spite of the fact that she let it all go by without blush or comment, their first date was their last.

Which is too bad. As Beckett was to so poetically underline—fart and Dante being joined in the same thought—"breaking wind" was not always so forbidden a topic. Our own Ben Franklin considered it at length in an address to the Royal Academy of France. And the French, ever leaders in cultural affairs, at one time worshiped Joseph Pujol ("Le Pétomane"), fartist extraordinaire, who outsold Sarah Bernhardt at the Moulin Rouge and became the highest-paid performer of his generation.

to locate the nose lately escaped from his face. If a nose were truly vestigial, why bother, why spend the two rubles and seventy-odd kopecks it would have cost to advertise for it? But Gogol knew the truth. He understood that the nose was the prince of organs, perfectly capable of independent existence. Dressed in a gold-braided uniform, praying in church, what need has a nose to relate to the noseless? Indeed, noses, Gogol assures us, had even built an entire civilization on the moon 138 years before Neil Armstrong's comparatively meager step for mankind. It's possible.

And we must recall Pynchon's lymphatic monster, the giant Adenoid, bigger than Saint Paul's Cathedral, a "horrible transformation of cell plasma quite beyond Edwardian medicine to explain," on its rampage through the East End of London. Metaphor, to be sure, but a signal that, like Alexei's, nose appurtenances in general may function protectively, trapping pathogens and devising antibodies, achieving immunity. Does not London need an immune system?

We must conclude, then, that while our olfactory sense suffers from upright posture plus sensor deficiency (dogs have 100,000 times as many olfactory receptors as humans), noses are not at all vestigial, an appendix of the face. Nor are those organs too ridiculous to be seriously discoursed upon. Why, one-third of American adults pick their noses at least once an hour.[22]

Eighteenth- and nineteenth-century anatomists developed the science of descriptive rhinology, a study prematurely discarded for reasons of political correctness. As the chiromancer could read the hand for character and destiny, and the phrenologist the skull, so could the rhinologist generalize character types from the structure of the nose. Johann Kasper Lavater's *Physiognomische Fragmente zur Beförderung der Menschenkenntnis und Menschenliebe* (1775–1778) (Physiognomical Fragments towards the Advancement of the Knowledge of Human Nature and Kindness among Men) asserted that it is the mind which shapes the nose, and thus that physical beauty implies moral goodness. And George Jabet's famous *Notes on Noses* (London, 1854) asserted that "the accurate observation and minute comparison of an extensive collection of Noses of persons whose mental characteristics are known justifies a Nasal Classification."

But none of Jabet's drawings or distinctions capture the character of Alexei's nose, his disposition, or his destiny. Was his pterodactyl snout his enemy, as in Gogol, or his friend, as with Beckett and Perkins? Or was it cruel only to be kind, as per Pynchon? Galen believed that nasal secretions signaled a "purging of the brain" that percolated through the base of the skull to the nose. Were there more nasal secrets whispering in

Passing gas is a field ripe for exploration. And indeed I have been forced into such researches by the nature of my costume. As you can imagine, plague doctors were much concerned with contamination and personal death as they went about helping others. The outfit I have inherited is essentially an ensemble of self-containment, impermeable to miasmas or fluxions from outside, and substantially containing my own.

The smell I must deal with. After studying the issue for the last five years, I have come to the following conclusions:

1. In general, I like the smell of my own farts; given the mask with its herb-stuffed beak, I never smell the farts of others.
2. Each of my fart episodes is truly unique in its frequency, discharge quality (blast), duration, humidity, qualitative odor, saturation, and degree of smelliness. Given the 49 strains of anaerobic microbes responsible and the vast combination of foodstuffs on which they may act, this variety is understandable. But not generally acknowledged is that some farts may smell as sweet as lilies of the valley.

Medical opinion is unanimous: on no account should farts be held in. Such gases convert within the gut to toxins like cadaverine, putrescine, and scatole. Franklin notes that "[wind] so retain'd contrary to Nature, it not only gives frequently great present Pain, but occasions future Diseases, such as habitual Cholics, Ruptures, Tympanies, &c. often destructive of the Constitution, & sometimes of Life itself." So out with them.

But one must be considerate of others. I don't know how many of my liberated intestinal gas events penetrate through the waxed material of my undertrousers and overgown, but just in case, on nights when I appear at public events, I do not partake of beets, attack beans, or other legumes. And I take my meals with savory, which I have found to reduce flatulence. I have not yet tried Beano.

As I do this work, I am entranced by the conundrum of why we fart furtively in public, but are proud and grateful to let 'er rip without restraint in private.

Public rejection? Well, farting is no respecter of rank or beauty; all become obviously equal in its domain. Society will never approve of that.

22. I cannot find a reputable source for this piece of data. I rather suspect that WH was guessing, as 73% of statistics are simply made up. With him, probably more than that.

our hero's ear? Was his brain the don and his nose the henchman? Was the sequence of his ever-larger noses working for or against him?

That the nose may be the enemy is hinted at by the peculiar Enigma of the Nose, to wit:

Why is it that our pets, in fits of reverent love, present their tushies to our faces? And why is it that we push them away? Their friends like it—why don't we? Alone in the class Mammalia, we by and large reject the odors of our most odorific parts, decline the information they purvey, purge them away with daily washing, deodorants, and scent. Do we know more than we admit about the Nose's inimical intentions? Are we aware of its potential power over us—its receptors pushing long fibers through the base of the skull, directly to the bulbs between the brows—those intimates of the limbic system—home of the emotions, of sexuality and reptilian drives—and from thence, riding the hippocampus, deep into Proustian memory? Here is nakedness within nakedness, vulnerability at the heart of the vulnerable. Do we trust the nose to take us there? That limbic system was originally called the rhinencephalon, the nose-brain. Does not that, in itself, set off an alarm?

Clearly so. Most of us are taught as young children not to sniff at someone else's crotch. Or at their armpits. It's not polite. And so our sense of smell remains uneducated, simple-minded (Mmmm! and Yuck!), and atrophies from lack of use. And thus vanishes—in the nick of time—the Enigma of the Nose, fashioned on our faces like Saint Peter's cross, upside down, humble—and betraying. Man reversed, divided within himself against himself. The Tarot's Hanged Man, the mysterious paradox of our lives, right there, phallic, protruding from our collective face. Truly, it's not polite.

Private approbation? For one, here is our lowest nature, often so cruelly suppressed, striving to express itself. Civilization discontent no more. But more importantly, farting is the secret instruction we have both of the ills that flesh is heir to, and of our universal human destiny. The paths of glory lead but to the grave. This we must be made to know.

4.

The Horror, the Horror[23]

23. Whew! After Professor Hundwasser's pontifical "Excursus," back to reality. Which is not to say that reality is best characterized by "The Horror, the Horror!" though in this time of evil there is certainly enough of it to go around.

Just as the '50s were infested with premature antifascists, so the early '60s were contaminated by Alexei Pigov, premature goth.[24] Jan & Dean were still belting out "Little Old Lady from Pasadena," and young girls were arguing over which was the cutest Beatle when he awoke one morning from disturbing dreams and found himself transformed into Alex Schreck, madman.

At fifteen, Alexei Pigov was a sophomore at the High School of Music and Art. His statistics were:

Drawings in his admissions portfolio: 35
Number judged as "weird" by his admissions committee: 6
Hours it took to ride on the subway to school and back daily: 2.8
Number of friends among the art students: 1
Number of friends among the music students: 2
Sexual intercourse: 0

Given twice as many musical as artistic friends, one might wonder why he had matriculated in the art division of the school. And that was precisely what young Alexei wondered. Especially since the focus of his attention, the object of his affection, the polestar of all his obsessions was his

24. An ignorant mischaracterization. I'll have more to say about this below.

First Love,

young Elizabeth Schrank. Yes, there had been Alice Mulvaney. But that had been when he was a child, awkward in his Groucho-nose and glasses. Now he was a . . . he was older, still awkward in his nose and glasses, but older, taller at least, with hair to be occasionally shaved and an almost consistent baritone.

Elizabeth was so beautiful, so thrillingly lovely, so flat-out stunning that it made him feel both fluid and electrical. And that charged runniness flowed blindingly upward through his eyes and brain and caressingly downward, engulfing his unmentionables. Especially when she played the violin. For him, she was (as they say today) "to die for."[25]

During free periods, Graulexei would pretend to be sketching while stalking up and down the practice-room hallways, searching out his Liz. He came to love the polytonality of sounds collectively filling the long, narrow space and thought of that cacophony as a Song of Songs, made of all the possibilities of tone and timbre. And he came to love the Prokofiev Concerto she was working on over her entire sophomore year.[26]

Most often, Elizabeth practiced alone, teasing out the difficult passages, working on phrasing and tone. Once a week, she met with Camilla Brogliano, a sweet but ill-favored pianist, known for her hairiness and her ability to sight-read anything. Midway through the term, Camilla disappeared. It was rumored that she had been further attacked by her adrenals and was hiding out in some convent in Little Italy. Elizabeth continued her practicing alone until one May morn-

25. The intertwining of love, sex, and death is of course one of the deepest, most moving themes in literature, and it is not surprising that Hundwasser would appropriate it early on in his effort to be on the *New York Times* best-seller list. The dying Tristan named that tune: "To yearn—and to die!" And well I understood it in Lily's presence. Lily Strauss—that name, that pure whiteness, flower of the Virgin, bouquet of chastity at home in funeral chapel or resurrection. Lily Strauss! Let me living die!

Elizabeth Schrank, Hundwasser? You name her Schrank? A cabinet instead of a bouquet? Good, Billy, very good. At least you don't insult her memory.

Lily's not dead, of course. I mean, I think she's not dead, though I've lost track of her. In fact, after high school I never saw or heard of her again. I

26. As will be apparent from his fictitious report of Lily's and my fictitious rehearsal, WH did truly like Prokofiev. He had failed at piano lessons as a child, but not before playing three of P's "Twelve Easy Pieces for Piano," Op. 65, and feeling appropriate, if aborted, twinges.

Hundwasser liked Prokofiev. But I *love* him. Consequently, I hate him. All that talent blooming into the talent of the toad, taming itself to match the grandeur of socialist realism. Those ghastly letters he wrote to the Soviet Composers' Union to get them to call off their philistine dogs: "It is the duty of the composer to serve his fellow

ing, he was horrified to see her shut in with . . . the back of . . . who was it? . . . Marciano! Pete Marciano!

As threatless as poor Pete was to Alexei, he was another male, another male engaged with his Elizabeth, enclosed in a small room with her, her! And the goddamn Prokofiev didn't sound all that bad either!

Through Graulexei's brain ran some archetype from the collective unconscious: "Hey, skinny, yer ribs are showing." "Quit kicking that sand in my face." "Shut up, you bag of bones." "Darn it! I'm tired of being a ninety-seven-pound weakling. . . ." He knew who he was in this scenario, but he couldn't remember what to do about it or where the story went from there. He thought he'd better find out.

Pageant Book Shop to the rescue! At the desk, eternal, sat old Sid, wise as Solomon.

"Hallo there, little Grouch, what can I do for you today?"

Graulexei queried.

"Atlas," Sam said. "You want Atlas."

Graulexei was doubtful. Atlas was mythology, or a map.

"Atlas, the Titan, also with a big nose, condemned to hold up the sky on his shoulders . . ." He led the boy up the stairs.

"And that's what you get for rebelling, you should take note. Holding up the sky," down the narrow aisle to the back of the store, "forever."

Sam left Graulexei bewildered in front of Pageant's foresighted comic-book collection, boxes of old, not-yet-valued ephemera, whimsically slipcased by bibliophiles. Worth little then and a fortune today.[27]

Graulexei recalled the feel of a comic book between his fingers. *Le temps perdu*. Are you an artist? Draw the pirate. Send away for. He pulled a *Tales from the Crypt* out of its plastic envelope, opened it, Hebraically, from the rear, and—bam!—there it was—the end of the story: a mail-order course, a punch in the nose. And "Oh, Joe, you're such a he-man!" Yes, he-man, *the* man, MY man! The sequence was inevitable.

expected her to be signed by some big record company and featured on their advertising in the new "sexy instrumentalist" category which seems to have taken over the music business. Or at least I'd expected to find her listed in the roster of some major orchestra. But I've checked the New York Philharmonic, Cleveland, Philadelphia, Pittsburgh, San Francisco, LA—not listed. I suppose I could try to track down all the rosters of the several hundred smaller orchestras—Grand Rapids, Little Rock—like that, down to whatever I could find of the community orchestras. But she was too good for a community orchestra, even as concert mistress. She couldn't put up with players who didn't practice five hours a day like she did. So where is she?

Might she be dead? Unthinkable thought. She'd be a gorgeous, talented woman now, a woman in her prime. And what could she possibly die of? Breast cancer? Such petite and shapely breasts (again I blush) could not conceive of such a thing. Leave that to her big-boobed, sight-reads-anything accompanist with her oddly-assorted hormones, whose name I don't remember. It wasn't Camilla. But if Lily were dying, I'd drop everything and run to her hospice to offer aid and comfort. These things really help. Even after death, I'm told.

For example, when Imelda's hus-

men, to beautify human life and point the way to a radiant future."

And what about the ugliness of life? *Kyrie eleison*! Is that not also to be painted—the better to understand it? Would Alban Berg have written such garbage to the Viennese Composers' Union?

"I am also guilty of atonality, which is often related to formalism, although I must confess with happiness that I began to yearn for tonal music long ago."

Guilty of atonality. A wonder he didn't puke up his borscht writing this line.

"The decision of the Central Committee of February 10, 1948, has separated the rotten threads from the healthy ones in the creative work of composers. No matter how painful it is for many composers, myself included, I agree to the resolution of the Central Committee, which establishes the condition for making the whole organism of Soviet music healthy."

So much for "innovationism." Mozart may have been an irresponsible, womanizing spendthrift, Beethoven a boor, Wagner an anti-Semite, Strauss a crypto-Nazi. But none of them deprived the world of the insights their genius could unfold. Even I have tried to remain faithful to my quest, and not give in to the blandishments of success. Why could not my beloved Prokofiev do likewise? I hate him. *Odo et amo.*

27. Wouldn't you know it—another obligatory gesture for entry into the McSweeney Brotherhood of Contemporary Hipness and Pop-Culture Distinction: a reference to comic books. Just a nod, a knowing glance, an indication that the author so deeply values them that he really needn't go into it.

But what good would bodybuilding do him? Elizabeth probably wasn't even interested in bodies. She was a soul-woman—you could tell. From her playing, you could tell. Did she hang out with jocks? Was she on the girl's volleyball team? Her dear skin would burn at the beach. Burn and peel.

He sat on the creaky floor, squeezed between tottering shelves of Americana, wondering what to do, where to go from here. And voilà, second synchronicity, Sid designed: just beyond his knees lay stacks of old *Life* magazines, beckoning. He searched for 1951, January issues, and there, staring seductively at him, from three days post his birth, was Betsy von Furstenberg, Society Girl, a rose clutched to her bosom.

Graulexei knew nothing of Betsy von Furstenberg, but he was certain she did not play Prokofiev. He leafed intently through the magazine. Communist forces in Seoul, an ad for the new Nash Rambler, $1,732, Fresh-up with Seven-Up! And on page 33, *Bozhe moi*! the answer, the real answer, the long-term and infinite answer:

There was a drawing of a young man, better-dressed and with a nose much shorter than Graulexei's, no Groucho-glasses with mustache, just a plain, ordinary fella who would probably love a date with Betsy von Furstenberg. He was twirling a stool in front of a small piano as four couples, looking gay but doubtful, prepared to listen. "Can he really play?" a girl whispered. "Heavens no!" Arthur exclaimed. "He never played a note in his life." And under this graphic introduction, the large type: "They Laughed When I Sat Down at the Piano But Then I Started to Play!"

> *Instantly a tense silence fell on the guests. The laughter died on their lips as if by magic. I played through the first few bars of Beethoven's immortal "Moonlight Sonata." I heard gasps of amazement. My friends sat breathless—spellbound!*
>
> *Then:*
>
> *"Jack! Why didn't you tell us you could play like that?" . . . "Where did you learn?"—"How long have you studied?"—"Who was your teacher?"*
>
> *"I have never even seen my teacher," I replied. "And just a short while ago I couldn't play a note."*
>
> *"Quit your kidding," laughed Arthur, himself an accomplished pianist. "You've been studying for years. I can tell."*
>
> *"I have been studying only a short while," I insisted. "I decided to keep it a secret so that I could surprise all you folks."*

band, what's his name? Fernando? Ferdinand Marcos died in '89, Imelda put him in a refrigerated casket which played a tape of Handel's Messiah 24 hours a day. Can you imagine how wonderful that was for him, assuming he didn't get too cold? There's not a note in that work which isn't truly inspired and inspiring, even if you're dead. Handel, after all, is dead.

And when the Philippines finally permitted Imelda to bury her beloved in his village, she changed the music to a tape loop of Mozart's *Ave Verum Corpus*, for, following Kübler-Ross, she had finally accepted the fact that her husband was a corpse.

But eight years post-mortem, there was a problem with an unpaid electric bill for the refrigeration and music. It was over 200 thousand dollars, and the family was unwilling to pay it, thinking that Hawaii and the Philippines kind of owed them. So Batangas Electric pulled the plug on the coffin. You may think I am making this up, but I'm not. If you look at it the right way, Ferdinand's final dissolution is everything Tristan or Isolde could have wanted.

But you know what the really big problem is? Elisabeth Kübler-Ross. What a happy-end swindle she pulled over the bloodshot eyes of the seventies. Grief does not end in acceptance except in New Age fairy tales. Grief opens the

Now, don't get me wrong. I love comic books too. Hundwasser and I used to share our collections of Archie Comics (to ogle the girls) and *Tales from the Crypt.* But really—what cultural infantalization! The diapering of America.

Harry Potter is the best example. All these chronological adults assuring one another that this is their kid's book, not theirs, "but it's really very good!"

Now, I haven't read Harry Potter. I'm willing to give it the benefit of the doubt. OK, it's "good." But it's especially dangerous in a society that idealizes youth and depreciates age and the wisdom that comes with it. That the release of a children's book becomes the central event in the literary year, that everywhere one goes, one sees grown-ups carrying thick hardcover books which are not *The Brothers K.* or *War and Peace* . . . but I don't need to go on.

Everyone clutching at their pasts, honoring—worshiping—their inner children. We now drink coffee out of sippy-cups. Where is this headed? This is not just dumbing down—this is a forced march, an active pursuit of dystopia. Our infantilization rejects any real-world activity that could better the lot of humankind. It postpones any attainment of authentic human desire, even if shallow or destructive. All this peterpandemonium, profiting the puppeteers and debilitating the puppets.

I went to a stationery store last Valentine's Day to buy a card for someone I'd fallen in love with. The first two I picked up read, FOR MY SUPER-DUPER GIRLFRIEND and TO MY HUNNY-BUNNY WIFE. I ran out, a Munch-faced adult. Andrea, admirable as she is, is neither super-duper nor hunny-bunny, never could be, nor could any other real woman. It does not take Simone de Beauvoir to understand this.

Then I told them the whole story.
"Have you ever heard of the U.S. School of Music?" I asked.

Graulexei had never heard of the U.S. School of Music. But he read on—about easily learning to "play ballads or classical numbers or jazz, all with equal ease!" Elizabeth might like that. Might love it. Three hundred fifty thousand people had already learned to play their favorite instruments.

There was no piano at home, and Nastya would never spring for one, no matter how cheap. "The floor will break," she'd insist, and she may have been right. But there, in a box at the bottom of the page, was a list of other instruments taught via mail by the U.S. School of Music. Many instruments. He couldn't displace Pisspot Pete by accompanying Liz on the flute, on the clarinet, or the trombone. But he could accompany her on—an accordion!—his father's very own ax, a classic keyboard instrument older and so doubtless more evolved than the pianoforte Beethoven himself had wrestled with.[28]

Was the U.S. School of Music still out there—or had it collapsed in the whirlwind of the '60s? Graulexei wrote the address on the back of his hand: 1031 Brunswick Bldg., New York City. He galloped down the stairs.

"Find what you wanted, Mr. Little Groucho?"

"You bet your life!" Graulexei answered, grouching his eyebrows up and down over his nose-glasses and holding up the back of his hand for evidence.

"You need a piece paper? I got paper. . . ."

"No, this is my system—ballpoint on flesh. Leaves no evidence when washed. But where in the name of Quacko is the Brunswick Building? Why don't they give the address?"

"If you don't know, you don't need to," His Omniscience replied.

"So how will I find it?"

"Ask me, why not? Corner of Twenty-sixth and Fifth."

"How come you know this and I don't?"

Sid Solomon smiled his most seraphic smile and waved the nose-glassed, mustachioed boy away, northwise.

sensibility for more grief in a positive feedback loop with exponential slope. Not just lovers die of grief—everyone does. The tree of knowledge is not the tree of life. No one can survive their eventual comprehension of universal grief.

Lily, dear Lily, if you are reading this, please contact me through my publisher and let me know you're okay.

28. I did play the accordion for quite a while. But it was not because the U.S. School of Music enticed me into it. When I was fourteen, I bumped into a Ukrainian festival over on East Seventh. In the midst of a cacophony of raucous music and dance, of hawking produce and foods, a beautiful young woman appeared around the corner from Second Avenue. She was on five-foot stilts with a long dress and braided hair. She played a song on a small accordion that was so lovely and tragic that the entire street went hushed, as if an angel were not just passing over, but had somehow come among us.

We Slavs have a saying: "When you hear an angel singing, you feel death near." I'm sure the crowd felt just that. A sad accordion folk song could never have done it alone. The silence. In the streets of New York City. During a festival. Not even the sound of ambient traffic. Something extraordinary was going on.

I wanted to be able to play that song, but by the time I had wrangled an accordion from my accordion-resisting mother, I had not the slightest memory of how it went. I never knew its name, so could never look it up. I went back to the festival the next year and the next, hoping to find the stilter. She never showed again.

But I did teach myself to play accordion. More than passably, perhaps with genius, as my father likely did. Some have called me "the Glenn Gould of the accordion." I like that. He too was a fighter against the plague.

It was a twelve-minute fast walk over to Fifth and up to Twenty-sixth. Unfortunately, there were four corners at that corner, three with buildings. He had to ask a passerby. He had to ask five passersby before one would answer him. Perhaps wearing Groucho glasses made him look weird? The answer he finally did get was, "Brunswick Building? I dunno. What's the address?"

So he thought he'd apply the generally accepted principle of empiricism and investigate them all. Since there was only one building on the north side of Twenty-sixth, he'd start with that one.

Bingo.

The Brunswick Building was a twelve-story, turn-of-the-century extravaganza, elegantly conceived. Graulexei found the front door, and the lobby directory, and there, on the tenth floor, there it was, 1031—currently the primest of numbers—the U.S. School of Music!

Elevator up. Ten. Long hallway. Eyes bugging with excitement through empty black frames. Long hallway, 25, 27, 29 . . .

The U.S. School of Music. National, perhaps international, in scope. Three hundred fifty thousand students. More by now, probably—that ad was as old as he was. He knocked timidly at the frosted glass window with the embossed lyre.

"Yeah?"

He poked his Groucho face in the door.

"Scram. We don't want any."

He closed the door, confused, and returned to the hallway. Maybe he should come in without his nose-glasses. But then there would be his nose—and that could be worse. But now he knew the place existed. Why not just write for more information? That way he'd have a chance to see the options, think about it, perhaps find an instrument, somehow, somewhere. It was May, and his love would disappear for the summer in less than a month. No chance to wow her before that. No chance—all right, little chance—she'd be ready to perform the Prokofiev before next term. He'd write away. He'd find an instrument. He'd use the summer to learn to play ballads or classical numbers or jazz, all with equal ease. And he did.

Soothing the Savage Breast

His black plastic very used Hohner Hohnica with seven nonfunctioning reeds ($30 at J&R Pawn Shop on Forty-seventh Street) reminded Nastya of Hawk's—and, alas, of Hawk too. Because of that, she approved of Graulexei's proposal and agreed to foot the bill for instrument and self-instruction. When it made its first sounds behind her son's bedroom door, she wandered around in the kitchen, then sat down and wept—in part for lost love and in part for fury at the unwanted child who dared revive such memories.

At school, Graulexei's "See you in September" farewell meant so much more to him than to Elizabeth Schrank. She took it lightheartedly; he meant it with the weight of a fateful agenda, a full program of both Norns and Muses—all three and nine of them.

"'Bye," she said.

He nodded his nose, mustache, and glasses at her, and lowered his lids.

Waiting at home was his secret charm, the Hohnica, the honey to attract his queen.

Over the summer, the hottest in twenty years, Graulexei did nothing but eat (little), sleep (less), read (metaphysical love poetry), and practice accordion (eight to twelve hours a day) until his back and shoulders ached. Nastya's pain on hearing him develop was massive, more than even she could stand. She was moved thereby to spend most of her nights with Antonio, her latest, a Tums for her tummy.

Her son, however, was blazingly inspired. It was good he'd not chosen the flute or trombone, for the mustache on his glasses would have compromised his embouchure. But his entire face fitted nicely above the bellows, and in a certain light, with certain cultural expectations, he even looked the part (he checked the mirror), a gypsy accordionist with a fascinating allure, black plastic instrument gleaming under black plastic frames, mustache fluttering seductively when he or his instrument breathed.

Breathing. That was the first thing he loved about the instrument. He would hold down the air button and just work the bellows. Inbreath whoosh and outbreath whooooo, much more expressive than his own sighing. Whoosh and whoooo, whoosh and whooo. He could do it all day, get into it, under it, surround it, embed.

When he was asked why he never wrote for the organ, Igor Stravinsky said, "Because

the monster never breathes." Graulexei's machine did breathe, and in breathing was then no monster, but some antimonster, cure and corrective to all that might pretend to be beyond prana. Alas, there was more than just pumping the bellows to be done.

From the U.S. School of Music Accordion Instruction Series Book 1, Level: Beginner, he learned the parts of his instrument, how the fingers are numbered; he learned the bass keyboard—all those buttons!—beginning with "A Bass Tune" and "A Chord Waltz," and then the piano keyboard. But who wanted to play "Merrily We Go Along" or "The Big Parade"? Not he. What did merriment have to do with his Liz Project, a happy one, to be sure, but so much more complex than merry? Learning "Charlie the Chimp" would not serve his purpose. He was already too "entertaining." He had to become instead . . . heartbreakingly compelling.

The speed drills he liked, outlets for his nervousness and manic energy. His fingers could fly, if only in one position. But why fly them on "She'll Be Comin' 'Round the Mountain" or "Golden Slippers"? If she ever did come 'round the mountain, she would not be drivin' six white horses or wearin' red pajamas. She would be floating in softest gossamer, playing Prokofiev. He would caress the violin scar on her lovely neck and tell her she was beautiful anyway.[29]

None—none!—of the selections in the U.S. School of Music Accordion Instruction Series Book 1, Level: Beginner was appropriate. All were not only a waste of time but a desecration of his love, a slanderous belittling of his great passion. "Little Brown Jug Polka" indeed! He would proceed directly to the heart of things—the piano reduction of the Prokofiev Violin Concerto in D Major, Op. 19. He got it at Patelson's, used, for a buck and a half.

Learning to play the accordion on a piano reduction of the Prokofiev First Violin Concerto is somewhat like learning to swim by swimming the English Channel. Unaided, as Graulexei was, one would either succeed or drown, with the odds greatly in favor of the latter. But the young man was floated and propelled full speed ahead by the image of his muse, his love, young Elizabeth Schrank, the most beautiful violinist at Music & Art, the sophomore angel already principal second in the school's famous orchestra. Juilliard will be lucky to get her. And so will I! he thought. If she, at fifteen, could be rehearsing her audition piece, he, at fifteen, should be able to master it too. Such is the arrogance of love. Come September, he would offer her all three movements, along with his heart, on a platter.

Joseph Szigeti, one of the concerto's earliest interpreters, had called the work "a mixture of fairy-tale naïveté and daring savagery." To those qualities, Graulexei would

29. Lily had a scar under her lower left jaw, where her chin engaged the chin-rest. Even though she usually wore high turtlenecks, perhaps to hide it, I'd seen it often enough to have to confront it, to confront its effect upon me.

First, and most obviously, who am I to object to a slight physical deformity in another? Well, I'll tell you who I am: I am someone exquisitely sensitive to the question of deformity, someone whose eye, heart, mind, and soul can laser in on it, whose mental tongue can taste it, whose ear can hear its melody and key. Deformity, for me, is not just another standard variation.

It was comforting to see that most of the forward-stand violinists and violists in the Music & Art orchestra also carried such stigmata. A string-playing friend told me it was called a violin or fiddle "hickey," and was a mark of pride for its bearers, a battle scar announcing, "Look how much I practice!" But what if the redness on Lily's swan-lovely neck were more than a dermatological condition? What if it were the scarlet mark of an affair, a wound of Cupid, and someone sucking—vampire-like—on her neck? Not possible. Too horrible to consider.

Others' scars were on duck necks, dog jaws, and ape chins. But a silver swan's neck and throat are sacred in a way no others are. Lily was surely the sacred wounded, like Amfortas, like Jesus, like any number of tortured saints. A scar on Lily was qualitatively different—an affront to all that is true, good, and beautiful in the world. The contrast with her unique loveliness was shocking. And at some level, and though I tried to hide it, I never ceased being shocked.

It is perhaps no accident that at my time of maximum mooning I was reading the Mann short sto-

add the longing lyricism of its opening, so romantic; the argumentativeness of its middle section (for argue they must); and its peaceful, dreamy, tranquil resolution, so evocative of his deepest desires. All those were Graulexei. Graulexei and Elizabeth, chagalled, entwined.

September came, and Graulexei was ready. For the first day of school, he was determined to make a killer impression. That morning, he washed and adjusted his nose so that it rode precisely perpendicular to the plane of his newly polished glasses. He brushed the pendant mustache with a new toothbrush—and his teeth too. He put on the dark-blue suit he had found abandoned on Ninth Street. His accordion case was Shinola-bright. If it didn't fit in his locker, there were plenty of hiding places in the old Gothic building. And given the hoity-toity mentality of the music students, who would want it? Who would steal it? What do you call ten accordions at the bottom of the ocean?—a good start. Ha ha.

No, his Hohnica would be safe—and unique. But there was a problem: how to introduce the subject. He auditioned various strategies:

"Well, hello, Elizabeth . . ." No, too formal. "Hi, Elizabeth . . ." Better to call her Lizzy? No, too familiar. "Hi, Elizabeth, nice to see you again." ("And nice to see you," she'd have to say.) "Say, Elizabeth would you . . ." No. No need to use her name in every sentence. "Say, are you still working on the Prokofiev?" Oh, no, what if she'd gone on to something else? The entire summer wasted! Endless hours, all that pain. No, she must still be working on it. It didn't sound all that good in June. Even though it sounded great. Fabulous. "Hey, how's the Prokofiev going?" Good. That was good. But it didn't get him into the picture. Suddenly he couldn't remember how he had decided to start!

Graulexei decided just to wing it. Better not to overrehearse. He stowed his accordion case in a broom closet on the fourth floor. The actual encounter went like this:

"Um, hey, you wanna play Prokofiev with me?"

"Oh, hi, Al. What do you mean play Prokofiev with you? You don't pl—"

"Oh, yes, I do."

"I thought you were an art student."

"Well, music is an art, isn't it?"

ries, "Death in Venice" and especially "Tonio Kroger." What can one conclude from these writings but that disease (a violin hickey) is the source from which all art (Lily and her music) springs, that perhaps all artists are diseased in some way, must be diseased if they are to be artists, and most radical of all, that disease is perhaps a good thing compared to bourgeois "health"—the factitious, superficial, decorative shallowness that pretends to be the world.

Lily's scar became clothed for me in ethical glory, both sign and signifier of the deeper reality Prokofiev chose to ignore, the reality Alban Berg embraced. And I embraced Lily ever more profoundly for it.

"Uh . . . I guess so. You mean you want to accompany me on the concerto I'm working on?"

"Yeah. Sure. Why not?"

"It's a very hard part . . ."

"I can probably handle it."

"Well . . . okay, I mean we can give it a try. When are you free?"

She asked me for a date, she asked me for a date! he thought.

"Oh, almost any time. I've got a really light schedule this semester. When are you free?"

She checked her new schedule.

"How about 2:15? Practice room 12 has a good piano. Let's do it there. I'll go sign it out right now."

"Great. See you then."

She stepped on down the hall, her violin case strapped to her back.

The Courtship of Graulexei Pigov

It must be admitted that surprise does not bring out the best in us. When he showed up at Room 12 at 2:15 on the dot, Elizabeth had not yet arrived, and Grailexei became Graylexei right there, in the hallway, obsessing on grayish thoughts, his morning's balloon leaking fast.

He had eaten little during lunch, so as to shunt no blood from brain and fingers to digestive tract, and now she wasn't even here. Their first date, and she had stood him up.

Oh, but there she was, coming down the hall! Gray turned to grace, and grace to gracias, gracias a Dios! and thank God too.

"Hi, Al. What's that you've got there?"

"What do you think?"

They went in. She was unpacking her violin.

"Um, a cat carrier?"

"No breathing holes."

"A huge typewriter?"

"Close, but not really. It's my piano."

He opened the case. Honey had never looked so black-and-white and shiny.

"It's . . . an accordion."

Let it be said, that even at Music & Art, where an accordion had never been seen, and where viola jokes were king, a small side chapel was reserved for accordion jokes. Even the exquisite Elizabeth Schrank was aware of the following story: "A man parks his car in a rough part of town with two accordions on the backseat, forgetting to lock the door. When he returns, there are three accordions."

Thus, her "It's . . . an accordion" was not a simple declarative sentence describing a local object. It was a tastefully understated disclosure of horror, of taint, of musical pollution, of which starry-eyed Al was oblivious.

"Right. A Hohner Hohnica. Top of the line."

"But I thought you said you played the piano."

"This is a piano accordion. There are button ones."

"I mean, this score is for violin and piano. Like this piano here." She pointed at the small Steinway.

He had an answer all prepared. "Say, which can do all the flute passages better, this guy here, or my guy?"

Not persuasive.

"But . . . it's . . . the part is too hard for an accordion. It needs the full range of . . ."

"Try me."

Groucho stood there like an accordionist landed on Mars, proposing to collaborate with a greatly puzzled and tentative Martian colleague. The seconds of silence seemed like minutes. He looked imploringly at his beloved.

"Well, okay, let's see what it sounds like."

Al harnessed up, feeling a bit undelicate compared to her. Honey was, after all, a machine—a music machine, but a machine nonetheless. Compared to Elizabeth's exquisite violin . . . But he knew he had her now. She set her music on her stand and offered him the piano part.

"No, thanks. I know it," he said.

He could see he had impressed her already.

"But what if we need to go back to a certain measure?"

"I know the measure numbers. Don't worry."

For her, the Martian, he had transformed from an alien earthling into a something from Neptune. Pret-ty weird! But okay.

"Ready?"

"Ready."

Graulexei laid down, ever so gently, a prelude, a soft aureole of sound to accompany her opening melody. All those accordion breathing exercises, techniques he had labored over: Cheyne-Stokes breathing, yogic, Kussmaul, and agonal. Days and days of bellows practice on these alone enabled him to provide a delicate setting for her gem of a melody. What a tune, he thought, what a face, what a body, that beautiful hair. Shimmering tremolandos of hair, shimmering tremolandos of sound. At the end of the opening statement, it was her turn to accompany him, and for the first time she looked upon her partner. What she saw was so surprising that she almost forgot where she was. He, Alex Pig-something—whatever his name was—he who never took off those stupid nose-glasses and kind of oozed around like a creepy teenaged amoeba, staring at whatever, was playing this, her favorite music. On some back burner of her consciousness, she was low-flame astounded. But Prokofiev was still on high, at the front of the range.

Come the middle section of the movement, the piano reduction of the orchestral score was bursting its poor seams to contain all that was going on. Fierce cross-rhythms, wild leaps of exclamation, prestissimo skittering of arpeggios and scales heading this way and that. First-rate pianists always had a hard time with this section and excused themselves with the feeling that, well, it was only an approximation anyway. But Alexei made it his own. His may have been the first hands to actually play every note in this maniacal display. They looked to Elizabeth like wild spiders high on speed and acid. And not just two. God knows how many there were—a clutter of them, a gaggle, moving so dexterously and so fast as to be a visual blur. Elizabeth's eyes widened attractively, her mouth opened seductively, and—not so attractively—a little bit of spittle drooled toward her chin rest. She quickly licked it back. But Alexei didn't see; his eyes were closed.

She played through the dreamy end of the movement staring at him in a kind of trance. Alexei's eyes remained shut, and a whole-body, beatific smile enveloped his being, the lips under his nose-mustache, the tilt of his head, the alternate rise and fall of his shoulders as he opened and closed the bellows, and the sway of abdomen over pelvis on the piano bench as he surrounded her, wind-like, harp-like, in delectable filigree. The final twisty flute run dissipated in the air like a wisp of sweet-smelling smoke.

He open his eyes and gazed at the woman to whom he had given this gift of love. She stared back at him. What was she thinking? She was thinking of this accordion joke: "What's the difference between an accordion player and a terrorist? Terrorists have sympathizers."[30]

30. I have noticed that Mr. Hundwasser, in his eternal quest for chiaroscuro, has rendered all the objects of my heart as cartoon villains, insensitive, if attractive, Jezebels which his hero, poor Alexei, has been unfortunate enough to encounter. This insults all my loves, every last one, but especially Lily. To be truthful, the majority of my misfortunes on the dating scene have been my fault.

Eine Symphonie des Grauens

Needless to say, her heart was still unwon. Even a smitten Graulexei could understand the intent in "Well, that was very nice. Maybe we'll get together again." But it was only when he sat down to practice again that his rage began to grow. His dreams that awful night were fearsome, with she the mare of his night, the evil incubus, the dark queen of the bitch-blackness, seizing him, squeezing his heart and lungs so they could no longer beat or breathe. Whooshing and whoooing drove his suffocation. Spiders skittering among keys and buttons, swarming over his face and back. Enough! Enough!

The next morning, Alexei found himself transformed, Groucho no longer. He wore his nose-glasses still, for a while, but rarely spoke and never joked. In his cryptic cocoon something was forming. What it was was still unclear.

Unclear—until in the *Illustrated History of the Horror Film* (a subject to which he found himself drawn) he discovered two things: in a footnote, Friedrich's (I kid you not) von Hollywood, and an entire chapter on *Nosferatu*.

Nosferatu. NOSEfeRATu! It was the combination of those words that drew him. Alexei had never seen the film—no matter: The stills alone brought about the change. Max Schreck as Count Orlock. Or was it Count Orlock as Max Schreck? Either permutation was persuasive. The gaunt, towering figure in his black frock coat, his bulbous head, his dermatologically evil appearance—diseased, contagious. His rat-like face with its sharp incisors—not canines but incisors, like Alexei's own! Above all, the unbearably creepy, dagger-sharp nails. Max Schreck breathed forth the air of some other planet, some dark world beyond, right from the page, without even scratching.

Schreck, German for "terror" or "fright." That was it: if he couldn't be loved, he could be feared. He was already weird. Now he could be feared too. Weird and feared—let them deal with that, all of them! Elizabeth and all of them. No more Mr. Nice Guy.

Miraculous, love's wounding. But how could he be weird and feared?

Lily's and my breakup—or, I still hope, only our trial separation (Lily, do write, c.o.m.p., if you see this)—did not occur at all as Hundwasser reports. First of all, it is literally impossible to play the orchestral reduction of the Prokofiev D Major Concerto on an accordion. We did do the opening section together, and she was pleasantly surprised and impressed, but after that, I had to beg off, with no "wild spiders high on speed and acid" or hands moving "so fast as to be a visual blur." The clever cycle-of-fifths arrangement of the bass buttons on an accordion, so useful for playing accompanying chords, absolutely precludes the kind of left-hand virtuosity necessary to approximate a good Prokofiev cello section.

We parted laughing, friendly, shaking hands. But not before I sprang the proposal I had planned to spring.

"Hey, guess what—I happen to have an extra ticket for Oistrakh playing this damn piece at Carnegie Friday night. Rostropovich conducting the Moscow. Wanna come along?"

It was an offer no one, no one, could possibly refuse, especially no one struggling with that concerto—to hear the greatest Russian violinist, a personal friend of Prokofiev's, perform that very work. And notice how cleverly I phrased it: not "Will you go on a date with me?" but simply "come along," tag along, why not fill the empty seat which happens to be next to mine? It did cost an arm and a leg for the tickets (orchestra, center, G 20 and 22), but I worked a deal of next semester's French tutoring for a dumb, rich 2nd trombone in exchange for the ticket price and a bit more in advance. Our date, though, was a manual of, a tragicomedy of, errors. The best-laid plans of mice and men . . .

We would leave at five after her orchestra practice. I used her rehearsal time to buy an elaborate "love bouquet" (her name!) of flowers. Turned out she was allergic, and spent the walk to the subway in uncontrollable sneezing—even after we had tossed the $14.95 item in the first trash can.

OK, off to 59th Street, and a walk down to the Carnegie Deli. Turned out she "had eaten" (when? During the horn chorale in Brahms' First?) and "wasn't hungry." Maybe she was a vegetarian and was just being polite. But they didn't have vegetarians in 1967. Or maybe they were just starting. In any case, she sipped her water and watched me eat.

Anyone who has seen a Carnegie Deli hot pastrami sandwich knows that watching someone eat one, especially someone with a big nose, is not a pretty picture. While she didn't exactly stare at me, her furtive glances did indicate some measure of disbelief. Perhaps disgust. What could I do? I was hungry. It cost a mint. Leave it on the plate?

We still had an hour to kill before the doors opened at 7:30, so we walked around, looked in Patelson's window, walked back to the park, and down Seventh Avenue again towards 57th. I carried her violin, the case strapped to my back. But then, but then . . .

Sitting on the sidewalk, with his back against that overembellished building on 58th, was a grizzled, ragged clarinetist beautifully playing some sinuously romantic melisma, his case open in front of him, brimming with bills and change.

When the need is greatest, help is nearest—as near as a footnote on page 81: "Nosferatu mask available from Friedrich's von Hollywood, 1503 Ivar Ave., Los Angeles, California 90028. Write for catalog."

Which he did.

And found that—for $7 each—he could obtain latex representations of the stars to pull over his miserable head: Chaplin or Keaton or Laurel or Hardy; Gable or Grant or Cooper or Wayne; Garbo or Harlow, Elizabeth Taylor or Marilyn Monroe. Debbie Reynolds—now, that might be weird.

But his eye flew over those photos and lit immediately on the richest lode: Karloff's Frankenstein monster, Lugosi's Dracula, Lon Chaney's Wolfman and Phantom of the Opera. And Friedrich von did not stop there, at Paramount and Universal studios. More appropriate to his mask-maker's art was the cinematic vision of the great expressionist monsters—Eisenstein's Ivan the Terrible; Peter Lorre as the child murderer in M; Conrad Veidt's somnambulist in Caligari's cabinet; the great gray, clay Golem. And crowning them all, Friedrich's masterpiece, a creation clearly in awe of its subject, was Max Schreck as Count Orlock, Nosferatu.

The mask embodied its own etymology, for the word "nosferatu" does not mean "vampire," "undead," or anything like that. It comes from old Slavonic: "nosufur-atu," itself derived from the Greek "nosophoros"—carrier of disease, of the plague. Alexei became both ill and ill at ease looking at just the small catalog photo. Let them all deal with it.

And as for me, he thought, who cares? Vileness demands as much self-renunciation as heroism. And I shall be vile, he thought, heroically vile, legitimately strange. Since by man came death, and all that, Homo monstrosus. Some girls go for that kind of thing, though I don't know any. But they'll come, he said to himself, they'll come. Together we'll bend the knee at Vice's shrine. Heh, heh, heh.

It was an unsatisfactory evil laugh. Anemic, pathetic. He'd have to work on it, turn it into a proper cackle, and work his way up to a terrifying roar. Heroic. Vile. Strange.

"He's riffing on the Brahms quintet," Lily informed me. "I love that piece."

"I'd love to hear you play it," I said as she sped up to get quickly past him.

"Wait," I said. "Could we hear a little more?" (It gave me a chance to touch her arm.)

She stopped, reluctantly, before we reached him. Maybe she was afraid. Maybe she didn't want his ugliness to taint her beauty. For me, it set it off all the more.

After another minute of exquisite listening, and partly to impress her, I pulled a quarter out of my pocket, and dropped it noisily in the case, so noisily in fact that the man stopped playing. He looked at me; he looked at the quarter lying next to what must have been a planted five-dollar bill.

"You a violinist?" he growled.

"Me? Oh, no, I'm a . . . I'm just carrying her case."

I indicated Lily, proudly boasting of the lady I served.

"Thanks for the quarter," he said, and began playing again, Kiji, I think, as if he knew it was Prokofiev that had knit us together.

"You're very welcome," I said. "It's a pleasure to hear you play."

Noble I was, noble and generous. We started off again toward Carnegie.

I'm not sure, but I think that guy stuck out his foot and tripped me—consciously and viciously tripped me. I mean, I don't usually go sprawling for no reason. Though he did say, "Excuse me," he never got up to help, and began playing again while I was still down on my hands and knees. A wind player's revenge? Jealousy of my date? A preview of the new world order?

I fell on my side, smashing her case (along with myself) on the cement. It ripped a seam in the canvas cover, and also in my pants. It is to Lily's credit that her first inquiry was whether I was all right. But her real concern was clear: Had I broken the violin? Even though it was no Strad, it was an early-19th-century German instrument with exceptionally fine sound. The bridge had been knocked over, the sound post had fallen, two strings had loosened, but the wood seemed intact. A bad start. Not the way to impress a would-that-she-were violinist girlfriend.

And then, can you believe this?—I didn't have the tickets. I'd lost the tickets! I had put them so carefully in my jacket that morning. I even kissed the envelope. Where the hell had they gone? Had the envelope fallen out when I hit the ground? Did someone take it from my pocket when the jacket was hanging over my chair at the deli? Could I have left it on my dresser after kissing it? Man, oh, man, what a loser.

I suggested we go to the box office, explain the situation, tell them the seat numbers, and ask if an usher would accompany us into the hall just before the concert to ascertain that those seats were not otherwise taken. We thought it would be better if Lily proposed this and not me.

Synchronicity! The box-office lady said no, but an usher was just then passing by, overheard the contretemps, and, probably smitten with Lily, and knowing I—the poor zhlub who was with her, probably

It took three weeks for the Schreck mask to arrive. During that time, Groucho hung on, the lamest of ducks, silent, grotesque in its silence, but nothing compared to his UPS'd successor.

Max Ming he called his new self, an initial-letter inversion of one of his favorite birds. *Ming* meant "bright," "clear," "brilliant" in Chinese. So said the Chinese laundryman down the block from his house. Its ideogram was the sun placed next to the moon. Romantic. And in a second inflection, it meant "the will of God, or Fate, or Destiny." Weighty. Surely girls would respond to that. Ming was better than Schreck as a name. Not so nasty-sounding. Oriental. Strange. Good.

Done.

Schreck's mask nose was larger than his own, and a good thing too, or he would have had to make a surgical incision in the rubber and allow his original nose to poke through—and that would have been too weird. A long black coat he already had. Its fur collar made it classier than Count Orlock's.

But wearing a full latex head mask was quite different from simple nose-glasses. Though there were nostril holes, it was harder to breathe. Moister. Almost wet. It smelled funny. And his voice sounded muffled, as if coming out of a crypt. This last was good; it added to the impact. The rest was a drag.

Though it did keep his hair dry in the rain.[31]

In order to thrive, Alexei believed, he would have to make Max Ming into a myth, something sublime—a force beyond the capacity for rational articulation, a creature encompassing the grandeur, horror, and power of nature, evoking some transcendent order of meaning behind the disguise of being. He painted Honey entirely black—including the white keys. In the hallways between classes, and occasionally in streets and parks, he played only in the key of F minor, often variations on "It's Not a Crime to Be Ugly as I'm," and he rehearsed disgusting little habits in order to impress girls, practicing hideous sneers and making wild and repulsive faces under his mask, violating all Principles of Appropriateness. Honey was not wild about his attempt at Orlockian nails—they clacked hideously and slipped off her keys. They made it hard to reach some

her disabled "client"—couldn't ever be competition, offered to help us "in the name of economic justice." After all, it was 1967. He promised to come back to get us at 8 on the dot, and if the seats were still empty, they were ours. The box-office lady frowned, snarled, but there was a line behind us and it was no skin off her back.

And of course, the concert was magical, and most helpful to Lily's playing. She listened with the same laser-like focus that I bring to the subject of deformity.

So we began the concert bathed in the soft glory of Lily's effective intervention, her save of the evening. In the cushy warmth of G 20, with her violin case between her knees, she was happy. I had made her happy. And when the curlicues of final sound wafted up past the chandelier to the high ceiling and yielded to silence, there was a few seconds' pause, breathless with adoration, and then the audience—including Lily—sprang to its feet in a tumult of unmusical clapping, bravos, stamping, whistling, shouting. And these were mostly old people. It wasn't very melodic. Had the Soviet Composers' Union been present, they might have pulled out their Kalashnikovs.

Now, 1967 was not yet the age of the idiotic obligatory standing ovation for no matter what. So a true standing ovation it was—that unique, spontaneous, entirely thrilling outburst evoked by something astounding and extraordinary. It was the music, the performance, and perhaps also a sense that the Cold War did not have to be so cold, that we, the enlightened musical public, could welcome them, the enemy, and take them to our hearts. Prokofiev, Oistrakh, the Moscow Philharmonic, world peace, music, queen of the arts, purveyor of beauty and truth. Isn't the world wonderful?

It was a spectacular moment, and Lily was truly grateful to me for having made it possible for her to be there. She even squeezed my arm. I think she squeezed my arm. Maybe she squeezed my arm.

But when I offered to take her home, she thought she'd rather go back alone. "I don't really want to talk. I just want to be in the Prokofiev." As if she wasn't there every day anyway. But she did get four stars for politeness and an adroit "thanks, but no thanks" to a would-be suitor. And apparently she got home safely.

31. This was my first real mask, awkward and uncomfortable. I have since become an expert in masks, likely clocking more hours within them than any three commedia actors combined, ever.

Wearing a mask is not about hiding; it is not normally about keeping dust or germs from the respiratory tract, though that was surely the plague doctor's intent. While a theatrical mask is used to subvert a viewer's judgment, to "send seismic shock waves coursing through him, to teach him his helplessness in the face of the powers that rule human life" (Artaud), the effect is equally great on the wearer, who, from the moment of donning it, experiences profound physical, emotional, and psychological transformation.

How this happens is difficult to explain. After all, the wearer sees nothing of the mask, not even its concave, often

unfinished inner surface. He may even have no mirror image to engage and recall if, like me, he abhors looking into a mirror. And yet there is transformation.

The restriction of peripheral vision, perhaps, the smell, the feel, the lack of breeze against the face—all combine to make one feel different, strange, and only loosely identified with the person he was before the mask. Though it may sound claustrophobic, a mask intoxicates, and offers radical refreshment to the spirit.

True, my masks have all been disguises, disguises thick and durable enough to let me be completely miserable behind them without affecting my effectiveness on others.

But do you, Mr. or Ms. Normal, think you are maskless just because you have never ordered from Friedrich's von Hollywood? You, with your face that is no face and all faces?

You, however, don't have the courage to take your mask beyond banality, beyond cliché into a realm of freshness, to enter frankly into tragic, hopeless revolt against your deformation, to go about a laughing-stock, if necessary, but in so doing, to master your flaws, to elevate your life into a work of art, to act out a script that transforms your truth into an ethos of reason and resolution.

Boldness—that's what's required, boldness. Danton's "*De l'audace, toujours de l'audace, et encore de l'audace!*" Tattoo it on your tattooed faces. A genuine boldness, though, not some blockbuster Hollywood version. Boldness in substance, in conception, in execution.

Know, however, that no matter what its expression, every mask is terribly sad—because it prevents a smile. I smile beneath my masks, I laugh. I am gay and charming. But who would know it? My situation is far more difficult than Pagliacci's. (Girls like a good toothy smile.)

I am often asked, "Do you ever take off your mask—even, say, when you are alone at home at night?"

I can't tell you. It's an essential part of my inscrutable

of her buttons. After three weeks of growing them, he clipped them off in private, in his bedroom, like Dreyer shearing Falconetti's famous hair for her performance in his *Passion of Joan of Arc*. (Ming, in his brightness, loved the fire at the stake, the signaling through the flames.)[32]

His nails, though now short, at least were filthy, for Filthiness, he conjectured, could very well be next to Godliness. Cleanliness was all well and good for casual observance, but did it not represent a worship of the material body, its wrappings and effects, as opposed to more salient concern with the spirit?

Once a neat child whose room was always spic-and-span, Alexei began to practice Filthiness with the zeal of a convert. He wore the same underwear and socks for weeks, months, even, until he was embarrassed to have his mother wash them. And so they remained unwashed. He refused to change his cat's litter box until Fyodor went on a strike worthy of the Wobblies, peeing and shitting all over Alexei's room and spraying all his lower-shelf books, which became too odorous and sticky for even King Filth to touch. Alexei took them to Pageant, but Sam, alas, would have nothing to do with them and kicked him lickety-split out of the store. He left his big box at the Grace Church rectory, hoping the church might use them for the library. They were good books.

As bookshelf space emptied, he took down two stories of boards and bricks and uncovered room for two art prints, his first ever. One was Domenico Ghirlandaio's Old Man and Child, which he worshiped for its statement of the human condition—the familial relation, underscored by the common red clothing; the unsmiling yet caring gaze of the old man at what must be his grandson; and the child's contemplation of the ecstatically rhinophymic nose of his elder not in horror, not even in curiosity, but rather with that questioning sense of his own facial fate "when I grow up." Ming loved too the odd, truncated landscape out the window, the churchly town with its manicured mountain-winding road, its placed and sculpted springtime trees. And lurking behind this civilized human construction, a mute and threatening mountain of sheer gray rock, perhaps even a volcano, capable of burying the village in smoke and flames.

The second print was from Victor Kamkin's Soviet Books on Fifth Avenue. It was a painting in new-style socialist realism, a Portrait of Zvezdochka, little daughter of the stars, the last of a group of remarkable dogs shot into space on the Vostok Sputnik 10. Alexei felt a strange affinity to these canines, earthborn creatures, the first to leave the planet.[33] Like them, he felt himself to be a preparatory, path-finding vanguard of a world unknown and yet to come. He knew there would be risks to the journey.

persona. It's in my contract. Let me simply say, with Georg Buchner, "We are always on stage, even if, at the end, we are stabbed to death in earnest."

32. Okay. I *am* tempted to identify with this great historical figure. She too was manipulated by others—her voices, the cheering of her fans, her interrogators, who knows, perhaps ever her manager or secretary of war. She too was a cross-dresser, as I am—of sorts—the both of us adopting roles far beyond what our mothers could have imagined. She too was punished for her leadership. I have not yet been burned at the stake, but we have both signaled through flames.

33. I would look at Zvezdochka's portrait with a mixture of awe and horror, an experience defining the word "sublime." Imagine the men who placed that doggie inside her capsule, there to slowly starve and die. A mammal like themselves, warm, soft, with a long snout, being sent off on a journey which can

only end badly. Why? She doesn't know. What's ahead? Arf, arf. "For the good of the People," the white coats say. How could they be so cruel?

And yet, I think of myself in tenth-grade biology, especially with a bevy of gorgeous, squeamish, long-haired, Music & Arty girls all around at the lab tables. High school biology is not a likely setting for the sublime, but as I look back on it now, it is the activity most awesome, most horrible. Frogs were the designated victims, *Rana pipiens*, amphibians that made the girls go yuck and me to show my killer manliness. Is it too obvious to observe that the combination of intelligence and force, science and testosterone, is an ominous one?

They called it "pithing." I would pick up a petted, relaxed, trusting frog in my left hand, its smooth white belly facing me, its legs hanging limply down, its eyes wondering what was wanted. "Hi, guy," I would gently say. With my left index finger, I would bend its head forward to expose the back of its neck. With my right hand, I would take a long dissecting needle, place its tip at the craniovertebral junction, then thrust the needle down into the spinal canal. The victim's legs would stiffen, its bladder discharge, and its eyes go quickly blank. Then I would twist the needle, reaming out the spinal canal much as Joseph K's assassins twisted the knife in his heart. Like a frog, like a dog. Like Zvezdochka. The once-frog then became a "preparation" to demonstrate some trivial biological trick—like a still-beating heart—and finally to be tossed into the trash.

How could a sensitive, long-fingered violinist or dewy-eyed, succulent-lipped flutist ever do such a thing? How could a long-waisted watercolorist or shapely-armed sculptress? They needed me—smart, fearless me—to do it for them. And I was, I thought, pithing-king of tenth-grade biology, hero of the damsels, hunter of the condemned, executioner of the innocent, Gawain and Sanson in one.

I can't believe now it was me. Where was the "real" Alexei Pigov? Who was the impostor double-performing—without a conscience—these unspeakable acts? What was my reward? I didn't get the girl. Surely *Rana pipiens* was the victim—but so was I for succumbing to brutality, so were those beautiful Music & Art girls for accepting and valuing it, so was the teacher for valuing such assistants. How were all these good, even innocent people sucked into barbarism? Presumably in service to the god of "Science," for the future "good of the People," and for ourselves, of course, as civilized, educated citizens to serve them. This story is not irrelevant.

I remember the first time I actually saw Krisa. My childhood friend. The rat. As he was sidling back and forth across my belly, I accidentally nudged open the closet door with my foot, and the two of us were suddenly illuminated by a long slant of light. We both froze. We looked each other in the eye. He looked somehow pure, lustrous in that luminous shaft. He looked—I couldn't say this as a four-year-old, but I realize it now—he looked moral—unlike me, who had been sent into the closet to be punished. I remember so clearly losing my bearings as a kid, a human kid. I was ashamed coming face to face with this animal, even this strange and, at least to my mother, repellent one. Under Krisa's gaze, I felt I was

He had wanted a doggie to go with the portrait and had gone so far as to locate a Zvezdochka look-alike at the ASPCA on Sixty-second Street. But the love affair was nixed by his mother—"Nyet, nyet, nyet!"—who felt she was speaking not only for herself but for the otherwise unrepresented Fyodor. Ming had to make do with a poster in heroic Soviet style: Zvezdochka, her ears alert, her eyes filled with utopian vision.

But Fyodor's contribution to a defining olfactory world was enough to initiate a practice that would loom large in Alexei's later life. He found he could stuff a small sachet of fragrant herbs between his own nose and Schreck-Ming's, distending the mask from within, thus creating an even more frightening image while masking the more repulsive smell-aspects of his spiritual quest. The wreckage of his room was a secret dividing line between him and the more orderly disorder of the "normal" world, one that, should he forget it, would remind him every night of the distinction.

In these days of gothic rampant,[34] Ming's image would be unexceptional. But at the time, he may have been the only young male in New York City dressed entirely in black, in a long coat, jabot, cravat, and cummerbund, all ripped and filthy. Even today, he would be the only youth consistently appearing in a Max Schreck mask. Did he wear it when he was all alone in his room? There is no way to know.

He never changed his clothes. But he did change his homemade buttons daily, cycling them around over the course of a month. GALLOWS POWER, said one, and ENEMY OF THE STATE, said another; I AM A GENIUS—OF SORTS, one proclaimed, AS SEEN ON TV, declared another. The button that summed it up for him was this: I'M NOT DEAD YET.

The overriding idea, the grand narrative behind all this, was to turn his life into a work of art, to demonstrate ironically the true monstrosity of the world in comparison with his own. Through such vigorous, systematic, fanatical practice, he would aspire to purity of heart. His mantra of "Conduct manic, aura Satanic," his carrying on in a generally loathsome way, would carry him—Ming—and the world, Faust-like, into Empyrea, the highest heaven, the source of light, the purifying fire.[35]

But the underriding idea was still to get girls. Especially when spring rolled its flowery way around. Ming in Spring—conduct manic, aura galvanic: he was charged!

being inspected by . . . Nature or something. By some huge, alien kingdom surrounding me.

Did we have anything in common, Krisa and I? Life? How was I supposed to react to this stare from a rat? I felt unnatural. Anti-natural. Like some kind of anti-rat. Yet I knew that some of my animal reactions were as natural as those of, say, Fyodor when someone stepped on his tail. I thought about becoming an animal. Or maybe a monster.

My relations with nature were terrible, lax.

34. Hundwasser hates goths. I think they scare him. And of course he's not the only one. A lot of straight people mock goth makeup and disparage their morbid attachment to all things dark and gloomy.

But I love goths. Or at least I like them. You just have to understand them. They are mostly just ordinary kids (including twenty- and thirty-somethings) who like to dress up and who have a lifestyle that is a bit unusual. People think they are satanists, or sadomasochists, or depressed, or violent. They think of them as a cross between vampires and zombies.

But most goths are well-educated, good students, hardly ever drop out of school. They're into classical education, history, especially medieval and art history. They're basically just weirdo intellectual kids who look at the world a tad differently. Did you ever hear them talk together? It's all about art, politics, H. P. Lovecraft, decadence, hairspray, Edgar Allen Poe. I don't know a single goth who is into graveyard destruction or cat slaughtering. They like graveyards and love cats.

And the whole black thing: they've just taken "black is beautiful" into another dimension, surely a necessary reaction to the druggo-disco colored aesthetic of the '60s and '70s. They're trying to take things society thinks of as evil or wrong and show them as special and attractive. They're the best of my fans—goth plague doctors, goth plague victims.

And there are many shades of black. I know there are the original Punk Goths, doomy and nihilistic, But there are also Cyber Goths, the tech heads; and Glitter Goths, with their glitzy makeup; there are Perky Goths, and the

35. Hundwasser's fictions notwithstanding, I did understand—from early on—the need for an all-out war on conventional wisdom. I knew from the beginning that I was to become the leader of a one-man movement for the overthrow of everything, for a perhaps Quixotic attempt to remake the entire system of existing reality.

I am, and always was a serious person, reasonable, subtle, noble, profound, bursting with poetic and musical ideas,

New Romantic Goths with their very elaborate dress; and Vampy Goths, like think Vampira and a full Halloween menagerie; not to mention Granola Goths, with hippie leanings and matted hair.

So get over it, Bill. You fall off a black horse, you get back on again. There's lots of good fish in the Gothic Sea.

—Miss Lonelyhearts

wanting to live purposefully and achieve something universally important. I once thought I could be Kant-the-child—humpbacked, or at least with a big nose—and nevertheless respected. No wonder I was widely disliked.

But the world was monstrous, is monstrous—ruled by infantile kleptocrats and full of wicked and ill-advised rabble supping on horror. There are some beautiful girls out there too, but what good has that done me?

Still, I am optimistic. Pessimism of the intellect, optimism of the will, *n'est-ce pas?* I saw a fan the other night with a t-shirt that read, THE GOAL OF REVOLUTIONARY ART IS TO MAKE REVOLUTION IRRESISTIBLE.

Well, the goal of revolutionary anything is to make revolution irresistible. I knew early on that my task was to live, to work in such a way that freedom, hope, becomes irresistible. And sustainable. Bill Hundwasser is ephemeral. Plague medicine is not.

In addition to more songs, he had rehearsed yo-yo tricks to show off to his Lady of Spain, Maria Tobosa, an attractive Puertoriqueña clarinetist from Spanish Harlem. She, he was sure, had already rejected the boulders from the Big Jock Candy Mountains so prevalent in her neighborhood. Or why would she have come to Music & Art? Good. One category of competition down. He didn't really speak Spanish, but he did have the basics common to all New Yorkers. She would likely be a passionate and romantic child of the Mediterranean. Ooo-wie! (And was she stacked! Double oooo-wie!) These people, raised in sunlight, are the most likely to be affected by an alluring image which speaks to the universal language of the eye. La Tobosa, he called her, not to her face, of course, La Tobosa de los Angeles.

He would not try to pass himself off as a monster; rather, he would allow her to see through a transparent monster-facade, to understand that even the mad are men of their time, concerned, above all, with amelioration.

Their first and last dialogue went as follows:

"Hi, want to play the Brahms clarinet sonatas with me?"

"No."

"How come?"

"You're too ugly, man. And you stink."

(He laughs.) "Brahms wasn't pretty either. And he smoked the worst-smelling cigars in Europe. It's Beauty and the Beast, Maria. An old and successful combo."

"Yeah, well, they're not for accordion. The Brahms."

"Give 'em a try."

"And you look like a monster."

"Well, yes, but appearances are deceiving. Diderot, in his *Éléments de Physiologie*, defined a monster as 'a being whose survival is incompatible with the existing order.' [He had rehearsed this as a pickup line and was pleased to get to use it.] Do I look like I'm incompatible with the existing order?"

"Yes."

"Implacable."

"What?"

"I said 'unpackable.'"

"Why did you say 'unpackable'?"

"I don't know."

"Besides, you have terrible handwriting."

"How do you know?"

"From the note you sent me in January."

"I thought maybe you didn't get it."

"Yeah, I got it, And I don't want to play the Brahms sonatas with you."

"I am seized by mal-de-siècle." (Another line he didn't want to waste, even if the handwriting was on the wall.)

"You're an idiot."

"All right, then. See you around."

"Not if I see you first."

Exeunt omnes.

La Tobosa de los Angeles was no more. He thought of her now as Maria Monstroso, aka Ms. God. He left a bag of salted pretzels on top of her locker addressed to "Lot's Wife." She probably didn't get it. Neither did he.

Perhaps it was time for another identity crisis.

5.

Cyranocchio

Max Ming was girlfriendless through high school,[36] and thus generally sullen and abrupt. He excelled in all his classes, for with no social life, what else was there to do but practice, draw, and study? His portfolio bulged with brutalities: violent charcoal evocations of interior events; nasty pen-and-ink portraits of schoolmates and teachers; and, stacked in racks and cubbies, oils and acrylics in black-and-white—fierce, energetic shapes, abounding in textures, exploding from gessoed canvas. His accordion remained at home, waiting to be attacked at any hour. And so, success—and utter failure.

It was a good thing he'd covered his tracks when releasing the rats from biology lab.

Immersed in *The Brothers Karamazov*, he felt that he too needed an act to define himself among his peers. Kolya Krassotkin had lain between the railroad tracks and let the train fly over him. But Alexei wanted to affect the world beyond. Repulsive and stupid though he imagined he was, he was not fixated on self. Ugly, yes; self-promoting, no!

Recognizing in his bitterness the need for compassion, he had decided to free the slaves on the fifth floor. At 4:30 one afternoon, with the building mostly empty except for the orchestra and practice rooms below, he opened thirty-six cages containing upward of a hundred rats. They wouldn't run out, jump out, or crawl out. Perhaps they rightly sensed a trap, some Nazi experiment ahead, some fat-handed teenager out to "train" them. Alexei had to place each, singly, on the floor, where they

36. This is not true. Or not quite true. It depends on what you mean by "girlfriend". If by that awkward term you mean a heart-throb whose heart throbs in return, why, then, I did have a very successful, moderately long-lasting relationship. To wit:

I had dropped by Oooo Marisa. (Yes, that is what it was actually called. My mother thought she might get more business if the name of her shop were in Hundwasser's book, so she gave him permission, in fact begged him to put it in. "Oooo Marisa", for the non-Cyrillic among you, is an accurate transliteration of У Марыса—at Marisa's place—in this case taking wordplay-advantage of the sexual overtones of both the initial preposition and of my sainted mother. It must have been coined by Mikhail Borisovich in a moment of passion, as she would never have thought of it. On the other hand, she might have.)

Anyway, I had dropped by Oooo Marisa to deliver a pastrami sandwich to a late-working Nastyamama, and there, waiting in the chair, waiting to be beautified by my mother, was a girl already so beautiful that the only post-makeover path was down. Curly-brown-haired she was, with huge eyes shining with sadness, and the delicate hands of a pianist. A figure so lovely and provocative, I don't even want to think about it.

What to do, what to do? How could I get to know her? There were chairs empty to her right and left, but it just seemed too . . . too obvious to sit down next to her. Besides, I had delivered the pastrami sandwich and was already on my way out the door when I noticed her. There was no reason to sit down. What could I have said to her? I would have lost my ability to speak.

wandered, confused, until he left the lab. After that, who knows? They had all disappeared by morning.

The trouble with this exploit was that no one knew it was his. So he called the *New York Times* and reported the event in a voice belonging to Maria Tobosa. (He was not above guileful revenge.) The reporter told him it was not the kind of story the Times generally covered. *The Daily News* was more accommodating, took "Maria's" description over the phone, and printed a small piece in the City section the next morning. The NYC Department of Health picked up on the story and sent an emergency team of inspectors to determine whether there was a public health threat from the escaped animals, and a Republican state assemblyman demanded accountability from the Board of Education and a possible cut in the budget of this unnecessary "special" school whose staff and students seemed unable to handle the responsibilities of scientific education.

The ensuing hullabaloo reached all the way from Albany to Melbourne, Australia, where Peter Singer was working on his master's thesis, "Why Should I Be Moral?" and whose ensuing report to the *Independent* was the beginning of his work on the philosophy of animal liberation, the book of that name, and of the subsequent formation of People for the Ethical Treatment of Animals (PETA), with their far more daring sabotage. Never had such a small act of teenaged *ressentiment* created such large cultural consequences. But Alexei couldn't put it in his résumé. And later on, he didn't need to.

But the heart of his darkness, the horror that was really getting to him, was simply this: Maria had been nasty to him and dear Elizabeth clueless, yes—but they really had nothing against him except . . . him. *He* was the cause, the fount and origin of his own isolation. Max Ming sat in his room and looked and smelled around him. The Bad Housekeeping Seal of Approval, to be sure. He inspected his Count Orlock suit. It wanted washing. His Schreck mask was breeding mold or fungus, and his original nose was scabrously inflamed by the suffocating embrace of Nosferatu's fiercer one. What girl would want to kiss that nose, to smell what might be emanating from its nostrils? Would the dainty, saintly Elizabeth Schrank want to stroke this flea-ridden coat with her violin fingers? Would even *puta* Maria want to unbutton his shirt or unbuckle his mildewing belt? Who would kiss these filthy toes or hold this grubby hand? Christ, even the Texas sniper had taken a deodorant stick with him in his siege provisions for the tower. I'm slovenly, he thought, or at least too unorthodox with respect to cleanliness.

And within, he felt audacity surge, flex its Atlased muscles. "I," he proclaimed, "am a ballerina of the spirit—but with a forty-seven-pound getup. I've got to change the costume! Clean up my act! Stop slinking! Leap! Fly!"

But I was not yet so in love as to have lost my ability to scheme. That evening, I asked my mother who that woman—her last customer—was. She didn't remember.

"Young girl. Sixteen, seventeen, curly brown hair, big eyes."

"Oh, that one. Elektra someone. Greek girl, parents come to Poland when she was baby. Fled from army."

"Why?"

"We don't go into it. Kommunisti, who knows?"

My heart was beating fast.

"Why you are so interested? She won't go out with you. And she don't speak good English, and you don't speak Polish. Or Greek."

So insightful, my mother, and so encouraging. That night, with Nastya soundly snoring, I stole by flashlight into her bedroom, snatched her purse, and brought it into my room for inspection. I did not take a cent, I swear. I was after bigger game—and I found it. There, nestled in amongst the tens and twenties, was a check for $12 from a Nicos and Elena Karanikas, 220 E. 27th St., New York, the amount of the check in a handwriting not that of the unreadable signature. It must be hers, Elektra's, her beautiful European handwriting. And she must be Elektra Karanikas, and she must live with her parents at that address. I memorized all immediately, and snuck the bag back into Nasty's room. I would woo her, Cyranoish, with letters. I would let her love for me build up before exposing myself to her—I mean my current persona, which at the time was still Max Ming . . . no, wait—by then it was Konstantine Karamazov, the fourth, generally unknown brother, dashing, devil-may-care, yet still intellectual and respectable.

And build up it did. I wrote her a quick note, thanking her for the emergency loan of the five dollars, and returning to her a spanking new $5 bill. If she were honest, she'd surely send it back with a note of disclaimer. And so she did—Elektra, my Elektra—in her elegant handwriting. I then wrote excusing my silly self for mistaking her for another (Elley) Karanikas, for losing her address, then sending the money to the most likely Karanikas in the Manhattan phone book. She wrote back forgiving me. I wrote back, remarking on her interesting handwriting. She wrote back telling me she had lived in Kraków most of her life, and had come here only last year with her parents, who were diplomats at the UN. Diplomats! How exciting! My ticket to a world unknown.

It's true, her English was not very good, and seemed cribbed from a Berlitz phrase book. But our letter exchange grew from weekly to daily, and sometimes to two or more a day. And her writing skill grew along with it. When she told me about reading the love poetry of Adam Mickiewicz, I knew she was hooked. And, so, of course, was I.

Was Elektra my "girlfriend"? Hundwasser didn't think so. For him, "girlfriend" implied some *sine qua non* below the belt. Or at least beneath the bra. But for me, this was damn good. Absolutely

He took off his clothing so as not to soil it further while cleaning his room.[37] From the maternal kitchen, bucket, water, mop, sponge, baking soda, Lysol, Mr. Clean. He released a suspicious Fyodor from his shit-'n'-piss-providing confinement. "Scat!" he cried. "And scat no more!"—and dismissed the beast with the three-fingered sign of the devil.

It took forty-nine hours—from Friday night to late Sunday on a weekend Nastya was at Tony's. When she returned home, she found her son sitting in his underwear, making up for lost time, practicing "The Flight of the Bumblebee" on the bass buttons. (It sounded more like the Flight of the Manatee.) The floor had been scraped and washed of dried-up poop, and the books, similarly cleaned, arranged in alphabetized sections on reconstructed shelves. Zvezdochka and the Nose Man were now tacked to the ceiling over the filial bed. The window had been cleaned, and the wall across the alley was now visible in all its brickish glory. His alternative pair of underwear and socks were nowhere to be seen, presumably in the hamper. Even his Schreck mask seemed to glisten. It was a consummation devoutly to be wished.

"Mother, dearest, you may enter my new room, Heliopolis. It has gone through the eighty ablutions of Mithra and is now affably bland. And my clothing will no longer employ the supreme principle of unmatched socks."

"You meet new girl," her Nastyaness replied.

"On the contrary. In attempting to pass myself off as a monster, I've experienced a kind of internal monstering. I intend to be Vampire Boy no more."

"Why you don't take off mask?"

"My nose is too big."

"I know what your nose looks like."

"You haven't seen it lately. It looks leprous."

"Want mamochka to give it kiss?"

"Don't you come near me. No, I want Elizabeth Schrank to give it a kiss. But she won't. She won't even play Prokofiev with me. But all this is about to change. I will put childish things behind me and make the leap—like Evel Knievel—to maturity. I'll get a new mask, adopt a new personage. My new nose will be an innocent nose, a purist's nose, a nose to ward off disease and corruption."

"What is Evil Kneeval?"

"Evel Knieval, *chère* Mama, is the closest anyone has come to being superhuman."

"I think you should aim lower—like just regular. *Normalnii*."

wonderful, in fact. I lived for the mail. I came home more, anxious to open the mailbox, or waiting for the postman on Saturdays. I practiced more, I studied more, I became less dissipated, as one does when the eternal feminine leads us on.

Was it time for us to meet? I kept putting it off, evasive when it came up on the page, wanting to be more certain that her love could withstand a face-to-mask encounter. And then one day, she stopped writing. Just like that. A month went by. I bombarded her with letters, cards, and notes. "I know you must be extremely busy. . . ." "Hi. Thinking of you at the Frick" (postcard of El Greco's Jesus whipping the moneychangers from the temple). Nothing. Then one day several months later, I got a note informing me that she had met a wonderful boy, a Greek. They went to Greek dances together, and for all I know got drunk on ouzo, and jumped nightly, naked, into bed, no doubt after Nicos and Elena had gone to sleep.

I did wind up an item unto myself. But she *was* my girlfriend, for a while.

37. I've always been somewhat ambivalent about cleanliness. On the one hand I am—certainly now but even then—a member of an austere community of one, devoted to reading, healing, and meditation, to individual and collective prayer, to the transformation of iconoclasm into a moral force. And I'm certainly aware that cleanliness—which is famously next to godliness—is even more important when godliness is inscrutable, and has perhaps absconded.

And yet, at times in my life, I have been transported by the bliss of filthiness. Simply dismissing fear about dirt and health is enough by itself to lift one's soul from a paranoid prison. The cleanliness freaks are led astray by purity. But filthiness is of the earth, of the great Mother who does not bother to wash behind her ears. And who better to grasp the essence of cleanliness than a filthy man? Fish do not know of water.

The aphorism "cleanliness is next to godliness" comes from the Talmud. "The doctrines of religion are resolved into carefulness; carefulness into vigorousness; vigorousness into guiltlessness; guiltlessness into abstemiousness; abstemiousness into cleanliness; cleanliness into godliness." Let us follow the plot here: care, vigor, innocence, self-denial, cleanliness, godliness. What's wrong with this picture? Bartleby was careful; vigorousness was not in his future. Dimitri K. was vigorous but far from innocent. Pantagruel was innocent but certainly not via self-denial. The monk Paphnutius denied himself, but rooting around for grubs and munching on locusts was far from clean. And Pontius Pilate was a consummate washer of hands, practically obsessive-compulsive, but godliness was not his thing.

Thus we see from eminent example that at every juncture the progression from carefulness through cleanliness to godliness breaks down and undermines believability. Or

"Human, all too human, you will always be. I, on the contrary, must find a way toward truth and love which does not conform to accepted practice."[38]

"Yes? Like what?"

"When I figure that out, I'll let you know."

Evel Knieval had a normal, Montana-type nose. Thus, after much thought, Alexei decided on Pinocchio as the vehicle for transformation. As the puppet had evolved from a stick of wood to a real boy, a beloved real boy, so would Alexei mature from a kicked-around rag doll to a faithful mensch, a beloved *molodyetz*—perhaps like Konstantin Levin—and eventually win the heart of a Kitty. Not Fyodor. A real Kitty, some Katerina Alexandrovna Shcherbatsky Schrank, aristocratic, charming, truthful, genuine, warm, loving.

There were several reasons why Pinocchio was an exemplary choice.

First, he would not have to improve too quickly; the transition from Count Orlock could be gradual. After all, Pinocchio's maiden act, once he had been given legs, had been to kick his father, the kindly Gepetto. His second act was to run away. These were inbred, homey themes, though it was Alexei's father who had kicked him and run away. His mother was not bad at it either.

But the deciding factor was—as ever—the nose, the nose on the mask, the nose on the mask in the new Friedrich's von Hollywood catalog. This was no cutesy-wootsy Disney Pinocchio, the charming little-boyish puppet even Bill Sykes would love to snuggle. This was the title mask from *Le Straordinarie Avventure di Pinocchio*, Fellini's second film, the precursor to *I Vitelloni, The Young and the Passionate*.[39] Long, pointed nose—not the "lying" nose so quickly pecked off by the Blue-Haired Fairy's thousand woodpeckers but a stiletto-long and stiletto-sharp pointed one, and a conical hat besides, worthy of a sage. It was certainly more attractive than Max Schreck's Nosferatu: it was a face some beauty might like to stroke, and enigmatic enough to hold her attention.

One thing though—the "lying" aspect of the image did have to be pondered. No girl likes lying or liars. The most important thing was that this mask's nose would not grow should Alexei tell a lie. Rather, it would hide any facial or physiological betrayal.

even the willing suspension of disbelief. *Credo quia absurdum est* may hold for Tertullian, but not for me. I can assure you that if you go long enough without a bath, you will transcend the need for such ablution, and even the fleas will spare you.

Mildew of the brain remains a problem. 

38. I must say a word about "accepted practice." And I hope you, the reader, will understand my words as more than mere kvetching. Franz Kafka was a kvetch. I am not a kvetch. Being a victim of accepted practice, I am attempting to do something about it, not just kvetch.

So what is "accepted practice"? It is "acceptable," I think, to know that the world is run by the man or men behind the curtain, and yet to follow their plans, declaim their lines, dance to their tunes, and thereby to consider oneself not only blessed, but fabulously original. Accepted practice.

Remember, this goes on while knowing—deeply and intuitively—the real situation: I and the world are run from behind a curtain. My self-management is shaped by Others' plans. Those Others are subtle—like Hundwasser. But Hundwasser too is run by them. No one wants to be a mere puppet. And the puppets want to become real boys and girls.

The Official Message is charmingly mixed: autonomy is good; too much autonomy is bad; rationality is good; too much rationality is irrational and bad; commitment is good, but you have to be committed to the right things; taking responsibility is good, but there are things that They, finally, must be responsible for.

In other words, even self-determination is tied to powerful systems of external control, coming from their sciences and pseudosciences and from their generally accepted religious and moral doctrines. They will have their way. The "consciousness industry" sells their attitudes and ideas as easily as their goods and services.

I have to say, though, that equating the general public to puppets is unfair to puppets. Read Kleist: puppets are deep and eloquent; the public is generally shallow and inarticulate. Puppets are honest and direct; the public is hypocritical and cagey. Puppets are who they are; the public is everything but.

How did things get this way? A hatred of history, for one thing. "The End of History" with its end-slogan: "Don't mourn, advertise." As we head toward a society chaperoned by the police, we might justifiably be terrified if things didn't seem so . . . inevitable.

I call for a Hegelian leap from accepted practice into the poetical.

39. What is this? What *is* this? I am a great fan of Federico Fellini, and I can tell you, I can assure you, that there is no such film. Fellini loved Collodi's book, thought it one of the great works, and even compared himself to Gepetto in the early stages of creating a film, when it would direct him and not he it. I know he always *wanted* to make a *Pinocchio* which would restore the violence and social

And he would never lie anyway.

But then, he wondered, what was so bad about lying? It was clear that "good manners" was just a euphemism for mendacity, a vehicle of falsehood which enabled oppression and undermined any radical form of dissent. And what had Picasso said? "Art is the lie that makes us realize the truth"? Yes, truth could be harsh, dangerous, even destructive, sometimes too simple for the world's complexity. What better way to evoke it, then, than lying, big-time lying, even hugely extravagant lying, weaving hopeful deceptions, enabling optimism in the shit-for-brains world?[40] Lying makes life worth living, no? Lies are more enlightening than literal truths, no? Literal truth-telling—it's like a mental problem, clinically abnormal, hey? We have to graduate from truth to meaning, to think more illuminating thoughts than the bullshit the world hands out. If I have to be a little bizarre to achieve that, thought Alexei, so what? He was an original person. He didn't think himself all that eccentric.

He spent $2.95 at Pageant for a copy of *How to Pick Up Girls*, and with it he armed himself for daily stalking in the main reading room of the Forty-second Street Library, Pignocchio Fellini, high school graduate, not yet ready for college. And there, among the elegant tables, not ten days into September, he spied his

First Love

Yes, the first love of his manhood. The first love of his postgothic life. This would be a serious love, perhaps—if all worked out—a life partner. There was only one problem: how to get to know her, how, even, to find out her name.

She was a tall blond young woman with a braid down to her waist. Regal. And even more so when she swept it up into a golden crown, revealing her long and graceful neck. That throat, he thought, that splendiferous throat . . . I could eat that throat, kiss it all over, sink my teeth into . . . No—that was Nosferatu. This must be his Blue-Haired Fairy, the mother he'd never had, the missing sister to unveil the mysteries of woman, the lover-to-be to lead him gently upward, onward. She.

How to approach her, what to say? It was one thing at Music & Art, where everyone knew everyone else. But here, one among a mob of readers, each a stranger to all—how to begin? Who was she, what to assume? He needed to prepare for all and everything.

commentary of Collodi and undo, if possible, Disney's sugarcoating, but he never did. The year before *I Vitelloni*, he made *The White Sheik*, and the year after *La Strada*. No Pinocchio. Ever.

Hundwasser seems to have made this film up out of thin air, probably to add one more feather to his name-dropping cap. "Oh, and he's a film historian too!" I can just hear the sweet young things saying. He also must have wanted an Aristotelian unity in his mask stories, some Occam's razor slicing things down to the simplest presentation, the wonderful mono-convenience of Friedrich's von Hollywood.

In fact, I did not get my Pinocchio mask from Friedrich's. I got it from Benny's Joke Shop on Christopher Street, when its windows were all gussied up for Halloween. There it was, a mask based right on the great Carlo Chiostri Pinocchio drawings Fellini so loved as a child.

I know this because I couldn't believe it when I saw Hundwasser's reference to a Fellini film I didn't know. I checked F's filmography in Baxter's definitive biography, and I looked at all the Pinocchio references in the index. Great quote I found: he thought Collodi's ending especially sad "because, losing his marionettehood, Pinocchio loses his childhood, the marvelous life of knowing animals and magic, in return for becoming a good, conforming idiot."

I will not be such an idiot. I will not disown my animal friends, mammalian or insect. I will not cease to believe in magical strategies for the Great Jail Break, even if it is I who must assume the role of magician.

All power to the imagination!

40. Even in his personal life Mr. Hundwasser usually avoids the inverse chic of foul language. So why this salty adjective? And whatever made him decide to use it?

That the s-word was hovering over the intelligentsia, whispering in its collective ear, was made plain by the phenomenal success of Harry Frankfurt's little book, *On Bullshit* (Princeton University Press, 2005). The 86-page book with wide margins and big print reached no. 3 on the *New York Times* best-seller list. It has been reprinted seven times, with well over a million copies sold—which puts it up there with the Bible in terms of non-textbook academic publishing—and Frankfurt even got to be feted on the Jon Stewart show.

The word "Bullshit" on the cover of a snazzy, low-cost hardcover, right up there at the register—since it would get lost on the shelf. "Oh, how cute! I have to get one of these for Uncle Roger." The book was a prime example of its subject.

What a marketing stunt! The graphic designers, the marketing folks who created the strategy to sell this project—it might as well have been a tin of "Indictmints" or a "Nietzsche Will to Power Bar"—the PR department who got it widely reviewed and arranged the book tours. It's worse than *The Nose*, which is at least a substantial, somewhat imaginative volume, and not a 25-page, dry-as-dust, overly intellectual academic essay tricked out as a must-read bauble for witty bookstore patrons.

He needed an attractive philosophy, some kind of attitude. Girls want someone with an attitude, not some namby-pamby dweeb.

The important thing was to buy new underwear, a three-pack of Fruit-of-the-Loom. For he had been shaken by a recent experiment: filling a white enameled wash-basin with warm water and soap, he'd soaked a pair of clean, folded underpants taken right out of his drawer. Why had he done this? His little finger had told him to try it. By the end of three minutes, the water was as gray as a corpse. Gray! This was from clean white underwear, mind you. Pignocchio was shocked, horrified. It was the strongest evidence yet of original sin.

Yet Fruit-of-the-Loom was no help. The prelapsarian look of the cloth, the feel of it on his postlapsarian loins, made things all the worse. He could never introduce himself swathed in such hypocrisy. It was a lie, a gnawing feeling of Sartrean bad faith—and he was a servant of truth. He returned to his old underwear and stared at her, daily, behind her back.

My mission must be to impose my will on her, he thought. I've got to convince her that I am the one, that I am what she is looking for, that I've got it all. I've got to demonstrate that I have a positive outlook on life and a superior demeanor. I will show her how astonishing the world is, how happy she could be with a guide like me. Not like me: me. But what if she blows me off?

The masked man sat gazing at her, sometimes frankly, but mostly over the pages of large, impressive books. When she looked up, or stretched her neck, he would snap his head quickly back into the pretext. Once he tore page 336 of a 1632 edition of Montaigne's *Essais* as his mask nose whipped around. Buried in his book, he would blush until his face, *submaskum*, actually hurt.

Sometimes he would get up, stretch conspicuously, and walk around behind her, willing her over and over to need to pee so he could bump into her, or examine her workplace more closely. Her handwriting.

But she never did go to the bathroom—at least as far as he knew. When she left, she always just left. *How to Pick Up Girls* did not cover libraries.[41]

Love's progress was slow, but Pignocchio's music advanced quickly. Dottore Squeezeboxo he had become, *il gran signore della fisarmonica*. And the Italian for "accordion" got him thinking: Why *not* a harmonica, a Hohner harmonica to add to Honey, his Hohner Hohnica, a little brother, as it were, but with the evocative power of a troupe of moaning ghosts?

What drove this slim volume to the *Times* best-seller list (jostling, I may add, the cookbooks, self-help books, and memoirs of women held as sex slaves by their fathers)? Yes, it's true Hundwasser's *The Nose* was on there for 26 weeks, so I can't be too snooty about it. But 86 pages, with sentences like "I shall next attempt to develop, by considering some biographical material pertaining to Ludwig Wittgenstein, a preliminary but more accurately focused appreciation of just what the central characteristics of bullshit are"—why? Why would *On Bullshit* become such a publishing sensation? The answer is symptomatic of a great national disease.

Slumming is the first answer—intellectual when a patrician moral philosopher says a bad word. Ooo—so risqué. And so tastefully printed in gold on red on black. Aren't we bad? For Frankfurt, it is "going downmarket", as they say on Madison Avenue, an academic trend that further coarsens cultural life; for his naughty customers, it has the dissonant appeal of a nun break-dancing, or the president crawling under a banquet table, looking for weapons of mass destruction. Bow-fucking-wow. Bad dog! Most newspaper reviews resorted to some coy euphemism or abbreviation for the title, posing as guardians of morality, wink, wink, nudge, nudge.

Frankfurt, the aspiring plebe, exactly mirrors Hundwasser, the wannabe intellectual—poseurs both. In a world catastrophically drowning in bullshit, they offer up their hyped-up analyses and faux alternatives to absolutely no avail. Except for the bucks they made.

But the Hundwasser dimension aside, I feel the issue is important, crucial. The first sentence of Frankfurt's book—before he gets all scholarly—is "One of the most salient features of our culture is that there is so much bullshit." And his central distinction between lying and bullshitting is that while a liar knows the truth and deliberately misrepresents it, a bullshitter doesn't care about truth at all. Truth is irrelevant.

For its truthicidal stance, Frankfurter feels that bulls—t is a far greater danger than mere lying. People talk all the time when they don't know what they are talking about. And they don't care if they know what they are talking about. (Hundwasser also doesn't care, but his talk is usually lying, or, as he says, exercising his poetic license.) And the public no longer thinks knowing what you are talking about is important. What's important is "sincerity," having an opinion, honest representation of one's feelings. "Sincerity is bullshit," the Professor remarks.

Almost everything is now bulls—t. The forest is bulls—t, the trees are bulls—t, the government is bulls—t, the news is bulls—t. When you turn on the radio you hear bulls—t lyrics set to bulls—t music. When you open a paper

41. Although I have by now collected a small library of "How to Pick Up Girls" books, I have to say that I've found them completely useless. Not one line in them has ever worked. No recommended tactic has ever succeeded. The girls and then women I was interested in would never fall for such nonsense as Hundwasser has me doing, and I would have had to be an idiot to keep on doing it.

you see bulls—t journalism surrounded by bulls—t advertising. Fish and water, coupled with a good dose of jaded cynicism and complacency.

This is our plague, and I must doctor to it.

What I do find useful is an approach suggested in Shunryu Suzuki's writings on attachment and nonattachment: Even though midnight is in one sense dawn, and dawn, midnight; even though calmness and activity are essentially the same; and even though in truth there are no separate, individual existences, still, dawn is also *not* midnight, calmness and activity are different, and there is an actual separate-from-me real girl out there.

So first I approach from the separateness side of things and think about an approach to bring our selves together. When I see that she is very unlikely to cooperate, I switch to the already-existing-oneness side of things approach—which of course is the same thing as the separateness side approach—and realize that I don't have to do anything to be united with the object of my affection. We are already soulmates, man and wife, flesh of each other's flesh.

It works almost every time, even if I wind up going home alone. And I've saved a lot of money over the years on carfare, concert tickets, dinners, gifts, etc.

He sold his collection of metaphysical poetry back to Sid Solomon. Who needed metaphysics? With the money, he bought himself a classic ten-hole diatonic Marine Band[42] and a holder to fit around his scrawny neck. His first piece to welcome Monty (full name: From the Halls of Montezuma) was a harmonica-and-accordion arrangement of Orlando Gibbons's "The Silver Swan," in honor of that swan-like neck, her neck, that throat, her throat.

The silver swan, who living had no note,
When death approach'd, unlock'd her silent throat;

O, that that silent throat would unlock itself to me, he thought. Why is it always I who has to begin? Why can't she come over to me? "Hello," she could say, "I'm Rowena Anne Billington, and I've been watching you for months. You're so different from anyone else in the library. Could we have dinner sometime? Sometime soon? I'd love to really meet you." Why couldn't she come over and say that?

Leaning her breast against the reedy shore,

That breast, her breast, and I the reedy shore. Could I stand it if she came up to me, then pressed my mask into her breast? The point of my nose might slide along her downy sternum without hurting her. I the reed, the thinking reed, the feeling reed, the reed to sway in her breeze. "Come to me, my little Pignocchio!" she might say. "Come to me quietly, do not do me injury. . . ."

Thus sung her first and last, and sung no more.

And now Monty took over in fantastic improvisation on Gibbons's melody, reflecting on its observation of the world and its sorrows.

Farewell, all joys; O Death, come close mine eyes;
More geese than swans now live, more fools than wise.

Who was speaking? Who the lover, who the beloved? They were twined in one, dying to the world, seeking peace and death in one another's embrace, fools, fooled, and fool-

42. Never. Never would I play a harmonica. My soul's hair stands on end when I hear one—a loathsome miscegenation between the ethereal human voice and a kazoo! Its barbaric note-bending threatens the destruction of all culture. Our civilization rests on distinctions: A is not B; B is not B-flat; B-flat is different from C. The tones are separate; they are not part of some thick soup sloshing its currents around, moshing one thing into another according to the will of the cook. Humans should not be given the power—or the permission—to break the barriers between things.

A mouth-organ! How little that Marine Band (excellent name!) toy resembles its mighty homonym, the instrument of instruments that thunders through our churches toward the infinite. The harmonica, pathetic and insidious at once. Damn the demons the instrument calls up! Tones are not made to be "bent."

I think Hundwasser put that detail in just to annoy me. You'll notice it doesn't appear in his report of the Fungus Pygmy performance.

ing all at once. *Wir sind der Welt abhanden gekommen*. Dead to the turmoil of the world, in peace now, together in their common heaven, in their love, in their song.

Matthias Hohner must have twitched ecstatically in his grave. Never before had his instruments been utilized to such effect. Not Abe Lincoln, not Wyatt Earp, not Billy the Kid or Jesse James—harmonica enthusiasts all—had ever produced such poignant sound. Even Nastya and Tony were impressed. Unfortunately, Rowena never got to hear it.

Though a traditional venue for accordionistas, money was scarce and hard to come by on the streets of New York. HELP ME BECOME A REAL BOY, read his sign.[43]

But there, in those mean streets, his repertoire expanded, and passersby, struck by something extraordinary and strange, dropped coins and bills and occasional condoms into his case, the latter an unintentional irony, deeply painful but productive of the very pain and passion that kept them coming. With income trickling in, he expanded his library of recordings, and his world of musical possibilities expanded with multiple big bangs, at red-shift velocity. When fortune hit, it hit this way:

Antonio Lionni, like many Italian Americans, was an opera fanatic. Though Nastya was initially indifferent, he had dragged her to the free weekend performances of the Amato Opera in its storefront, piano-accompanied operations, then on Twenty-third Street. *Il Barbiere di Siviglia*, *Cavalleria Rusticana*, *Rigoletto*, *La Traviata*, *Pagliacci*. He'd whisper what was going on into her Cyrillic ear. The intimacy was contagious, with not a facial gesture missed, and Nastya got into the soap-opera swing of things. Their occasional attendance high up at the Met was disappointing in contrast.

In one of his rare appearances at Nastya's apartment, Antonio overheard Alexei practicing the love duet from the first act of *La Bohème*, with Monty as Rodolfo, Honey as Mimi, and Pignocchio as the entire Teatro alla Scala Orchestra. Tony was vaguely aware that Nastya had had a son by some other man, and that that was his room, in there, like Gregor Samsa's, but now, all of a sudden— whammo: "*Dammi il braccio, mia piccina.*" "*Obbedisco, signor!*" His erection was not from looking at the currently bedraggled Anastasia.

It was at that moment that Nastya's son entered his consciousness as a high and treasured part of *la famiglia*, Alessandro or Pignocchio or whoever he was. And for Alexei, Antonio Lionni became the first of his mother's lovers who had a face and not just a

43. "HELP ME BECOME A REAL BOY" turned out to be a brilliant slogan for my street-musician work. Matrons felt motherly and opened their purses. Beautiful young girls were amused, giggled in groups, and put little treats in my accordion case. Young guys tended to scorn me, but older men, even men in suits, must have gotten a whiff of the good old days before they'd settled down, like Pinocchio, to conformist idiocy. They were the best contributors. You can really make a living out there with an accordion. And yes, there were condoms. I always offered them to the sneering punks, who always took them.

I should relate one incident Hundwasser for some reason omitted. Which was strange, because he was very, very interested in this story. I have my theories about why the interest, and why the omission.

It was some time in the early '70s, so I was nineteen or twenty, and would have looked fourteen if anyone could have seen me under my mask and Pinocchio gear. For some minutes I had been aware of a silver Bentley parked at my curb, apparently occupied, its motor purring softly. I was in high form that day, performing some tunes and arrangements I dare say no other street accordionist could manage. Lots of coins and bills in the case.

When I had finished up the Grosse Fuge, to the applause of a small, astonished crowd, the rear window of the Bentley rolled down and a silver-haired gentleman joined the acclaim, thrusting his jewel-laden hands out the window to clap. One hand withdrew and reemerged with a $100 bill. He asked if I could put it in the case for him. "Or maybe better not," he said. "Someone might swipe it while you're playing.

"Play some more," he said.

Another ten minutes of late Beethoven, and it began to drizzle. As I was packing up, he invited me into the Bentley. I asked if it was true that the loudest sound you could hear was the ticking of the clock. "That's a Rolls," he told me. "You don't hear *any* sound in a Bentley. The clocks are electric. Want to see?"

HELP ME
BECOME
A
REAL
BOY!

"Sure, why not?"

He told the chauffeur to head for the park, and we drove around for an hour, talking about Beethoven and listening to the silence.

"I like your sign," he added. "'A real boy.' Is that what you want to be?"

And then he started in, talking about the oppression of real boys, the sexual oppression, as if young people like me couldn't make informed choices about their sexual experience, couldn't give informed consent. As if intergenerational intimacy were outrageous and criminal, as if the cradle of our civilization hadn't practiced boylove as a norm.

Although he was still at the far end of the car seat, I was getting the picture. And the shameful thing is that I didn't ask him to stop the car and let me get out. I was too flattered by his admiration of my playing, too entranced with his offer to speak to his friends about me, too captivated by the possibility of being "discovered," with its emoluments of fame and riches.

He wanted me to be his "special young friend." I hemmed and hawed. He asked me to take off my mask. I refused. He wanted to know why. I explained as best I could. He pleaded with me and offered me another hundred dollars to take it off. I told him no. So he reached over suddenly, knocked off my hat, and pulled my mask off my head.

Revenge is sweet. His jaw dropped. He was probably disgusted by the smell too, and of course horrified at the dermopathologies. Ravaged faces are hard to look at. He had the driver stop the car, and let me and Honey out at 72nd Street. He said nothing as the car sped away to the west. I pulled my Pignocchio mask back on. Hey, I was two hundred bucks richer. I walked all the way home in the rain.

pecker. It was only natural that when Sofia, Tony's beloved little sister, got married, Pignocchio would be hired to play at the wedding.

A gig! His first real gig! One where there might be—would be—single girls, desperately seeking. He'd have to play tarantellas. He studied up. He studied the music—the normal tarantellas, Napoletana, Calabrese, Sicilian. But in addition Liszt's frantic "Tarantella, Venezia e Napoli," Chopin's, Rachmaninoff's, and Schubert's at the end of "Death and the Maiden."

He studied tarantulas too, his spider fingers itching with joy. For the dance had originated as poison control for *tarantatas*—women from Taranto bitten by the hairy beasts. Neighbors would surround the victim, play and dance, and watch the movements of their patient. Once the correct rhythm, speed, and tune were found, survival was certain. Using Pignocchio's arachnid hands to denature tarantula venom seemed a genuine homeopathic interaction, *similia similibus curentur*. Sam Hahnemann would be proud; no one at the wedding would know.[44]

His performance strategy was simple: one of contrast and surprise. He began his wanderings through the reception hall playing Gesualdo's "Moro Lasso." Only he knew the secret words and their referential meaning. This is your life, Alexei, and all of you out there:

Moro lasso al mio duolo,
E chi mi può dar vita,
Ahi, che m'ancide e non vuol darmi aita.
O dolorosa sorte,
Chi dar vita mi può, ahi, mi da morte.

The music was extravagant, emotionally shocking, early-seventeenth-century chromaticism not heard again until Wagner and Strauss. Some passages included all twelve notes in a single phrase, anticipating Schoenberg. Sharp dissonances of pain, violent rhythmic contrast, uncomfortable harmonic juxtapositions, as of A minor and D-flat major at the beginning of the piece. Wedding music it was not.

But to set up a wedding—what could be better? Pain—then release and joy, a sequence highly recommended by the sages. At a signal from Antonio, Pignocchio let rip a medley of the hottest tarantellas from every region represented in the room. Even dotards left their wheelchairs to dance. Groups formed, chains spun clockwise and counter-. The puppeteer puppet sped them up and slowed them down like some

44. Studying tarantellas and subtly applying them was my first experience of being a healer. Hundwasser kept a tarantula in a terrarium in his lab as a conversation starter for the "pretty young things in their white lab coats" he enjoyed cultivating. I began with Herman.

Herman was a dancin' fool. He (?) would jump out of hiding—or hibernating, or estivating, or whatever tarantulas do for sleep—at the first peep of the accordion, and would then stand thoughtfully, taking the music into his ganglia. Then he would begin to sway, and after a minute to dance, and to dance appropriately to whatever I was playing, almost in rhythm, but definitely fast for allegros and slowly for adagios. When I stopped, he stopped—and waited. He could outwait me. When I left, I just left him there, waiting.

I figured if a spider person could react this way, with so few nerve cells, human persons must be able process those signals with far more complex consequences than simply dancing.

As you probably know, Beethoven suffered chronically from abdominal problems and severe intestinal inflammation. Fortunately Hundwasser suffered from similar symptoms. An experiment was staring me right in the face. The famous *Heilige Dankgesang* in the A minor quartet, the "Holy Song of Thanks from a Convalescent to the Godhead," was written after Beethoven had recovered from a serious bout with abdominal pain. Surely the tones, the great ideas of that movement, beyond being "proof of the existence of God" (Huxley), the successive integrations of disparate elements, must have something to do with disease, and with (Beethoven's) stomach disease in particular. It was worth a try.

I made an accordion arrangement of the three adagio sections, and played them daily to Hundwasser during lunch break. We used the animal room for privacy. He just sat and listened. I suppose the rats listened too, but I had no parameters to measure the effects on them.

Hundwasser, however, had lots of parameters. Or, like the hedgehog, one big parameter: we would

demonic personal trainer. Children danced descants around the grown-ups. The Pied Piper wouldn't have been more successful. In fact, several rats were seen dancing in the kitchen. And these were New York City rats, normally ironic and blasé.

During a break, and following their Milanese tradition, the best man, Harpo-like, snipped the groom's tie into pieces—to great cheering—and the pieces were sold to pay the musician. Pignocchio was bravissimoed into the spotlight, the crowd undaunted by his mask, and presented with over a thousand dollars in checks and bills. Among them were business cards scrawled with "Contact me for more work." When asked to comment, he could only say, "*Grazie, grazie*. I wear not motley in my brain,"[45] a remark that left them—for some reason—laughing and applauding.

As the blood-alcohol levels ascended into heaven, Alexei wandered the tables, boosting hilarity with his sneezing song which began with a verse set to Mozart's dark minor variation on "Twinkle, Twinkle, Little Star":

Twinkle, twinkle, starnutire *[note: Italian, "to sneeze"]*
Oi, my eyes are getting bleary
And my ears are getting stuffy,
And my nose is getting puffy . . .

Suspended on the dominant, here he broke into a polka chorus much fitted to his instrument:

Achoo!
Achoo!
Achoo, achoo, achoo!
Ah-ah-ah-ah-ah-ah-ah-ah-ah-ah-ah-Achoo!
Scusi.

The guests, protected by invisible alcohol shields, didn't seem to mind being sneezed on. Perhaps they thought the germs couldn't get beyond his mask. How did they think he breathed? In any case, they laughed and laughed, and slapped him on the back.

The dance hall was filled with eligible dark-eyed beauties, many friends of the bride. And Pignocchio had memorized six killer pickup lines. Surely one of them would work:

count the number of Rolaids he popped each day. It took a week or so before R began to drop. From an average of 20 to an average of 12. On weekends, no music, R rose again. Come weekdays, it began to fall by Tuesday. In a sustained three-week experiment, no days off, R fell to 3, then climbed to 12 again with a week off. We were on to something. Neither of us had the time for a full and lasting cure, but after we stopped the experiment, he bought a record of the Budapest playing it and has used that routinely to calm his symptoms. Saves him money on Rolaids, and he can listen while washing the dishes during the rare moments that he washes the dishes.

Flush with success, I looked more closely into the tarantella situation, the *Antidotum Tarantulae*. I would need to study the phenomenon first-hand.

But there aren't a lot of tarantula bites in Manhattan. There aren't many tarantas to whom I could offer treatment—especially if it were just an experiment by a newbie. What to do?

Herman to the rescue! If I could get him to bite me, and then, in the heroic tradition of the great doctors and medical researchers, I could try to cure myself. I admit such research is small potatoes compared to the guy who shoved a catheter into an arm vein and guided it up into his heart, or the guys from Walter Reed's team who invited malaria mosquitoes to bite them so they could test drugs, or even the guy who gave himself ulcers so he could prove it was bacteria that caused them. Small potatoes unless I died. But I knew that though tarantula bites were toxic, they were not often fatal.

And of course, we have to remember Dr. Curt Conners, aka the Lizard in Spiderman Comics, who lost his arm

45. A remark from my favorite of all Shakespeare's characters, Feste, the clown in *Twelfth Night*. "I wear not motley in my brain." The man is a slave to the whims of his noble patrons. They can dismiss him at will to wander and starve; they can order him hanged should he too much offend; he has no family, no friends, no history, no personal life: he is alone. A clown who makes no one laugh, for he is never funny. He lances the boils of the plague of his time. And yet in his mind, he is free.

What does Feste say? "Many a good hanging prevents a bad marriage." Now, that's cutting to the real heart of things.

And his song at the end of the play, his summation of human life? When that he was a tiny little boy, even amidst the wind and the rain, any foolish thing he did was only a trifle.

But when he came to be a man in the wind and the rain, the world shut its gates against his foolishness.

And when he married, he could get away with nothing.

And on his deathbed he noticed that the drunks were still drunk. Nice. The Ages of Man.

A great while ago the world begun in the wind and the rain, but now it's all one, and the play is done.

Sometimes I wish that I too might take no prisoners.

"If you were a new hamburger at Burger King you would be Burger Princess.

"I wear Fruit-of-the-Loom underwear. What kind do you wear?"

"I'll be Beethoven, you be Mozart. Let's have a conversation."

"That's a cool outfit. You look like Eudora Welty. I'll bet everyone tells you that, right?"

"Is it hot in here, or is it just you?"

"I miss my teddy bear. Will you sleep with me?"

The first three provoked laughter wherever applied. The next two were met with vacant stares, while the last, uttered in desperation toward the end of the evening, elicited from one *bella ragazza* only: "Excuse me, I have to throw up."

Perhaps she had drunk too much chianti.

As she staggered away, Pignocchio felt a tugging at his sleeve. He turned to see a shriveled old man beckoning to him. Leaning over sideways so as not to bash the ancient with his bellows, he put his ear to the speaker's mouth.

"*Più in alto che se va,*" he croaked, "*più il col se mostra!*" The higher you climb, the more your ass shows. It wasn't clear to whom he referred.

But Alexei felt upbraided. He recalled an incident from early childhood when his mother had taken out after him for giving his checkers wild rides in his little red wagon instead of playing quietly with them. A "high fanatic," she had called him, some mistranslation from the Russian, and he had stood there, truculent, swearing to *be* one when he grew up.

Was all this nose-mask stuff truculent? Fanatical? Others had big noses. The girl who'd had to throw up had a big nose. True, not as big as his, but . . .

No, he must persist. As Rimbaud had said, "*Tant pis pour le bois qui se trouve violon,*" and he was both wood and violin. Accordion.

He'd heard someone whisper, "*Che brutta faccia,*" as he had approached to sneeze on her. Perhaps he needed a less ugly face, a nose not so threatening, not so stiletto-like, and perhaps a change of hat. Perhaps he should no longer do his marvelous impersonation of an imbecile. Enough of Piltdown's Progress. He would put puppets and their lies aside and, like the mature Pinocchio, the bad boy cured, but not too cured, he would henceforth embody rationality, commitment, responsibility—and thus become a real boy. Man.

There was that side to Pignocchio—a capacity for enlarging oneself, questing for new sensations, exploring hidden pleasures, secret fantasies, dangerous excess. He felt internally redeemable. It would just mean moving on from here. *Ciao, caro. Andiamo.*

in a war and experimented with reptilian DNA to try and grow it back, a great example of being less-than-careful what you wish for: the therapy caused him to mutate into a creature half-human and half-reptile. He became a villain too, and even uglier than I am. I wondered if I might turn into a tarantula person—from the saliva—but it wasn't very likely.

I knew this self-experimentation would be looked down on at Berg, even though experimental physiology, surgery, and pathology was exactly what I was doing. So it was 1 A.M. when I let myself into Hundwasser's lab, took Honey out of her case, and aroused Herman with the traditional slow, lamenting introduction to . . . Borodin's Polovetsian Dance no. 2, "The Wild Dance of the Men." Out he came on cue, staring at me through the Adagio, and when the fast part started, he gave a shiver, and went into nothing short of a frenzy, leaping high off the terrarium floor, doing 90-, 180-, 270-, and 360-degree spins in the air, landing on his feet, rolling over on his back, and dragging himself miraculously by hyper-extended forelegs reaching up, over, and behind his head, engaging the sand. It was so amazing, I almost forgot what I had come for. He must have been a Polovetsian spider, or at least have Polovetsian blood, perhaps from the Russian steppes.

When the both of us stopped to get our breaths, I thrust my left arm into the terrarium, and, though normally a pacifist, he leaped at it, and sank his fangs in midway between wrist and elbow. Good Herman! I had to pull him off. Within a minute and a half, I was, as they say, possessed by the spider.

Though somewhat atypical, I was that night afflicted with all the typical tarantula-bite symptoms: feelings of prostration, anguish, psychomotor agitation, clouding of my sensory apparatus, difficulty standing, stomach cramps, nausea, paresthesia, muscular pains, extraordinary itching, and, best and worst of all, vastly heightened sexual desire. I took a cab home; the cabbie thought I was way-drunk.

Lying in my bed, I felt wounded and weary, and aware of the deep tediousness of all things. Still, after a short sleep, I was able to drag Honey out of her case and begin a medley of tarantellas I had learned.

Somewhere toward the end of the 1490s, the great Neapolitan scholar Alessandro d'Alessandro described the treatment of stricken *tarantas* by the local folk musicians: "they play different dances according to the nature of the poison, in such a way that with the victims entranced by the harmony and fascinated by what they hear, the poison either dissolves inside the body and dissipates, or else is slowly eliminated through the veins." And with (wouldn't you know it?) one of the Neapolitan tarantellas, I could feel just that effect, a veritable exorcism, a return to life, possibly to love. By the next day I was weak, but feeling basically normal via my iatromusical practice.

Plague doctoring is not so much different, though I suffer less, and my patients suffer more. 

Still, he was shy. He couldn't get a girl because he was shy. How to honor that shyness and at the same time make progress? The mask was critical. Adopting a mask-generated script seemed absolutely necessary since he alone, with his original nose and his history, was clearly doomed to failure. The new Alexei would live the good life. He would not be just another pretty face. He would be shy but effective. He would be . . . Cyrano! Why not?

Friedrich failed him here. All that was in the catalog was a full head of Jose Ferrer as the big-beaked bard. Alexei liked the hat with its feathery plume. But the nose was unevocative. Unstimulating to women. Large, to be sure, with a slightly bulbous tip. Perhaps when that nose was eighty, like Ghirdlandaio's *vecchio*, it might have gravitas, but now . . . he needed something more.

Something radical.

Something really radical. He would consult Frank Mangiafuoco, MD, Plastic and Reconstructive Surgery. If the *dottore* liked his accordion playing half as much as he'd scrawled on his card ("*Prestazioni magnifico! Dieci mila grazie*!"), perhaps he might help. Off-putting forces can lurk in a mask. Women can be repelled by one. Perhaps he would go without. Go without!—but anatomically modified. Maybe that was going too far. But too far was often insufficient.

The Good Doctor . . .

So he trudged out to Queens one snow-gloppy day to the residential office of someone he'd met at the wedding. He'd called the office that morning to be sure the doctor was in. He'd told the pleasant-voiced receptionist he would rather discuss his problem in person. She was understanding and made him an appointment for three months later. Three months was not what he had in mind. He wanted to be seen the same day, and would be.

Before leaving home, he took off his Pignocchio mask and wrapped his poor, scaling face with gauze—like Boris Karloff's Mummy, so beautifully depicted in Friedrich's catalog. People gave him their seats on the subway.

He climbed the stone stairs to the second floor of a three-story house shingled with asphalt and, with a ding-a-ling, entered the foyer outside the waiting room. Sitting at a

Victorian desk, on a swivel chair stacked with PDRs and a pillow, was a most glamorous profile of a most unglamorous achondroplastic dwarf.

One of the students at Music & Art had been a dwarf, a term now considered offensive but at the time merely descriptive. Arianna Pobelle had a most remarkable alto voice, the resonant product, perhaps, of her abnormally large head, and at her senior recital had provided Alexei with one of the supreme aesthetic thrills of his life with her performance of Mahler's *Kindertotenlieder*, his Songs on the Death of Children.[46] It was as if she were her own mother, mourning her own monster birth, or herself mourning herself, and mourning every child she would never have because of her deformity. It was hair-raising—and so was she.

But this Queens receptionist turned toward the newcomer a face so shockingly lovely as to be hair-raising in itself. While Arianna's face was typical of her genotype—prominent forehead, low nasal bridge, and an underdeveloped midface with scant evidence of cheekbones—here, facing the mummy, was a stunning, fine-featured face, delicate, rosy-cheeked, and impish. Her body was typical of her condition, with a narrow torso and disproportionate shortening of upper arms and thighs. The contradiction between head and body was metaphysically frightening, as if the Teilhardian imaginings of science fiction had come to pass and the human race had left body behind and adopted the noosphere as home.

"May I help you?" the Face politely asked, apparently unfazed by all his gauze.

"I've been in a terrible accident," he said, "and I need to see the doctor right away."

"Name, please?"

"I'd prefer to keep that private for the moment."

Noting the lack of blood on his bandage, the steadiness of his posture, and the firmness of his tone, she asked him to have a seat and gestured with a hyperextended finger to the waiting room on his right. Facing him in a chair opposite was another mummy in a getup almost identical to his own. He nodded his bandages at hers; she nodded her bandages at his. She returned to her *Life*, and he took up an old issue of *Boating*. She was called before he was, and twenty minutes later walked out the front door with a far less bulky dressing.

Alexei watched the dwarf slide out of her chair onto a footstool and then to the floor. She waddled into the waiting room and beckoned him to follow. She was less than four feet tall, with a swayed back and legs grossly bowed. Her raven hair, glinting deep

46. Friedrich Rückert, the poet who lost two tiny victims to diphtheria, and Gustav Mahler, whose wife warned him in vain against tempting fate (their own child died shortly thereafter) report a far more complex journey than Elisabeth Kübler-Ross's fraudulent New Age itinerary of Denial, Anger, Bargaining, Depression and Acceptance.

In the five songs of the *Kindertotenlieder*, a grief-stricken parent meditates in the early morning on the loss of his children during the night. His first profound impression is one of irony: in the midst of his pain, the sun will soon come up and shine brightly on all, all the to-be-happy-today people. "Only I have experienced this horror this night." Does he deny? No. He strengthens himself against taking night into the center of his being; he tries to see his pain in the truthful context of oncoming, but ironic, light. Thus, the first stage for an enlightened soul is not denial, but expulsion of the threatening pathologic.

In the second song, Rückert and Mahler understand the premonitory two-facedness of the light sparkling in their children's eyes. They are flames of concentration, arrows of longing for the larger world from which they had recently come. Thus, the deeper second stage is not anger and tantrum, but an intuition of the complexity of spiritual space-time.

In the third, most painful, song, triggered by a small event, understanding and intention give way to outpouring anguish. Father is sitting in a room. His wife comes in, stands in the doorway, and father looks not at her face, but at the empty space at her side where the child's face should have been. The horror of that emptiness leads Mahler to what is perhaps the most painful phrase ever composed, extended and again extended to the limit of singer and hearer alike—what depth of human pain is there, pain of transience, pain of finitude, pain of mortality, the universal senselessness of the human condition. And thus, the third stage: not bargaining, but shattering. One must truly die to be born again.

Kübler-Ross is right in this: humans often try to trick themselves, an activity similar to, yet more complex than simple denial. But as Sartre points out, and as Mahler and Rückert already know, lying to oneself, walling-off of consciousness is a tricky, improbable maneuver.

The fourth song illustrates the double perspective of true suffering: "I often think that they've only gone out for a walk. They've just gone on ahead, up into the bright sunshine above the clouds." But the griever sees himself thinking it, knows it to be a story, but a story with consoling power. No depression

blue, reached down below her knees. They entered an office that Norman Rockwell could have rendered, unchanged.

The doctor put down a sweet-smelling pipe, stood up, and shook the patient's hand. He was an enormous man, at least six foot six inches, with a substantial beard, black as pitch, yellow teeth, and glowing eyes. Alexei was amazed he'd not noticed this giant at the wedding. Yes, the mask had limited his vision, and he had been concentrating on the women, but still.

"What can I do for you, Mr. . . . ?"

Alexei handed him his scribbled card.

"My God! The genius accordion player?"

Alexei nodded.

"What happened?"

"Can we be alone?"

"Certainly. Miss Robinson, could you . . . ?"

She left, reluctantly. Alexei explained his situation apologetically, tentatively, as best he could. Dr. Mangiafuoco listened carefully, puffing on his briar. At the end of the story he asked, "Why is your face bandaged?"

"So I could get in to see you today."

"You're in a rush?"

"If I had to put it off three months, I might not do it."

"Not many people ask for a nose augmentation. It usually goes the other way."

"I'm not many people," the patient said.

"I knew that from your playing."

The doctor knocked ashes from his pipe into the authentic half-skull on his desk.

"Thank you," Alexei said, genuinely moved. "But would you be willing to do something like that? A nose augmentation?"

"Why not?"

"Are you good? Will I look good?"

"Did you notice Miss Robinson's face?"

"Yes," Alexei said in vast understatement.

"Do you know what a typical achondroplastic dwarf looks like?"

"Yes."

"I did that. I did her. She's the feather in my cap."

The doctor filled his pipe and tamped it down with a huge finger. Beyond the sweet

here, no self-deception, but a soothing opiate, like the woman pouring oil on Jesus' head, the conscious use of imagination to lighten suffering.

Just before the end, in the fifth song, a reactive brush with anger, an externalization of the psychic storm within, a true, passionate and crucial assertion: "it's not my fault!" "I wouldn't have sent them out in such weather—they were carried out, against my will." Man hat sie hinaus getragen. Who did the carrying? Man—they. Who is they? Everyone, everything that is not me. A cry from ego in an ego-despising universe.

And with this fierce and futile protest, the true light dawns. An eerie, chromatic d minor is transformed into the gorgeous sunrise of D major—the sun that was rising, but superficially, at the beginning of the work. From ironic light of sky and predictive light of eyes, through emptiness of absence, past tender light-imaginings and stormy darkness to the genuine light of spiritual understanding—that is the path our tour guides take us.

Are we too cynical for this journey? "No storm can frighten them now? They're resting in God's hand? Baloney!—they're just food for worms, and pity me!" If we are unable to see by the dark light of the *Kindertotenlieder*, then we are truly the shallow, deprived souls observed by Kübler-Ross who angrily deny, plead and whine, get depressed (and on Prozac), and finally, often by dint of inexcusable forgetting, "accept." The deeper we breathe in this music, the more we will understand when our own time of sorrow comes.

This is dangerous music the dwarf had sung—dangerous because so transforming and beneficent.

tobacco smell, Alexei whiffed a strange sensibility in the air, some inchoate, Rasputin vibration. His fingers began to twitch.

"But do you think it's ethical to do this—just because I want it? I mean, will you get in trouble with some medical board or anything like that?"

"You see that bust over there on the bookshelf?"

Alexei nodded.

"You know who that is?"

Alexei got up and examined the statue. No name. He placed it back on the shelf next to *An Essay on Liberty*, *Essays on Politics and Culture*, *The Subjection of Women*, *Utilitarianism*, and *Principles of Political Economy*, all by—

"John Stuart Mill?" Alexei guessed.

The doctor nodded and lit his pipe.

"I don't give a flying fuck what the Board of Medical Practice thinks. I care about what you think, what you want, what you need. We need a new Millean Declaration of the Rights of Man!"

Alexei was astounded—as much by the doctor's conviction as by his profanity. Who had ever cared what he might need?

"There's a sanctimonious bullying, a conformist spirit out there which you and I can help defeat. Mediocrity ascendant. The modest nose. The nose in sensible shoes. Screw that. I loathe mediocrity. I loathe faintheartedness."[47]

He puffed away thoughtfully.

"You know who that other bust is, the other bookend for Mill?"

Alexei examined it.

"No."

"You should. It's Don Carlo Gesualdo, Principe di Venosa."

"The Gesualdo I played? 'Moro lasso'?"

"The Gesualdo you played. The assassino."

"What do you mean?"

There was a knock at the door.

"Later!" the doctor called out. "The murderer. He caught his wife *in flagrante delicto* with a lover, slashed them both to death in bed, carried their mutilated bodies to a Napoli piazza, and left them there to edify the population concerning the sanctity of marriage."

He leaned back in his chair and relit his pipe.

"Why are you telling me this?" Alexei asked.

47. By this time I should have noticed that the man in front of me was, how shall I put it? Megalomaniacal? But, my God, I was, what? 21, 22 years old? My judgment was colored—and shrouded—by his huge impressiveness—his size, his voice, his language, his self-assured manner, his vision of himself as a multi-talented artist and anatomical engineer, in the mold perhaps of his countryman, Leonardo da Vinci.

After this, our first meeting, and considering I might be spending considerable time under the tutelage of this gentleman, under his influence and under his knife, I thought I might at least look into the featured hero of his bookshelf.

I did happen to have a not-yet-read, un-peed-on copy of Mill's *On Liberty*, in an edition small enough to have been stashed on one of my upper shelves. I had picked it up for a dime at Pageant, and had filed it in the "How to Pick Up Girls" section, figuring it might come in handy, either to give myself permission to go ahead and try, or as a possible topic of conversation, or even as a source of good opening lines.

When I opened it at random, the first sentence I came to was "It will not be denied by anybody, that originality is a valuable element in human affairs." Great, I thought. This may be a treasure trove. That

"Because you already know it from the music. Because you chose to warn the bridal couple and their guests. Because you don't believe in mediocrity."

"So you will do it?"

"The augmentation? For you? Of course I'll do it."

Alexei inhaled and exhaled deeply, his nasal gauze flapping like a flag of surrender. He sat back down in the leather chair.

"But you'll have to take off the bandages. And you'll have to do it in front of Miss Robinson, and you'll have to answer her questions."

"Why? Why can't I just do it with you?"

"Delia Robinson is a very great artist, both with her pencil and with her camera. I'll need her sketches and photos to plan our strategy. You'll need her skills to capture the essence of the face you want. Not only the letter but the spirit of your new nose. Her sketches will be my road map. You'll have to trust her as you trust me—she's part of our fight against conventionalism and constraint. She, herself, is something new, something previously unknown—and she will be more so."

"What do you mean?"

"When I am done, she will be a real woman, a real girl, free of her genetics, entirely marvelous, stunning, bewitching. Your nose is child's play in comparison. She is the spirit that will lead both of us on. Get used to her. And you and I can make beautiful music together."

"What do you mean? What kind of music?"

"All kinds. Surgical music. Medico-cultural-political music. Music music."

Another relighting of the pipe. Alexei was getting nervous. This was more than he had bargained for.

"I want to play with you," the doctor continued. "We can make a band, play gigs such as no one has ever imagined. We can help keep marriages together—like Gesualdo."

He smiled warmly with tobacco-yellow teeth. Alexei began to fiddle nervously with his bandages.

"Marriage is a sacrament," the doctor continued. "*Non è vero*? But half of them dissolve. You know why?"

Groucho's ghost welled up uncontrolledly.

"The chief cause of divorce is marriage," an old Graulexei muttered.

"Unh-uh," declared the doctor, shaking his bushy head and blowing out sweet-smelling smoke. "You may not have played enough weddings to realize this, but mar-

single sentence would point to my originality, its greater meaning and value in human affairs, the originality of my choosing my target as a target, and at the same time would subtly suggest the theme of having an affair. I studied *On Liberty* diligently for the next two weeks.

Doing so made me better understand the man with whom I was to have many encounters, one particularly fatal. We will cross that particular bridge when we come to it. But also it helped me confirm my self to myself, and justify the singular path I had chosen. Mill condemns the conformity of crowds exercising choice only among things commonly done. Detestable. Any peculiarity of taste, he observes, is shunned as if a crime, and people abjure their own individual natures until their full human capacities are withered and starved, and there is little nature left to reclaim. "They become," Mill observes, "incapable of any strong wishes or native pleasures, and are generally without either opinions or feelings properly their own." I couldn't have said it better. And this path was not for me. Over my independence, my right is absolute, and I am sovereign. If you don't like it, go take it up with John Stuart Mill.

It was a good start on my relationship with Francisco Mangiafuoco.

But it turns out I should have considered more carefully the Leonardo dimension, and as I would learn, his Wagnerian self-image as *Gesamtkünstler*, entitled to fashion worlds.

He and Leonardo did, of course, share many values. He, like Frank, was an artist-engineer who wanted to help create some more sensible rational order, one in which his acute intelligence, might bring original nature under the sway of the human mind. His "Great Bird" was not just an example of failed early aeronautics, but a projection of the human soul to free the earthbound human body.

But Leonardo's bread and butter came from the Duke of Milan, a man more interested in warfare than in bread or cloth production. And so we have the outpouring of ingenious designs for war machines including armored tanks, propelled by hand-cranks, and revolving scythes, advancing in front of a horse-propelled vehicle, to mow down the enemy.

Still, Leonardo, seemed to have enough moral scruples to object, unlike Frank, to his own output. Although he, for example, invented the submarine, he deliberately suppressed the invention "on account of the evil nature of men, who would practice assassination at the bottom of the sea."

And unlike Frank, he had bad dreams. In a letter to a friend he recounted a gigantic, subhuman monster he might have designed, one impervious to attack:

> *Alas, how many attacks were made upon this raging fiend; to him, every onslaught was as nothing. O wretched folk, for you there availed not the impregnable fortresses, nor the lofty walls of your cities, nor the being together in great numbers, nor your houses or palaces! There remained not any place unless it were the tiny holes and subterranean caves where after the manner of crabs and crickets and creatures like these you might find safety and a means of escape. Oh, how many wretched mothers and*

riages break up because of wrong wedding music. Stupid music. Nazi Wagner music as the bride comes in, Jewish Mendelssohn music as she walks out. *Lohengrin*: sorcery. "Here Comes the Bride!" Marriage aborted ten minutes later. *Midsummer Night's Dream*: lovers drugged, lost, unfaithful. Whoopie!"

More puffing.

"My little theory, ragazzo mio. How can marriages survive such confused beginnings? We're lucky that only 50 percent split up. You and I will play the right music, unimpeachable music, music designed uniquely for each wedding pair. Healthy marriage birthing is the divine right of musicians, and we have never been allowed to exercise it." He broke into a hearty laugh. "And it'll be fun. *Un scherzo glorioso*."

"What do you play?" Alexei inquired.

"*Kontrabaß*. Juilliard, '47."

"You think that will go with accordion and harmonica?"

"Yes. Brilliantly."

More smoke.

"How did you . . . ?"

"Einstein Med School '53. I was impressively tall. Five years of residency at Jacobi."

"Why did you . . . ?"

"Couldn't make any money as a musician. Smoky jazz joints unhealthy. Beethoven's Fifth aside, why would anyone want to play professional bass?"

The doctor leaned back and studied his patient through his wrappings.

"I'm going to call in Miss Robinson, all right?"

Alexei was too confused to resist.

. . . and His Nurse

Delia Robinson answered the intercom, promptly appeared in the office, and the three of them made their way into the neighboring room. Alexei sat on the papered table, the doctor switched on the examining light, and Delia clambered up on the table and stood next to the patient.

"Are you ready to take off the dressing?" the doctor asked with a practiced tone.

"Dr. Mangiafuoco, I . . ."

fathers were deprived of their children! How many unhappy women were deprived of their companions. In truth, my dear Benedetto, I do not believe that ever since the world was created there has been witnessed such lamentation and wailing of people, accompanied by so great terror. In truth the human species in such a plight has need to envy every other race of creatures . . . for us wretched mortals there avails not any flight, since this monster when advancing slowly far exceeds the speed of the swiftest courser.

I know not what to say or do, for everywhere I seem to find myself swimming with bent head within the mighty throat and remaining indistinguishable in death, buried within the huge belly."

One might consider his military work as affording him the luxury of having bad dreams, and thus exercising his suppressed moral scruples. Given his disdain for the Board of Medical Practice, Frank had no such correctives lurking around his work: he was pure Mill: "There is always need of persons not only to discover new truths, and point out when what were once truths are true no longer, but also to commence new practices, and set the example of more enlightened conduct, and better taste and sense in human life," a yang without a yin. But neither of them ever sought to ask whether intelligence alone, however directed or decontaminated, is adequate for shaping the needs and purposes of life.

The Wagner element is interesting. I knew nothing of Wagner then, but my *Götterdämmerung* experience both forced me into, and gave me time for the intense study needed.

One might imagine that the Leonardo would be interested in the contrapuntal fluidity of Renaissance music—which he was, and that the Mill man would privilege eighteenth century forms and clarity—which he did. So where did Wagner fit in? Power, that's where. Wotanish, shape-changing power, swirling modulations directed anywhere, and preferably impacting the deepest caves of the human heart, and the interstices of the human soul.

When *On Liberty* is blended with mechanical engineering in the context of a weird kind of personal war, and the two of them fused with an insatiable lust for power, the mixture becomes explosive. As Ahab, in a surprising moment of self-knowledge: "All my means are sane; my motives and object mad."

"Call me Frank."

"And call me Delia," the dwarf added sweetly in Alexei's ear.

"I'm embarrassed," Alexei offered. "I haven't shown my face to anyone since fifth grade."

"Some people don't show their faces for their whole lives," Delia remarked. "This is a privilege, you know."

She began unwrapping the bandage, leaning far across him as the bandage came around. "Easy, now," she whispered at the penultimate layer. The gauze end dropped free, the culmination of a remarkable striptease. What was revealed, one must say, was at best grotesque, hideous enough to raise an unacquainted gorge. It was not the nose—though that was upsetting enough. It was the condition of the skin, marinated for years under life-denying latex, oozing, flaking, shriveled, red, its melanin kaput.

Alexei was unaware of Frank's skillful eye assessing the dermatological component of his task. What he was conscious of was the warm, soft breath of a lovely face next to his own, the deep blue of her eyes, the graceful eyebrows, the exquisite lashes, the soft curve of her lips. The face didn't seem offended by the smell of his putrefying epidermis. Rather it surfed along on its current, tipping from side to side, lovingly surveying the scarred and pitted landscape.

Dr. Frank fetched the Polaroid and handed her the camera. Navigating around the narrow table, surefooted as a mountain goat, she snapped three photos from different angles on each side. Alexei squinted against the flash.

"What shall we call you?" the doctor asked. "You haven't given us your name."

"Umm . . . Cyrano. Call me Cyrano," Alexei essayed.

"Ah. An excellent choice. A noble character. A majestic nose. An incomparable swordsman. So . . . Cyrano, would you mind lying down on the table so Delia can get some frontal shots?" He pulled up a stool and lit his pipe.

The dwarf shot from way back on the table extension and from each of the stirrups, extended out at 45 degrees. The camera delivered its pictures. Delia handed them to her captain and savior, and he handed over a sketch pad in exchange.

"What do you think?" the doctor said, handing the photos to their subject. Cyrano was aghast. All mirrors had been banished many years ago. He had felt the state of his face, by hand and by proprioception, but the visual impression was overwhelming. He would never, ever, ever, be loved. He would never, ever, ever, be happy. What was he thinking, imagining he might go without a mask?

"Here's how we'll do it," the maestro began. "Delia will make sketches while you free-associate, incorporating the lengths, shapes, images, expressions, and attitudes you evince. We'll approach it by successive approximation until you are completely, 100 percent satisfied and big-time enthusiastic over your new image—whatever it is. We should be able to sculpt life as we sculpt stone, right? So don't stint. Go for it."

"And then?"

"Then, depending on how long and what shape you want your nose to be, we'll have to find the cartilage or bone somewhere else in your body and extract it. Part of a tenth rib might be perfect."

"You're going to cut out my rib and make it into . . ."

"A nose. Not a helpmeet. Unless you consider your nose a helpmeet. And only part of the rib. If you want to grow your nose an inch or less, we can just implant the distal rib cartilage and—once the skin heals some—stretch the soft tissue over it. More than that, and you'll have to join Delia in my skeletal distraction group. I've invented a small machine—you know how the car jack works, the rotary kind?"

Cyrano shook his head, never having owned a car.

"Well, there's a long screw topped by a gear which engages a bevel gear to shift the turn axis by 90 degrees." He sketched the device as he talked. "If we turn the bevel with a small Allen wrench, we can get the primary screw to shorten or extend a threaded sleeve to any given length. I'm going to do this shortly with Delia's leg and arm bones, and she'll wind up as tall as you—and far more beautiful."

Delia primped theatrically—a self-mocking display.

"Your case, while overall more simple, is technically more difficult. That is, we don't have a nice long-shafted bone in which we can implant the lengthening screw and sleeve. At the moment, it's not clear to me how to anchor it at the skull and support it at the tip. It could be a pretty droopy cantilever there."

With a forefinger he gently tweaked Alexei's nose.

"The distractor might be miniaturized and driven by some small, magnetically controlled servomechanism implanted in a maxillary sinus so we could extend your nose without repeated incisions and gear-turning. But as I say, it depends on how long you want it. We could probably extend the soft tissue by a millimeter a day. So for two inches, that would be about a month and a half, two, of daily adjustment—provided all went well. Once all was stable—bone hardened, cartilage well-adhering, no stretch marks—we could extract the motor and the extender, and there you'd be, whatever you want, a work

of art, beyond public opinion, beyond its skull full of bugs and desiccated peelings. All power to the scalpel and the screw."

He raised his pipe in toast.

"All power to the scalpel and the screw," Delia echoed, and raised her penciled fist. "And to the pencil."

"So what do you think?" the doctor asked. "Or would you like to take some time to think it over? You can just work with Delia for a while and see what you two come up with."

"How much will all this cost?"

"For you—*niente*. Right, Delia?"

She nodded.

"Consider it a trade for the marvelous music, and for getting me back playing again."

"How is that?"

"Our band—don't you remember? The Fungus Pygmies? The magical cure for the plague of divorce?"

What was there to lose except twice-weekly carfare to Queens? Cyrillano imagined it as a form of free, focused psychotherapy, allowing him, perhaps, to make sense of his inchoate desires. Would he engage the scalpel and the screw? That remained to be seen. The pencil, however, might do him some good.

Cyrano Unbound

For all the nose stuff early on, the part of Rostand's play that most engaged our Cyrillic hero was Cyrano's delirious life-summation at his death. Here was exactly the swashbuckling shyness that called to him. Here were cataloged the great enemies he must fight. Here was—at least in format—the woman of his dreams: the faithful Roxane, passionate but chaste, living in a nunnery, coming at last to know the identity of her lover.

Night is falling. The ambushed Cyrano appears at the convent,[48] in great pain but acting cheerful as ever. When he repeats by heart the last words of the man she loved, Roxane realizes that it was he, Cyrano, all the time, ashamed of his deformity, hiding behind another's handsome facade. For the first time, she kisses him, and for the last

48. A Hundwasserian reference, no doubt, to my Convent Ave. apartment. Cheap student apartment. "Room" would be more like it. More like a cupboard than a

time, thus inspired, he leaps up to brandish his sword at his eternal enemies—the very same enemies list as Alexei's: Falsehood. Compromise. Prejudice. And greatest enemy of all, the final fiend, *la Sottise*, Stupidity. Can he defeat them? No. *Mais on ne se bat pas dans l'espoir du succès!* One doesn't fight with any hope of success. *C'est bien plus beau lorsque c'est inutile!* The struggle is far more beautiful for being useless. Cyrano's only triumph will be after his death: saluting God with the one thing left him, the thing never stained, never compromised, the one thing maintained pure in spite of all his foes—his panache, his feather, his flourish, his dash, his swagger.

What a way to go! Alexei, with his feverish Russian-gypsy DNA, would go that way too. And at the end, too late, his Roxane might kiss his bandaged brow.

No wonder he was attracted to Jose Ferrer's hat with its great white plume. A white plume he too would have, a counter to the great white whale, a feather to dust away the mendacity and stupidity around him. And to attract girls.

But the nose had to be bigger and better than Ferrer's. Grander and more inspiring. "There is no excellent beauty that hath not some strangeness in the proportion," said Francis Bacon, and the former Pignocchio was thus encouraged. Why be the victim of wrong-minded tissue when one can master and exceed it?

These thoughts came to him during his afternoon with Delia Robinson. He talked, she sketched. He remembered, she projected. He discovered generalities, she captured details. As Cyrillano's visions became more militant, she quietly cautioned him with lines painted into one of her favorite versions of Hick's Peaceable Kingdom:

The wolf did with the lambkin dwell in peace,
His grim carnivorous nature there did cease.

Cyrillano began to warm to this strange creature with her malformed body and perfect face. He could not call her "Delia," even though invited to, for that felt too forward, too intimate. He did notice the soft moistness of her lips, the gentle depth of her gaze, the sleek blue-blackness of her hair, and the sensitivity of her interpretations.

But then he would become aware of the abnormalities below her neck, of her determinate non-nubility, her for-him repulsiveness, and his feelings would harden into objective neutrality. Nurse Robinson was performing her specialized function, normally paid to do so by her employer, normally compensated by Blue Cross Blue Shield.

place to live. In fact, I think it was a walk-in closet in its previous incarnation. Cot, tiny desk, and chair, that was it. Bathroom in the hall. I used to sit in my Raskolnikov room and worry about authenticity. It seemed impossible for me to meet the demands of Dasein and at the same time go shopping for Mounds bars and milk. I was more afraid of going to the dentist than of *le Néant*. Me—consciousness in a Pinocchio hat, eating Cheerios at my desk. It was an existential scandal. How was I to bring meaning into the world and then try to sneak into the subway? Well, what do you want? Stupidity is inevitable. So much dirt! So much garbage! The angels shrug.

When his musings were finished, her drawings done, and several approved, they began to discuss next steps. Would he settle for a simple cartilage augmentation, or would he like to join her over the rainbow in experimental land?

Very conflicted he was. But in the end, the mere mereness of a naked nose, of a nose that was perhaps modeled after some larger character but was finally his alone, seemed insufficient. He thought of the oceans of goodwill and toleration his nose-glasses had brought him, the millions of laughs he had inherited by adopting the Groucho persona. And he valued the spine-tingling excitement provoked by Nosferatu, the great questions of life and death the vampire raised. Would a simple big-nosed Alexei have such force? No, he'd just be the freak he was. It was his masks, their resonant characters, that carried him through. Pinocchio was good. "HELP ME BECOME A REAL BOY" had attracted many dollars to his instrument case, and some few women, a few at least, might have felt motherly toward him. His own nose had had the opposite effect, especially with his mother. But Pinocchio was not good enough. Too puerile. Limiting. And finally, ineffective. "Excuse me, I have to throw up," one sweet young thing had said.

No. He could not go barefaced. Ever. Even with nasal augmentation. He would always need a role he could piggyback on, a role that would call forth thoughts and emotions larger than his own. Cyrano it must be—Cyrillano—with the Friedrich's mask enhanced. With such a face he would stand alone, aloof, a planet among planets, attracting, perhaps, a moon. From top to bottom, from panache to boot, he would demonstrate an aristocracy of spirit if not of looks, a heroic originality and superiority of dress, demeanor, and personal habits. True, he was shy. But so was Cyrano with Roxane, content to stay in the shadows. Shyness, though, was key. Shyness was attractive. Shyness brought out women's mothering instinct —though not in his own.

Not wanting to take work time or space for the proffered freebie, Delia had invited Alexei for an evening consultation at her small apartment just around the corner from the office. She listened to his thoughts, and he adjusted her sketches toward the perfect Cyrillano face, even though—as he now informed her, to her surprise—it might be hidden under a mask. After a cup of tea, she offered him a facial, with special herbs and lotions.

"You'll have to take off the bandage," she said.

"I'm sorry, I can't do that," he said. "I'd love to, but I can't."

"Why not? I've already seen your face. I've photographed it. I've drawn it. Can you still be embarrassed to show it?"

"Yes."

"May I say something?" she asked. "From a medical point of view? Your skin is terrible—macerated and infected. These bandages are a good rest from the masks, but if you don't really heal it, it will start to putrefy—and then, mask or no mask, you're really in trouble. You've got to heal up, really heal up, before you become Cyrano."

"Cyrillano. A Russian type Cyranno."

"Cyrillano."

Her hair glinted blue in the shaft of late-afternoon light.

What could he say? She clearly was right. If even *he* found the smell inside his mask intolerable, what would Alice or Elizabeth or Rowena or Roxane think?

"What do I have to do?" he asked. "And will there be any charge?"

"Of course not. Just take off your bandage and lie down on the cot. I'll do the rest."

She gazed at him so pleadingly as to dissolve his hesitation. He didn't want to say no. He didn't want to say yes either, but if he were to be Cyrillano, he'd better begin his chivalry right now.

While he unwrapped his face, she draped a clean sheet over the bedding and a towel over the pillow. Alexei lay down and mused as she changed into a bathrobe, collected items from the bathroom and kitchen, and filled a bowl with warm water.

As for most of us in acute situations, his thoughts were diffuse and flitting.[49] He wondered about sneezing with a greatly enlarged nose. More mucus membrane within meant more . . . what the Germans so poetically call "*Nasenschleim.*" Could be a problem. On the other hand, he wouldn't want *not* to sneeze—at least occasionally.

A recognizably prominent nose, he recalled, had gotten Louis XVI guillotined. But he and his medical team could fashion a trustworthy nose, a flirtatious nose. He should surely mate with a short-nosed girl as a complement and geometrical easement, maybe some cute, bawdy Irish wench. On the other hand, wouldn't a large-nosed, say Italian or Jew, better understand him? He wanted somebody innocent, though, someone who could discover him even as she discovered herself. People had seemed interested in his noses from time to time. True, they were judging by appearance, which is both good and bad, but . . .

"You ready?" she asked.

He was brought back to the odd-enough present.

49. It's true. I have often been perplexed by the firings inside my skull, the turbulent display of thoughts that appear before my mental eyes, which accounts for many of my failures with women—as when I fatuously brought up the metric system with Emma Robiner in junior high. In that acute situation, it was what came to mind.

But often these straying thoughts involve bodily functions, the spirit weighed down by the flesh—and I don't mean just pooping or peeing. My hand itches. I wish I could spread my toes more—signals from highly innervated body parts. The best example I know is that of the factory lad who is led out to be executed just before Pierre Bezukov. Tolstoy writes, "When they began to blindfold him he himself adjusted the knot which hurt the back of his head; then when they propped him against the bloodstained post, he leaned back and, not being comfortable in that position, straightened himself, adjusted his feet, and leaned back again more comfortably."

If I were taken out to be shot, I'm sure I'd be adjusting my mask, making certain my nose was pointing straight forward toward the guns, placing my feet in third position, and then scratching my neck if my hands weren't tied.

I know many people wonder how they might react in this situation. 

"Um, I suppose. . . . Thank you for doing this."

"Thank you for letting me do it."

And with that, she placed bowl, jars, and bottles on a cot-side table, positioned it appropriately, and clambered up onto his chest, all sixty-five pounds of her.

"That feel okay?" she asked.

He didn't answer for a moment. Sixty-five pounds on the chest is a tolerable load, especially if one is an abdominal breather. What he was more unused to feeling was a woman's thighs spread over him. Their size made him think of the wedding with its spread of sixty Cornish game hens, laid out for the taking. Perhaps he could think of them as child-thighs. But no, they were definitely a woman's thighs, and that made him very uncomfortable.

"Let me check your pulse before we start," she said. "Your heart seems to be skipping right along there."

She leaned forward to feel his carotid. He could feel her pudenda against his chest. White-bathrobe tachycardia!

"Okay, just take some deep breaths. In and out. In and out. Just keep it up. Easy does it."

And she rode his chest like a child on a merry-go-round, rising and falling slowly, rhythmically. She sang to him as she rode.

Doucement, doucement
Doucement s'en va le jour
Doucement, doucement
À pas de velours . . .

New York City, the language crossroads of the world. Not the carotid massage but the song worked upon him. The French song. His heart rate slowed, his breathing relaxed. . . .[50]

"What's that?" he asked.

"Mom used to sing me to sleep with it. *Un chanson de Dordogne*."

"You are French?"

"My parents run a B&B half an hour from Bergerac, right on the river."

"From Bergerac?"

"Mom's parents were from there."

"So you wouldn't be mad if I became Cyrano?"

50. Congreve thinks that "music hath charms to soothe the savage breast/to soften rocks, or bend a knotted oak." Well, maybe—at least the first. To soften rocks, you'd probably need intensities present only at certain rock concerts, right up close to the speakers. And as far as the oak is concerned, I don't know that it's been tried, and why would one? Violins are made out of spruce and maple.

Oh, wait, there were those experiments back in the '70s on the secret life of plants, you know, the physical, emotional, and spiritual relations you can have with your chrysanthemum. If I remember, they like Mozart string quartets and hate Led Zeppelin—as if one couldn't guess. They didn't like the "William Tell Overture" either.

My own feeling about music is more like Jessica's in *The Merchant of Venice.* Lorenzo is feeding her

"Cyrillano."

"You wouldn't be mad?"

"No. *Il dottore* might be—he wants to fix you. He wants you to be you. But I would be mad if you became all ulcerated and necrotic."

Her face was so lovely as she uttered these words. She felt his carotid again.

"Our first job is to clean this mess up. When was the last time you washed your face?"

"I don't."

"Doesn't it feel . . . slimy?"

"Yes. It's part of the price. The trade-off."

"Trade-off for what?"

"For being able to build castles in the sky."

"That is important."

"The most important."

"So will you mind if I, um, debride your face? Get out some of the dirt and dead tissue so you can start to heal? It may hurt a bit."

That it would hurt made it seem more, not less, acceptable.

"Go for it," he said.

She laid several warm, wet gauze strips on areas of his face that had crusted over and let them sit for several minutes while she wiped the grease and filth from others. When the scabs were softened, she picked them off with tweezers and wiped the entire surface with soap and water, removing dead skin and flakes of latex. It did hurt some, but not too much.

"This is your cleaning and anti-infection session. We'll do another in two days to bring down the inflammation and a third to speed healing. Then we'll see from there."

She dipped her finger in a jar and spread something thinly across his face and forehead.

"What's that?" he asked.

"Honey. My witch's antiseptic and osmotic device to draw out poisons. Just a ground layer. Sweets to the sweet. Now for the heavy hitters. Myrrh, like for baby Jesus' diaper rash, a cleanser, counters putrefaction, antibacterial and antifungal."

Her tiny fingers caressed his face as she applied each cream and gently rubbed it in, as if he were a clay figure being shaped.

"Does that feel good? And now some Goldenseal cream, anti–everything bad, including viruses, and restores tissue tone besides. You're not bad-looking without your masks, you know. What does Cyrano say? 'A large nose is the mark of a witty, courteous, affable, generous and liberal man.'"

lines about "soft stillness and the night" and the "touches of sweet harmony"—great pickup strategy, by the way. She says simply, and I agree, "I am never merry when I hear sweet music." But his balloon will not be pricked, and he goes on about "the sweet power of music." The man is like an ad for aspartame.

He begins his pushy male dismissal of her profound statement by telling her, "The reason is, your spirits are attentive," and in this case only, I think he is correct—mine too are attentive, and that is the reason music makes me sad.

But Hundwasser's reporting here is both untrue and not to the point. My spirits are attentive, yes, but to what? Not Delia's *Doucement, doucement, à pas de velours*, but to their usual object of attention: myself.

I don't mean to appear egoistical. The question is: What does music move, when it "moves us"? The answer clearly must be: "us." We are the vibrating reeds, or strings, or membranes, or columns of air. Sound waves may enter from outside, from Arlene Premper's (Hundwasser's Arianna Pobelle) no-neck throat or from Lily's graceful violin, but it is we who vibrate, plywood boxes or Guarnaris that we are, according to our particular resonance.

In other words, we hear only ourselves.

I am saddened because what I hear beyond all sound is music "about something that will never happen, or something else that is not." These were the words of the great Charles Ives describing what came pouring forth from him in "Hawthorne."

Something similar is a permanent state in me, a feeling of deep nostalgia for somewhere, something I have yet to be, for some state or entity deep in my interior dreamworld, never, perhaps, to be reached.

Musical expression as generally conceived—Lily's Prokofiev, Arlene's *Kindertotenlieder*, Delia's *Doucement, doucement*—all that is child's play compared to the visionary hearing I know is in there, down there. Nobody has ever yet heard Mozart or Mahler or Wagner or Beethoven or Bach as they really are, unveiled, beyond the notes, beyond the compression and rarefaction of the transmitting medium. Few except the masters have ever yet really heard themselves.

Deep inside my masks, compelled ineffably inward, I have been better-equipped than most to listen for "the intrinsic essence of the world." Accordion or no, I am still the musician I was—and will always be.

"And of someone no one will go out with."

"How do you know it's your nose? Maybe it's your masks that put them off."

"No! They love the masks. It's the only thing about me they love. Groucho made them laugh. Schreck gave them shivers, got them excited, and Pignocchio brought out their pity."

"Is pity what you want from a woman? Okay, now a little coneflower, aaaaand some tea-tree oil to make you offensive to fungi. There! That should do you for a couple of days. I'm going to put these hydrogel sheets on top to keep things moist, and if you don't mind, I'll rewrap you in some clean gauze and see you on Thursday."

At the door, he reached down and shook her hand.

"If he makes your arms longer, will he make your hands bigger?"

It might have been one of his pickup lines.

"Good question," she replied. "We'll talk about it soon. And I'll also try to prepare him for your decision to continue with the mask."

"I thought that was one of my options."

"It was. He'll be miffed anyway, since he wants to develop a microdistractor to deal with your nose."

"He could do that anyway, no?"

"He could. He's a little irascible, though. Don't worry. I'll deal with it."

After two more sessions, with coatings of turmeric, bromelain, comfrey, and aloe, his skin, while still a little red, looked better than it had since Nosferatu; the odor was gone, the itching had stopped, and the trade-off was losing its grip. She'd put him on Vitamins A, C, and E, and he was feeling as much improved as he looked . . . as he looked, that is, under the gauze.

The Fungus Pygmies

It was in his newly arrived Cyrillano mask—its nose distended to the limit of the latex—that he came the following week to inform *il gran dottore* of his decision.

"You look horrible," the doctor said, as his patient walked into the office, "preposterous, ridiculous, laughable. And take off that hat."

Cyrillano sat down timidly in the facing chair and placed his *chapeau* on his knees. The great white panache fluttered with each Cyrillanostril breath.

"I'd rather not go without a mask."

"I know. She told me. She also told me you had discussed it, and that your decision was okay with her. She also told me that after talking and spending time with you, she no longer wanted me to make her into a long-limbed beauty."

Cyrillano had not heard this.

The doctor sucked on his pipe and puffed out a mouthful of smoke, its remnants rising from his great black beard. His left hand, palm up, beat a steady, nervous rhythm against the desk with a huge gold ring on the fourth finger.

"That your wedding ring?" his patient asked, hoping to deflect the subject from the one he had come to deal with.

"No longer married."

"So how come you wear a gold ring on your wedding finger?"

"Wouldn't you like to know?" Mangiafuoco asked.

"Well, I was just asking. I'm sorry, I . . ."

"I meant you would like to know," he asserted.

"Why is that?"

"You know *The Ring*?"

"Which ring?"

"*The Ring*, the *Ring*—Wagner's *Ring*. Of the *Niebelungen*."[51]

"No."

"I didn't think so. This is Alberich's ring."

"What does that mean?"

He smiled. And sucked on his pipe. It seemed the end of the conversation. Cyr got up to go.

"Stay where you are!" the doctor ordered abruptly. "*Porca madonna*, you know in the old country you would be killed for treachery."

Alexei sat meekly down again.

"I thought you said I could make up my mind—"

"Not without consulting me. I'm the doctor. You're just the patient. There's more at stake in this than your piddling nose problems. The future of nasal repair and prosthesis may

51. I have not been fair, thus far, in reducing my remarks concerning Wagner to the issue of power. Let me say a bit more.

Hundwasser knew nothing of Wagner except the joke "What is the question to which the answer is 9W?" (Answer: "*Herr* Vagner, does your name begin with a V?")

So, though I was a Wagner newbie myself, I had to tutor the musical ignoramus on all things Wagner, take him to see every Met production, and rent for him the video starring Richard Burton so he could appear musically sophisticated enough to sprinkle Wagnerian names along the course of his book.

What really turned him on was a graphic novel of *The Ring* which featured sexy superhero babes as goddesses and Rhinemaidens and, wherever possible, naked or well on the way. Siegmund and Sieglinda's incestuous mating left nothing to be desired in terms of Olympic musculature and Playboy flesh. Hundwasser's take on this reunion of Plato's separated halves, on this fusion of yin and yang, was, "Yeah!"

(I have to admit, that I too found the drawings stimulating.)

But *The Ring* is about much more than sex, drugs, and gods: it is also about money—and that was

rest in our hands. You know how many nose jobs are done daily on this planet?"

"How many?"

"I don't know. But a lot."

"I thought you said not many people want bigger noses."

"That's just the point, *stronzo.* There could be a huge market out there. Hundreds of millions of dollars. I would be the only one doing them. I'd get into *Time* magazine."

"I'm sorry. I thought you said—"

"I was only joking."

"About my having a choice?" Cyrillano asked.

"Just now, I was only joking. I always joke around—*sono fatto così*. I'm not mad at you. When do we rehearse?"

"I'm sorry Delia changed her mind. I mean maybe it's good for her. . . ."

"Maybe not."

"But we never talked about it, I swear. It wasn't my fault."

"I said I wasn't angry at you. When do we rehearse?"

"I hope she didn't say we talked about it."

"Delia wouldn't do that. She likes you. A lot. *Moltissimo*."

"I know. It sort of weirds me out. When I came in just now, she ran up and kissed my hand."

"Look," the doctor said, "Pinocchio walks into my office, and I just want to be a good fairy and make him into a real boy—with a genuine big nose—capisci? But if you don't want to be a real boy, you don't have to. You can remain a wooden blockhead, and I will leave you hanging on the tree like Our Lord." He took a great puff from his pipe. "*Scusi*. When do we rehearse? The Fungus Pygmies. I have a gig lined up for next month."

Cyrillano didn't need to check his date book. He wasn't doing anything anytime.

"This Cyrano stuff is all wrong for you, you know," Frank added.

"No, it's just right. Cyrano was shy. I'm shy. He was swashbuckling. I want to be swashbuckling."

"He was a virgin when he died. You'll be a virgin when you die."

"No, no—girls love musicians. Look at the Beatles. But Ringo can't get anyone because he has a big nose."

"Yours is bigger, *cazzo*."

"That's why I need the mask. I never did have a customary nose."

something Hundwasser was extremely interested in. In fact, he went so far as to identify (at least tentatively, and momentarily) with Alberich, the evil dwarf (pituitary, at least in a miniature superhero way, in the illustrations) who steals the gold from the Rhinemaidens, thus setting the gargantuan 16-hour clock into its motion unto doom.

I don't know if he didn't get it (it's certainly obvious enough) that Alberich could go for the gold only if he renounced love, and Hundwasser was still in hot pursuit of Jessica Kornblum, the Siren of Neuroanatomy, though renounce her he soon would, for fear of her boyfriend, Pablo. But in general he was definitely into "love," and far more successful at it than I. At least in getting it returned. At least for a while.

But I am meandering. *The Ring*, Wagner's *Ring*.

Eventually Hundwasser, nouveau-riche in musical knowledge, would maintain that *The Ring* was "a symphony of Jungian archetypes" "hiding its truths behind a poetic veil"—yet another level of mythological bullshit, and indicative of his bourgeois denial of its implications:

Wagner published his first written version of the story in the year 1848—the year of the *Communist Manifesto*. No coincidence, that. Anyone who thinks that *Rhinegold* is "a symphony of Jungian archetypes" would be quite disabused of their opinion by reading Wagner's essay "Art and Revolution," in which context *Rhinegold* is clearly a socialist tract. The third scene, where Alberich whips the helpless dwarves slaving for him underground, mining, refining, and working the gold, is an accurate metaphor for the sweatshops of ruthless early capitalism.

It took Wagner twenty-eight years to complete the four operas. That's four seven-year cycles, for me, four changes of mask. If there is any central theme embedded throughout the monster work, it is the conflict between love and the lust for power symbolized by the Rhine's accursed stolen gold. Is that not my very own story?

Here I am, quite rich and quite famous, my riches and fame stolen from a society of rubes, a confederacy of dunces called "America." I would love—that's for sure. I do love, eternally, repeatedly, immoderately—and yet like Alberich chasing his nixies, I seem forever doomed to loneliness.

Small compensation to be treated as a god by many. What does *The Ring* say about gods? In the opera, their power—that Power I spoke of—is based on an evil deed, Wotan's own theft of the Rhinegold from the thieving Alberich. The gods can be saved from the consequences of that crime only by some pure being who will take the crime upon himself, and expiate it through his death. Sound like Christ? Think again. It is quite another thing from the Christian Lamb of God who taketh away the sins of the world. Rather than expiate the sin of humankind, Siegfried's task is to expiate the sin of the gods! *They*, my fans, may actually be superior to me, sinwise—an abysmal and depressing thought.

Do I, like Wotan, actually desire to be destroyed? Has my power to rule over fanatics come at the cost of forever giving up (returned) love? If so, do I want to go on?

"Look, you could be the Glenn Gould of the accordion. He was an extreme introvert, like you. But he didn't wear a Cyrano mask."

"Cyrillano. My nose is bigger than Cyrano's. I want to turn my life into an exemplary work of art. This mask will modify my socially unacceptable behavior—I'm shy."

"Shyness is un-American, Alexei. This is the land of the free and the home of the brave. Back in the old days, shyness might have kept you from getting saber-toothed, but now it will only inhibit your career. One must not slay the albatross of self, my boy. It could be fatal."

Francisco Mangiafuoco[52] was a somewhat strange man. He had been the tallest baby in the bassinet and stayed that way in carriage, on tricycle, and tooling around the streets of Milano. He was handed a full-sized double bass in his *scuola elementare* orchestra because full-sized was the only bass they had, and he was the only student hefty enough. It became his friend, the only one who would play with him on a regular basis.

They called him "'Pazzo' Mangiafuoco," but he wasn't crazy—just different. In a postwar time when all things German were repugnant, he chose to study German, and made a deep teenaged exploration of German music, literature, and philosophy. No sappy Bottesini or Dragonetti concertos for him. He went right for the Bach suites for solo cello, difficult enough for an instrument tuned in fifths and some say almost impossible for one tuned in fourths. He took on the Beethoven cello sonatas and, like Alexei, had worked up the Brahms double concerto with a lovely violinist he was interested in.

As a bass player, he was extraordinary. One could cite huge hands and giant, instrument-enveloping height as responsible. But no. What characterized his playing was delicacy and stunning clarity, with long, lyrical lines of an almost vocal quality and seamless changes of bow. His sound was clean, clear, silky, focused. From early on, he was winning all the local competitions, and then the national ones.

When all his hormone-steeped friends were going gaga over Puccini and Verdi, he found himself far more attracted to the great Germans: Handel, Gluck, and Mozart, *Fidelio* and *Freischütz*, Strauss and Berg. And especially Wagner. He loved the masterly Hans Sachs, Parsifal the holy fool, and his even more foolish son, Lohengrin. He shared the unwelcome *wanderlust* of the Dutchman and Tannhäuser's wary relationship to love. He understood the sweet poison in Tristan's chromatic passion. But above all else, he loved *The Ring* with its infinite meditations on lust, greed, and power. He felt himself Wotan,

Wagner was particularly attached to the Wanderer scene at the beginning of the third act of Siegfried. Wotan is at the height of his powers, the apparently all-powerful playwright and director of his cast of humans, gods, and dwarves. But in reality he is fearful that in the coming together of Siegfried and Brünnhilde, which he imagines inevitable, the rulership of the world will pass from the gods to the human race.

In perplexity, he summons up Erda, the Earth Mother, mother of the Norns and the nine Valkyries, she who rises from the earth only when she senses impending disaster. But her only advice is "Yield!" and she soon sinks again into the deepest sleep. Of this scene, Wagner wrote:

"We must learn how to die, how to die in the complete sense of the word. Fear of the end is the source of all lovelessness, and this fear arises only when love has already begun to fade. . . . Wotan rises to the tragic grandeur of willing his own destruction. This is all we have to learn from the history of mankind: to will what is necessary and to accomplish it ourselves."

Has my capacity to love already begun to fade?

Hey, I just remembered a good Wagner joke from Music & Art: "Wagner is the Puccini of music."

52. This is an exemplary recursive confusion on the part of Hundwasser, who obviously substituted a two-minute description of mine for having actually read Collodi. Frank's last name was not Mangiafuoco—convenient for Hundwasser's pseudo-Wagnerian final contrafactual conflagration—but, truth being stranger than fiction, Settembrini. It was the reason I decided to get in touch with him in the first place. A humanist with an upward-curving mouth, in fact, anybody who might be even human to me, was what I needed. It's true his unfortunate death did make him a mangiafuoco, but it was cruel for Hundwasser to use that correspondence with Collodi for his literary purposes.

It is also a slander on the original character of Mangiafuoco. Although his appearance in the book (cribbed by Hundwasser)

> His beard was as black as pitch, and so long that it reached from his chin down to his feet. His mouth was as wide as an oven, his teeth like yellow fangs, and his eyes, two glowing red coals. In his huge, hairy hands, a long whip, made of green snakes and black cats' tails twisted together, swished through the air in a dangerous way. . . .

is designed to fill one with horror, he turns out to be a kindly man, and one of Pinocchio's saviors along the way.

Alberich, Fafner, Siegmund, Brünnhilde, Siegfried, Mime, and Loge all in one. They made him that much more huge. Especially Wotan.

He read Kant on the categories of the mind, and Schopenhauer on the will. And beyond all, enthroned in parallel to Wagner, he discovered the madman Nietzsche with his projection of the *Übermensch*—the perfect companion for his six-foot six-inch frame—and a subtle and not-so-subtle indoctrination.

Given his audition tape and record of achievement, he was a shoo-in at Juilliard. And another one at the Albert Einstein College of Medicine. They liked well-rounded applicants.

Hysterica Musico

Rehearsals were a gas: nitrous oxide. Much laughing. Each reveled in the other's technical skills and unorthodox musical imagination.

And some of the laughter was chemically induced by a different gas, bananadine. The doctor had a prescription for curing shyness and much else, including stage fright, and for liberating the daimons within:

1. Take 15 pounds of ripe bananas, eat, and save the skins. [Frank consumed two-thirds, his partner the rest.]
2. With a sharp knife (of which the surgeon had many), scrape off the insides of the skins.
3. Put all scraped materials in a large pot, add 4 gallons of water, and boil until material has attained a solid paste consistency (3–4 hours).
4. Spread the paste on cookie sheets and dry it in an oven at 300 degrees until it turns to fine black powder.
5. Smoke it.

They used a two-hosed hookah Frank had obtained on his last trip to Cairo. Three or four puffs did it, though Cyrillano thought his high might have something to do with having eaten five pounds of bananas.[53]

Far from burning him, as threatened, he gives him five gold pieces to help support his poor father, Gepetto. It is true these gold pieces almost wind up killing Pinocchio at the hands of the cat and fox assassins. But that brings me to two important points.

One, the most crucial formulation of Murphy's Law: No good deed goes unpunished. And two: The ancient saw, so well-enunciated by Chaucer's Chanticleer in the 14th century, *Radix malorum cupiditas est.* The first needs no elaboration; its truth is obvious. The second, however, requires some commentary.

"Cupidity is the root of all evil" is often misquoted as "Money is the root of all evil." While one might argue that the former is cousin to the Buddha's First Noble Truth concerning attachment, I would maintain that in this case, it is illiterate folk wisdom that gets the cigar.

The Fox and the Cat convince Pinocchio that planting his coins in the Field of Wonders will yield money trees increasing his investment a thousandfold. But if the puppet had lived beyond the cash nexus, if he were involved in a bartering culture, he could not be convinced to plant his small herd of sheep to obtain a larger one. Nor could his herd of sheep have been hidden, dishonestly stashed, to tempt the assassinating fates. No, it is the money itself, that portable concentration of wealth, which leads to all the *malorum* in our lives. And now that gold coins have been superseded by electron-sized virtual numbers, well, look at the results.

I think we may well say here that small is not beautiful, but potentially evil. Would that the same might be understood about noses.

53. I did actually test this hypothesis, unfortunately without controls, since I was, and am, unwilling either to do the

experiment or to suffer the results a second time.

Method: I used 5.0 lbs. (after peeling) of optimal-bouquet Chiquita bananas bought at Gristedes. I ate them without beverage over a fourteen-minute period.

Results: Symptoms began to appear at 22 minutes from the last swallow. They were not those of the bananadine high, but rather broadly localized intense abdominal distension and cramping, intermittent, in bouts of 3 to 6 minutes.

Interpretation: One can definitively conclude that bananas themselves do not cause psychoactive symptoms. Whether they caused the abdominal crisis is more problematical, since they did not at the other two ingestions. So my clinical experience may have been simple white-coat bowel hyperactivity. It struck me, though, that eating that many bananas may put one at risk for cancer and genetic mutation. I did discover that if you insert your little finger into the end of a banana and apply pressure, it divides itself longitudinally into three equilateral triangular solid strips.

Not many people know this. 

The gig was the wedding of an elder colleague's daughter. There would be plenty of women there of many ages—enough for both of them. The couple had expressed no particular inclinations concerning the music—"Just something to come in on, and something to go out to. And whatever at the reception." Nice. Easy. The Fungus Pygmies felt free to call the shots.

Frank suggested the *Meistersinger* march as a processional, a completely positive, C majorish work, with none of the catastrophic destiny of "Here Comes the Bride" in Lohengrin. Cyrillano thought this might be a good introduction for him to the dreaded Wagner, so he took out the score and brought to the first Pygmy rehearsal the remarkable accordion and bass "deorchestration" he had made. The good doctor found it more than satisfactory and was sure it would increase the chances of a solid, if C major, marriage. For a recessional, they worked up a version of the imaginary Kije's wedding, reckoning that since marriages subsist primarily in the imagination, the couple would have a salubrious send-off. They tacked on the "Troika" so as to get everyone the hell out of the church asap so they could pack up and get over to the Elk's Hall for the reception.

Since "whatever" was the only guideline for the reception music, and there would be plenty of alcohol and plenty of talking, they felt free to be more devil-may-care. So they worked up a medley of Looney Tunes, followed by some Hoagy Carmichael for relaxation, then on to a rendition of the orchestral suite from *Lulu* (since the bride, Frank assured his partner, was a lulu), followed by some faux Liberace for interlude and culminating, while people were plenty drunk but still standing, with an improvised, but elaborately planned *Sinfonia Discordia* in five movements: Chaos, Discord, Confusion, Elaboration, and The Aftermath. The idea was to create something completely unharmonizable—sounds no system could encompass. High on bananadine, they were sure Confusionism would lead to liberation. And sure the party would love it.

At the end of the third and last rehearsal, Frank said, "You know, *figlio mio*, you are *magnifico*, terrific. There's nobody like you."

The accordion player explained that that was because he had been born parthenogenetically, without a father. That bananadine was good stuff.

Tarantella con Fuoco

Cyrillano had never played a wedding service before. A reception, yes, but never the service. In fact, he had never even been at a wedding, much less a Catholic one. This was his first. He was impressed.

The *Meistersinger* processional went well, though the Pygmies could play through only half of its nine minutes before the two sets of parents, all the good, better, and best men in their tuxedos, and all the bridesmaids, spilling like overstuffed couches out of their matched satin gowns, and finally the bride and groom had assembled themselves seriatum in the apse. Were they as surprised as Cyrillano by the opening homily?

"Dearly beloved family and friends, we are gathered here today in the presence of God to celebrate one of life's greatest moments, to witness and bless the joining together of Robert and Emily in holy matrimony. In Romans, Saint Paul has told us that it is better to marry than to burn, for we are carnal, and sold under sin. You may see by the bride's dress that she is barely able to contain herself. You may follow the eyes of the groom as they caress the exposed flesh of his beloved. How rightly, then, are we gathered here to sanctify the union of this man and wife in heart, body, and mind. They stand here, I may add, in the nick of time.

"No sniggers, please. For we are all sinners, and I trust that in sharing joy with Robert and Emily today, you will take time to reflect on your own concupiscence as Robert and Emily have on theirs, and ask forgiveness, and for the remission of your sins. Let us pray."

Wow, Cyrillano thought, this is serious stuff. No mealymouthing here.[54] The apse people just smiled blandly, and didn't blink an eye.

The bride, in fact, was a lulu. Cyrillano might have fallen in love with her on the spot if she hadn't been up there in that preposterous dress, holding hands with that dick-head, Robert.

He's probably a junior salesman at some car dealer. Just shows she's not all that bright. Better not to get involved.

He and Frank sat through the service without interrupting, though Cyrillano thought it might be beneficent of him to answer the call for objections and try to put

54. I hate hypocrisy. I hate misrepresentation. I hate ignorant stupidity. It is hard to know which to hate most in the vast majority of wedding services that use Paul's First Letter to the Corinthians, chapter 13, as a text.

At the time of Hundwasser's Fungus Pygmies (our group was actually called Einstein's Nose, after Frank's alma mater, and my own grant from Mom and Dad), I hadn't been to many weddings. Since then, of course, I have been to hundreds, invited as a guest of honor, and introduced as such, by my fans. I even have a *Dies Irae* processional tune reserved for my entrance, though no one else, of course, would ever use it, and I have to distribute parts in advance arranged for various combos. Nevertheless, to the point:

asunder—before death did them part—such an ill-starred coupling. But instead the Fungus Pygmies waited for the primordial kiss, marched the couple out to sounds that Kije might have heard had he ever existed, and sped them off in the troika, though it was August, and there was little snow.

The reception was a whole other affair. First of all, it was National Accordion Day, so Cyrillano couldn't have been higher. Except that he *was* higher because Frank had insisted on a good hit of bananadine before loading up Grane, the Alf. Yes, they had traveled from house to church, and church to Elks Hall in a top-down 1962 Alfa Romeo silver convertible, with the instruments lording it up in back on the red leather seat and the bass, at least, surveying the traffic with its scroll. R. Gus Fungus had a canvas case, of course, but when taking him around in good weather, the Captain liked to give him a chance to take in the view. Good dog.

The band set up amid a moderate din of conversation, backslapping, and complaining about this and that. There would shortly be more to complain about.

They began with their medley of Looney Tunes: compounding the leitmotifs of Bugs Bunny, Daffy Duck, Porky Pig, Elmer Fudd, Road Runner, Tweety, Sylvester the Cat, and the recently censored Speedy Gonzalez in a mix worthy of Richard Wagner. In fact, it *was* Richard Wagner, adapted, as might be expected. The effect of this—as planned—was to introduce the revelers to the notion that there was actually a band there and that, if they chose to listen, they might enjoy it. The melodies triggered the child genes of many and disposed them to be friendly.

After the slight applause, Cyrillano took to his feet and wandered the tables with his rondo variations on "Stardust"—fox trot, waltz, czardas, and polka—while Frank studied the revelers' faces with an eye toward reconstruction. The children made fun of the accordion player's mask and pulled at his feather. Cyrillano parried the thrusts.

It was during this walk that he saw her—the Reason for the gig. "Stardust" went onto automatic. What he was thinking was Do I look all right? How is my hair? I shouldn't have worn these shoes. Why would she pay any attention to *me*? Maybe I could ask her for some stock tips. He blushed inside his doublet and hose, he felt hot, suffocating. His spine dripped with sweat; his heart fluttered and tumbled. He was faint, giddy, confused. He held his eyes askance in the Samuel Perkins peer.

She looks so innocent, he thought. He was always attracted to the vulnerable, and the

I *Corinthians* 13. Read it in Greek if you can, in King James if you can't. Chapter 13 is the answer to the questions raised in Chapter 12: How can I be part of the body of Christ if I am not an apostle, or a prophet, or a teacher, or a worker of miracles, or a healer? If I can't speak with tongues, or interpret the diversity of languages? If I'm just an ordinary moron?

Paul gives the answer about how even *zhlubs* can be part of the body of Christ: "I show you a more excellent way." The answer is to have love—not the hots for someone, but—and here he chooses carefully among three Greek words which we simplistically translate as "love." Of eros, philia, and agape, Paul uses the last, agape, precisely to separate it from that stewpot of sentimentality and lust which brings most people together in marriage, that which we call luuuuuv.

Agape. That is what I *Corinthians* 13 is about. Not luuuuuv.

Agape, as in "Those who love (agape) Jesus will do what Jesus taught." *John* 14:15, 23.

Agape as in "if a person has material resources and the love (agape) of God within him, his heart will take care of his brother who is in need." I *John* 3:17.

Not agape as in "I agape you, a bushel and a peck." But Agape, the transcending of the particular, passion without need for reciprocity, unilateral, if necessary, impartial respect for another person qua human being in the abstract.

King James wisely translates the word as "charity," a truth-speaking too blatant for our modern translations. You will never hear the word "charity" in a wedding service. You will only hear about love, viz. luuuuuv. But the text is *in contrast to* luuuuuv.

So, misrepresentation. Either intentional, which is sinful, or ignorant, which is even more so.

And then to quote Paul at all! Paul, the raving misogynist. Jesus' egalitarian view of gender relations was destroyed by Paul, who imposed patriarchy, taught that women were inferior, were to blame for sin and the fall of humanity, and were to be excluded from ministry. Veil your heads and go sit over there. "It is better to marry than to burn" (I *Corinthians* 7:9—only a couple of chapters back).

No wonder marriages break up when initiated with such intellectual dishonesty. I wouldn't even send Paul an announcement for my wedding. But then again, I am not likely to get married.

But if I ever did, I would have the opening movement of *Wachet Auf* for my processional, with Nicolai's great summons, "Wake up, Jerusalem, it is midnight, and the bridegroom is coming."

innocent. "The chemistry, the chemistry—I can feel it!" The situation was too much for him. "I'm unattractive and unworthy of attention," he sang, sotto voce. "I'm a hopeless case." And he accidentally bumped into her chair.

"Oh—you frightened me," she whispered.

"What happens . . . if you get scared half to death twice?"' he asked. She pulled away.

Oh no, oh no—no hits, no runs, all errors, he thought. Only errors. I've freaked her out. This is me, you. Inside the outsider. Why won't you love me?

But he never knew any women. Never knew any girls. No sisters, no mother to speak of. No lovers. No one to practice on. Better if he had just hidden away with some canned food and bottled water, and maybe a gun to protect himself.

For the moment, he'd better just kneel down at her feet and serenade her with his "Shyness Song."

"This one's for you, dear."

The Grand Old Dork of Yuck
He had ten thousand yen,
But since he couldn't speak Chinese
He died a bum. Amen.

She laughed, reached into her little pink purse, and handed him a dollar.

After he stumbled back to the stage, enchanted by her laughter, he heaved a great sigh, and the Pygmies began the major work of the first set, their suite of impressions from Alban Berg's opera *Lulu*. The bride did not realize that the performance was in praise of her and looked over briefly, perhaps to wonder whether the musicians might need something to eat.

She also didn't realize that the composition had been created not only in praise of her vivacious beauty but as one more of the doctor's determined attempts to save the institution of marriage. As he played Lulu's song in high harmonics, accompanied softly by his partner's unnerving bellows-shake, he mentally offered to Emily the text it set: "Even if men have killed themselves [and one another, he thought] for me, that doesn't change my worth."

The performance was elegiac and filled with the distinctive yearnings of man and boy. When they were done, Emily, practicing for her role as housewife, brought over a plate of cocktail franks. The Pygmies took a short break to wolf them down and then,

preceded by a chorale prelude on "What a Friend We Have in Sneezes," returned for a second peripatetic interlude, a reprise of the once-Pignocchio's "Sneezing Song," with its new coda of "Liar, Liar, Pants on Fire." This last was merely an excuse for some pyrotechnics newly fashionable among the latest shock bands. These kids!

They had rehearsed it well enough. While Cyrillano was touring the tables with his squeezebox, sneezing in the food, Dr. Mangiafuoco would sneak behind him, Looney Tunes–fashion, and wet his pants with a solution conspicuously labeled LIGHTER FLUID. Like some vaudeville villain, he demonstrated the can to the guests, who hissed him in return. In rehearsal he had used lab alcohol, which burns with a cool flame, will not ignite cloth, and evaporates before it can damage skin.

Cyrillano thought it strange that the alcohol didn't smell the way it had at rehearsal. Perhaps it was his always-cantankerous nose acting up, but damn if it didn't smell like something else. At the table of the bride and groom and their families, Mangiafuoco lit the match and applied it, as they had planned, maximum entertainment for those who'd paid the piper.

Cyrillano's faux-satin knee-britches shot up in flames, as did the curtain just behind him. The flames jumped high, athletically, to engulf his panache and began on the hat beneath it. Thinking quickly, our hero grabbed a fluted glassful of champagne and poured it over his head. He couldn't roll on the ground because he was strapped to the accordion—but "Roll! Roll!" shouted the guests. Instead he tried to smother his rear on the already burning drapery—a bad move. The curtain came down from its brackets and threatened the wedding party and its guests. Alexei climbed a side table and sat down in the punch bowl as the fire spread to adjoining tablecloths, and all began to panic. He struggled out of his accordion and splashed what was left of the punch all over himself. Soaked but no longer flaming, he surveyed the scene with horror.

Mangiafuoco grabbed his arm. "Come on, let's get out of here."

"But what about the others?"

"They'll take care of themselves, or they won't. No point in our being incinerated too. First principle of the savior: save thyself! C'mon!"

"The bass! The accordion!"

"You can buy a new one. C'mon!"

Allegro Agitato, con Fuoco e Appassionato

The giant pulled a struggling little Alexei with him and threw him into Grane's backseat. He pulled away with squealing tires and made for Queens Boulevard, lowering the top against the wind.

"It's the obligatory car chase, my man," the driver said as he put the pedal to the metal. "A one-car car chase, though, an excellent money-saving innovation."

"Can you slow down, Frank? This is dangerous."

"You are *con fuoco, ragazzo*. Name is destiny."

They sped along side streets, to lose any pursuers, and emerged, innocent, on bucolic Queens Boulevard.

"You remember that Cyrano had many enemies, all trying to kill him?" the doctor yelled back to his passenger.

"Yes," Alexei yelled back. "They dropped a huge log on his head."

"Well, you know, *chi pissa contra vento*. . . . Do you have any opinions about unhappy endings in film and literature?"

"Uh . . . no. Frank, will you please slow down?"

Now that they were no longer being chased, he did.

"I find unhappy endings more realistic," the doctor said. "More descriptive of this postlapsarian pisspot of a planet. You know, last year I was visiting Napoli, and I made it a point to lie in the bed, the very bed, in which Gesualdo slew his nymphomaniacal wife and her lover, the bed in which he himself died, that great prince, the enigma, the immortal composer, betrayed. Like me."

Frank began to sing:

"Mo . . . ro las . . . so . . .

"That's how we met, remember? You played Moro lasso for a wedding, and I knew."

"What? What did you know?"

"That I wanted to give you my ring. Alberich's ring. Here."

He pried the great gold nugget off his finger and handed it back over his shoulder.

"I really don't want it. I mean, thank you, but I won't be able to play the buttons with . . ."

"I want you to have it," the driver said.

"No. I'm fine. Really. Thank you."

"You okay?" Frank asked.

"Yes," his passenger answered from the rear. "I'm fine."

"Good. Because I'm going to kill you."

"What?"

"I said, 'Good. Because I'm going to kill you.'"

"What do you mean? Why?"

"What I mean is dead, and why is because you piss me off—terminally. You and Delia."

"You mean just because we didn't want—"

"No. Just because. But don't worry, this is my last ride too. And Grane's. Just a few more blocks."

Alexei was dumbfounded. What did this madman have in mind? He surreptitiously tried the door.

"Locked," the driver assured him.

They drove along Queens Boulevard, going with the lights. Frank signaled and switched over to the right lane.

In Kew Gardens, on the corner of Seventy-eighth Avenue, the Colonial Garage had been closed for the day for refueling and a huge Esso tank-truck was still parked on site, a tableau which Frank had noted on the way to the gig. He sped up, ran the light, swerved to the right, yelled "*Evviva coraggio*!" and rammed the tanker belly-on. He was killed instantly, Wotan, Alberich, Fafner, Siegmund, Brünnhilde, Siegfried, Mime, and Loge all at once, colliding with windshield and wheel. Alexei, in the rear, had no such luck. There was a huge explosion, and fast-spreading orange flames ate at Grane's top but opened an escape route for its traumatized, flaming passenger, choking in satanic smoke.

Alexei awoke at Queens Mount Sinai with oxygen feeding into his real nostrils, his left leg and arm in casts, and the upper right side of his body badly burned. With contracture scarring of his right hand, his accordion career was at an end. Which was just as well, as he no longer had an accordion.[55]

55. Frank Settembrini's life, alas, did end in a flaming crash, accidental and alone. His flight from the wedding gig, his unintentional (one hopes) act of arson, the two dead guests that resulted from it, the

6.
Scarabmouche de la Mancha

threat of an attendant investigation—all led him over the cliff of ever-threatening alcoholism and to the burning car crash and fall from the Pulaski Skyway which led to his awful and sensational death. Hundwasser, the ghoul, was waiting in the wings to give the story just enough variation to adorn the "literary fiction" of *The Nose*.

But his sad end had nothing to do with me. I still have my right hand, unscarred, and Honey 6 sits in her case in the corner, waiting to be called on if ever I feel the need to call on her.

Why does one stop playing an instrument one has mastered? Why does one stop playing music at all? Because one has stopped singing, internally, in the head, in the heart. That's one reason, and perhaps the deepest. But there are ancillary abysses.

More trivial perhaps, but for a musician also decisive, is a feeling that there is nothing left to do, no piece you haven't mastered. Some accordion players can fill their lives with being the life of the party, playing polkas and horas and tarantellas and jigs, making events happy for dancers young and old. A lovely gift on both ends.

But my approach to the machine was not that social, that altruistic—it was about the music, matching the unique capacities of an accordion pushed to its limits, to some of the world's greatest compositions. I did advance the art, and few, if any, have been able to follow as far. But many, even most, close to all the great works are simply not playable on even the most advanced accordions with huge numbers of stops. Rimsky's orchestrations, Stravinsky's polyrhythms, Bach's multiple-keyboard fugues, Mahler's huge concatenations of sound, and even most of the piano literature are simply not playable—even by me. Buttons and their necessary geography are not keys and theirs. Breath and phrasing are slaves to the univocal in-and-out of the bellows, so how can one even approximate simultaneous crescendos and diminuendos between voices?

I worked out and played what could be played. I added previously unthought-of details. But after that? It was just the same thing over and over. Been there, done that, as they say. Onward. The telling symptom was my deep weariness at taking Honey and her ever more expensive successors out of their cases, of putting my arms through the straps, of unsnapping the bellows-holders. Did I want to keep doing this? Not really, and then no, and then not.

"If music be the food of love, play on"? But what if my music never succeeded in feeding love for me, if every one of my encounters using it was a failure? Then its treasures become mere excess, surfeiting appetite and killing it.

As for the Duke of Illyria, music for me is "not so sweet now as it was before," and like him, I cling now only to the general shapes of fancy, which "alone is high-fantastical."

In the Mountain

Mount Sinai would be strangely like Tannhäuser's Venusberg: two females—both unwanted—suing for Alexei's affections while around them, white-garbed nymphs and satyrs bustled, busy with corporeal tasks.

One of them, very short, her white dress indicating no specific training but only that she had worked in a doctor's office as a "nurse," was busy laying out string around Alexei's hospital bed. Her size made it easy for her to creep under the high-tech affair to follow its rectangle where it abutted the wall.

"What the hell are you doing?" he asked with a combination of curiosity and annoyance.

"I'm making *koshere fodem*.[56] One of our Brownsville patients taught me."

"On the floor?"

"Well, it's usually done around a grave."

"I'm not dead yet."

She crawled out from under the bed, dragging a trail of string behind her.

"Therefore I adapt. It should still work." She seemed quite confident.

"What is it, and work for what?" he queried through his bandages.

Delia continued playing out the string along the bed's perimeter.

"It is *koshere fodem*, I told you that, and what it does is help you get better more quickly. It's part of a system."

"Which is?"

"Which is yesterday I went over to Machpelah Cemetery, and I found the grave of an old rabbi who died of cholera in 1849 . . ."

"I'm not Jewish."

"But the string is. And this rabbi, you will be happy to know, is situated right next to the grave of Harry Houdini, which was so crowded with tourists waiting for him to escape that no one noticed me measuring out Jacob Brownstein's grave with string. How's that for a system, dear?"

He hated when she called him "dear."

"I still don't get it."

56. I don't know where Hundwasser picked this up, but the koshere fodem story is clearly invented, since I was never in the hospital. I believe he is Jewish, and I know he grew up in Brooklyn, so this may have been some neighborhood lore. But that Delia practiced so many little oddities, and believed in them without any skepticism, this was true, and this, I think, was the thing that kept us further apart than we might otherwise have been.

I'm a rational person—presuming there are rational processes. I'm not superstitious. If anything, I'm *sub*stitious—laboring under oppressive spiritual forces, the general soul-destroying tendencies of our culture. I'm not trying to be dramatic here, and I don't anthropomorphize the evil abroad in the shape of a red guy with horns and cloven feet. But that something satanic is going on, and has been for a while, that is clear. There are great forces at work, mythical forces beyond and prior to our ability to articulate them, forces bound up with the horror and power of nature as well as the more comic monstrosities of humanity as seen on TV. I'm talking about the plague. I'm not a plague doctor, but thanks to Hundwasser, I must play one for the world—and I take my role seriously. If there were a plague medical school, I would enroll, but there isn't, so just consider me a very serious, talented autodidact who at least sees the problem. Gide said talent is fear of failure, and I am afraid, and my fears constantly assault me with an evil smell.

But Delia—God knows why she does what she does. Having defeated the fear of ridicule, she appeared all-around fearless, and yet was attached to all sorts of superstitions to ward off or cure this or that.

It was probably just another example of Skinner's pigeons, one of the great demonstrations of human

"The system is that I braid the string from the rabbi's grave with the string from around your hospital bed, and I make a candle wick out of them. And when I burn the candle, the smoke goes right to the nostrils of God, or if you prefer, the Universe—"

"The universe doesn't have nostrils."

"Are you kidding? You think our stink doesn't get noticed? Goes right to the nostrils, and the Powers look directly down upon Queens Mount Sinai, room 546, and you heal faster."

"How do you know this rabbi had such connections?"

"He probably died from ministering to the sick during an epidemic. Very holy."

Oils, creams, ointments, and diets were one thing. But this! At least her creamy thighs weren't spread out across his naked, pimply chest.

Delia was winding the kosher string into a ball when the second Venusbergian peeked in, the mean quean herself, a somewhat bedraggled Anastasia Pigov. Visiting hours are open to all.[57]

"Alexei?" she inquired. "Nurse, is here Alexei Pigov?"

The nurse, her string-winding arrested, checked with her patient before answering. Alexei raised his head with some difficulty.

"Yeah, Ma. You can come in." Like Tannhäuser, he called on the blessed virgin, Elizabeth Schrank, to protect him—from his visitors both.

Nastya surveyed the scene and moved an armchair to his bedside.

"Nurse, I want to be alone with son. You go, okay?"

"That's not a nurse, Ma. That's my girlfriend, Delia Robinson. We're practicing dancing freak to freak."

Delia gave him a friendly whack.

This was a delicate moment for Nastya. It was much to take in. Would she accept this misshapen woman into her family, she, the great Russian beauty? On the other hand, she was conscious of being not quite as attractive as she once had been, and in spite of the many resources of *Oooo Marisa*, the best she could come up with was a skunkish streak of white down the middle of her black-dyed hair. Though her customers thought it "fascinating," she had enough natural taste to realize it was iffy. But she couldn't imagine the dwarf naked—a test she applied to all humans, male and female, friend or foe. So what kind of a girlfriend would she make? Not one for her, certainly. But could she really catch anyone she wanted anymore? She was almost forty. She had split with Tony. If she was still glamorous, it was only in a Russian dance-hall kind of way.

"Girlfriend." "Freak to freak." Delia also was a bit perplexed. She didn't know

irrationality, except it was pigeons. But still. Skinner put pigeons in a feeding machine which dispensed food at regular intervals completely independent of the birds' behavior. But if the pigeon was wing-cleaning or turning clockwise when the food came out the slot, it would wing-clean or turn clockwise to bring on the food, figuring that it was influencing the food-god by so doing. The paper can be found in B. F. Skinner, "Superstition in the Pigeon," *Journal of Experimental Psychology* 38 (1947). Delia no doubt thought that her mantras and incenses and horoscopes and quirky little behaviors—fear of the number 17, for instance, or never opening an umbrella indoors, or always going through a doorway right leg first—that such doings would somehow create a locally better world. Pathetic.

It's pathetic to say "pathetic" about someone the world at large already considers pathetic, but what else can you call this kind of activity? OK, maybe "delusional."

57. If I ever achieve a position of real power, the first improvement I will make will be for hospital visiting hours to be open to all except mothers. I was recently looking in on a fan at Kaiser Permanente in San Francisco, a young woman who had broken her leg plague-dancing at an appearance of mine at the Fillmore Auditorium. We were discussing this and that, many topics ranging from ontology to fascism, when into the room burst her mother, who began swinging at me with her purse, me, the Plague Doctor, quietly sitting bedside in my classic regalia, helping her daughter pass the time improving her mind as well as her tibia.

"Out!" she yells, "Get out of here! Stop bothering my daughter! Stop polluting her mind." My fan protests, but that only makes things worse: "See? She prefers you over me!" Completely hysterical.

Preserving my dignity under her Vuitton assault, I made my way out the door and past the nurses' station before security could be called. Had there been a confrontation, it would have been I, no doubt, who would be seen as the aggressor. Mama, in this case, was applying the principle of being cruel only to be kind.

I have also experienced the converse. When I was seven, my own Lillith-ma took me on the bus to the New York Foundling Hospital (nice little barb, there) "to get my tonsils looked at." It was only when I was about to be gassed that I understood the betrayal. "They just go to look at them," she had reassured me. "They don't even take off your nose-glasses." On that day the die was cast between us. In this case, Mama was applying the principle of being kind only to be cruel.

In all my visits ministering to sick fans, I have never seen fathers perform such a function. Granted, fathers may act this way occasionally, but I, for one, have never seen it.

whether to be delighted by the former or dismayed by its sarcasm. The latter was questionable too.

"You are his girlfriend?" Nastya demanded, not hiding her scorn.

"He was only kidding," Delia admitted, not least to herself. "I'm just a friend."

"Why you are in nurse clothing? What is string?"

"I . . . I work for a doctor. Another doctor. Your son's old doctor. Or I did. . . ."

"You had doctor?" Nastya asked Alexei. "You were sick? How you pay? You have insurance?"

"The doctor was treating him for nothing," Delia said.

"Treating for what? Why he treat for nothing? Here America—*nothing* for nothing."

She plopped down in a chair.

"Actually, he didn't do anything, Ma. I was just talking to him about—"

"About what? You are sick? Nurse, you will leave. I talk to my son."

Delia threw up her little hands and left to sit in the waiting room.

"She seems dumb as fish. Bad nurse."

"Ma, you just walk in here, you don't even ask me how I am or what happened, you—"

"I know how you are, what happened. There was article in newspaper. I come as soon as possible."

"I've been here almost a week."

"I don't see paper. A customer brought. Yesterday only. Why you always hate me? Why we always be like cat and dog? Why we live on this volcano?"

Perhaps she was upset, seeing her son in bandages.

"I am sad old woman, old as world, alone as finger."

Perhaps not.

In any case, Alexei felt as he often did in her presence—like a rat fighting with a lioness. Six times bitten, twelve times shy, he was most wary of engaging.

"What you look like under bandage?"

"You know what I look like."

"You look like your father."

"With a Fibonacci nose, aggravatingly large. And it's your fault."

"Is not my fault. And don't be clown."

Alexei felt a strong native resistance to this suggestion.

"Why? Everyone—except you, maybe—loves a clown. But nobody will go out with one."

"That karlik will go out with you. Because maybe she can't get no one else. How you are feeling?"

"I'm okay. Where's Tony?"

"Where's Tony? Is just what I want to know. Not there for a month. Doesn't answer telephone. Never home when I go over. *Ischezatii*. I am abandoned."

Alexei sent hearty telepathic congratulations to Tony.

"And you will be abandoned too," she continued, a Slavic Cassandra. "When you go, out of hospital, believe me, many misfortunes await you."

"Thanks, Ma."

"No. I am being truthful like mothers. Many misfortunes await you. Many."

"I know you're being truthful. You're always truthful."

"You are right. I leave now. I just wanted to see you. Make you a little happy. Don't go out with that *karlik*. I warn you. Many misfortunes."

Out she stormed.

And in peeked the other. Intrusive, he thought, both of them. Even dangerous to my health. Alexei, who just wanted to be alone, plotted murder. Of both.[58] And found himself wondering if killing himself might not be easier, less complex. Why was he so bad at handling these things? Had he so neglected worldliness as to be a mere babe vis-à-vis babes? And these weren't even babes. They were his mother! His mothers!

"What do you think of these?" Delia asked, climbing a chair and thrusting her sketch pad in front of his eyeholes.

They were, in fact, remarkable sketches of the recent invader—pointing, threatening, standing hands on hips, sitting with sexy legs.

Alexei thought of those 144,000 virgin males with God's seal on their foreheads, those who did not defile themselves with women, the only ones who could learn the song of rushing waters and pealing thunder. And then of the female virgins promised by Allah: eleven thousand Elizabeth Schranks and Saint Ursula herself. Oh, wait. Elizabeth wasn't Muslim. But Saint Ursula would be enough. Maybe he should become a Muslim martyr, do something martyrish, with a turban. . . .

He didn't say a word. His heartmind was in a swirl. It was unsafe to talk. Delia shrugged, patted his hand, and sat down to draw. Though nurses, techs, doctors with students, and cleaning staff swarmed through her sketch pad, a bandaged patient in a hospital bed, seen largely from below, loomed as the primary subject.

58. In the investigation around Delia's suicide, I was one of the first people interviewed by the police. Why, I don't know, but I did know I had nothing to fear from interrogation. And the polygraph exam was most useful to me in developing my current theory of personality types. I failed. Why did I fail? Did I push her out the window? No. So why should I fail?

I failed because I knew which questions were trying to trap me. They ask lots of neutral, innocent-type questions, and you answer with simple facts. Then every once in a while, they slip in a more tricky question, and you know, you just know, that this is the question they will try to get you on. So naturally, your heart rate goes up a bit, your skin starts to sweat. Then, once that happens—if you are imaginative enough—you begin contrafactual speculation: What if I *did* push her out and just don't remember? What if I really am a killer, not a healer? You spin all this out into a novella while some fat, redneck detective is barking other questions at you, and lo and behold, you are a techtonic star, goosing the polygraph with 6.0 readings on the Richter scale. So the questions get tougher, more insinuating: "Did you *do* it? *Did* you push

The next day was a big one: at 8:15 in the morning Alexei was unwrapped like some Christmas present, perhaps unwanted. The nurse's aide held the bandage gingerly, between two fingers, as if it were icky. But for Delia an hour later, it was Valentine's Day, and her heart leaped throatwise to see his naked face again.

"Don't you look beautiful!" she exclaimed. Nobody had ever said that to him. "Like an exhumed god." Nobody had ever said that either.

His face was still macerated and hydropsical (not far from its usual submaskum state), but medically ready to meet the air, undefended.

"And I have just the thing for healing and propitiation," she added.

From her backpack she took four beeswax candles and set them—each in a small, brass candleholder—on the bed table, the IV pump, the food trolley, and the sink. Her Zippo did the rest.

It was the Mount Sinai Hospital debut of *koshere fodem* therapy, the open flames quite against fire regulations, especially in the oxygenated setting of the burn unit. But kosher is kosher, from the Hebrew, clean, proper, fit for use, and the four candles, with their flexile smoke and pervasive, prayerful scent, may have been the only treatment fit to infuse the dimensions of Alexei's case. Four candles lit, a few Robinsonish mutterings, and four candles pinched out and back in the bag before the next nursing visit or first explosion. Delia imagined the fragrance would reach God's nostrils before those of the floor supervisor.

"What's that stink?"

In barreled the head of dermatology, a behemoth of nasal acuity.

"What stink?" Delia asked.

"I don't smell anything," the patient asserted.

The behemoth sniffed, snorted, and left the room.

"What *was* that stink?" Alexei asked. Delia rejoiced in their collusiveness.

"Genezareth balm, incense from Cape Gardefui, labdanum, silphium, and aristolochia—the inspiring vapors of Delphi."[59]

"On Mount Sinai?"

"Yes, of course. I believe in one God, don't you?" And nobody had ever asked him that either.

Perhaps the question was only rhetorical, but it would have its consequences.

She sat that morning and sketched him from many angles, a miniature paparazza of

her? *Why* did you push her?" and you sweat like a pig and your polygraph goes out of its gourd.

You think of all sorts of things and their extrapolations. Like Hundwasser's assertion that I had plotted the murders of both Delia and my mother. Maybe I *did* plot them. Maybe I *did* them. Maybe I did them in some vague fugue state when I didn't know what I was doing. How could I be so *cruel*?

If they hadn't lacked any evidence at all of my being a murderer, I surely would have been convicted based on polygraph evidence alone. As it was, Delia was listed as the suicide she was. As was *ma mère*. And more on all this later.

59. It was this kind of statement from Delia that would continually drive me up a wall. OK, maybe she had found some list of the herbs used by the Delphic oracle to put her clients into a receptive state. But where would such a list come from? Did the oracle keep notes? And even assuming it were accurate, what was the precise mixture

pencil scratches, not clicks. He stared dead ahead, silent, aware of her but not aware, his mind wandering through the forest of her question. One God? Hmm.

Naked-nosed, resembling more and more a natty albino rat, he lay there for days among the solemn odors of shit and disinfectant, of flesh mortified and decaying, amid strong and serious smells of depth and darkness, whiffs of the grave, perhaps, and yet something of the wind, weighty odors amid the flash of white uniforms and the squeaking of rubber-soled shoes. And always her pencil scratched, and her pages flipped, and neither of them spoke.

And then, obscurely, life stirred below his waist. It occurred to him that he was still alive. The forest gave out upon a dream of escape—from the dark of the wicked world along paths of light and love. Marat, Robespierre, and Danton all had scarred, scary faces, and it didn't stop them. Wildly desirable. Fully realizable.

Whither, then, do the wings of the gate open
Thou knowest it not?
INTO LIFE!

Neither of them spoke until one day he said to her, "I would prefer it if you didn't come anymore."

"Why?" she asked.

Given no answer, she packed up her sketch pad and left.[60]

La Commedia è Stupenda!

Three days later, he was discharged, and into life he went, mask-free, nose to the wind, the warm west wind of Central Park in June. He mused about a condition of pure authenticity.

Dogs, dogs, dogs. A pair of ferrets. An iguana on a leash. Thousands of well-heeled children. And emanating faintly from the direction of the Great Lawn, the rhythmic whack of a high-pitched drum. As Alexei wended his way, rat to the piper, a Renaissance madrigal snaked its way into his ear.

O, occhi manza mia . . . gioia mia bella . . . fa mi contento . . .

Yes, alas, his beloved's Elizabeth-eyes were still out there, haunting, though he had

to produce what result? Very unscientific, very unquantitative for a woman supposed to be a healer.

The whole aromatherapy industry stinks to me of fraud. Where are the studies? What are the controls? This is science? And besides, what exactly is the aromatherapy industry trying to do? "Promote" health and well-being? "Promote"? Sounds like a certain acquaintance of ours whose name begins with H. We don't need these little, unproven, smelly-gods cluttering our medicine cabinets. What we need are the potent smells of freedom, of originality, of deep authenticity. We need to be able to smell the inalienable meaning of things, to smell new possibilities instead of ultimate catastrophe. Conversely, we need to know the smell of bulls—t, as Professor Frankfurt might say.

Perhaps I am just a limit-case, an outstanding example of Heidegger's "heroic naïveté." Perhaps I am simply seized by mal-de-siècle. But I am a *philosophe,* an honest man; I cannot speak dishonestly. It made life difficult with Delia, for she could be dishonest—mostly to herself.

On the other hand, how easy it is to believe oneself a god.

60. I am always amazed at the power of insult when such insult refers to one's mother. And yet even I, Mr. Rational (presuming again there are rational processes) was alienated when my mother was disparaged. I do have hot Roma blood, I suppose, and it must have been that blood, unmasked, which even years after my mother's death boiled into rage at an innocent remark of Delia's: "She was pretty self-absorbed, and she wasn't very nice to you."

Well, that was certainly true. So why should I ever have gotten furious about such remarks? Why, for instance, should I

little joy of her, and still less contentment. But the day was gorgeous, the western wind was gently licking his face, the wind, her eyes . . . what a tease, what a tease. . . .

In the distance, four singers, Renaissance-garbed, the men in doublets and tights, the women in low-necked, puffed-sleeved blouses and flowing skirts. And behind them, the stage grew. A raised floor was assembled, a backdrop hoisted on poles, and last of all, a proscenium banner was flown: THE SAN FRANCISCO MIME TROUPE. Alexei joined the gathering crowd and plunked himself down in front to welcome the cross-country visitors.

The singers and builders assembled on stage. The men donned masks, the women not, the drum beat for a dumb show of the story to follow, and a caped announcer came forward to address the crowd.

"*Signore e signori!*

"*Mesdames et Messieurs!*

"Ladies and gentlemen . . .

"*Il Troupo di Mimo di San Francisco,*

"Directed by R. G. Davis,

"Presents for your appreciation this afternoon

"A newly restored commedia,

"*La Servante Amoureuse*—The amorous serving-maid!"

The entire cast danced the stage, each in character, each playing a characteristic instrument—drums, tambourine, recorder, sackbut, crumhorn, small button accordion—and exited behind a scene of Venice.

From the dumb show, Alexei had some idea of the plot, a typical commedia intrigue where ruse is piled upon ruse and the characters snared, snarled, and discombobulated—before all is disentangled.

Flavio, it seems, is in love with the beautiful Leonora but knows not how to woo. A well-paunched Pantalone scorns him as a son-in-law, preferring Miles Gloriousus, the thrasonical blowhard with good connections. Black-garbed Scaramouche would thwart Pantalone by teaching Flavio the way to Leonora's heart—by demonstrating wooing technique on an unsuspecting Columbine, the title servant. But she, all too vulnerable, falls heels over head for Scaramouche, the cynical scoundrel, incapable of love. Disguises, deception, confusion reign until at last, Pantalone is thwarted, Miles humiliated, Flavio and Leonora united, and poor Columbine left abandoned, an exception to the rule of happy endings.

Let the play begin: Alexei was ready. He was especially ready to devour (with his eyes)

have told Delia at the hospital, "I would prefer it if you didn't come anymore," a line snagged by Hundwasser in complete ignorance of its Melvillian overtones. Why?

I do not want to be a riddle for you, the reader, to solve. So let me take you backstage in my being.

Why do I get mad? Guilt, that's why. Children always feel responsible for the suicide of a parent. What was I to my mother but some tragicomical parasite sprung from her womb, a source of shame whose existence limited her own, around whom she might organize her cynicism? Sharper than a serpent's tooth is a big-nosed child. And I have to admit that I often wanted to kill her.

The reader may be interested in the details of Nastya Pigov's death. Perhaps it was an accident. Perhaps it was a simple urge, like Ishmael's, toward water when she was overwhelmed by the November in her soul. One early-vodka evening in 1981, wearing a gray-blue dress, she undertook a walk into the oncoming traffic on the West Side Highway. She had a brief encounter with a Chevy Impala.

Maybe it was an accident. It seemed like suicide to me. Perhaps over me.

the *servante amoureuse*, a Columbine whose loveliness put both Leonora and columbines themselves to shame, a slim, red-haired beauty whose breasts danced alluringly under the thin white cotton of her décolletage, who floated on half-toe, high off the boards.

The company played with broad, exaggerated gestures, straddling the line between farce and feeling, playing hard into the wind, punching each moment to demonstrate the play to those too far away to hear. As the scene came in which Scaramouche woos Columbine for Flavio[61] behind the arras, and she falls desperately in love, Alexei felt himself falling into her pleading eyes. It was as if she were his very

First Love

"C'mon," any sane reader will say, "we've had 'first love' three times already." But love is not quite sane, and first love far less so. Besides, thought Alexei, this is my first true love, the first love as me—not as Groucho or Pinocchio or Cyrano. The occhi of his once Lizzy *manza mia* were fading into the orgone-laced air, bleached away by the shining eyes of the here-present Columbina.

Meanwhile, Back at the Great Lawn,

Scaramouche danced and fondled, sang and danced, and . . .

. . . slipped! Slipped! Turned his ankle and fell with a howl of pain. Much of the show was improvised, and Columbine's first thought was that Scaramouche was trying out a new technique to evoke pity and perhaps a caress from the object of his alleged affection. But no—this was the real thing, a third-degree tear of the talo-fibular ligaments, and an evulsion fracture of the lateral malleolus. The actor crawled behind Venice. It was RICE for Scaramouche—rest, ice, compression, elevation—and surgery thereafter.

The show must go on. But how? How, indeed! Alexei leaped to his feet and onto the stage.[62] Not knowing what to say, he snatched the concertina from Flavio's hands and began to make for his love a song without words. She stood there, looking confused, not knowing whether to go with the flow or call for the police. Alexei ran backstage, emerged

61. Although it may not concern this particular situation in the least, it may not be entirely useless to relate a similar event.

I have never been fond of Longfellow as a poet, nor particularly attached to "The Courtship of Miles Standish." But I was quite taken with Pricilla Mullins's response to John Alden when he wooed her for his friend: "Why don't you speak for yourself, John?" she said. He did, and she did, and married they were.

It was easy to identify with John, the substitute wooer. In fact, I fell in love with the only Priscilla I'd ever met just for her name and the possibility that she might say something similar to me. My own superstitiousness, I admit.

One summer afternoon, I was in Central Park, leaning against Alice's mushroom, when up onto the statue bounded a sprightly, bubbly young woman. "Mind if I share your mushroom?" she asked, and of course I moved over with joyous anticipation. A lovely woman come to me! Leaning next to me! She told me she was watching out for a friend, and climbed up on the cap of the mushroom right next to Alice for a better view.

62. I did leap up on that stage. I modeled mine on that famous 1943 leap of my hero, Leonard Bernstein, when he jumped in to replace an ailing Bruno Walter at the NY

in Scaramouche's black cape and long-nosed mask, and returned to play the scene. His right hand was too scarred and stiff to manage a keyboard, but he could manage fairly well the three short rows of buttons. His left hand fell right into the patterns he knew. While Scaramouche the First lay in pain backstage, Scaramouche the Second played his scene in front.

He played to win the heart of a woman—not just Columbine but the red-haired beauty who stood behind her. He would win her by the tenderness of his playing, with melodies never before heard, with Gesualdian modulations which could crack the skull of Goliath and open the heart of a Shylock or Scrooge.

It seemed to be working. The scene began to play again, and the actors saw their chance to bring the afternoon off in spite of the calamity. Columbine was suitably wooed, Pantalone thwarted, Miles humiliated, and Flavio and Leonora united. A surprised Columbine was joined at the end by her black-masked wooer, and the audience applauded even harder for a joy-day unalloyed.

Would they take him on? He could play Scaramouche until the actor was better—and be their music director. He could live on very little. He would have a chance to really meet—her—to have her get to know him, and learn how lovable he was.

But what if she didn't really love him as she pretended in the play? Especially when he was without his handsome Scaramouche mask. What if he transformed after the show into just another ugly guy—a good concertina player, maybe, but leave me alone!

The players thanked him effusively, sincerely, even his First Love. And then they started to pack up, everyone busy with practiced tasks, now including those of Scaramouche, in addition to getting him medical care. There was no time to pay Alexei more attention. He was shunted aside. The handwriting was on the wall. But not all the handwriting. The fallen actor was pretty much out of it, still writhing in pain with any movement. And since each actor was personally responsible for his costume, instrument, and mask, in the general haste and new confusion, the packing of Scaramouche's were forgotten.

Alexei stood at an ethical crossroad. Should he or shouldn't he? On the one hand, it was theft, and while the cloak looked like a Salvation Army Halloween special, the mask might set them back a pretty penny. On the other hand, they had taken in a good deal

I asked about the friend, and she told me it was her sweetheart, Tod, and I told her that *Tod* meant "death" in German, and that she'd better think twice about marrying him. She said she wasn't planning on getting married, she was in second-year medical school, and he lived in Philadelphia, in Germantown, and he was in law school and felt the same way—the usual talk-around from the immature who can't deal with commitment. I asked her name, she told me Priscilla—and everything went wild.

I went into hyperspace mode, madly inventing a Longfellowish plot. I knew a Tod from Germantown, I said. What was her Tod's last name? Klimowitz, says she. Tod Klimowitz? He was my best buddy in high school. Wonderful guy, you should grab him before someone else does.

And I went on and on about how great he was, about all the things we used to do together, and how I knew that he must really want to marry someone like her, but was no doubt too shy to ask. I told her how secretly bashful he was. I gave her plenty of openings for a Priscilla Mullins line.

Then—how could I not have expected it?—Tod comes around a curve, and she climbs down off the mushroom, jumps onto the ground, runs to meet him, rubs her bosom against his, kisses him fiercely, and pulls him back toward me.

Phil. And what did he conduct? *Don Quixote*, with Schuster as cello soloist. *Don Quixote*! And he had never conducted it before.

He was an instant success, and that leap changed the course of musical history. Without it we might still be Mahlerless here in America. Without it, American musical comedy might still be stuck at *Oklahoma*! or *Carousel*. I thought perhaps I too might make that kind of leap. I was so excited.

"Honey, look, surprise—it's (whatever name I told her; I don't remember which mask I was wearing) from Germantown." Tod looks at me, I look at him.

"I guess it must have been the other Tod Klimowitz from Germantown," I said.

"There was no other Tod Klimowitz in Germantown," says he.

I looked at my watch, made a big deal about being late to something, and made my escape. I probably got them to marry.

You never can trust poets.

of money from the crowd—all of which he felt was due to his efforts. For surely, had they stopped the play halfway, no one would have thrown money into the hat. The cloak and mask might be seen as a small thank-you for his saving the show. The troupe would still make a good net profit—even after the mask and cloak were replaced. And he didn't need the concertina.

But did he need the mask? That was the question. He stood amid the packing-up chaos, among the thronging Sunday crowd, mask wrapped in cape, the ensemble making a small black parcel easily overlooked. Should he just walk away into the park? He'd never stolen before.

Here were his considerations:

- She seemed to love me when I wore the mask. She let me touch her, stroke her hair. My hand brushed across her breast. On the other hand, once I took the mask off, I was just another person, practically in the way of the packing up. I practically stopped existing for her.

- I know our romancing was only part of the play, but at the very least, she was not positively repulsed by me when I had the mask on. I couldn't say the same for when I took it off. It's a beautiful mask.

And indeed, it *was* a beautiful mask, one imported from the Paduan workshop of Amleto Sartori, a creation of water-sculpted leather which seemed alive even alone, before being donned by an actor. Black it was, but shiny, with light-reflecting surfaces and an unquenchable resilient life of its own. The nose was five inches long, longer than any of Alexei's previous adornments, but manageable, he thought.

63

When later he stood before his mirror, gesturing, he felt courageous, full of thoughts. Anarchic breezes blew through his soul. "I demand everything," the mask said. The only question was, what is everything? Together he and Scaramouche could make an all-out war against conventional wisdom. "We oppose everything!" "We call for excess and rampage!" That should get him somewhere. Where?

That he had made off with some poor actor's mask, someone working for beans for some poor mime troupe, he set aside. Did not real life trump theater?

Warm wind on the face was a lovely thing, but some things in life are more crucial

63. This hiatus between the lines is the single most scandalous thing in the shameless monstrosity that is *The Nose*. Between "... he thought" and "When later ..." lies the clear implication that I stole that mask from an impoverished mime troupe, taking advantage of a performance disaster.

Am I the kind of person who would do such a thing? This is not a rhetorical question—am I? From what you have read in my commentary, do you think I—whose intention was to save the show—would have rubbed salt into its wound by making off with the troupe's most valuable possession?

It's true I was tempted. That mask might have been more valuable to me—if it enabled me to catch my own Columbina—than to them, who could easily find some other mask for the role. But being a devoted situation ethicist, I understood it was merely *eros* tempting me, and that I must ever be guided

only by *agape,* the ultimate law, the foundation of all moral truth. Absolute, unchanging, and unconditional love only! Stealing the mask might advance *eros,* but would it maximize *agape*? No.

I left it on top of Scaramouche's neatly folded costume, stage center, where it could not be missed. Regardless of what that scoundrel Hundwasser implies, may he be trampled by a herd of stampeding pigs, I will have you know that I bought my mask from the museum-store catalog of the Museo Internazionale della Maschera Amleto e Donato Sartori in Padua. Cost me a pretty penny too, and at a time when I could ill afford it. I might even be able to find the receipt if you want to see it.

than sensual pleasure. However he was not some classical commedia figure; he was not some limping actor's clone. He would be his own creation: not Scaramouche but Scarabmouche, the sacred dung beetle mated with the mundane fly, resurrection and escape.

On Sartori's stately forehead, anterior to the sixth chakra, he painted a scarab[64] -tilaka in fine enamel. It would activate his center of will and clear the way to enlightenment. It would strengthen the nerves and prevent the loss of brain energy. It would open his third eye. Green on black it glowed, and in the center of its dorsal plate, an oriental red "S." S for Scaramouche, S for swaggering and seditious, S for *sacer*, *Scarabaeus*, and sacred. S, finally, for the Superman he would be. Scarabmouche. He'd slay the girls in such a getup.

Swashbuckling– the Theory

In Shakespeare's time, a "swash" was a boaster or bragger, someone who moved flamboyantly through the world, violent and noisy. A "buckler" was the small shield to deflect the blows that inevitably came at such a person. Although terrible at swashing, Alexei might have used the buckler.

He consulted Sabatini's swashbuckler, Scaramouche: "He was born with a gift of laughter ["I can laugh if I try."] and a sense that the world was mad. ["Well, that seems true enough."] And that was all his patrimony. His very paternity was obscure. . . ." ["As is mine, as is mine. It's an omen this is the right path."]

Using his stolen mime-troupe mask, and Sabatini as a guide to costume, he outfitted himself as a skirmisher, a dangerous fellow going deviously to his ends "in a close-fitting suit of a bygone age, all black, from flat velvet cap to rosetted shoes, a small-sword at his side and a guitar slung behind him." It was, in fact, a ukulele, more easily picked at and strummed with his scarred right hand.

64. The dung beetle is without doubt my totem animal. The ancient Egyptians believed that *Scarabaeus sacer* existed only as a male, and reproduced itself by depositing semen into a rolled ball of dung. Given my girlfriendlessness, and substituting an old sock for a dung ball, that could be me—in which I and the dung beetle resemble the great god Khepri, who creates himself out of nothing. That would be me too. And fashions his mates by his own shaping. Who else? I, like the scarab at the Great Temple of Luxor, might represent transformation, renewal, and resurrection.

I made a pilgrimage to the Great Scarab when I appeared at the Valley of the Kings in 1998. I could feel the vibrational resonance. I wished Delia had been there.

Thus dressed in Sabatinian glory, masked and nosed à la Sartori, with an arrogant tilt of his head, he could be impish and caustic, slyly intriguing. He could set folks, especially girls, by the ears. He would be impudent and aggressive, a knight errant unerring, combining insubordination with a kind of gentle brutality. He would be playful and horribly good-natured. He would realize great poetry in everyday life.

He looked at himself in the mirror. "*Je est un autre*," he declaimed, "*parce que la vraie vie est absente*!" The mask makes the man, he thought, "I long to fly, to howl. I will not be caught in the snare of the normative world's insanity. He who desires but acts not breeds pestilence."

But I still need some good pickup lines. What can I say that won't sound cooked up, cheap, presumptuous? "Acquisitiveness is the curse of mankind." How's that? She's got to agree, no? And once we agree on something, we can start talking about other things. No. Too intellectual. I need to be both fisherman and fish—the catcher and of course the caught.

Fish! That's it. Why didn't I think of fish before? The new Aquarium at the Bronx Zoo. I'll go down to the Fulton Fish Market, find a pretty girl who seems seriously interested in fish, and tell her about the new aquarium. Ask her if she wants to go see it. Clever.

Expectation, expectation. Was this a mere personality disorder? But, mocking reader, it worked—it actually worked. Polly McMurtry was at the Fulton Fish Market, and besides being a gourmet cook on the prowl, she was a biology grad student who had worked at the Woods Hole Oceanographic Institute, and she was interested in fish, and she hadn't been to the new aquarium since it had opened, and she had been meaning to go, and she did think it would be interesting to go with a masked stranger in black. In New York City, many things happen.

Love me, desire me, choose me, Alexei had thought at first sight. I need you. And when the gutted perch on display seemed to interest her more than his presence behind her back: You ignore me, you disdain me. You destroy me. I hate you.[65]

But he didn't hate her for long because it was she who backstepped into him and in her embarrassment began telling him about the mating behavior of perch, a subject of some interest. Scaramouche's "unassailable conviction of the general insanity of his own species" teased his fish-drunk senses. And she was a looker!

65. I take this moment—though I could have taken any hundred others throughout Hundwasser's self-acclaimed masterpiece—to draw the reader's attention to the author's compulsive idée fixe about my motivations. Were you to believe him, you would think I was motivated solely by "getting girls."

Everyone wants a girl, of course—unless he or she is gay, in which case, "girl" may be understood metaphorically. That is, we all want companionship and the various kinds of warmth that attends it. Most of us, maybe. Some of us might not.

But because I have these perfectly normal motivations, natural urges, you might almost say, does

Swashbuckling—the Practice

"Pater-noser. Gross-snoter. Stand me in good stead."

They met at the Paul Manship gate, Scarabmouche and his Polly. Their names alone sounded piratically embraced. Pretty Polly.

Walking with Scarabmouche toward the welcome fountain, she made her first mistake.

"Yikes. It's a herd of squirrels. I hate squirrels."

"You hate squirrels? Why?"

"They remind me of rats. High-class rats with improved tails."

Scarabmouche thought of his old friend in the closet.

"But they're planting trees," he countered. "They're warning their slower friends—rabbits and raccoons—that our vicious dogs are coming. Look how they come to you for friendship."

"Friendship? They want food. From the cuteness-dupes."

Things were looking doubtful.

"Listen. You don't want squirrels against you. None of us can afford to have squirrels against us. 'Cause there goes our electricity, our pipelines, our water and gas. Everything chewed through. The top ten silent, the stock quotes dead, the toilet unflushed . . ."

How hard it is to connect. The silence that followed prophesied no good. What could she be thinking? What could he?

All right. She doesn't want cuteness. If she wants ferocity, Scarabmouche can dish it out. They climbed the steps and proceeded past the big cats.

"But it is war, of course," he began. "We've captured all these beasts and brought them here against their wills, and caged them up to demonstrate our control. Capitalist demonstration of the taming-and-entertainment use of the instincts. Sexuality, motion, desire, play—there they are behind bars, trapped. The very desire for freedom displayed for our enjoyment.

that mean that I am driven exclusively by them? Even if getting a girl is the most important thing in the life of a person who doesn't have a girl—worse, never had a girl—does that mean that that person has no other *raison d'être,* that he might as well just give up all other activity and go live with his parents?

I have a friend who desperately wants to get a girl, and he spends all his time reading and writing personal ads and answers, and waiting for the envelope or email that never comes. He's lost his job for doing it on work time. He just sits at home in his underwear and obsesses over this or that face or presentation-of-self.

Am I like that? Do I not have greater things to pursue in the world than my own sexual and emotional happiness? On the door to my apartment, I have hanging a portrait of Chairman Mao, and under it, his great slogan, 为人民服务, whose characters I have reverently copied out, though I know no Chinese. The neighbors don't know what to make of it—but it's my apartment, I bought it with my hard-earned money, and I can do whatever I want with it, right? "Serve the people!" the sign says, and that's my motto, not "Serve yourself."

It's true I have experienced many loves, each of them "first loves." But ask yourself, is not every love a first love? First love of the particular love-object, first love of the who-you-are-now, a qualitatively new experience deepened by the others that preceded it. Hundwasser milks my heart-leaps for a running gag, winks at me, and cackles as he heads for the bank, and then home to some new sweetie. What could be more manipulative and cynical? Does he think he is Dickens and I the lovelorn Uriah Heep?

I choose this moment to make this point because it illustrates yet another aspect of Hundwasseriana. "I hate you," he has me thinking about Agnes (his Polly McMurtry). This is a passing and even trivial example of the treatment he gives my complex feelings about Delia.

I did often find her hostile and hateful, but why? A real author—Proust or Henry James, for example—would explore rather than assert. Inasmuch as she offered her particular person, Delia was hostile to my need for the archetype, for the Platonic idea of woman. Inasmuch as she was one woman, she was not Everywoman, Goethe's *Ewig-weibliche*, whom I needed to draw me on. As such, she represented a threat, a limiting factor to that part of me which would transcend limits.

There was also what she looked like. I addressed this issue in passing in Notes 13 and 29, but it is a deep human problem, far beyond my own.

Those of us who are the good-lookers, the nines and tens on a scale of ten, have no problem attracting and propagating their own, producing more nines and tens, a small, elite cohort, a physiognomically-gated community whose members are chosen via secondary narcissism.

But what about the rest of us? What about the twos and threes like me? Are we to be relegated only to our own breeding ground, once again gated, not to protect us but to keep us from escaping into the world? Fat for the fat, big-nosed for the big-nosed, deformed for the deformed? "Stay in your place, boy, or you'll get what's coming to you!"

"Look at that cheetah," he continued. "Seventy miles per hour? Look at him pacing. You know Rilke's poem about the panther? A 'great Will'—stupefied. 'For him it's as if there were thousands of bars, and beyond those bars, no world.' And there he is, next cage—a panther. Black. Powerful. Performing slavery for us. Just like in the good old days on the plantation.

"We hate wildness," he informed her. "We hate wild things. Extinction is best. The silence of death where only cash registers ring. Listen. Can you hear them? The choruses of antelopes, of ostriches, of hawks and bats, of llamas and donkeys and eels and kiwis? No. Nothing. Are the spiders singing, or the starfish and baboons? We've killed them. You've killed them. Here, I'll perform for you the croaking chorus from *The Frogs* of Aristophanes:

Brekekekex, co-ax, co-ax, brekekekex, co-ax
Slimy offspring of the swamp
Sing we flute-like, dance and romp
Dionysus can relax
Brekekekex, co-ax, co-ax.

He leaped about, swirling cloak and waving hat. He hopped around the circumference of the fountain. He grabbed the ukulele banging on his back and punctuated his croaks with fierce strumming. The seals barked. The children were frightened.

Brekekekex, co-ax, co-ax.
Brekekekex, co-ax, co-ax.
Singing of the Furies, croaking of the frogs!

"Do you hear them anymore? No. It's a helluva price to pay for your mascara. Don't you think? Huh? Huh?"

But there was no answer. In fact, there was no Polly. And they hadn't even seen the new aquarium.

This I cannot tolerate. Why should I not be able to mingle my essence with the most beautiful souls, the most graceful bodies? Who would not want to do so? You can see why I might be ambivalent about hooking up with Delia.

Nevertheless, between us there was definitely more than Hundwasser reports or may be capable of reporting. Our relationship was quite other than some eternal Sadie Hawkins day, with Li'l Abner me being chased not by the luscious Daisy May, but by the ugliest woman in town. Delia was a beautiful soul and a wonderful woman. And she had a lovely face even if her body took some getting used to. We spent much precious time together—as friends.

A Scarabmouche of Rueful Countenance

Women! Pygmies in Africa allow anyone, at any time, on any occasion, to break spontaneously into dance. So why not me?

Maybe she thought I was just showing off. What a dullard! But this was no haphazard pilgrimage; this could have been Turning-the-Brain-Upside-Down Day. A quest. We could have abandoned country, honor, riches, the delights of this sinful world and all kinds of trivial pleasures to achieve purity of heart.

Girls! Never inflamed, as I am, with the need for perfection and saintliness! Never a dream of a wildly desirable yet fully realizable world. Is it wrong to demand everything?

That's the thing about being a guy, I guess: rejection. Into what, o Rector, have I been *geworfen*?

Though Scarabmouche had dreams of rebellion on all fronts, he wound up for a year an "Italian" street musician with a little squeezebox he could manage, singing texts from the *Principia Discordia*, haranguing passersby about Miserableism, the depreciation of reality, the rationalization of the unlivable, and the certain Confusionism that must follow. Instead of a monkey on a leash, he had with him, dressed in a little red hat, G. Garza, a rat.

7. Pantalone

Dark Angel! triumph over me:
Lonely, unto the Lone I go;
Divine, to the Divinity.
· LIONEL JOHNSON

Q: Is thirty-seven too young for a late-life crisis? Raphael was dead at thirty-seven, and Mozart was already two years moldering. Mendelssohn had a year to go.

A: No, thirty-seven is not too young for a late-life crisis.

It wasn't only the girls, or lack of them. It seemed to Alexei that his life was continually held in check, under check, that he was forced to flee from square to square to avoid being mated—much as he might desire it.

Groucho, Schreck, Pinocchio, Cyrano, Scaramouche—how much more could the world want than that collection of schnozollas? Alice Mulvaney, Elizabeth Schrank, Rowena Anne Billington, Columbina de la Mimetroupe, Pretty Polly McMurtry—where among the stellarium of such worthies would there be a star which might double-dance with him? It was constant humiliation. Am I so useless, he thought, so unfit, so unteachable, unhealthy—and now unyoung—as to be so unwelcome? Dull ruminations. Feckless brooding.

He stared at Scarabmouche, with its glowing pineal emblem. In his mind, he saw it creasing up, crow's feet growing at the eye holes, its nose swelling and shredding as in Ghirlandaio, its chin loosening and mouth drooping. Why not? he thought. Time for another transformation, right, Garz? The rat squeaked.

"Sweet GG, servant of the Living God. You keep the Lord's watch against the adversary, and every house is incomplete without you. You little mix of gravity and waggery! Plus, you can creep, and are smart, my only friend."

G. Garza squeaked once more.

Alexei placed the Sartori masterpiece nose-down in a large pot of water, added a cup of white vinegar, and soaked it overnight. Not much change. Better try boiling it for a while. A few minutes' rolling boil and an afternoon's simmer, and the metamorphosis was achieved.

Masterpieces breed masterpieces. Smash Michelangelos, cut Grünewalds into pieces, and you wind up with masterful shards. The new mask was also a masterwork, retaining its genotype if not its phenotype. It stayed within the family and would be instantly recognized by the cognoscenti as—presto change-o—Pantalone. Pantalone, *il vecchio*, a comedian *della farte*, long hooked nose, codpiece in hand, for where else could it be? Pantalone, panting alone for some unknown *principessa*. How appropriate.

He put on the mask, and frightened GG, who burrowed into his newspaper shreds. Already Alexei's breath felt heavier, his muscles weaker, his brain more ridiculous. He took a walk around the block: the street seemed longer; his legs seemed shorter. Perfect. I am old. Why not? Ancient. I am beyond it. Yay.[66]

Pantalone needed a costume. A dirty satin bathrobe from the Salvation Army and bedroom slippers without backs. Black silk stockings for a touch of class, embroidered with gold clocks to remind him of you know what. He carried G. Garza around in one pocket and actually felt weighed down on one side. Listing, he thought. More mass he had, and less energy, sluggish in a world of toil and toilet. That world seemed broken and absurd, not his anymore, belonging only to others. Move, check, move, check, stymied. And for all the costuming, he was essentially invisible.

I am now only what I am, he thought, and not what I may become. The past is prologue—to more of the same, less of the same. A scab, I am, a scar, like my hand and arm, passable but useless. Eh, sonny? What's that you say? I will never conquer the world? I smell bad? I look like a crank? Time for a walk. I'd better go practice my shuffling.

Out he scuffed, GG in pocket, and not just around the block but up to Fourteenth Street for a breath of the relatively unaccustomed.

66. Yay and boo too! And quite more boo than yay. "From hour to hour we ripe and ripe." That's the yay part. "From hour to hour we rot and rot." That's the boo part. "And thereby hangs a tale"—my tale.

I know, I know—to everything there is a season, a time to love and a time to rot. Hundwasser (at my prodding) makes an attempt at catching this, but in his attempt to sell me as a "lifetime burning in every moment," he under-relates the depths of my on-and-off despair.

Who really wants to grow old, even if he can deflect his own and others' attention behind the façade of some eternal archetype? Yes, I boiled a valuable art object, ruined it, and called myself a hero. And yes, even that devolved mask performed its mask-magic: this I established by controlled experiments comparing times to walk around the block with and without, resultant heart rates, visual acuities, and ability to remember random 10-digit numbers.

But Pantalone-chic aside, who really wants to grow old? We are as helpless before time as before the dismissive gaze of a beautiful woman. Our bodies wither like grass, and food tastes like ashes. Naked, without my masks, my fans would snigger at me, no doubt, not worship.

Sacred scarab, indeed! "Transformation, renewal, and resurrection!" I wonder what I'll be in my next incarnation. A rat's liver? A cockroach's middle leg?

Ah, progress! Progress monthly, weekly, even daily, as old businesses were replaced by those more upscale, mom & pop nudged across the river to the cemeteries in Queens, semi-sleaze sanitized, skid row outliers forced out. Fourteenth Street Wireless, the Garden of Eden, Daphne's Caribbean Express, Todd English's Olives, Payless Shoes for the financial survivors of Todd's and Daphne's, Circuit City, How Creative, the Fourteenth Street Framing Gallery, Throb . . . ah, yes, the dry violence of progress.

And look, a second-floor establishment he had never seen: Between two granny knots, THE ~2 AC. In the windows above, some startling lovelies on spinning machines, no grannies they. ~2. A sign-maker's mistake? Tilde two? Makes no sense. Oh, wait. The logic sign for not: "not too AC."

He climbed the stairs, the curious old cat, and U'd around to street-side. And there it was, behind a thick steel door, the Not-Too-Athletic Club, www.ntac.com. Not-too-athletic—that's me! It was always me, and will remain me. This must be my door. He opened it.

And closed it again as many tens of decibels assaulted his ears. Electric guitars screaming, electric drums beating, electric diaphragms whomping it out, urging the adrenaline of the not-too-athletic, goosing them on to ever greater runs of nonathleticism.

He shuffled quickly down the steps and over to Duane Reade on Avenue A. Coughs and Colds, Dental, Eye and Ear, there we go. Ear plugs, orange. Roll 'em up and let 'em expand in utero, thirty-three decibels. Not enough, but better than nothing. I've got to get back there before those lovelies finish their workout.

The two of them were coming out the door as he reached the top of the stairs.

"You be here tomorrow?"

"As usual."

And they danced past him down the stairs, balletically if not athletically.

They're here every day. I'll have to join. He inserted his earplugs and opened the door. All eyes turned upon him. He could feel the laughter collecting in their lungs.

"Hi!" screamed Cindy, her name magic-markered on her name badge, the "i" dotted with a smiley face. "Can I help you?"

"I . . . how much does it cost to use the machines?" Pantalone screamed back.

"It's ten dollars a session—you can stay as long as you like. Or you can become a member for fifty dollars a month."

"Is there a senior citizen's rate?"

"Oh, of course. It's only five dollars a session, and thirty-five dollars a month. Do you have ID?"

"I don't have it with me," he yelled. "But I can bring it back tomorrow."

"You're welcome to give it a try today—free of charge. We have some abandoned running shoes you can try on."

"No, thank you. I mean yes, thank you, I'd like to try it. But no, thank you, I'll keep my slippers."

"Okay," Cindy said. "They must be very comfortable."

"Yes, they are."

"Here's a towel. The men's locker room is over there."

"It's very loud in here. Can you turn the music down?"

"Loud? Hmmm. You think so? But sorry, no. That's the level most of our members like."

Pantalone (and GG) shuffled off to the locker room. The old man chose an empty locker, took off his bathrobe, and hung it up in the smelly confine. GG squealed in protest, so Pantalone put his bathrobe back on, hung up his towel, and shuffled, unchanged, out into the cardio room. He chose an Exercycle on a side wall so he could surreptitiously survey the room for interesting members. By now all were ignoring him, or pretending to, appraising him only fleetingly and side-wise. There were two men and three women.

Of the former, one was completely hairless. Not shaved but even eyebrowless, simply without an idea of hair-making. Puffing away on his stepper, he seemed—comfortingly—not-too-athletic. In contrast, the other was a midfifties cross between the Marlboro cowboy and the Hathaway shirt man. Tall, tanned, bearded, muscular, he seemed more-than-athletic, and a swoon for any maiden, eighteen to sixty. Bad.

The women were alarming. One was a peasant-type blond beauty, the picture of goodness and health. She seemed athletic enough on her treadmill. The second was a fierce woman who bordered on scariness, so Charles Adams-y was she, but whose body was the most inviting Pantalone had ever seen. On the other hand, he wouldn't want to meet her in a dark alley, even if that dark alley harbored a discarded mattress. The third . . . the third, oh, no . . . was this it?

First Love[67]

This woman was something new, never before encountered, perhaps the first real indication of how a mature, understanding, lasting partner might be embodied. Here was a being with Rowena Anne Billington's elegance, her braid now turning silver with wisdom. Here a woman as spirited as Columbina—he could tell from the glance she shot him—and as educated as Pretty Polly—and it was not only her minimalist granny glasses that told him so. Finally, and most disturbingly, here was a potential mate as virginal as young Elizabeth Schrank—she displayed no rings or jewelry—and as musically sensitive, if he were to judge from the face between the earbuds of her iPod. For all he knew, she could have been listening to the latest performance of the Prokofiev Violin Concerto, to compare it with her own. Some might call it treason, treason to Lizzie, the ur-beloved. Did he accept the charge?

No. At this stage of his life, he had to be pragmatic, to understand the archetypes in operation. The woman on the stepper represented the actualization and fulfillment of Lizzie's seed, and thus his first real love, not a projection.

How would he meet her? Should he flash G. Garza? His cohorts at the ~2AC must be thinking the squeaks were coming from one of the machines thirsty for WD-40. But Pantalone knew the secret of their rhythm: they came each time his right leg kneed GG's haunch. He thought it was cruel, perhaps, and he opened his bathrobe to allow the garment to drape less kinetically alongside him. But the squeaking continued as though GG were trying to alert him concerning the woman across the room, that visitation from the angelic orders. He stroked GG to calm him down and received a gestural nip. Oh, God, he thought, is this like Lassie barking at the farmhouse door when old Fred gets pinned under the tractor? Was GG trying to tell him something? Are you trying to tell me something, GG?

The open bathrobe now exposed his filthy undershirt, roadkill he had found on Ninth Street last year, a ~2-attractive enticement for his ~2-athletic prey. He closed it again and transferred GG's pocket to over his crotch to spare him the rhythmic kicking.

67. "First Love" again—oh, ha, ha! According to Bergson, one of the chief springs of comedy is the revelation that the human soul is prisoner to a stupid, mechanical body—as when one slips on a banana peel, or sneezes while proposing to a loved one.

A running gag, then, is doubly pathetic: a mechanical presentation of robotic imprisonment. And thus I, as the subject of Hundwasser's running gag of "First Loves," am even further debased in the reader's mind. I'm sure it was part of his plan.

Nevertheless, I must protest once more that life is always new, and that in a deep way, all loves are first loves. Thirteen-year-old $Alexei_1$ in 1964 is surely not the same person as a 39-year-old $Alexei_4$ (or is it_5?) in 1990. Therefore, the woman on the stepper was truly $Alexei_4$'s first love, i.e., Pantalone's first love, and I urge the reader to grow up and stop sniggering just because Hundwasser wants you to.

While I will forever ache for my true beloved, Lily Strauss (Hundwasser's Elizabeth Schrank) just as she was at fifteen, as I grow older I am ever more alert to the deeper beauty of older women. Christ washed the feet of adulterous wives, and licked the toes of lepers. Am I to be repulsed and flee at the sight of a few crows' feet about the eyes? They are signs of smiling. The wrinkled brow reflects experience, compassion, and the ability to survive tragedy. Et cetera. Agape does not flee such signs, so why should eros? My Slavic lyricism rejoices in such landmarks on the road to death. Love and death, the awe of it, awakening from mere life-as-prescribed to the deeper realities of human existence—for all this I can offer some remedy, some physic for the fatigue of soul and body, a glimpse over the horizon of conformity. And conformity, Ben Shahn noted, is simply "a failure of hope or belief." Truer words were never spoken: hope and belief are exactly what I bring.

All loves are first loves for another reason, the inverse of the first: human love is really one single passion, made up of an infinity of successive loves and losses and jealousies, any of which may be ephemeral, but in their uninterrupted multitude revealing their deeper continuity and unity. Thus, in loving my stepper sweetheart, I am the same eternal me, loving the same eternal other, each of us growing richer by accretion. First love and last.

Of every girl and woman I've loved, I've asked only one thing: not to persecute me, but to love me! Is that unreasonable? I don't have to be limited to my history of failure. If

The angel's Stairmaster stopped its rhythmic churning, and he watched her sink to floor level with a pneumatic hiss, a seraph returning to earth. She gathered up her towel, took the earbuds from her perfect ears, and turned in his direction. Now it would come, the Annunciation, he Maria, she the whisperer of truth. He smiled at her, but his mask did not. Pantalone's mouth remained shriveled and toothless, his nose edematous and droopy, his jowls unsightly and slack. The angel passed over. The angel of life passed over—into the women's locker room.

The signs on the facing wall read MIND, BODY, and SPIRIT. The monitors they framed were pumping out conflicting sounds to add to the throbbing din. Some kind of new sporting event was eliciting cheer after cheer as announcers shouted out contiguous home runs, touchdowns, jump shots, knockouts, goals scored of some kind of new über, all-and-everything event, which Alexei thought must be "postmodern." The other TV featured circus music, a screaming studio audience, and some kind of wheel that was spun to send contestants in some contest into a species of frenzy. The ooohs and aaahs floated on top of the acoustic tumult like mating calls in bedlam.[68]

Mating calls! Pantalone jumped off his Exercycle, ran into the locker room, took a quick shower, climbed back into his underwear, bathrobe, and slippers, and slipped quickly out of the gym. He would secrete himself in a hallway alcove in visual contact with the stairs. He would almost bump into her heading down, excuse himself charmingly, and initiate a conversation . . . about, oh, say, the labyrinth of life, or the value of a classical education in forming a nobler citizen.

There she was, lyrically dressed in embroidered peasant garb. Oh, my Slavic soul, thought Pantalexei, can I bear this? Out he rushed, after she had made the turn onto the stairs. His left shoulder brushed against her right, intentionally, gently, but in a way that couldn't be ignored. "Excuse me," she muttered, though she had nothing to be excused for. The masked man spun back upon her in oleaginous excess of contrition. "Oh, no, no, excuse me. It was my fault, I'm so sorry, please forgive me, please . . ." All this half backward—or three-quarters—he didn't know exactly how to position himself—a step or two below, proceeding quickly down the stairs, not daring to impede her exit while very much wanting to do so.

But bedroom slippers have minimal traction, and stepping backward in backless footwear easily looses the foot. Down he went, on his left side, down half a flight of wooden stairs, his hip clipping each step along the way, his bathrobe riding up behind him, his yellowed underwear on display, his dignity largely compromised. G. Garza

nothing else, I can re-create myself and become an object of morbid fascination. I realize that I am no longer a king going off to war—but neither do they any longer model a face that might launch a thousand ships. It is therefore best for both of us to mingle the resources of our decomposition, the best of our deeper selves which has not yet been reached by mortality's fungus. My skin may be bad, but my heart is still intact. Regardless of what Hundwasser's running gag may imply, my yearning for older women is anything but ontologically promiscuous.

Alas, I have to call her "my stepper sweetheart" because I never went back to the gym again. I am not really interested in the physical body, and aerobics is too hard, and it would have brought up memories of GG.

68. Hundwasser fabricated this incident based on one of my occasional rants about contemporary culture. Perhaps you'd like to hear it. If not, skip.

Two years ago, getting paunchy under my gown, needing more naps, and feeling generally logy, I took myself off to the local gym, a set of rooms filled with standard weights, machines, and aerobic trainers. To steel my will toward such activity, I bought a two-year membership, counting on my penny-pinching to keep me attending an activity already paid for.

The most important piece of equipment I knew I'd need was a box of earplugs, those roll-'em-up-and-let-'em-expand-in-the-ear kind, top of the line, 33-decibel attenuation. No surprise for one who needs sound control more than sunscreen. The best is silence.

Silence, of course, was not to be had at my gym, or at any other I have sampled over the years. Health clubs, like department stores and supermarkets, dentists' offices, and elevators, come with sound as standard omnipresence, fulfilling functions obvious and arcane, and by now expected by two generations wired to their earphones. No problem—or not much. I resolved to use my earplugs and tough it out, as usual. The world is too much with us not to travel with earplugs always in the pouch.

All was going well enough, my aural tampons enabling me to tunnel through the sonic battering, until one day I received a four-color postcard from the gym advertising its services "for body, mind and spirit." What? Had I missed two-thirds of my membership benefits? Had I been clenching my teeth and tensing my astral body against some healing wisdom?

And so I began to pay attention (through my earplugs) and to peek (up from my treadmill reading) at the mind and spirit aspects of my training. And what I heard continually, unless I could blot it out,

squealed and squeaked, escaped his (luckily right-sided) pocket, and scampered up the stairs like gray lightning, between the legs of the beloved.

She rushed down to the figure sprawled at the bottom of the stairs.

"Are you okay? Are you all right?"

"Oh, yes, yes, I . . ."

She held out her hand to help him up. There it was—her touch, the magic touch that might have launched a bloodline. But on that hand a ring. Why had he not noticed it before when she'd gripped the bars of her Stairmaster? Hysterical blindness? Dazzled by aura? She'd left the ring in her locker so as not to sweat under it?[69] Wagner's *Ring* was less weighty than this one gracing the delicate hand gripping his own.

He was deflated. His authority deserted him with a sizable, silent, psychic Stairmaster hiss. That ring . . . there was no more to say but "Thank you."

"You sure you're okay? Want to try walking?"

He did, and pretended not to limp. She left, satisfied, with a "Sorry." But he was far sorrier. He reached unconsciously into his right bathrobe pocket to pet GG, to assure the two of them of the stability of the world. Gone! The change of life was ominous. The only being offering him unconditional love—except for the too-present dwarf—was gone. And finding a particular rat in New York City was not a task for the fainthearted. Which Pantalone now was—childish and senile at once. And limping in truth, besides. The long death march is begun, he thought. Progressive interior decay, with deterioration and emptying of self. I must sit down. Which he did.

The whir decayed, the street came into focus: Fourteenth Street emerging from the cocoon of its old ways into the butterfly world of the present. Suits and bums, bag ladies and power dressers passed by him as if from Mars. My new role in life, he thought: a stupidly proud naysayer from another world. Were I to reach out to touch them—any of them—my hand would pass right through. Is it the hand or they which are discarnate?

I am shrinking. Shrinking in space, filling up with time. My reach is short through the bars. I need something, some great enterprise which cannot be accomplished, my only chance left for dignity.

He croaked out a tune he had written in his concertina days, now a cappella:

Strange are the streets of the City of Pain
Silent in their hurly-burly,
Playing fields of emptiness
Rilke-y dilke-y, diddley-tiddley-dum.

were voices screaming unintelligibly from behind a curtain of metallic, intentionally distorted sound. (I recall the psy-ops strategy of forcing ex–President Noriega, via such sound, out of the protective arms of the church.) The beat was driving, unvarying. Cymbals punctuated every offbeat, so beats were never off, but only on. There is never relaxation into three, that lovely mode of minuet and waltz, the natural shifting of weight from left to right and back again. Never three, only four, or rather one, one, one, one—fierce, aggressive, driving, militaristic. There is no breathing, no breath, no rhythm. Only meter. Meter and no melody, meter and no harmony, meter and no counterpoint of intertwining voices. I assume there are words—I can't hear them through my earplugs. Perhaps they add something positive. But it seems to me that no words screamed to penetrate distorted decibels can carry meaning much greater than the screaming itself.

And how is my heartmind to find the pace of my exertion, the rhythm of my own breath, when I am so assaulted by external, insensitive bullying? A gym is no zendo, to be sure, but still there is inbreath and outbreath to be monitored and explored, and the pregnancy in between. Brahms' sinuous sensuality of three beats against two—all right. There is a rhythmic tweaking of the spirit, Pythagorean, intentional, finely offered. But the arbitrary cross-rhythms of say, my steps on the treadmill and the beat harassing me, fifteen against seventeen, seven and a half against four, jittering me up into numerical irrationality—this cannot come to good.

69. Could it possibly be that my SS took off her wedding ring at the gym specifically in order to entice one of the men there? The Hathaway Marlboro man, for instance?

No, she was too innocent and guileless. What a weirdo I am to even think something like that! The demons that disseminate the holy evil of love must have hold of my inner ear. It's because of the principle of infinite agitation.

In the aerobics room, in addition to the CD-fed speakers, there was sound emanating from two television sets, often tuned to different stations. Now, I am a great fan of Charles Ives and his fantastical polytonal, polyrhythmic, polydiscourse canvases. But with them, Ives does not pretend to be healing body, mind, or spirit. He uses them, rather, to demonstrate the booming energy of American expansion or, more quietly, to evoke some mysterious, fleeting interstices of existence. Nothing like the random, continual cacophony of MTV plus great moments in sports plus game shows plus rock. Plants would not thrive in such a sound environment.

I don't own a TV. The gym was my first exposure to what's evolved since Groucho's *You Bet Your Life.* L'enfant sauvage, moi. All I can say is "My goodness!" And "This can't be healthy for children or adults." I have actually timed the cutting rhythm of the MTV shows. Between one and three seconds per cut. Sometimes less, practically subliminal. Flashing lights, sped-up, surreal violence, but rarely even enough to grab on to for the ride.

A suit threw him a quarter. Thank you.

But with that quarter unexpectedly came—G. Garza. His absence. Beneath the mask, a tear? In his pocket, the little red hat.

Alexei shuffled home,[70] stiff from his Exercycle, aching from his fall, and heartbroken from his encounter with the possible. There was mail in his box. One letter, hand-addressed, he should at least open it.

The page unfolded to reveal a five-by-five grid of a beautifully drawn alphabet, A to Z, Illuminated manuscript-type letters with beasts curling around uprights and lolling on crossbeams, with pastoral scenes framed in the spaces, minutely worked and beautifully rendered. No message. No signature. What the hell . . .

Wait a minute. Five times five doesn't equal twenty-six. Something was missing. Linear scan. U! U was missing. Missing from? Or was this an "I miss you" card? It was from Delia! She misses me, he thought, but is afraid to say it. As well she should be. The strumpet shall sound. That woman is hostile, intrusive, and dangerous, he told himself. "I'm going to get a restraining order on her. Entrapment contemplated by another nixie who wants to nix me."

Why am I like this? She loves me. Like G. Garza. Or like G. Garza did. The wise man is the one who knows the causes of things. Guess I'm not one. But I'm too old for her now. I need a younger woman. Hermippus developed a technique of life-prolongation by inhaling the breath of young maidens.

"That's for me," he said to himself. "I need more life force, more caffeine. Sag and gag and water on the brain. I'm for a spot of tea-zero. With Excedrin."

I could kill her, he thought. Make it look like natural causes. Dwarves don't live that long. But maybe they do. I have to look up the life span of achondroplastic dwarves.

Do I need an antipsychotic? No, I normally cut respectable capers. Perhaps I just need circulation pills, high dose. If I don't take them, I may stop circulating. What are circulation pills?[71]

And the sports. Not a sport, but sports—all mixed together and showing only home runs, touchdowns, goals scored, baskets made. Here, three- to five-second cuts, but no conceptual breathing space because of the continual, non-contextual switch of activities.

Zen training has a concept called "monkeymind." When one begins a meditative practice of any kind, the first goal is simply to still monkeymind, the associated twitching of thoughts and images that keep one from concentration and inner quietness. Were I to design an environment explicitly to *promote* monkeymind, I could do no better than this in my gym, now claiming to strengthen mind, body and spirit. There I am on my treadmill, counting 12 against 7 against God knows what else, with lights flashing in my eyes (should I raise them from my book) at rhythms fit to drive epileptic fits. Body, mind, and spirit indeed!

I've talked to other gym members about this. Many older ones agree but feel the cultural situation is hopelessly determined. Many of the younger people love the chaos, feel it raises their adrenaline, makes them more able to pump. I suppose this is to the good—their good. But the benefit, if any, rests entirely in the realm of body. Mind and Spirit are not so cajoled.

So this old curmudgeon takes refuge in his earplugs and treadmill Kierkegaard. Back to hear no evil, see no evil, my monkey hands shielding me as they can from monkey mind. I'm feeling stronger and less logy—but spiritually polluted. Noxious rhythm, toxic noise, heavily made-up women ogling over cosmetics, contestants winning more money than I would ever want to earn for mastering admitted trivia. These are not the offerings of a health club worthy of the name.

70. This was an eventful trek. Something happened to me over those few blocks, and I felt, and still feel, shaken.

It seemed the streets, Fourteenth St. especially, was uncommonly filled with men asking for handouts. "Spare change, mister?" Maybe it's just that they noticed my disheveled, downcast face, and thought I'd be an easy mark.

I had a pocketful of quarters left over from a recent laundromat excursion. I gave one out, and then another, and then a third, and then a fourth. At the fifth request, I looked ahead and saw six or seven other men, young and old, sitting on the street, with cans, or a hat, or an empty coffee cup in front of them. Some had signs to spare them active begging.

I had only two more quarters. I could give a quarter to number five and one to number six. But what about seven and eight, and ten and twelve? They would get nothing. Just because they happened to be in that order on my path.

71. Is William Hundwasser trying to implicate me in Delia's death? It's true I have not yet been indicted, or even investigated, but maybe even now they're gathering evidence against me. Maybe they're not. It's been two years since *The Nose* appeared.

Pantalone sat in his room for four times forty days and nights, wondering and growing older. Like Beckett, he sought consolation in the thought that it was now, if ever, that truth might dawn on a mind in ruins, in its exploration of the tangled relation between memory and self. The outside world was delusion and fool's play—that much was clear. But the inside world . . . Whence arose his needs and repulsions? Why Elizabeth Schrank, who ignored, and not Delia Robinson, who doted? He thought about his mother. He bought a plastic human skull from Carolina Biological Supply House. He contemplated it in the light of the candle he waxed onto its crown. It looked like many people he knew. Its eyes were the eyes of all the black-eyed beauties he had admired. Its jaw was strong, and its smile attractive. Its nose left something to be desired.

Back to Carolina Biological Supply for a rat skull. Protruding from the human nasal hole, it made an admirable contribution to nosedom, far better than a carrot in a matroshka's face. Man and rat and rat and man, a match that's made in Heaven's plan.[72]

He slept a lot, as old men do, both to knit up the raveled sleeve of care and to invite encounter with the gods. To purify himself for entering Morpheus's temple he washed with burdock tea and discharged any spermatozoa he felt pulsating within. If chastity was foreordained, he might as well be chaste. His rectal management was precise. He was preparing to meet his maker—not his mother, not his fictive fickle father, not the woman who would make him by leading him helplessly to her bed, but the Maker of Us All, the One in the Sky with the Big Nose, the biggest nose in the world.

An indistinct angst came over me: I was facing something morally threatening, something impossible: I might have to suspend my agapean empathy with panhandlers. I, who so often had been in their place, would have to take on the role of the despised, stone-faced passerby, steadfastly ignoring their existence.

I'm sorry. There were just too many of them. And here was the aporia: this conclusion meant that morality was impossible! Because morality must be the same for all, not different between number six and number seven. That would be unjust—and so, immoral.

All of a sudden, the world seemed alien to me. I felt ensnared by some clear and present miasma of evil, trapped in a civilization rooted in stupidity and the glaring depravity of power.

As a child, I had resolved to be a fanatic. That would mean quarters for every single encounter, not this-one-but-not-that-one. But now it seemed impossible to reconcile the moral law within with the half-baked order of this land of Abracadabra, with its death-by-government

But what was the author's intention in assigning me these murderous thoughts?

I could sue him for libel, maybe. What's the definition of libel? He thinks he can get away with it because I am a public figure—but he was the one who made me a public figure, and the whole thing is like the murderer of his parents asking a jury for mercy because he is an orphan.

And the skull reference in the next paragraph? Another hint of my guilt? The fact is that I love the Carolina Biological Supply catalog. It is one of my favorite books. And I have bought many things from them—charts and specimens and sets of microscope slides. I own a rattlesnake skeleton I got from them. Beautiful.

The skull was a direct reference to Rembrandt's *St. Jerome in a Dark Chamber*, a citation obviously beyond Hundwasser's ken, a tiny etching represented my psychic state after losing the possibility of morality.

St. Jerome sits in a room almost entirely dark. You can barely make him out, or the furniture, or the staircase, or the skull. And yet that room has an extremely bright window in the upper right. But that's impossible, right? Why does the light not enter the room? Why? Because the artist had just lost his beloved wife, Saskia, and that chamber was a portrait of himself, a vessel of darkness which no light could penetrate.

72. Another dig at me, this time below the belt. Did he think I wouldn't get the reference to *Mann und Weib, und Weib und Mann/Reichen an die Gottheit an*? Man and wife, the combination that evokes divinity, a state I may never attain. Go ahead, rub it in.

I am not one who sees *The Magic Flute* as the apotheosis of Mozart's genius, "a work of grandeur, majestic mystery, intoxicating eloquence, with its sentiments of moral philosophy,

and placid violence. You can see why I arrived home a jittery mess and was perhaps hyper-reactive to the letter in my mailbox.

its nourishing criticism of the world, its dialogue that springs from the heart, and above all its great magic that makes the impossible appear as truth." Great God! I am always irritated when I hear this kind of blather, this wishful categorizing of *Die Zauberflöte* as Mozart's great swan song, the transfigured wisdom of a late work—divine simplicity, etc., etc., and not what it was—a last-ditch attempt to get out of the red. *The Magic Flute* is not terribly important among Mozart's works. My 2¢. But of course, it's heresy to say this. It has to be great, for geniuses are great, especially just before dying young.

Die Zauberflöte is, in fact, just a sentimental old Singspiel, a dumb little play with music—good music, yes, but basically a low farce with an infantile emphasis on special effects, an exotic plot, animals, magic tricks, reversals, improbabilities, unmaskings and remaskings, a patchwork of absurdities plundered from myth and Masonic mummery. Why are we supposed to worship this farrago of stunts and vulgar clowning, this pandering combination of the serious and the goofy? In a way, it reminds me of *The Nose*.

On the other hand, on the other hand, I do identify closely and painfully with many of the characters and situations. Papageno's ardent desire for a little Papagena to call his own. And Pamina! If I may be allowed to see myself in a female character without being slandered—this poor, wise, honest girl, tormented by a man who won't speak to her, who would honor a vow of silence in the face of her pain, her aria . . .

And I had lost something greater than any Saskia, though I wish I had had one. I had lost my innocence.

And why is H. so interested in implicating me? Is it possible that he has something to hide? Is it possible that he was involved? This bears looking into.

And then one night, it came to him in a dream, his calling . . .

. . . Along with His Nurse.

Not coincidentally, Delia Robinson, dwarf goddess, also appeared in that dream—the terror object from which he was fleeing. Delia Robinson, she of the gorgeous face and stunted body, she of competence and kindness, she, the artist who would share and record his life, Boswella to his Johnson, if only he would allow it. While Alexei retreats, let us reconnoiter:

She, unlike he, was born tush-first. Opting against a C-section, which she considered a particularly offensive American intrusion, her French-born mother entrusted her to the obstetric skills of the St. Elizabeth's Medical Center in Utica, New York, a parochial institution inspired by Saint Francis of Assisi and faithful to the teaching of the Roman Catholic Church. Her husband, Delia's father, sped her at the classic 3 A.M. from their home in Clinton, eleven miles in eight minutes, screeching the Peugeot's brakes into the ER pit stop. The Franciscans triumphed, as they often do, and Danielle Robinson, née Loiseaux, brought forth, tush-first, a healthy, six-pound baby girl.

Clinton was home to Hamilton College, a small liberal arts institution, where Charles Franklin Robinson was, at thirty-five, a tenured professor of French literature and four-time winner of the annual student polls for best teacher, a status reflecting both his flair for the dramatic and his classes' enthusiasm for it.

Hamilton likes to broaden its students abroad, and it was on one trip he led in the early '70s that Charles met Danielle, a svelte and graceful long-haired beauty ten years his junior whose English, at the time, consisted of a few choice phrases which he found meltingly charming. "Zat make me sheet" was his favorite, a direct rendering of "*Ça me fait chier,*" which, issuing from her charming pout, made him want to hug her. And she

Ah, I feel it—vanished
forever is love's happiness!
Nevermore will you return
to my heart, hours of bliss!
Tamino, see these tears flowing
for you alone, beloved.
If you do not feel love's yearning,
I will seek peace in death.

. . . what is this but my story, the story of a soul longing for finality?

The opera is a wild mixture of styles and moods, like the succession of my noses and personae. Like me, a priest looks forward to a day when earth will be inseparable from heaven, and mortal men will be like Gods. Like me, Mozart spins out sincerest reverence for conjugal love.

Can you see why I am sensitive to Hundwasser's cruel dig?

liked that. For Charles Franklin Robinson was tall and handsome, a great-great-descendent of Benjamin, whose Francophilia was no doubt spawned by a decade of alliances and dalliances in the court of Louis XVI.

She followed him home across the seas, did Danielle, moved into his tweed-jacketed young professor's digs, and soon became the bewitching toast of the French Department and the envy of French majors of both sexes. They would make beautiful children together. Their first was not long coming.

They named her Delia, he after his grandmother, she after the face that might in the future launch a thousand ships. Danielle was amused at the larger breasts she'd always wanted, and settled right into nursing her beautiful new infant Delia, a name she'd thought was standard East Coast American. The new mother had become American with zest, and after producing an American child, she decided the child needed an American pet to grow up with. At the Clinton farmer's market, she found a sweet black kitten and brought it home along with the champignons and asperges. "I want to call it an American name," she told her husband the professor.

"Like what?" Charles asked.

"Jasper," she announced decisively. "Jasper-minou." Jasper-minou grew, like the American he was, to be violent, unpredictable, and semipsychotic and had often to be reprimanded for biting poor baby Delia.

At several months, their gorgeous new child began to give them cause for concern. She didn't lift her large head as early as the books predicted. And she never crawled the traditional way but rather snowplowed across the floor, propping up her rear end and pushing her head forward in front of her, rubbing her forehead raw on the rug. Alternatively, she would sit upright and scoot herself forward, pulling with her legs, dragging her butt across the floor. "Some children never crawl before they walk." They'd heard that somewhere. Einstein had never crawled—or was it that he had never talked?

At two, Delia was walking, about a year late. But she swayed back and forth and side to side in a kind of waddle, with her tush sticking out. Her arms and legs looked short. "Cephalocaudal development." Charles had picked up that term in college biology. "She'll be on the track team yet." But that winter, Charles and Danielle knew something was definitely wrong.

Hitherto, they had done their own infant care for a child slow to develop but otherwise charmingly normal. The self-care movement was in high swing, and Danielle's peasant roots and skills served admirably. But six months of coughing, crying, breathing problems, and ear-tugging led them to the college infirmary and then, by reticent refer-

ral, to the pediatrics department at St. Elizabeth's. There the signs all came together: Delia was very likely an achondroplastic dwarf, manifesting the childhood problems of her type. An MRI showed that her large head with its noble brow was not hydrocephalic and even more "normal" than usual, a mutation, perhaps, within the mutation. Charles and Danielle were warned of eustachian tubes too tiny to drain well, predisposing to constant ear and sinus infections. They heard about small airways which with any bad cold might become life-threatening. They were shown X-ray films of her narrowed spinal lumen, which might later squeeze the cord and result in problems with her back or legs.

This was not what they had bargained for. Actually, they hadn't "bargained" for anything: they'd felt clearly destined for a high-end, attractive child, fiercely smart like both of them, a child who would make them proud of their transatlantic genetic achievement. They left the consultation confused, depressed, carrying a daughter with tubes in her ears and a prescription for antibiotics. "*Ça me fait chier*," Danielle said. Charles said nothing.

Delia celebrated her fourth birthday in bed—her back had been aching when she walked, and the tingling in her legs was getting worse. Her present from Grandma and Grandpa Loiseaux had arrived all the way from France, the most beautiful doll she had ever seen, a delicate Mary with blissful ceramic smile, in soft blue robes and white headdress. With it, a note to Danielle and Charles: "*Un antidote puissant contre Barbie*." Always protecting—although it wasn't clear to their daughter what level of irony was intended, for Mama had been a reluctant Catholic and Papa a doubtful one. Still, the doll was lovely.

Another week of bootless bed rest sent them again to St. Elizabeth's, where Radiology confirmed spinal stenosis and recommended a surgical decompression of the spinal column best done at a major dwarfism center like Johns Hopkins. Three months' potential hospital stay, complications possible—infection, nerve-root injury, permanent numbness or paralysis—news unwelcomed by worried parents.

Grandmère Loiseaux responded with an offer to fly Delia and Danielle to Lourdes to see what might be accomplished. Four thousand instantaneous and permanent cures had been attested to by the Bureau des Constatations Médicales, she informed them, and the Church had recognized sixty-seven of those cures as miracles.

"But this is genetic," Charles objected. "It's built into her, fated on some chromosome in every cell in her body. It's not some hysterical disorder which can just vanish. She's not about to go into spontaneous remission. And what are the odds? Thousands

of sick people go to Lourdes every day, since what—1860 or something? Four thousand alleged cures out of millions of sickies? And you are expecting Delia to be one of them?"

"I'm not expecting anything," Danielle said. "But it can't hurt. A free trip. She'll get to see Mama and Papa, get to see France, get to hear more French . . ."

"Get to have a long, exhausting drive to New York, get to sit for hours and hours on an uncomfortable plane, get to be jet-lagged, all so she can dunk in some holy cold water—for nothing?"

In a contest of wills, they were evenly matched. So young Delia was asked and made the decision: she wanted to go see Grandmère et Grandpère.

The trip was a great success. The little trouper survived the travel, was feted by her grandparents, and loved the car ride into the mountains, the church at Lourdes, and especially the grotto with a statue of her doll, Maria. She worried that people might be staring at her in the crowd at Lourdes, and on the streets of Paris. "No," Danielle assured her, "they were just looking at your pretty dress." Even though her back pain and paresthesia let up a little, she was not, hélas! the sixty-eighth miracle cure. But she could speak better French by the time she came back home.

After several months Delia's symptoms disappeared, and she walked more comfortably and confidently—but alas, toward the next crisis: school.

In 1976 Clinton, NY, population 3,010, was 96.4 percent white, with its black and Hispanic populations "significantly below state average" and its median household income significantly above. In brief, it had little acquaintance with diversity. Like Lake Wobegon's, all its children were above average and tended to be trim, fair, and good-looking in a *Saturday Evening Post* sort of way. Its tree-lined streets and Victorian homes were immaculately kept, and all was always as it should be.

While her immediate neighbors were aware of Delia's condition, the younger citizens of Clinton Elementary were unprepared for a dwarf as peer: they were downright cruel as only children can be.

Dwo-orff, Dwo-orff
Ugly, stupid dwo-orff!

was the chant, in that universal singsong whose usual text was nya-nya, nya-nya, nya-nya-nya nya-nya.[73] Delia had never heard the word "dworf" before, but she had heard the words "ugly" and "stupid" and was shocked that they might refer to her, as pointing fingers might indicate. She was hurt. And frightened.

73. Does this interest you as much as it does me—the universality of the childhood mocking tune? If not, it's probably because you weren't mocked as much as I was. And it's not just children who use it.

Thirds have great power, changing melodies from happy to sad merely by twitching this way or that

A school visit by outraged parents did little to scotch the clamor of ridicule, which simply downshifted to whispered taunts and drawings on spitballed notes. At week's end, Delia was transferred to St. Ann's Academy in nearby Kirkland. The demographic was the same, but the nuns would not put up with teasing.

"What is a dworf?" she asked her parents. "Am I one?"

It was a moment of truth for Charles and Danielle. The answer, as it often was, was "Let's go to the library." And there they found a coffee-table book of Disney's *Snow White*, took it out, and sat with the drawings and the tale.

"Those are dworfs? Dopey and Sneezy and Grumpy? I'm not like them, and I'm not a dworf, and I don't want to be a dworf, and I'm not a dworf!"

"There's nothing wrong with being a dwarf," Danielle said.

"Then *you* go be one. I'm not going to be. I'm going to be Snow White."

She told the nuns she had changed her name to Snow White, but that didn't fly. Delia Robinson she remained—at least on weekdays from 8:30 to 3. And on weekends, the game she liked most was when Papa would carry her on his shoulders, and she would wear Mama's long raincoat draped around the both of them, and the giantess's head was eight feet off the ground, and her name was *La Géante*, whose Baudelairian song her father would chant as he stomped the giantess around. She knew it by heart but didn't know what it meant:

Du TEMPS que la NaTURE en sa VERVE puisSANTE
ConceVAIT chaque JOUR des enFANTS monSTRUEUX,
J'eusse AMIÉ vivre AUPRÈS d'une JEUNE géANTE,
Comme aux PIEDS d'une REINE un CHAT volupTUEUX.

The nuns had had no experience with dwarfs. They did not pick up on her hearing loss, and without admitting it—even to themselves—took her physical difference for lower intelligence. After her hearing was tested in the second grade, she was moved up to the front row. Her intelligence improved markedly—a miracle.

And so they mainstreamed her—she was treated like all the other students, just as she wanted to be. They didn't anticipate her size difficulties in the girls' bathroom, or her back pain after physical education. Delia understood these as the cross she had to bear if she was to grow like all the others.

She used her four daily prayers to pray for growth, passionately willing it, waiting for her body to stretch itself. She watched her friends lengthen before her eyes, and grow in

half a step. Bernstein thinks the mocking tune is universal because it engages the first notes in the overtone series. Kids' self-started tunes almost always begin with descending intervals. Check it out. But I don't really get it.

If you have a good theory, let me know via my publisher. Send a picture of yourself, as I like to see who I'm corresponding with. Whom? I hate being pedantic.

And frankly, I don't even understand mocking. Why would anyone want to mock anyone else? 

power as they did so. She watched them then move on from her toward others their own size. Delia had to play with kids much younger and by the fourth grade had become a "little mother" to first and second graders. She spent every recess alone, hanging from the monkey bars, not swinging along, just hanging.

"What are you doing?" a girl might ask.

"I'm growing," she would say.

One day she responded to Danielle's "*Comment ça va?*" with "Fine. I am scheduled to grow next year. The growth spurt associated with the Big One-Oh." Danielle burst out laughing. Delia was hurt. When she was grown, she'd move away from here to where no one would know she had ever been a dworf.

The Big One-Oh or not, she thought it prudent to help her growth spurt along nutritionally. She had watched Jasper Minou stretch out from a little black ball of fur to a huge, sleek, powerful tom, much feared by all. When he slept on a chair, he would sometimes do "long-arm," allowing one front leg to dangle toward the floor. It was astounding. It almost touched. She would go for long-arm too, by eating his Science Diet food. Just a little every day, nibbled unseen, right from the rolled-up bag. It didn't taste too bad. It didn't taste great, but it was worth it to increase the odds for long-arm when she would move away. She discovered Plastic Man Comics and took to wearing red, black, and yellow. Why? Her parents never knew. When teased about her big head, she thought, Big head—more brains, but was too polite to say so. For she was actually beginning to like herself. Somewhat. To a degree. A little.

As she studied the lives of the saints in class, she was particularly impressed with the story of St. Christopher and asked her parents to buy her a medal—which they did, and which she wore. Again they could not imagine why—and Delia would never tell because she knew she was thinking something bad, conflating herself with that child almost too heavy for the giant man to carry. Heavy because grown huge—though that was never depicted—heavy because that child bore the weight of the world on its shoulders. The nuns explained Christopher as a symbol of the struggle of the soul taking on the yoke of Christ in an un-Christ-like present. How prophetic they were!

When Delia Robinson entered seventh grade, she stood three foot ten. Her arms were short enough to make for difficulties in wiping herself; her legs were so bandy as to

permit her large head to pass between them should she choose to try it when standing at attention. Her limbs had stopped growing by age eleven.

She studied her mother's long, thin body, made up half of legs. She imagined the length of Danielle's bones and made little diagrams of what they must look like compared to hers. She watched her mother's walk—how the long legs just swung right out and back while the hips remained facing forward. She tried doing it that way herself and found it comically inefficient. Waddling, for her, was the way to go. She pondered her mother's breasts, just hanging out there off her chest, floppily independent, while her own were just oncoming mounds of fatness on her already thick torso. She came to the inexorable conclusion that she was different, that she would and could never grow into her mother's shape, that some dwarf had closed around her like a restricting suit of armor.

And she knew there were places where "different" people were kept—mental hospitals, carnivals, prisons. Prisons. All were prisons—like her body—separating the prisoners from a world of normal folks whom they might disturb.

Delia did disturb other people. She knew that. Some were simply curious. But she was also a constant object of ridicule, of staring and pointing and comment. She would get angry when people looked at her, and even angrier when they wouldn't, treating her as if she were invisible.

She sat once at the table of a thirteen-year-old birthday girl. Her patent-leather Mary Janes dangled two feet off the floor, for she was perched on three phone books so as to comfortably reach the food. As the cake was brought in and the party broke into "Happy Birthday," she heard a woman standing back against the wall say softly to her neighbor, but loudly enough to be audible over the singing, "I can't understand why they invited her. She completely spoils the beauty of the party." Delia knew to whom she was referring. She wanted to take revenge, but at the end of the song, when the candles had been blown out, the guests had shifted enough for her to be uncertain who had said it. Besides, what revenge could she have taken?

Thirteen, fourteen, preadolescence, the height of self-consciousness. Nicole, her eight-year-old little sister, was a head taller than she, slim and beautiful, like Danielle. She had watched Nicole grow, hating her for doing so and hating all the others guilty of the same transgression. She still sat in her old children's furniture and had even inherited some of Nicole's. What was more, Danielle had to sew her clothing specially to fit, starting with children's garments and modifying them to look more "grown-up."

Delia was expected to be polite and friendly to strangers at all times, a public figure

and ambassador from the land of dwarfdom, a credit to its kingdom. And indeed, that was the most fruitful way to go, the path of most benefit for least effort. Yet the cruelty of her peers, while more sporadic than before, could be even more intense: "What are you studying math for? You should just go into a freak show."

Though she had some friends, she was shunned by others, and even her friends were quick to abandon her when more attractive connections might be made. Why should she not just hole up? Go to school, come home, and hole up? Work on her sketching and painting and singing? No, she thought, she had to go out and try to do things, to meet different kinds of people, and not use her strangeness as an excuse to . . . to what? To avoid difficulties? To avoid being a grown-up?

She stared at herself in the mirror and found her face to be slightly pretty, an at-least-intended mixture of Charles and Danielle, her eyes, his brows, his nose, her lips, their combined intensity. Yet what was south of that face—of that, she tried not to think.

Her parents took her to the LPA convention—Little People of America—one year when it occurred in Schenectady. She took three steps into the convention hall and fled. "I'm not like that. I don't look like that. All those awful-looking people, hundreds of them, thousands, wanting to make out, to hook up." She was disgusted.[74] And in shunning a thousand of her peers, she experienced a soul-chilling loneliness, bitter yet tonic, like a cup of her ginseng tea. If she was inferior to the normal world, at least she was superior to them, the damaged ones all celebrating their impairment. She didn't need them. She didn't need anyone.

Still, at Holy Name High, it would have been nice to be asked to the dances, to actually dance and not just prepare the hall and chaperone. But the phone never rang on Friday or Saturday nights, and rarely Sunday through Thursday—and then always for help with someone's homework. Even little Nicole got more calls.

Delia had fantasies of meeting a boy, a man, of marriage and family with normal children, but then again, she wouldn't want any boy who would want *her*. What kind of weirdo would that be? And the artist in her could never tolerate someone more hideous than she, some thalidomide unfortunate, or a victim of facial burns.

She was popular—in a way—and had a circle of friends and protectors. As a junior she was elected class treasurer, and in her senior year class president. But still no one would ask her out, and the reverse was unthinkable, too certain of rejection.

Once a friend tried to fix her up with Nortie Gusky, a shrinking violet who sat out all the dances, gazing longingly at girls through thick glasses. Physically pushed on Delia to dance, he ran away to the humiliation of both. Occasionally a popular jock would

74. See? Does not Delia here express the very same feelings I have to make excuses for? But because she is a child, and even better, "a crippled child," you are all very understanding, aren't you, ready to mentally take her hand and say, "There, there. That's all right. I understand. Let's go get an ice cream cone."

offer her his hand. But she always refused, knowing it was only on a dare. "No, thank you," she would say. "I have to stay free in case something comes up." Standing on her stool in the girls' bathroom, she looked in the mirror and saw a Delia Robinson in a green velvet dress, a face almost pretty enough, intelligent, sad, and very lonely.

Into the bathroom stomped Bunny Greenacre, cheerleader and ingenue star of the last three Holy Name musicals. "Wrong dress, wrong dress!" she raged as she adjusted her shoulder straps to make herself look more fetching. What would she have done, Delia thought, if it was not her dress that was wrong but herself?

"I think you look beautiful," the dwarf said.

"Yeah? So how come Tim has been dancing with Gay Tierney all night?" And she stormed out, revamped, unto the breach once more. Delia was glad she wasn't that attractive.

"I think I'll get a big dog," Delia concluded, in a fit of (quite consequential) non sequitur. She had never had a dog. She had always denigrated dog owners as superficial, sentimental people requiring fawning devotion and obedience in their pets and compared them invidiously to cat lovers, who admired the flawless grace and self-sufficiency, the aloof beauty and philosophic repose of the immaculate, sleek beings who chose to be their guests.

But now she would ask for a dog—for graduation—a big one. Not so much to be its master as simply to balance out the combined size and poundage of man plus beast. Woman plus beast. Beauty and the beast it would not be—unless the dog were the beauty. And the dog would *be* a beauty, a Bernese mountain dog—not quite as big as a Saint Bernard but far more handsome.

She named her dog Lotte—because there was so much of her, especially for one as small as her mistress. Body black, with a white nose and chest and brown lower legs with adorable white feet. Lotte was a beauty. And her beauty attracted the consequence of the non sequitur above:

First Love

Alexei had no monopoly on this phenomenon. And who wouldn't have fallen in love with Jens Jensen? A transfer student at Hamilton, new in town, a music major, blond-

bearded and superbly handsome, with a wire-framed, intelligent look. It was love at first sight, at least between their dogs.

"Whoa," said Jens as his golden made a powerful beeline for Lotte. He offered embarrassed excuses for almost having trampled Delia in the scramble. They wound up walking the dogs together to the Village Green, picking up after them when they pooped together on the October lawn ("How romantic!" Jens remarked), and spending an hour in animated conversation—till he had to go.

"Gotta get to a rehearsal."[75]

"What sort of rehearsal?" she wanted to know.

"Hamilton Vocal Ensemble. Pretty terrific. A grad student in the music department pulled together a group of singers to do early music. Nice bunch. Pure voices. No vibrato. We're working on a Josquin mass."

"What's that?" Delia asked, her musical knowledge going back to Bach and no further.

"A Josquin mass? Josquin des Pres? You don't know him?"

Delia blushed, an odd response but appropriate to the moment.

"Greatest composer of the Renaissance. 'Swing and sway with Josquin des Pres'—that's our motto. Do you sing?"

"Well, yes. I do."

"Soprano, alto? Probably alto, right?"

"Yes."

"Can you sight-sing? Just sing off a page?"

"Yes. Pretty well."

"Well, hey, maybe you should come by. Monday, Wednesday, Friday, 12 to 1 at the Chapel. Know where that is?"

"Yes. My father teaches at the college. French."

"Who's that?"

"Dr. Robinson."

"Really? He's terrific—at least I hear."

"He's a great dad."

"I'll bet. Wow, Charlie Robinson's daughter... So do you want to come? To Vocal Ensemble? See what it's like?"

"I'll think about it. I've got a lot on my plate."

"Okay, then. See you when I see you. Great to meet you."

75. Have you noticed how fixated Hundwasser is on musicians as love-objects? The man himself was a low-grade guitar player like them all who, as a teenager, had a garage band imaginatively called the What. It's unclear if the What ever got out of the garage. I know Jessica, at least, had quite a torchy voice. But the way to Carnegie Hall is via practice, Bill, not copulation.

I, in contrast, a quite accomplished musician, have loved widely, and not just as a musical wannabe. For research purposes, I have tried to make a list of all the women I have loved, if not possessed. Out of the thirty-four I can remember, only seven were musicians, though my high school was teeming with them, and my subsequent accordion playing attracted much keyboard-player attention.

The earth, you know, breeds many sorts of flowers.

The fact is that Delia's plate had just been licked clean by a large golden retriever and its master. And she spent the next several days—and nights—thinking about nothing but the latter. But did she have the courage to step in that direction? A week had passed. She had glimpsed him once when he and his Woody had been leaving the green as she approached. She would not yell out, or run after. But when her father delivered a reminder-invite left for her in his departmental mailbox—that was too much to bear. On an early November afternoon, she pulled open the great white door to the Hamilton Chapel, and then the door into the sanctuary.

This was the miracle. She had walked into the middle of a miracle—*Et homo factus est.*

The central moment of the Nicene creed is the mystery of incarnation: *Et incarnatus est de spiritu sancto, ex Maria virgine*. And the center of the mystery, the miracle at the heart of all miracles, is evoked in the next line: *et homo factus est*, he was made man. Josquin had transcribed his heart-stopping awe at this event, calling a halt to his unmatched weavings in musical space-time and proceeding quietly, on contrapuntal tiptoe, as it were, to describe the mystery. It was much the way Delia entered the chapel—hesitant to presume or to intrude. The effect of Josquin's awe on her own, of his tentative, breath-holding witness on hers, was staggering. She had never heard anything so beautiful in her entire life as the sounds that caressed her from those echoing walls. She groped her way into a pew and dropped down onto the kneeler. From her hidden position, framed by wood and velvet, leaning her head against the hymnal, she absorbed the crucifixion, the death—and, with a shock, the spirited resurrection. And with that ascension, she was pulled back from the deep and shot outward, an arrow of longing, toward the source of the sound. At the Amen, she scrambled herself up onto the pew until the rehearsal was over.

"Delia!" Jens cried out when he noticed her at the back. "Hey, you came! Have you been here long? What did you think?"

What was she to say?

"I came in when Mary gave birth to Jesus."

"Is that in there?"

"*Ex Maria virgine . . .*"

"I don't know Latin. But I guess, yeah, Mary, virgin . . . okay."

"You mean you sing this without knowing what it means?"

"I only know how beautiful it is. Incredible. That's enough for me."

She could have left him then and there, before it even started. But she didn't.

Instead, she joined the chorus and spent the next months of dog-walking sharing with him what she had gathered in twelve years at Catholic school, her last two years of reflection, art history classes at the college, and her own studio work exploring religious and spiritual themes. He, in turn, shared with her his deep appreciation of early music, from chant to the most complex Flemish polyphony, and allowed her to glimpse yet another face of God in the world.[76]

Notwithstanding their friendship, and in spite of what she felt but did not speak, they were far from being a couple. It was sharing "The Little Mermaid" one night that pushed them into dangerous territory.

Jens, being of Danish stock, had of course been brought up on Andersen. One April day, poking around in the music library stacks, he had come across a recording of Dvorak's little-known opera, *Rusalka*, the story of a Slavic water-nymph similar to Andersen's tale, but darker. He suggested they listen to it together—which they did, following the score, at his apartment, on his high-end stereo. After listening, they discussed the differences between Rusalka's fate and that of the Little Mermaid, and Jens was shocked to learn that Disney's happy-end version was the only one Delia knew. He grabbed his *Tales* from the shelf and read her the original, the painful, strange, and horrifying one. And then they talked of that.

Delia shared with him her feelings of sisterhood with the Little Mermaid—a normal human head and face ("The head of a Botticelli angel," Jens commented—at which she blushed) and a body below which she felt might as well have been that of a codfish.

"No," he said. "You're just . . . small. You have your own shape, but so does everyone. You're a . . . beautiful girl." He looked her up and down, assessing her body really for the first time. The May night blew a caressing wind through the open window, the gibbous moon threw its shadows, Rusalka was a death-spirit, and the Mermaid was foam on the waves. A magic moment, somewhat rash.

Perhaps it was pity on his part; perhaps it was an act of pure friendship, a prompt to her self-esteem. But it soon became something else as blood and juices flowed, and Woody looked on and panted. There was no penetration, but there may as well have been, for her soul reached out and enveloped his in a way that was shocking to each of them. They both came, whether physically or spiritually or both it was hard to tell. And then he pulled out. He pulled his soul out, straightened his clothing, put Andersen back on the shelf and the CD back in its case. He offered to walk her back home.

Being small does not mean having small joys, inconsequential pains, or stunted

76. Delia's is a true story up to this point. At least according to her. She'd never give me the details about what happened with her and Jens Jensen, whose real name, I believe, was Hans Hansen.

This brings up the poignant question: Why is it that Hundwasser treats *me* so differently? The early Delia episodes seem to be correct even in detail—the trip to Lourdes, the Baudelaire poem, etc. So we know WH is not a pathological, involuntary liar. He chooses to lie only about me. Why?

First, be it said that I have an inborn gift for selecting the wrong collaborators. This would include parents, employers, and beloveds as well as Hundwasser. Nevertheless.

My theory is this: it has paid him well to voice the bankruptcy of our culture in order to become an "important" literary figure. As a successful cult author, Hundwasser has exhibited the triumph of a basically working-class person over the vicissitudes of competition. The principle of salability demands that he be committed less to truth than to the public taste for odium.

I'll have to admit that the silliness of his serio-comic novel is a preferable alternative to the glamorizing of crime, high-powered capitalism, and take-no-prisoners business/military tactics. On the other hand, he exhibits an unstable grasp of reality, especially mine, and reprehensible indifference to the suffering he has caused with his terrible and lasting form of cruelty. To me.

His frank trolling for a Hollywood contract—such as with the chase sequence, fire, and explosion at Mangiafuoco's fictive end—may be excused as starry-eyed boyishness. I've already spoken at length about his pandering.

But cruelty is not a warm puppy, and a closed mouth gathers no feet, my friend. 

dreams. Having a childish body does not necessitate juvenile thoughts. She looked at Jens with pity.

Delia dropped out of chorus to alleviate their mutual discomfort, since it seemed she was dangerous to those she loved. She understood how people—especially men—might shy away from her, from her power of contamination. Even shoe salesmen avoided touching her feet. People she surprised coming around a corner jumped back in visceral fear. One woman had even shrieked—as if she had seen some troll under a bridge. She couldn't get a job. She couldn't get a job, and she couldn't get a job, and she couldn't get a job, a real job, for years, until she was hired by Frank Mangiafuoco, MD, largely for her strangeness—and her ability to sketch.

By then, she felt nourished by people's disgust, feeling in some way superior, intriguing, an obviously beautiful soul in a tortured body. She grew to enjoy the wary attention she commanded and was even tempted to ham it up, to play the cheerful cripple or the friendly freak, using her body as a shield and a weapon. She did have arthritic pain, and back pain, and leg pain, and tingling from spinal compression. Why not cash in on them and renounce her endless quest for normality?

And then in Frank's office, she met Alexei Pigov, a soul in worse shape than her own, a being whose otherness was even more evident than hers. And once again love called, but in the opposite direction—downward, toward caritas and mercy. But he and his mother wouldn't have it.[77]

The Way of Perfection

In his dream Alexei was running, running from Delia Robinson because Delia Robinson represented entrapment in the flesh. Like him, she was trapped in the oddness of her self, her body, made so much worse in contrast to her face. Her snared beauty peeked out appallingly from behind the wall of the otherness that was she, and conversely, her ugliness itself was imprisoned by the irony of beauty at its top. But worse than her own recursive entrapment was her potential to ensnare him, to smother his quest in what? a dwarf woman's love, a woman dwarf's lust, in her needs, in the bantam folds and membranes of her flesh?

No, he must be free, he would be free to live a life of perfect purity, not in order to

77. If I may be allowed to factuate yet again concerning the fictions of Mr. Hundwasser, I have to say that his book exists in an unreal, grotesque atmosphere, and is covered with soot. I have said it before, but let me insist: Delia's and my relationship was characterized by a gentle, moral feeling of love, as in *The Magic Flute*, each of us seeking the blessings of care and companionship and not simply sensual abandon. We were both shy, we were both awkward. But Hundwasser has extracted from me only my most extreme gestures, and never, ever presents as wholesome my vigorous, unique, legitimate strangeness.

It's true, as I've said, that in the beginning Delia took some getting used to. I was positively disposed to achondroplastic dwarfs via my experience with Arlene Premper, the young woman who sang the *Kindertotenlieder* for her senior recital at Music & Art. I was an outcast myself, and well aware of the suffering of those who are physically "different." But for some reason, I just couldn't see myself with anyone but the most beautiful, angelic, ethereal girls in the school, girls who would go off to Sarah Lawrence to dance or write lyric poetry. Is it a crime to admire the Botticellian female beauty of swan necks and long limbs?

Delia did not have a swan neck. Hers, like Arlene's, was closer to no neck. And as for long limbs . . .

escape the real world but the better to apprehend it. This was not the mere egotism of the humble.

The Talmud notes that man is born into this world with his fists clenched, as if to say, "Watch out, here I come, this world will be mine!" But he leaves this world with his palms open, as if to say, "There is nothing left. I am empty-handed." Alexei was ready to leave empty-handed; he wanted only to understand where he'd been.

There are no atheists, they say, in foxholes; neither do they exist in burrows. And like a mole pursued by the enemy, Alexei would dig down and build himself an impregnable storehouse, and that storehouse would be sanctity. Dora may have destroyed the end of Kafka's story, but Delia would not destroy his.

Sainthood. A saint for our time. That shouldn't be so hard. Alexei's wants were small and not burdensome. Wait. Wasn't he only imitating some Dostoyevskian character—Alyosha or Mishkin? The Underground Man or something? No! Unlike any of them, Alexei would bring to straying humanity a presentiment of something irreplaceable, some glimpse of the great mysteries. He would show the way, a king of only-the-essential.

There is a significant text in which St. Thomas exhorts kings to imitate God's government of nature: the king must create cities just as God has created the world; he must lead man toward his finality. And what is his finality? Is it physical health? No, says Thomas. If physical health were the finality of man, then he would not need a king but a physician or a personal trainer. Is it wealth? No, because then a financial consultant would do. Is it truth? No, answers Thomas, because truth can be had from teachers or scientists.

No, he says—man must be inspired by a being who can lead the way to heavenly bliss through conformity on earth to what is *honestum*, a spiritual king to lead his fellow man toward *honestum* as their natural and divine finality. Honesty, integrity, virtue. Empathy, fairness, love. Alexei was ready to abandon honors, riches, the delights of this world, and all kinds of pleasures to grow into his role. He would become Saint Alexis Honestum, the Vagabond of God, and he would emanate slowly, via paths arcane. For was not the strategy of the Hebrew holy texts to hide within its consonants? The seeker was responsible for supplying the word sounds, scanning each root for all possible meanings, and adding vowels that teased his understanding. What lay hidden behind the mask of consonants? What lay hidden behind the mask of Saint Alexis? The more mysterious he could be, the more profoundly challenging to this world in need of rescue. He would found a religion

well, let's not talk about it. So I have to admit that her physical appearance did set limits on how close I allowed myself to get to her. What if she fell in love with me and expected me to return those emotions? What would I say? "Gee, Delia, I really like you, but couldn't we just be friends?"

I have always been allergic to using words commonly spoken by others. And unlike others, I was most wary of rushing from desire to satisfaction and, satisfied, to have to yearn again for desire. That facile treadmill was not for me. So I kept my distance, and Delia and I were nurse and patient, then friends and confidants, and finally each others' trusted advisers. There was nothing sordid between us, no hanky-pank, not even a late night's tipsy experimentation. She accepted my wish for distance with practiced humility, and I valued her proffered warmth, intelligence, and depth.

I once accompanied her on accordion in her singing of Thomas Ford's exquisite Elizabethan song:

Since first I saw your face
I resolved to honor and renown thee.
If now I be disdayned I wish
My heart had never known thee.

What I that loved and you that liked
Shall we begin to wrangle?
No, no, no, my heart is fast,
And cannot disentangle.

I felt, true or not, that she was singing about my face. She was one of the few people to have seen it post-puberty. And I felt we both understood and accepted the fact that though she loved me, while I only liked her (only!), our relationship was, and would be beyond disentangling. It was a supreme moment of beauty between us, one which I will always remember, closer and more intense than sex. Probably.

which would lead the twenty-first century from its sordid, waste-heap reality to another, from death to life, from time to timelessness.

This would require a certain transformation of the self—for access to truth cannot be achieved without purity of the soul. Pantalone would have to go. There could be no secret concupiscence. What was the yardstick of concupiscence? He'd solve that later.

So Saint Alexis Honestum, still disguised as Panatalone, haunted once again the great reading room of the New York Public Library, studying the lives of the saints, especially those whose martyrdom involved the nose, in nonstandard volumes. He discovered, for example, Saint Ignosius of Kiev, martyred in 1152 for making a nuisance of himself smelling crucifixes, even those pendant upon bosoms. As he hung by the nose in the courtyard of the Basilica of Saint Sophia, that appendage grew to extraordinary length, prompting some to declare a miracle and fueling a series of copycat transgressions, like that of Saint Aloysius of Sipupus, who also was hung by the nose in 1681, but this time for smelling the dress of Princess Anak Agung. When he was brought down from the scaffold, his nostrils were draped over his ears. Fascinating but not applicable. Alexei's path required sexual abstinence, not sniffing—sexual abstinence and physical privation. The self was a great snare, a spider's web spun out of the bowels. He would reduce himself to nonbeing before nonbeing claimed him as its own. No pain, no brain.[78]

Physical privation turned out to be easy.

78. My turn to religious consciousness was not as silly as all this. William Hundwasser, in spite of his Nietzschean pretensions, is merely a facile kind of agnostic, and so trivializes this and most other dimensions of my inevitable spiritual quest.

Why inevitable? You might think that a person with such an idiosyncratic path as mine would evade "inevitabilities." But why shouldn't I allow myself an ordinary thought now and then? Why must I always strain to pursue things new, unseen, and astounding? Why can't I be ordinary, be like the rest, and experience things that have been experienced for millennia?

As there is normal moral development in children, so there is normal religious or spiritual development in most adults, and not simply from acknowledging one's own mortality, but because of a wider understanding of the dimensions of existence. We grow in our concerns from individual to community, from community to planet, from planet to universe, from universe to Infinity—if unimpeded. That is the soul's normal progress.

At birth it is only me, me, me. Then me and her, that one, the titty-lady. Then family and larger family, and slowly, nation, world, and often cosmic consciousness. If at birth we were as broadly conscious as an adult, it's likely that by the age of five suicide would be widespread, even a question of honor. But we are *not* that conscious, and a good thing too. Fascination with the *mysterium tremendum*, with the weird Portentous, must come only when we are ready. Many educated people come slowly to tuck

8. Feeling Nasty

"faith" away in some back corner of their brains. On deep reflection, they may find it again later, or by an effort of memory.

For instance: "To know that what is impenetrable to us really exists, manifesting itself as the highest wisdom and the most radiant beauty which our dull faculties can comprehend only in their most primitive forms—this knowledge, this feeling, is at the center of true religiousness" (Einstein). Compare this to Hundwasser's glib reporting.

"Our dull faculties"—there is the key to the religious difference between Hundwasser and me. My faculties are as dull as his—but I *know* it, while he assumes his are razor-sharp and all-seeing. Even Bill, however, would admit that we do not see the UV seen by bees, or hear the pitches heard by bats, or smell the olfactory world of dogs. Our senses compared to theirs are dull. Do we say those electromagnetic frequencies do not exist? Do we deny the existence of high-pitched sound, or the odors-effects of micromolecules? No. We simply say they are "invisible" to us, to our senses.

Why then is it so hard for people like Hundwasser to admit that there may be other energies in the universe outside most systems of detection? Some of us have antennae tuned to these, and they fill us with boundless awe and wonder, and enrapture our souls. And the Hundwassers go pooh-pooh, pooh-pooh.

We un-Hundwassers are entranced by moving closer to the Thing we sense behind all things, the Force responsible for their creation, movement, and growth. Like Einstein, we nose our way towards the mystery of conscious life perpetuating itself through all eternity, the marvelous structure of the universe which we just dimly perceive. We try to comprehend an infinitesimal part of the intelligence manifested in nature.

Though I want to become a saint and a holy man, it may interest you to know that never at any moment in my life have I "sought God." I saw the problem of God as one for which humans here below could obtain no data. Consequently, I translate that word in Tillich's language of "ultimate concern," or better "ultimate ground of being"—that which underlies everything that is.

Related to not believing in "God," that is, the God of theism—God limited by man's finite conception—I have never allowed myself to think about life after death. I believe that the instant of death is the center and object of life, and that in that instant, in that infinitesimal fraction of time, pure truth, naked, certain, will become apparent. When one hungers for bread, one is not given stones.

I have an extremely severe standard for intellectual honesty and thus belong to no church except my own. And I feel I must fight against the idolatrous deterioration of religion into arbitrary dogma.

Hundwasser may discredit all this—we all disbelieve facts and theories for which we have no use.

But is there no use for faith? Well, as William James so effectively demonstrates, faith can make facts happen. For example, a whole train of passengers, each individually brave enough, can be looted by just a few highwaymen simply because the robbers can count on one another, while each passenger is afraid

Anger I sing, the wrath of Alexei Pigov.[79]

How many blows can one psyche bear? Continual rejection from the XX set and too much shameful pride to access the XXX, loss of a musician's right hand and the meager living that might come with it, pursued by an ardent unwanted infatuate, abandoned by a ditzy mother, just kickin' down the cobblestones, feeling nasty. Emerson notes that "we boil at different temperatures," and Alexei's boiling point was now well below 98.6 degrees.

It may be that hatred is the most steady and reliable emotion, far more dependable than love, especially when nourished by physical privation. So Saint Alexis Honestum, still disguised as Pantalone, sat out on a blanket on Astor Place, an inexplicable object, accordion in lap, but silent. And hungry. And hating.[80]

An occasional coin was dropped into his case by some passerby who—who knows?—appreciated his Cageian silence? Liked his drooping nose-mask? Was thinking of something else? And the buck or two a day enabled him to survive from soup kitchen to soup kitchen, provided he had the energy to get there.

Experimental left-hand meanderings among the button chords or pitches seemed to have a negative effect on his income. Too much bass clef? Alienating enharmonic modulations? Eventually Honey, like the Christ child, became too heavy to lug to Astor Place

that if he resists, he will be killed before anyone else backs him up. But, says James, "if we believed that the whole car-full would rise at once with us, we should each severally rise, and the train-robbing would never even be attempted. There are then cases where a fact cannot come at all unless a preliminary faith exists in its coming, where faith in a fact can help create the fact." And QED, I say.

What is the fact I want to create by faith? I am one with God and Jesus and Muhammad and Buddha and Confucius in demanding righteousness and justice in individual, social, and political life. Plague doctoring offers to treat the disease our culture is now suffering. I am more than the preposterous huckster William Hundwasser has made of me. My intent and my practice transcend the snake oil with which he has lubed his career. With these notes, I will break free of him, and then we shall see how far this train can travel among the highwaymen.

79. Yeah, yeah, if I may be permitted a descending minor 3rd of two positives adding up to a negative. So now he's equating his own H with Homer's.

80. I do not hate. I have never hated anyone. Ever. Not my leave-taking father. Not even my mother. I never hated the kids who teased me at school. What was my response to them? I tried to make them laugh. Hatred is H's projection.

As the reader will see, Hundwasser will go into writing *The Nose* immediately after being rejected by Jessica Kornblum, the Siren of Neuroanatomy. He started to put her into his earlier novel and assign her the part of the

from wherever he had spent the night. He needed something lighter, something easier to carry around. Pan pipes would be good.

And then one day at the Salvation Army, he discovered not only a damn good mulligatawny (or what he imagined was mulligatawny) but a beastly $25 violin and almost hairless bow, lying in their scruffy hand-built case, looking for a home.

Now, $25 was more than he might make in a week of passive begging, but if "salvation" was on offer, this was surely it: he walked out with the beast under his jacket, feeling he had helped the Lord's Pentagon advance its stated goal. Perhaps he would be saved. He might be. He was on his way to sainthood.

Left-Handed Violinist

In der Beschränkung zeigt sich erst der Meister, Goethe observed. It is in confronting limitations that the master first shows himself. In German *vol*, Italian *vil*—the violin is tied fiercely to the will. And what is more fervent than the will of a forty-two-year-old, hungry, angry, frustrated holy man?[81]

He sat on his blanket during the warm days of June and explored Beast's range of tones. The rosinless, hair-depleted bow could hardly draw forth a sound, so he concentrated on his left hand, the hand fate had allowed him. At first he merely played with Beast, then on him, and within a week, he simply played Beast, at once the instrument and himself, for they had fused. He'd quickly found he could do more than pluck the open strings. By striking fingers sharply from above, he could sound any pitch, play any scale, or eke out any tune. He sang silently while playing, duplicating pitch, or adding counterpoint. The Beast was his voice, in soft percussion.

Slender fingertips explored the range of tones: he danced them over every inch of ebony. He found ways all his own to strike and pick—his first and second fingers stopping notes, while ring finger (without a ring, alas) and pinky plucked away up front. Thus he could play a kind of one-handed lute, slowly at first, then ever faster, his rediscovered agility in service to his soul.

Slow Byrd Pavanes and Sweelinck Fantasies he played; and then Scarlatti, floating off in air, and finally the heavenly Bach—a music taught by deepest faith: that readiness—so like his own—to enter unafraid into the beckoning darkness.

willing *amour* of a six-foot white rat—and that's not counting the tail. While he makes a big, honorable deal out of his changing her name in his never-completed *What a Rat!*, you'll notice that in *The Nose*, he names her straight out. It would not take a Sherlock Holmes to go through the Berg Institute directory and find a Jessica with an address on the fourth floor. Does an author have the right to point a fiery public finger at an innocent person who is not a public figure?

I happen to know Jessica Kornblum. I took great pains to meet her when I found out that she had turned down Bill Hundwasser and might therefore be available. Far from being an "eff-ass," she is a beautiful, gentle woman, wise beyond her years, and savvy enough to say thanks-but-no-thanks to that scheming Lothario. She was not interested in anything more than a friendship with me because she already had a boyfriend, a dashing Mexican postdoc named Pablo Rudomin.

Jessica is a truth-seeker. Among other things, she was interested in the truth-value of the proposition in vino veritas. Don't get me wrong: she was not a wino. Rather the opposite. She had never been able to drink anything stronger than Ethiopian honey wine because she hated the taste of alcohol. She had never been drunk. Perhaps unwisely, she invited her new friend Pablo to help her experience whatever veritas was to be had from a bottle of tequila. As was predictable, she hated the taste, so he brought her a large box of Ritz crackers for the experiment. One sip, then one cracker to cover the taste. After three sips she was dizzy, after five, she conked out. That was the end of their second date.

What convinced Jessica about Pablo was that, hot-blooded as he was, he did not take advantage of her unconsciousness. He let himself quietly out the door, though she looked particularly fetching. That's how she knew he was for her. Had she tried to two-time Pablo

81. Again, projection. *Hundwasser* may have been frustrated—about Jessica, about the huge literary and business project he had taken on, so above his natural abilities, perhaps even about the state of the world at the turn of the millennium—for he did have a social conscience, kept well-sequestered, of course, as the dollars rolled in.

Was I frustrated too? No. I was in a state of suspended tantalization, a kind of tense, excited awaiting with no clear object, an inverse, blissful unphobia. I had had my accordion for income, and the use of both my hands. I did buy a violin for $25 from the Salvation Army as an *aide-mémoire* of Lily when her image began to fade in and out of my aging

with H or me, we all would have seen another Pablo, I'm sure, a black belt in machete.

All this to say that Mr. Hundwasser was red-faced, wild-eyed, and furious five days a week, and sometimes on Saturday, when he and Jessica would pass in the hall. With Rudomin, he was cautious.

So which of us was the hater?

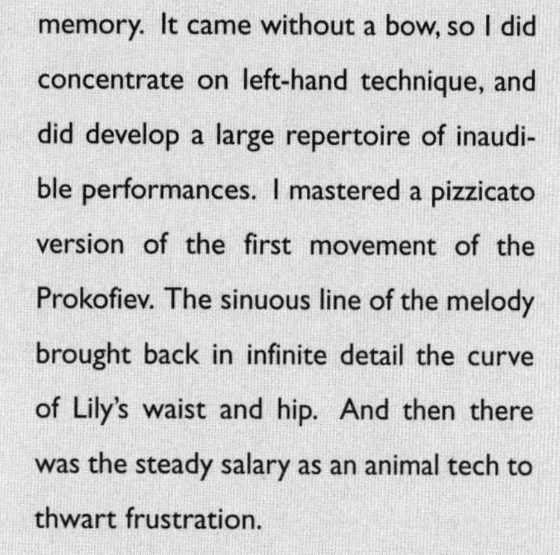

memory. It came without a bow, so I did concentrate on left-hand technique, and did develop a large repertoire of inaudible performances. I mastered a pizzicato version of the first movement of the Prokofiev. The sinuous line of the melody brought back in infinite detail the curve of Lily's waist and hip. And then there was the steady salary as an animal tech to thwart frustration.

Frustration is generally related to the denial of gratification by external reality, i.e., by not getting what one wants. Now, if the concupiscent reader chooses to equate my inability to "get girls" with all gratification by external reality, that is his or her (usually his) right. But he will be wrong. Frustration, as every fifth grader knows, may be definitively eluded by sublimation.

Do you think that had I been awash in the normal post-pubescent soap operas, I could have learned four languages or read 200 books a year? Its original motivation aside, if I had had to spend my weekend nights romancing, could I have mastered the accordion as I did?

The need for immediate instinctual gratification is associated with severe ego weakness. If I had indulged that weakness would I be where I am now?

The saint enjoyed each scintillating sequence and the next, and loved the passage work, the leaps and double stops! He managed scales in high positions with purity of intonation never matched. He mastered complex passages on one string while plucking lower or upper ones, and often sang a third, unearthly cantus. He rejoiced in left-hand pizzicato, arpeggios and chromatic runs whose every note was crisp and spaced. His lightning trills were silver, trembling, a shiver of delight, thrilling, tensionless, imperative. His melodies were elfin in their playfulness—or shattering in profundity, reflecting the strength of his Russian soul within. He would incline his head and bend his left ear to the instrument, attention reaching out. In the tiny sounds he heard an inexhaustible richness, a movement, shape, and motion which left him in serenity and wonder. His neighbor ear, close-inclined of course, was the only one to hear them.

KISS ME, I'M LEFT-HANDED—a button he'd bought for a dime at St. Vincent de Paul's. The symbolism of right hand and left—the former, doer, now defunct, the latter, dreamer, sinister, enabler of the future. Perhaps there was something sinister at play—his uncanny intonation, the icy glitter and demonic virtuosity of his trills, his almost supernatural dexterity and diligence.[82] It might have spooked some people, frightened them. But no one, no passerby, even those who dropped him coins, ever experienced the exalted, passionate music. Amid the din of traffic, it remained, of necessity, his own.

While the sight of his left-hand gymnastics brought in a bit more cash, the passing of summer revealed the weakness of his situation. He could not expose Beast to rain, his fingers would freeze in the snow, and he'd need a place to sleep. Saint or no, he'd likely need a job.

But sainthood does have its perks: the fates tend to favor it, and virtue is not always its own only reward. Walking along Fourteenth Street one raucous autumn afternoon, Saint Pantalone noticed a sign in the window of one of the "Crazy Eddie"–type discount stores still struggling for survival, windows filled with watches, cameras, and electronics with wildly lettered prices; street tables piled with polyester clothing, sunglasses, and souvenir t-shirts; stacks of Naugahyde luggage. The establishment was Punch's Discount Enterprises Center. Its motto was "Everything You Need for Less! Small Appliances, Perfumes, Clothing, Black & Decker, Sony, Calvin Klein." Its submotto was "Guaranteed Lowest-Anywhere Prices!" The sign in its window said, STREET SALESMAN WANTED.

"Hey, you! You with the nose . . ." the guy with the belly shouted from the entryway.

82. To inspire myself to learn the bowless violin, I thought of Paganini. Not that he had no bows; he had many. I saw one of his bows on eBay starting at $25,000. But he, like me, began his virtuoso career relatively late in life, and devoted much time to practicing and introspection. He, like me, had quite a big nose. He, like me, pursued many women. He, like me, became a superstar and was well-off late in life. He, like me, died of laryngeal cancer. Well, I haven't died yet, and don't intend to, but let's just say wrestling with LC is my current sport. And suffice it to say, I've become quieter.

His great rival, Louis Spohr, described him as "a strange mixture of consummate genius, childishness and lack of taste, so that one is alternately charmed and repelled." I've pondered this famous characterization for many years, and thought about myself within it. I'll admit to some sort of genius, however short of consummate, and a constant devotion, as they say today, to honoring my inner child. It is the "lack of taste" that leaves me anxious. Has anything I've done been in bad taste?

My problem is that if any one thing turns out to be tasteless, my entire life, every mask, every character, every thrust and parry, may turn out to be tasteless too. This is a proposition no single person should be asked to consider.

Even someone like John Belushi, who made a career out of being tasteless, must have had a private, tender side, a time for pillow talk with Mrs. Belushi—if there was a Mrs. Belushi other than his mother. He must at some time have reached down to pet a dog, or dandled some friend's baby. But my life, I think, has been more of a piece, and my tender moments probably fewer.

On the other hand, my possible bad taste could not be anywhere as bad as, say, John Belushi's—like asking a comely late-night groupie to inject him with a heroin-cocaine speedball, and then *dying* from it. Talk about bad taste! The poor thing was charged with murder, which, I can assure you, is not a pleasant experience.

"Me?" Saint Pantalexei asked.

"Who else got a nose?"

"Um . . . every . . . Ooooh—you mean this nose," he said fingering his Pantalone proboscis.

"Yeah, that one. You like noses?"

"What do you mean?"

"C'mere. C'mon in. You wanna job? With a big nose?"

Could Deus Ex Machina Christus have spoken more generously or to the point?

"Yes. Sure. I mean, what kind of a job?"

"See that sign in the winda?"

"I did see it. But . . ."

"But what?"

"But I didn't think you would want someone with a big nose."

"Hey, we want someone with an even bigger nose."

Punch's Discount Enterprises Center had lost its barker, the guy who stands out in front sizing up the street, talking up the merchandise, and watching out for thieves. The shtick was that Alexei was to wear a Punch mask—and the one on hand was not the British Punch of the hooked nose but his progenitor, an old Pulcinella from Napoli. The Antari boys didn't know what they had—if they had known, they would have sold it. To them it was just an old prop, a shticky attraction to lure poor suckers off the street and into the store. And the mask could hide the eyes of the countershoplifting operation.

"Trade you that mask for this one," Louie Antari said. "Five bucks an hour. No bennies. You keep up the chatter."

About the chatter, Alexei didn't know. But about the mask, it was yes, yes, yes. And $5 an hour. That was $40 a day, $200 a week, more if he worked on weekends. He'd have enough for a room on Avenue C.

"Okay, I'll make it $5.35," Louie offered, generously upping the salary to mini mum wage.

"I'll give it a try," Alexei said.

The Saint of Fourteenth Street. He could imagine an opera with that title. Saint Punch, yes—a snappy appellation. So he took the mask, swapped it for his own, showed up at Punch's at 9 the next morning, and climbed the soapbox at the front of the entry way.

Pedestrian traffic was still light. He had a chance to warm up and practice. Louie was watching him from the doorway, making him nervous.

"Ladies and gentlemen," he said.

"Louder," said Louie.

"Ladies and gentlemen, step right up . . ."

"No, no, no," said Louie. "This ain't no '50s carny. You gotta get their attention."

"Like how?"

Louie took his place on the soapbox.

"Hey, you idiots," he yelled, "live it up! Shit's on sale! This shit's on sale!"

And the crowd began to form.

"You. Yeah, Mr. Plug-Ugly, you! You better get your ass in here and buy that Hawaiian shirt to distract 'em from your face."

And believe it or not, Mr. Plug-Ugly did just that—bought a Hawaiian shirt in late September.

"See?" Mentor asked his pupil.

"I guess so," Telemachus said.

The teacher went in to ring up the sale, and the pupil remounted the box.

He stood there, dumbly surveying the now streaming workers and shoppers. All he could think was, Fourteenth Street. I wonder if I'll see my sweetheart from the gym. And then Saint Punch spoke softly into Alexei's ear. And the novice holy man understood that seductive women were merely fiendish instruments of misdirection, and his Punch part thought of Judy, and how she looked like Delia, and how he'd like to kill her with a stick.

Saint Punch

We have spoken before of how the mask can make the man, how the exterior lineaments of an applied face can leak inward and penetrate the tongue, the brain, and finally the soul. And an angry Alexei Pigov was particularly permeable to Punchness.

Braggart, thief, liar, coward, the embodiment of villainy and violence—the monster Punch is always victorious; crime always pays; he rides out every storm, innocent of guilt.

And when Saint Punch surveyed Fourteenth Street, the gentrification, the oppressed mixing impotently with the oh-so-innocent oppressors, he could easily feel Punch as the personification of present power. Power that could be his!

So he started with lines he imagined from the play, naked lines whispered to him by the prompter enveloping his skull. To a beautiful Irish lass, examining the sandals:

When the heart of a man is oppressed with cares

he announced,

The clouds are dispelled when a woman appears. . . .

She smiled up at the man in the long-nosed mask. She shouldn't have. "What a pretty creature. Ain't she a beauty?" Punch asked her cohort shoppers.

I love you so, I love you so,
I will never leave you, no, no, no
If I had all the wives of wise King Sol,
I would kill them all for my pretty Poll.

This was getting a little weird for her, so she gave up on a handbag hunt and moved on toward Sixth Avenue, a fish that got away. And too bad too, for Saint Punch was already half in love.

Love! A wife! A family! There was one—over there, complete with babe in backpack.

"Give that child to me!" he yelled to the shocked mother. "I can take care of it as well as you!" The baby, preternaturally threatened, began to cry.

"What's the matter with it?" Saint Punch demanded of the crowd. "Poor thing! It's got the stomack-ache. Get away, nasty baby, before I whack you one with my stick." Not very Papageno.

A stick. He needed a stick to be more convincing. He ran into the store and reemerged with a carved African fetish staff to wave around as a cross-cultural threat. Mother and child had disappeared. "If it doesn't stop crying, she can always get another one," he reassured those left behind.

As yet, he hadn't forced one sale or inconvenienced one shoplifter. He might need another strategy. So he ransacked the pile of stacked luggage and built a rudimentary

puppet stage: a camp-trunk upended for a base, two Samsonite Pullman cases for uprights, with a luggage carrier extended between them, supporting two Pierre Cardin carry-ons to complete the proscenium arch.

"Ecco—voilà!" Saint Punch declared with a flourish as he completed the construction. Now what? A puppet stage with no puppets and no script. His mask kept prompting: kill the baby, kill your wife, kill the constable, kill the crocodile, kill the doctor, kill the hangman. Get him to show you how to put your head in a noose. Kill the devil that comes to claim you. Free yourself, free yourself and free the world! Thus raved the Punch-drunk saint. Internally.

But he had no props. There's a doggie walking along. If only it would bite his nose, he could complain about his nose, his pretty little nose, his beautiful nose—and get them laughing. But dog and master went on by.

There was one prop in the entryway. It wasn't a traditional Punch-&-Judy prop, but he could use it maybe for one of the old scenes. It was the Antaris' monster boom box for playing their disgusting come-on loop of top hits. Saint Punch grabbed it and put it stage center on top of the trunk. He and it could do the bit, *mutatis mutandis*, and call even greater attention to the store.

"Now that I have been elected mayor of the great city of New York," Saint Punch announced, "I have decided to declare a new public policy to reduce the ambient noise level so as to preserve, protect, and promote the public health, safety, and welfare and the peace and quiet of our inhabitants."

Here he turned the boom-box volume up from 5 to 6.

"And also to prevent injury to human, plant, and animal life and property, to foster the convenience and comfort of our inhabitants, and to facilitate the enjoyment of the city's natural attractions."

Volume from 6 to 7. Those Antari boys should be really loving this now.

"Why do this? you may ask. Anybody want to know?"

"Yeah," shouted several in the crowd.

"It is my feeling that every person is entitled to ambient noise levels that are not detrimental to life, health, and enjoyment of his or her property."

Volume from 7 to 8.

" So I hereby declare the making, creation, or maintenance of excessive and unreasonable noise a menace to public health, comfort, convenience, safety, welfare and prosperity, and that all perpetrators . . ."

Volume to 9.

". . . will be apprehended and held as terrorists under section 319 of the USA PATRIOT[83] Act . . ."

Volume to max.

". . . until such time as . . ."

The Antari brothers were, in fact, enjoying this. They stood together ten feet back in the doorway to the store. They were enjoying it right up to the point where Officer Not-So-Friendly stormed in through the crowd, grabbed Saint Punch with one hand, and with the other pushed the $300 Aiwa ghetto blaster off its stage and onto the cement, smashing it into silence.

"Hey, that's our . . ."

"You wanna make something of it, Mac?"

Obstructing a police officer in the course of his duty is a felony offense.

The Antari boys were ticketed for violating the noise ordinance, and Saint Punch was hauled off to the station to be booked. And that was fortunate for him, for after being let off with a warning, the police let him walk away with his priceless mask. Of Deus Ex Machina Christus it might well be said that His yoke was easy and His burthen light.

The ambient temperature was dropping daily as Saint Punch's personal temperature was rising, and furious as he might be about all or most things, he still needed a job. He doubted the Antari boys would take him back after paying out $500 for his *Beschränkung* creativity. He wandered the streets, and his mask sang to him The Song of the Unrepentant Murderer.

And now I hears the bell,
And it's me funeral knell,
And I'll see youse all in hell,
I hopes yer frizzle well,
Damn your eyes.

By the time he had stalked up to Thirtieth Street, he was feeling Ishmael's grimness at the mouth, and made quite consciously for the East River. And sitting on a bench on the generous campus of the NYU School of Medicine, eyeing the pretty young things in their white lab coats (who may, in turn, have eyed him as a wandering psychotic), he

83. Acronyms, I think, bring out the worst in people. For example, the USA PATRIOT act is not an act for American Patriots, as it would appear, but rather the U.S.A.P.A.T.R.I.O.T. Act—Uniting and Strengthening America by Providing Appropriate Tools Required to Intercept and Obstruct Terrorists. Act.

Imagine the wordsmithing over that one. Imagine how many taxpayer dollars went into the choice of those acronymic wonders.

And the marvelous mendacities therein—"uniting," "strengthening," "appropriate," "required"—all hidden behind the mask. Truly a work of the devil.

There are masks that hide, like that one, and masks that reveal, like mine. It's important to distinguish them.

overheard a conversation between two of them that changed the course of his life, and for four years the life of cultic America.

"Prosser's totally pissed," said one.

"Oh, it's not so hard to find lab techs," said the other.

And they passed by.

That was enough. His Alexei brain clicked into action. Sounds like a job opening. A white coat might go well with his sainthood. Purity, shrouds, the whiteness of the whale. Could he fake some science credentials? That remained to be seen.

An inquiry at the main Bellevue Hospital building indicated that there was in fact a Dr. Irwin Prosser at the Berg Institute for Experimental Physiology, Surgery, and Pathology just around the corner. Dr. Prosser was out for a few minutes, but an obliging technician affirmed that, yes, there was a job open for a lab tech, involving mostly animal care, that the position had just become vacant and was not yet posted, but that if Mr. . . . ? Punchino interviewed with Dr. Prosser and was accepted, Prosser would see to the paperwork afterward. Getting someone couldn't really wait, as the rats would starve and things would get nasty.

Good omen—nasty. His mother's sobriquet. His feeling about Homo sapiens, especially girls and women. And rats. Rats! Taking care of rats! Who better than the abandoned, forlorn ex-housemate of the most wonderful G. Garza?

Prosser was impressed with Al Punchino's passion, as who would not be? They quickly hit it off: Saint Punch was hired on the spot. He could start work tomorrow at a salary low for whitecoats but off the charts for him. In the elevator going out, he met the lab tech who had set him up so well.

"How did it go with Prosser?"

"Superbly," the lab saint answered. "I start tomorrow."

"What's the pay?"

"Ten-something an hour."

"Well, that should shoot skyward after your six months' probation."

"You mean I'm only on probation? I can just get fired?"

"Hey, it could be a bad match. Want to pop in across the street for a quick drink? I usually do that before I go home."

"Sure, why not?"

At Pedro's on First Avenue, Bill Hundwasser let Al in on what was going on in Suite 401 of the Berg Institute for Experimental Physiology, Surgery, and Pathology: some research on *Yersinia pestis*, the agent of bubonic plague.

"No real danger—at least in our part of the lab," he explained. "The buggers are still exquisitely sensitive to tetracycline, so even if you got it, you could be cured for 25 cents a day for ten days."

"What about them, the buggers?" the saint asked. "I mean, what's to research?"

"We're just looking at how to cooperate with the fleas in growing them. But the guys up on 14 are playing around with the DNA. Some military project we're not supposed to know about. They got a level-four operation going up there, and . . ."

"What's that?"

"Oh, you know, special containment techniques for superhazardous infectious agents, negative-air-pressure rooms, positive-pressure personnel suits, everything done in biological safety cabinets—Fort Dietrich kind of stuff."

"What's all this for?"

"You think they'd tell us? Biowarfare, I suppose."

"Does Prosser know?"

"Probably. But who can tell? They keep things very compartmentalized."

"What about the fleas?"

"Oh, we've got them too, next room. They're part of the deal."

"Ah."

They left the shop talk at that.

"So you're an accordion player?" Bill asked. He'd overheard the end of the interview.

"Sort of," Al replied. "I burned my hand, so I can't really play. And you?"

"Once played a little guitar, but nah, I'm just a lab tech. And a writer. I'm working on a novel."

"Oh, yeah? What's it about?"

"A guy who works on the plague with lab rats—what else? Write what you know, you know?"

"So what happens?"

"Oh, like the rats take over the lab, and my guy winds up in a cage. Stuff like that."

"Science fiction."

"Yeah, sort of. There's a love interest, of course."

The saint's ears pricked up.

"Somebody in the lab? I mean is she patterned after somebody in the lab?"

"Well, yeah, sort of. You'll meet Jessica."

The saint felt his Scorpio rising.

"That your sweetie?"

"I should be so lucky," Hundwasser said. "She won't give me the time of day. But I get my revenge—she becomes the sex slave of the alpha rat."

"Really?"

"Yeah. See, the lab has been doing hormone experiments, and this main rat gets really big, human size, kind of the sleek, strong, silent type. Adrienne—that's Jessica—gets off on him. It's all very hush-hush, but little by little the relationship leaks out. Terrific ending. Symbolic of Faustian overreach and the bestialization of man."

"So what happens?"

"I don't know yet. I'm waiting to get inspired."

Since it takes two to do the *Yersinia* tango, Al Punchino became not only master of the rats but master of the fleas. He would keep the rat farm healthy, happy, and holy and introduce and harvest the fleas on selected populations. He did his own little experiments, investigating flea breeding as a function of rat diet. His results were published in the *American Journal of Laboratory Animal Research* 127 (June 2005), pp. 77–78. For this, he was given a raise.

But more important, he found a new G. Garza—Max—a most intelligent boar with the brightest of eyes. And more important than that, he took his first steps in creating the Famous Flying Flonzaly Flea Circus Company.

The FFFFCC[84] began with a small infestation of escapees from room 401B, which showed up in his bed at his new apartment on Second Avenue. As long as he was fated to have fleas, he thought, why not really have them, own them, use them, make them as beloved and famous as they deserved? What other animal can jump four hundred times its own height? And train them. Train them not to bite inappropriately, to wait patiently for regular feedings.

Yes, Virginia, there really are such things as trained fleas and their employments. Flea orchestras have played audible flea music for flea dancing couples in dresses and frock coats at great flea balls. Other fleas have been harnessed to miniature coaches or warships, some costumed as Napoleon and the Duke of Wellington. Flea circuses were featured in circus sideshows in the United States for decades. Given the size of the per-

84. My reverence for the flea is unmatched, even by my reverence for Paganini. Like Paganini, fleas are gargantuan performers, stars of astonishing, high-jumping feats, trillions of tiny Stefan Holmses, buoyed on the supreme winds of the insect soul.

It may not be apparent to the reader, but my training achievements with the FFFFCC were made not with common dog and cat fleas (*Ctenocephalides canis* and *Ctenocephalides felis*)—, as were the achievements of previous flea-circus masters—but with the fleas endemic to Berg's fourth floor, i.e., *Xenopsylla cheopis*, the rat fleas responsible for transmitting bubonic plague. *Xenopsylla cheopis*, truly one of God's wonders. *Xenos*, foreign, strange, as in "xenophobia." The strange flea *cheopis*, coming perhaps from Egypt, land of Cheops, the king who built the Great Pyramids, one of the Seven Wonders of the Ancient World.

In this world you take what you get, even though it was the redoubtable fourteenth floor that was

formers, the potential audience at each show was tiny, groups in a few chairs surrounding a small table—but up to fifty times a day.

Low-level "training" involved rigging the insects up with wire harnesses so they could only move in a particular way. If necessary—say, in a flea orchestra—the fleas might also be glued to their seats. And what did PETA have to say about this? There was no PETA then.

But fleas from the Berg Institute for Experimental Physiology, Surgery, and Pathology deserved better than that—and they got it: genuine Pigovian conditioning of the flea belief system, developed from scratch by Saint Punch, Master of Fleas, based on his own life experiences with women. Here, for example, was his method of teaching them to hang out. The achievement was far greater than creating a herd of cats:

Through Dr. Prosser, Al Punchino was able to have constructed a two-foot Plexiglas cylinder with a finely calibrated piston for a ceiling. Without its top, a hundred fleas would simply jump free within seconds. With the ceiling, however, after a period of smashing themselves, they would jump less high, less hard, so as not to bang their little heads, and then less and less high and hard, until they veered off with a half inch to spare below the lid. The ceiling was then lowered—a foot and a half, a foot, eight inches—and each time the same lowering of insect expectations occurred. At six inches, the saint removed the roof entirely—yet not one flea chose to jump free. The cohort of one hundred would remain that way for the rest of its life, believing it unwise to jump more than five and a half inches high. This is real training. He published his results in the *Journal of Applied Behavior Analysis* 34 (Fall 2006), pp. 43–46. Again he received a salary increase.

Fleas can and must be trained, not wired or glued. Without proper training, they have no idea what to do: they'll just hop around all over the place without ever accomplishing anything. But with the pedagogy of the emerging Famous Flying Flonzaly Flea Circus Company, they could tightrope-walk or dive from a high board into a saucer of water; they could jump through flaming hoops or be shot from cannons into tiny nets; they could pole-vault and ride in bareback teams on mice.

Saint Punch published his results in *Spectacle: An International Circus Journal* (Fall 2007), 11–13. This was not a peer-reviewed publication, so there was no increase in salary.[85]

responsible for the choice. Whether this made my task harder or easier I don't know. But since originality and imaginative exaltation have never flourished among fleas, I think we can assume the three species are IQ-equivalent.

Xenopsylla cheopis's role in transmission of the plague is as much that of martyr as of perpetrator. Their poor tiny intestines become blocked when loaded with *Yersinia pestis* cells, and they can't feed normally, and are thus forced to attack humans, against their wills. They do have wills, you know, as any flea trainer can attest. Yet via martyrdom, they carry the full totemic power of the plague. According to the historical literature, these little guys have brought on ominous portents: heavy mists, falling stars, blasts of hot wind from the south, blood spots on freshly baked bread, even stranded whales. My very own sweeties! Well, not alone; of course there are the bacilli—

Have you heard of the deadly bacillus,
The deadly bacillus
that threatens to kill us?

Ring around a rosy. *Yersinia pestis.*

And of course, the rat, *Rattus R. rattus*, the middle R standing for "Rat" and thus the famous three Rs, aka R3, of which G. Garza was a prime specimen, and for all I know, may still be.

Rats, too, are amazing. A single pair of rats could—given three litters a year, with ten young in each, abundant food, shelter, and zero mortality—increase in five years to something over 940 billion. Do the math. And this could be small potatoes: in NYC, the observed record reproductive rate was seven litters in seven months. Do *that* math!

If it weren't for overstuffed New York dumpsters filled with half-eaten Whoppers and pizza crusts, rats would control their own population by cannibalizing one another. But as it is, New York City embodies the highest realm of rat heaven. There are buildings with third-level subcellars, structures that date back to the Revolutionary War. And in them, revolutionary rats, R2, perhaps the original Founding rat Fathers. Even *I* would hesitate to visit. But man, rat–New York, whooie! You get rats coming up out of the toilet bowl—Mark Spitz, Esther Williams rats. Alive.

The fourteenth floor, for their own ominous reasons, seems to be working on bubonic plague. When a human contracts bubonic plague with no antibiotics available (much

85. You can see I was well on my way in the wondrous world of *Wissenschaft*, and might have successfully worked my way to the top of the lab-tech career ladder but for a fateful conversation one happy hour at Pedro's. Hundwasser, it seemed, had had a brainstorm. I will report it verbatim, since it has burned its way,

of the world has no antibiotics available), there is a four-fifths chance he or she will die within two weeks. The incubation period runs from two to eight days. Then, flu-like symptoms, with high fever. Then, buboes—black welts and bulges—in groin or armpits, varying in size but all extremely painful, and diarrhea and vomiting don't help. This is the crisis stage. If one kicks it now, one kicks it. But four out of five enter the third stage—pneumonia and respiratory failure, heart failure, internal hemorrhaging, or exhaustion. In the '80s there were three documented cases of bubonic plague in California. Not enough for floor Fourteen, I guess.

Back in the good old days, there were no fourteenth floors. In cottages and slums, windows were closed and covered. The upper classes hung thick tapestries. (Those late-medieval tapestries in the Cloisters were functional, not just decorative.) Frequent bathing was seen as dangerous—one's pores might open to receive the miasma of venomous atomies.

The miasma! Or whatever it was: if not some bad astrology involving a conjunction of Saturn, verbatim, into my life. Are there such things as fourth-degree burns?

We sat down at the bar.

"OK, man," he said, "enough of this lab-tech stuff. You and I are gonna get filthy rich: it came to me in a dream."

"Yeah, yeah, yeah. Does that mean you're buying?"

"No, man. I said we're *gonna* get rich. We're not rich yet. Pay for your own."

"OK, let's hear it."

A mistake, perhaps, for me to ask, but consequential.

"I have a dream, man. And here it is. You're a funny guy, you know? Not ha-ha funny, just peculiar. With that Punch mask and all, and your left-hand fiddle, and your non-girlfriends, and your rats and your fleas."

"So?"

"So put 'em all together, they might spell a million bucks. I mean, you're a character, right? We should market you. And we each get fifty percent."

"But there's only one of me. What do you want to do, put me up on eBay? An adorable Al Punchino doll? To compete with Barbie and the Hulk?"

"Damn straight. But we're going to go them one better—First there'll be a book . . . a novel. A real big, long adult novel. Complex, literary, full of references and things like that. Philosophical. With Faustian overreach—you know. Symbolic. The bestialization of man."

"(!)"

"Weren't you already writing something along those lines?"

"Oh, I don't know, it didn't really work out. The rat-gets-girl thing was getting too skanky, even for me."

There was something vaguely intriguing about all this. Maybe it was just amusing. Still, I was wary. Who wouldn't be?

"Bill, may I ask you something?"

"Sure."

"You won't get mad?"

How I Long to Be in That Number

Shortly after this disappointment, Saint Punch of the Fleas received a square envelope in the mail, on heavy paper, addressed in a familiar hand:

Almighty God,
Creator of heaven and earth,
sovereign ruler of the world,
and the most glorious Virgin Mary,
queen and princess of the heavenly court,
invite you to be present at the marriage of their Son,
Jesus, King of kings and Lord of lords, to Miss Delia Robinson.

What in the name of Beelzebub was going on? His pursuer going off with someone else? Becoming a nun or something, was she?

On the one hand, he felt relieved, but the other hand was more disturbing. Not quite jealousy—who could be jealous of the King of kings?—but some inchoate mix of insecurity and self-blame, a momentary loss of self-esteem, perhaps resentment that she, and not he, had been able to open the godly door, and finally a tinge of pity that she would never experience the putative joy of carnal intercourse, which still awaited him. Why would a woman ever want that?

Perhaps it was he that had driven her to it, the loss of his affections, the alienation from what she must have thought his great worth that had driven her to this extreme. So with the cuckold's loss of self-esteem came a compensating flood of awe at how wonderful he might appear to some, to at least one woman, even if she were a dwarf. He felt like crowing, but didn't.

Mars, and Jupiter, then probably some Jewish conspiracy. Jews, as was widely rumored, might spread the plague by poisoning wells, like Yippies putting LSD in the reservoirs.

Various news organizations reported rainstorms of frogs, serpents, lizards, scorpions, and many other kinds of venomous beasts, like color-coded threat levels. Why was all this happening? There were different theories of cause, usually centering upon indecent clothing, corrupt clergy, disobedient children, and the general immorality of the populace. Where have I heard that before?

People prayed to relevant saints—St. Roch, tended by his faithful dog (no doubt covered in fleas), who had recovered from the plague; or even better, St. Sebastian, slain by multiple arrows, which, metaphorically sharpened, became associated with the plague-arrows of God.

Aside from no bathing and the stink of rotting corpses and their buboes, things didn't smell so good anyway. Many people bathed in urine or stood for a long time in latrines so that they might repulse the bad air with odors still

"Shoot."

"Um, except for Faustian overreach and the bestialization of man, do you think you, like, know enough to write a complex, philosophical literary work? I mean, your language, the way you talk, is . . . well, it just doesn't seem like you could . . . "

"You don't have to write like you talk. Too pedantic. You ever hear Saul Bellow talk? Do you write like you talk? I'm much smarter than I talk. Way well-read. Besides, you can help, contribute ideas, references, some of your polysyllabic words. Sesquipedalian, ha! You can edit the book even, help ghostwrite it. Tell about your childhood, like that. You and I can get together, do some hash . . . look what hashish did for Walter Benjamin. We could write like that. Benjamin, Foucault, Baudelaire—hey, Louisa May Alcott was a hash-head. We could have another *Uncle Tom's Cabin* on our hands!"

"Who is Walter Benjamin?" I asked. Maybe I should have gone to college.

"Who is Walter Benjamin? Don't get me started. Where you been, man? The major intellectual force of our generation. And Foucault? You heard of him?"

"No."

"Christ, man, I don't know if I *want* you as a writing partner! He's the philosopher of our time. Like what's the role of power in shaping ideology, in shaping our sense of self. Is that important, or what?"

"I guess I'll have to read them."

"I guess so. There'll be a quiz on Monday."

"And Walter Benjamin and Foucault are going to sell the adorable Al Punchino doll?"

"Yeah, sure. The book'll open up a new market—educated, upscale parents who apply their kids to Harvard in utero. Benjamin. Foucault. We get reviews in the *New York Times*, the *New York Review*, they'll get excited and buy the doll for the kids. And that'll be a first, a cultural phenomenon, and we'll sell it to Hollywood."

It was true that Delia had been somewhat pissed by Alexei's mother asking her to leave his bedside, but it wasn't that, or his diffidence, that had started the ball rolling on her journey toward the Holy Spirit. Rather it was a chance conversation she had overheard on the Third Avenue bus, on her way from her final hospital visit, and an overhead poster she'd stared at as she'd heard it.

She was sitting in front, in the seats reserved for the elderly and disabled. Though she considered herself neither, she knew that she took longer to descend the steep steps at the front of the bus, and that things went faster for others if she could make an early start on her exit. A beefy young woman across the aisle was addressing her cell phone.

"Y'ever notice how they keep Christ on their crosses? Don't they know He's risen? What are they doing, worshipping death?"

Her interlocutor must have agreed, for the speaker continued,

"Yeah, it's weird, Catholics are weird. And y'know, they worship Mary—like she's a Goddess."

The conversation changed to finding a time to get together, but Delia contemplated the religious contentions all the way from Fourteenth Street to Fifty-seventh. She had never thought about the different crosses. In all the churches she had been in, the cross was just the cross. Some had bodies on them, some not. Some were modern and arty, some plain and self-effacing. But she realized the fat woman was right. All the writhing bodies were in Catholic churches or carried by Italians in their Catholic parades. What was that? Why was that? What did non-Catholics want, Easter Sunday without Good Friday, having-risen without crucifixion? The tenanted cross seemed so much more evocative of the painful world she knew.

And then the Mary thing. Wasn't it good for Christians to have a woman figure to venerate? Didn't it soften the world of sternness and sacrifice called forth by other sects? Wasn't the Catholic world—for all its denial of priesthood for women—more valuing of women than the Puritan world that had martyred Hester Prynne and her descendants? Weren't the Catholics at the forefront of liberation theology, the professors of "a preferential option for the poor"?

While having these thoughts, and to avoid appearing as if she were listening in on a private phone call, she kept her eyes raised to the space over the fat woman's head, the line of advertising posters with their 800 phone numbers and websites. A little to the left was a poster that caught her eye, a bucolic scene sponsored by the Poor Clares of Perpetual Adoration in Rahway, New Jersey. VOCATION, NOT VACATION, it announced, in spiteful negation of its neighbor, an ad for Princess Cruises.

more foul. It was really hard to get together over a meal.

The good old days without fourteenth floors. Who would you rather have generating miasmas: God, or guys with PhDs?

Have you noticed how interested we have gotten in plagues? Perhaps my own appearance began it. But then, since 9/11, John Adams's recent opera at the BAM based on Bergman's *Seventh Seal*; the hugely popular Met exhibit of plague art, "Hope and Healing: Painting in Italy in a Time of Plague, 1500 to 1800"; Steven Tanis's and Fred Wessel's latest paintings; the re-publication of Camus's *The Plague* as an Oprah selection . . . all this attests to a state of corrosive public anxiety in an age of biological WMDs—anthrax, smallpox, or avian flu. Certainly those who breathed the odors near Manhattan's "ground zero" must have experienced an atavistic shock of historical recognition. Many people, prompted by the yellow media, seem to be spending their days trying to control their fears. For a while we thought that "Science" had all this under control. But now we are edging back toward the good old days of incompetence and helplessness.

Bill sucked on his Bud while I sipped my club soda.

"Why would anyone want to even know about me, much less have a doll of me?" Obvious question, no?

"Well, I've got that figured. It's true: you're not very attractive as you are. Or even interesting. But this mask stuff, and the rats and the fleas—what does that make you think of?"

"Al Punchino at the Berg Center."

"No, man, think out of the box. Out—of—the—box! Mask, rats, fleas: a *plague doctor*! You ever see those pictures of the medieval plague doctors with their big beaks and thick glasses, and wax-covered gowns, and gloves and wands? You'd look great in a getup like that."

I would, I thought; I might very well look great.

"And the nose would be bigger?" I asked.

"The beak, yeah. It could fit right over this one."

He tweaked my Punchly snout.

"You know what the beak was for?" Bill asked.

"Not really."

"They stuffed flowers and plants in there—to keep out the germs or whatever they thought it was, the stink of the rotting buboes, the gangrene. . . . "

"They didn't know about germs," I said. "They thought it was miasma—some kind of poisonous atmosphere, maybe a punishment from God."

"There you go—see?—you're improving it already. *Miasma*, that's great. Great word. *Miasma*. We'll get miasma in there."

"In the novel?"

"In the novel, sure, but also in other ways. Like we can have miasma events like in movie theaters at midnight, with lots of people dressed up as plague doctors, doing plague doctor healings, singing plague doctor songs, dancing plague doctor dances. You can make all that shit up, right? And we can sell them the plague doctor costumes, like in an LL Bean catalog, incorporate Miasma Inc.—or Ltd., that'd be classier. A line of goggles, of plague doctor wands. There'll be plague bands, miasma music like the *Grosse*

Now, Delia's middle name was Clare. She rarely used it, and most often to fill in the blank for middle initial: C. So she was in a sense a poor Clare, without a job, without a significant other, without a family this side of the Atlantic, and with only a middle initial.

A vocation sounded good. Delia Clare Robinson put on her glasses to read the finer print:

> We live in poverty, chastity, and obedience in community life in a spirit of joyful hope and servant love. Our spirituality is based on the Augustinian tradition of religious life in the Church and emphasizes a special love for Jesus Christ in the Holy Eucharist. Our daily prayer includes Mass, Liturgy of the Hours, meditation on Sacred Scripture, Rosary, spiritual reading, and devotion to the Blessed Sacrament. Join us?

"Joyful hope and servant love." It was those words, on the Third Avenue bus, that tweaked her in a direction that would transform her life. She didn't know beans about the Augustinian tradition, or whether a "special love for Jesus" represented some sort of heretical turning away from the doctrine of the Trinity. She felt predisposed to poverty, was seemingly assigned to chastity, and might not be bad at obedience if there were a someone or something worthy to obey. From Forty-sixth to Fifty-seventh, it seemed to her as if she had the right psychology for commitment. This poor Clare would love to give herself humbly and wholly to a cause, to surrender up the dross of her existence. She would love to be in love, to marry herself to her beloved forever. But was Jesus the right guy? Becoming a nun would pay the rent, but did she really want to live in a convent with a whole bunch of "sisters" she hadn't chosen as friends, much less as roomies?

Such were the aleatoric and humble roots of the invitation Alexei held in his hand. Slowly, but with gathering speed, Delia began to explore them. Web searches at the public library, writing away for materials, correspondence with the vocation directors of several orders—each day made the possibility of a cloistered life seem more attractive.

> Reverend Mother Prioress
> Carmelite Monastery of the Sacred Hearts
>
> Dear Reverend Mother Prioress,
> I am a twenty-six-year-old woman who is seriously contemplating applying to your convent as a novice. My mother was a skeptical Catholic, but she did once take me to

Which makes my analysis and presentation of the current plague that much more crucial and significant. Using the costume and metaphor of the old, I make the primitive appear progressive, I ask the public to understand its transformation to the new, to acknowledge the sublimation of disease from the physical world into mental, cultural, and political dimensions. Let us attend to the plague that really matters. I am at present its one true prophet, as necessary to the contemporary West as Jeremiah was to 6th-century B.C. Jerusalem.

But I was talking about my pet fleas.

One of the dangers of climate change is that as the ice sheets melt, and bacterial spores and viruses defrost, we could see a public health catastrophe should they then spread bygone bacterial strains to which we have absolutely no resistance. Civilized order would collapse, social forms disintegrate, and any and every infringement of morality prevail—with its attendant psychological disasters. Christ would certainly die in any new pandemic.

That is why it's so important to meditate on fleas and spend time with flea circuses. Fleas are cute. They're relatively smart. They demonstrate massive innocence. They allow one to examine more correct dimensions, as I do. Oedipus, after all, brought plague to Thebes *without* rats or fleas. And our *Fuge,* you can go on *Oprah*. Everything will sell everything else—the novel sells the doll; the doll sells the novel, and the accessories, doll accessories, and costume accessories, like for Halloween for the kids, and tony parties for the grown-ups. And then we can pitch a movie, maybe an underground documentary first, documentaries are big now, and then a high-budget production with big-name stars. You know, a chase sequence and explosions. I'm telling you, this is a million-dollar idea, a hundreds-of-millions-dollar idea. It can't fail—it's just too weird to fail."

I had to admit this was some pretty advanced thinking—for Hundwasser. And not entirely unappealing.

"It's true it wouldn't take much investment out front. We could both keep our jobs. . . ." I said.

"Right, until we say bye-bye to Prosser and Berg and eff-ass Jessica, who, believe me, will be sorry as shit she didn't grab me while I was available. . . ."

"But if it didn't work, we'd still have our jobs."

"It's *going* to work, man, it's got to work. Who is weirder than you? And weird is good, right? Weird is in. Everybody is tired of straight and normal. You'd be the ultimate retro, man, the black plague—thirteenth century . . ."

"Fourteenth."

"See? Good work! That's what an editor is for."

"So, uh, what do you see me doing?" I asked.

"First thing is we have to get you a plague doctor costume. Maybe you don't wear it at work—that might be a little too weird. . . . "

"Or I might explain it as part of a rat and flea experiment."

"Yeah, sure. Everybody gives you a wide sway by now. See, man, I knew you'd love it."

"All right, so then what do I do in a plague doctor costume?"

"Who knows? You fight the plague. You find plagues and

Lourdes in an unsuccessful attempt to transform me from the achondroplastic dwarf I am to a "normal" child. My experiences on that trip have remained with me and now seem to be blossoming as my religious understanding matures.

I would like to pursue with you the possibility of entering the Carmelite novitiate. Although I am in great sympathy with the service orders of the Church, at my age, and with my "disability," it feels more correct for me to seek out a contemplative life. I have been a nurse and am an artist drawn more and more to religious subjects. While I have never lived in an intentional community, I know many who have, and was drawn to their stories. I do think I am the right psychological type to succeed in such a situation.

I need help in making such a large decision. May I write you further?

Sincerely,
Delia C. Robinson

Carmelite Monastery of the Sacred Hearts
8540 Kenosha Dr.
Colorado Springs, CO 80908-5004

Dear Miss Robinson,

You are old enough to understand that, simply put, I am not the one to help you make this decision. Only you can answer the question that Jesus is now putting to you—you in conversation, deep, face-to-face dialogue, with our Lord.

Though you feel confused, your immediate path seems clear—to deeply examine God's role in your life. What is God's will for you? Not what do you want, or how can you best serve, but what does HE want? The way to such an answer is to truly seek Jesus in your heart, and to build an ever-stronger prayer life in concert with Him. He will guide you to the truth you seek.

The secular world can never fill a heart that was made for Christ alone. If you find that yours is such a heart, I would be happy to correspond with you further concerning your joining us and planning an initial visit.

Sincerely,
Sr. Margaret Doyle
Prioress, Carmelite Monastery of the Sacred Hearts[86]

Correspond they did, and the visit to Colorado Springs was productive. Perhaps it was the return to sea level after a week at six thousand feet that made her sanguine enough to seriously consider the letter that arrived from Dordogne:

plague is above all a kind of psychic entity. It is our spiritual pathology we must attend to.

fight them. You send out press releases. You have a blog, a website, you do interviews. We get you out there."

"And what do you do?"

"Hey, it's my idea. And I write the book and get it published. We can figure out what you do in the book—you can make suggestions—and then you do them, do those things. Only what you feel comfortable doing, of course. I'll get you gigs. I'm telling you, the papers will eat it up. That costume. They'll do think pieces on you, on the contemporary plague, or what did you call it? The poison?"

"Miasma?"

"Yeah, miasma. The contemporary miasma. I'm gonna write that down."

You think *The Nose* could have become a big hit novel if he had put that conversation in there? If the fans knew how cynical the whole scheme was? But I guess Wilde was right: nothing succeeds like excess.

Strange as it may seem, I felt less angry at the world after this session at Pablo's, less nasty. It wasn't so much the plague that inspired me as the idea of healing, *tikkun*, healing the broken world. Maybe I'd been wearing a lab coat for too long, but the notion of becoming a doctor at my age—without even bothering with medical school—seemed most alluring. Hey, Dr. Bronner also wore goggles, and was somewhat less weird than I was—and *he* got rich. So getting rich was not out of the question—though getting rich, per se, no longer interested me. Just getting by was fine, if I could do some good in the world. A living wage, right livelihood, that would be enough.

And a doctor would be more likely to succeed than a saint—though I have to say that doctors at the University of Paris, citing Aristotle, attributed the plague to a conjunction of Saturn, Mars, and Jupiter on March 20, 1345, at 1 P.M.

86. I wish I had known about these letter exchanges. Having had similar thoughts at a similar time, I might have been of some help.

It is fascinating how people who have shared important experiences on one level may henceforth find themselves involved in other parallel ones—as if two

Auberge Littéraire
44 Rue du Petit Sol
Bergerac, 24100 France

Dearest Delia,
We loved the mountain postcard, and will follow with interest your further engagement with the Carmelites there. Pikes Peak is surely preferable as an object of veneration to Cheyenne Mountain, home of much that drove us back to France.
But Mother and I both had the same idea: if you are considering a closed Carmelite convent, why not go for broke and investigate Ste. Thérèse's old place at Lisieux? It's only a day's drive from here, and we'd love to be close enough to see you occasionally, if only through a grille.
You know, of course, that Ste. Thérèse was called "The Little Flower," a name that always reminds us of you. And she pursued her lovely "Little Way," discovering the holiness in routine and ordinary things of everyday life, without living in fear of God's judgment. Again, much like you, I suspect. And remember your Virgin Mary doll?
We want to invite you to come visit (we'll pay), and we'll all go together to Lisieux to visit the convent and set up appointments for consultation. What do you think? Give us a call.
Love,
Y'r dad

So visit she did. The Auberge Littéraire was Charles and Danielle's playground, a project Delia had heard much about but had never seen. Six and a half guest rooms, each fashioned around a defining author of his century. Villon's room a prison cell, with a gallows looming in a faux window; Rabelais's a monk's cell in the Abbey de Thélème, with "*Faites ce que vous voudrez*" over the door, a room in which many things, presumably, were accomplished. La Fontaine's room was fitted with a huge statue of Jupiter, as per the fable, and Diderot's was lined with books and a reprint of the *Encyclopédie.* Baudelaire's featured a huge clock, "*dont le doigt nous menace et nous dit: Souviens-toi!*" Beckett's was the Endgame room, complete with throne but fitted out behind a screen with Proust's narrow bed. The half room was up in the attic, Alfred Jarry's room, its ceiling five feet high, to be shared with three stuffed owls and a terrarium full of chameleons. Perfect for weirdos, masochists, and tiny Delia, who was neither.

Once each month, in one of the rooms, the guests would sprawl on beds and floor while Charles held a seminar on the literary century evoked, complete with dramatic

separate wire strands, once braided, must somehow share the same current, regardless of in what directions they separately head from their encounter.

A kind of spiritual induction process, apparently, ranging from typical parental misguidance to the timeless inspiration of true love.

"For Jupiter, being wet and hot, draws up evil vapors from the earth, and Mars, because it is immoderately hot and dry, then ignites the vapors, and as a result there were lightnings, sparks, noxious vapors, and fires throughout the air."

This does not inspire my confidence in medical wisdom. And doctors in general have a bad rap these days. They make too much.

But, I thought, what about the combination of a doctor *and* a saint? That might turn out to be a winner. *Similia similibus curantur*, they say: like cures like. So a beaksome doctor might cure the disease of too-much-money, even in the face of society's obscene forces of recuperation, while a saint might address the metaphysical etiology. Together, I thought, the two might embody a lyric of nonconformist healing of our cynical sentimentalism. To paraphrase Hegel, "the beak that inflicts the wound may also be the beak that heals it."

After all, remember the not-too-distant news story of the Chicago bus driver who, being bored with his job, just decided to drive to Florida? He gave those who wanted to a chance to get off at their intended stops, and then headed southeast. The kicker was that seven out of the nine passengers elected to go with him! They were stopped in Indiana, and he was arrested. The passengers were transported back "home."

I take that as proof conclusive that the plague doctor's time has come. People are ready to cast aside the fetters of everyday routine, to escape the chains of the reality police, to disremember the present, and to set out on a heroic adventure to unravel the future of the Future.

Doctor-saint: a pregnant strategy, don't you think? It embraces the much-valued upscale, mobile lifestyle of a macho hero, a lifestyle revolving around leisure, centered on looks, images, and consumption. Whereas—at the same time!—I *have* no looks, and I don't consume. And thus I

readings of selected works. Danielle gave French lessons three times a week—part of the service complète. All this was a big hit on the intellectual Elderhostel circuit.

In 1955, its first year of operation, the Auberge Littéraire (Jarry's room) had housed the ex-prisoner Jean Gênet, whose play *Le Balcon* was inspired by its program. There is now a plaque to that effect in the entrance hall.

Delia, raised bilingually, dusted off her French, and the family, minus Nicole, now a professor of linguistics in Beijing, had a gay old time in the Citroen on a leisurely, picnic-filled excursion to Lisieux, a trip that would result in a six-year rite of passage.

Evolution of the Bird

Great minds against themselves conspire. From would-be saint, to would-be Nobel Laureate for Animal Research, to wannabe healer and even—strange as it may seem—Plague Doctor became Alexei's tortured path over the next few months. His first problem was to pick a name.

The historical Paphnutius, the eyeless, kneeless fourth-century bishop, had little to do thematically with Alexei's ultimate choice. If anything, Alexei suffered from an organ surfeit, not its opposite. However, the name called him, and strongly so. The "noosh" clearly pointed in the right direction, while the "shuss" sounded as familiar as the airflow through his chronically congested nose. "Nutius" sidled up against "luscious" on the right and "nauseous" on the left, an accurate evocation of his understanding of the world. And "pap"—for one who had longed so long to caress even one of them—need more be said?

Paphnutius, then, it was, Paphnutius the Plague Doctor. Should he be Dr. Paphnutius? No, for then he might be confused with some common MD of Mediterranean origin, some practitioner from New Jersey. That such a name would be too complex for the mouths and memories of his fans, he could not have predicted. The world would come to know him simply as "The Nose," while he would know the secret shorthand involved. Paphnutius the Plague Doctor it was and would be, internally and eternally, till death might him part from this plague-ridden world.

Next came the costume. There was good historical documentation on which to build: on the head a hat, and goggles to protect the eyes, the face covered with a birdlike mask—a long-beaked bird like an ibis—and in the beak, a potpourri of odorous

exercise the power of being fully inside a tradition—while at the same time marshalling all its resources with the paradoxical intent of undoing its terms.

My saint-part, of course, is attached to Nothing. A saint first renounces evil, then men, and, breaking off bits of the world, finally lets go of everything in himself that is not Virtue until he himself is only Nothingness, relating to God alone. This is still my agenda—with its strong association with flea-like martyrdom, an overriding value in an age of whiny victimization.

Of course, everything in this world does disappoint, even sanctity. Nevertheless I, St. Dr. Paphnutius, would proudly wear the scapular of the Order of Impossible Salvation.

Why is God so dull, so feeble, so inadequately picturesque? Not to be immodest, but He might do well to learn some tricks from me. Humility does have its contradictory pride.

medicinal herbs to filter the inbreath. Below the mask, the body enveloped in a long black linen gown, waxed on the outer surface to repel sticky fluids; under the gown, high leather boots with built-up soles to raise the wearer above contamination. In the hand, a baton for palpating contagious victims, for moving clothing aside, and for repulsing those who would approach too near.

Hundwasser and Alexei found that black oilcloth would save them the trouble of waxing and that normal Japanese geta sandals could be strapped to standard army-navy store hip boots—a footwear style that generated the characteristic gait of serious Nosies.

The creation of the mask fell to Alexei alone. It would be necessary for him to start from scratch, as no nose in history had even approached Paphnutius's in magnitude—fully out to arm's length.

He sculpted the head out of clay. Papier-mâché would not be strong enough to support the cantilevered weight of ibis beak plus stuffings, and the paint and varnish would not tolerate its projected use for long periods in all weather. He did not know the Sartori family's secret process with leather, but he'd heard of another solution.

Celastic® is a resin-impregnated fabric available in theater-supply stores which, when dipped in acetone, can be laid on any shape, wedged into its angles for fine detail, and left to dry. In fifteen minutes, one can lift off the Celastic® and have a lightweight, perfect mask, easily gessoed and painted, weatherproof, waterproof, permanent.

This Alexei did. The eyeholes were large enough to accept industrial welding goggles. The mask was a masterpiece far exceeding any he'd previously worn.

Finally came the slogan and the associated deportment training. Paphnutius suggested, "Voracious consumerism and corporate greed have created a plague corrosive of culture." Hundwasser thought it too long.

Paphnutius: "Why is there such a fearful stench all over the world that one has to stop up one's nose?"

Hundwasser noted that this was six words longer.

"The world preaches a million sermons on vanity while millions of bureaucrats are diligently plotting death!"

No.

Finally they agreed on something short and punchy: THE PLAGUE IS EVERYWHERE![87]

The rest is history.

87. And of course, the plague is everywhere—the emptiness plague, the devotional plague, the promotional plague, the plague of militarism and planned undoing of others. But none of this would be possible in an ever more savvy world but for the underlying plague of plagues: the plague of BEING SCRIPTED BY OTHERS.

9. Plague Doctors

It takes only a small class of others—armed with the vast power of mass media and advanced techniques of thought control—to direct not only what we do, what we buy, but actually who we are. Hundwasser got to make me up, to imprison my life in his idiotic dungeon. But that's just the tip of the iceberg for the larger problem of scriptwriting for the many by the self-chosen few.

We all postulate our internal freedom, our ultimate sovereignty, our sensibility and admiration of beauty, our passionate seeking of the world, our tensions and bedazzlements. But that freedom has as much reality as an animated cartoon, the animation done by a micro-megastudio of "animators"—those who give us life, and show us its menu—two kinds of crust, thick or thin, and a small choice of toppings.

I know—you are thinking of skipping this ranting note, but believe me, this is late wisdom. Hundwasser wrote an exploitation novel: these are not exploitation notes.

However, this is also America, and you are free to go back to Hundwasser's Oprahization of my life and complex thought. Go ahead, buy the latest Nose merchandise and spend tonight at a Nose event instead of reading Foucault.

Foucault? Why, you can just read old Mumford waving to us from 1956:

> If the goal of human history is a uniform type of man, reproducing at a uniform rate, in a uniform environment, kept at a constant temperature, pressure and humidity, living a uniformly lifeless existence, with his uniform physical needs satisfied by uniform goods, all inner waywardness brought into conformity by hypnotics and sedatives, or by surgical extirpations, a creature under constant mechanical pressure from incubator to incinerator, most of the problems of human development would disappear. Only one problem would remain. Why should anyone, even a machine, bother to keep this kind of creature alive?

That's what they want, the good-hearted leaders and their myrmidons—they want all their problems and yours—but mostly theirs—to disappear. And it really isn't that important to keep the creature alive, unless he and his will buy the goods of, and fight to the death for, them and theirs. But—*nota bene*!—fully 70% of the world's population is economically insignificant, and thus, disposable. Write their scripts, and write them off. Them could well be you.

But of course you know this. You think. You think, therefore you are not. For

Thoth was the genius god of the ancient Egyptians, depicted not in sweatshirt and white hair but with an ibis head and beak. The inventor of writing, the first historian, "Lord of the Divine Books," he inscribed human reality on tablets and taught it, Moses-like, to his people. His name means "Truth" and "Time," and he was thus associated with healing. The Book of Thoth, or "The Key to Immortality," contains the secrets of remaking humanity so that it may behold the gods. Ibises are known to kill crocodiles.

All this Alexei's new beak fed back to his face, and he was awestruck, filled with wonder, reverence, and dread. He reviewed in his mind what he understood as his new vocation: its dependence on technical skill, its responsibility to his community, its need for an understanding of history, literature, and the arts, its demand for personal integrity and faith in the value of life, the need to alleviate suffering, and finally its mandate of humility. Which leads us to the topic of

your "thought" is an obstacle to authentic existence. ee cummings put it most succinctly:

> Almost anybody can learn to think or believe or know, but not a single human being can be taught to be. Why? Because whenever you think or you believe or you know, you are a lot of other people: but the moment you are being, you're nobody-but-yourself. To be nobody-but-yourself—in a world which is doing its best night and day to make you everybody else—means to fight the hardest battle which any human being can fight, and never stop fighting.

But go ahead, forget it all and sing the Ronald McDonald song, or the Plague Doctor anthem. But while you're being "bold and Foucauldian," you might actually take some time to read him.

Who exercises power on whom? How? Who makes decisions for you? Who is programming your movements and activities? That is what Foucault wants you to think about. He shines his light on the strategies of power, its networks, its mechanisms, the techniques by which its decisions become accepted—by you.

His overall conclusion? That you—you, your very self—are produced by specific technologies of manipulation and formation. You are in Power's grasp for Power's maximum control of the world. Your individual "psyche" is a deceptive abstraction conjured up by Authority to satisfy its needs. Your body and your mind are subjected to constant inspection, measurement, and classification. Even—especially!—your sexuality calls for management procedures. Contraception, anyone?

But, dear reader, out-and-out repression is not the most subtle or pervasive form of domination. That award goes to creating your belief that you are *resisting* oppression, whether by self-knowledge or by speaking the truth. What better support for Them, what better way to hide the real working of Power? Go ahead, protest. Be my groupies, or Che Guevara's. They love it.

But I, The Nose, call for new techniques of the self—techniques that will allow people to perform real operations on their own bodies, on their own souls, on their thoughts, their conduct, to modify, even transform themselves, to achieve a quasi state of perfection, of happiness, of purity, of even supernatural power.

The human species, now a mere herd of sheep asleep at the slaughter, might be so individuated that differences between man and man could become far greater than those in the animal world. Between Beethoven, the free man, and

First Love

The reader may feel loath to enter into this topic yet again, or that the author is suffering from excessive fits of formal consistency and that such consistency is, as is so often noted, the hobgoblin of small minds. But let me point out that Emerson was referring only to "a foolish consistency." If there is such a thing as wise consistency, that would be Alexei's—a continual, repetitive openness of heart.

But that would account only for love. What was first about this particular manifestation? It was the first directed at all and everything, the first ur-love, Platonic, not *eros* but *caritas*, a passionate, Saint Teresa–like love for the entire created world.

It's true that at one of his early public appearances, he was temporarily smitten with a sweet young long-braided thing in an undershirt home-stenciled with HUG ME—I'M A POOH BEAR. But a short postlecture discussion with her on the topic of art and disease convinced him that she was, perhaps, a bear of little brain and not worth pursuing.

No, *agape* it was, *cujus regni non erit finis*, amen. This, then, was the new object of forty-nine-year-old first love, and of last.

In His Steps

For Delia, it was much the same. The family trip to Lisieux had left her enchanted. The legacy of Saint Thérèse was overwhelmingly attractive: the "little Way," the Way of the Little. She interviewed and was accepted as one of four sisters of the novitiate for a time of trying out. It was a wise system: although the cloistered world of the Carmelite is focused on silence and solitude, it still meant living in close community with twenty-six other women, ages nineteen to eighty-six, some of whom were far from easy to abide.

our leaders, *Homo monstrosi*, there is a chasm greater than that between a tiger and a worm, an eagle and *Yersinia pestis*. And where do *you* fit in?

Do you ever feel like you are living in End Times? Epidemiologists publishing in the *Proceedings of the National Academy of Sciences* found that a rise of just 1.8° Fahrenheit in springtime temperatures has led to a 59% increase in plague prevalence around the world. Yes, that kind of plague, plague as in "Bring out your dead!" The researchers focused their study in Kazakhstan, where the primary host is the great gerbil.

I am not making this up. The gerbils carry fleas, which carry *Y. pestis*, which gets transmitted to humans via flea bites. Lots of flea bites in Kazakhstan. *Yersinia*, of course, triggered both the Black Death, which killed more than 20 million people in the 14th-century, and a 19th-century pandemic in Asia that killed tens of millions. Depressingly, both outbreaks occurred during warm, wet climatic periods. Hmm, warm, wet climate . . . sound familiar? If you need us Americans, we'll be in the bunker, hiding from the gerbils.

Thus prophesieth The Nose.

Carmelite life had been reformed in the sixteenth century by Saint Teresa of Avila, a mystic but mystically practical administrator who founded little "deserts" where closeted religious men and women could seek out God, privately and in communal prayer, while working in an atmosphere of friendship and joy. Love was to take precedence over everything, including any horrid practices of mortification.

In the late nineteenth century, this particular convent in Lisieux had been graced by the humility of one young woman who'd joined it at age fifteen and died in her sisters' arms nine years later in 1897, at the age of twenty-four. "The Little Flower," as she was called, went on no missions, founded no religious order, and performed no miracles or great works; yet only twenty-eight years after her death, she was canonized—Saint Teresa of Lisieux. The reader will understand why after reading her diary, *Story of a Soul*. Her spirit still infused the tiny convent and smelled most sweet to our life-aching achondroplastic seeker. At the end of her interviews, Delia was ready to undertake that walk through darkness all contemplatives must encounter, and the sisters were ready to let her try.

The Sanctuaire Sainte Thérèse was a quadrangle building with a garden in the center surrounded by four light and airy cloisters. Delia's room was a ten-by-eight-foot cell with a bed, a desk and chair, a lamp, a clock, and a cross on the wall. Its challenge to her was simply this: "Do you wish to be here forever and ever?"

At the reception ceremony, Mother Catherine concluded with the following caveat, one Delia pondered much upon: "Though peaceful, our life is not designed to escape the yoke of the cross. We measure freedom differently here: here, everything is upside down; in order to gain, we have to lose; our victories come through surrender. We wish our new postulants much joy."

There was a long road ahead, and the four could bail out anytime until the end. During that period, they could be asked to leave if the community found them unsuitable. They were to spend the next nine months as postulants forming their initial impressions of the sisterhood, and the sisterhood of them. After that, the sisters would invite them—or not—to enter the novitiate as members of the community. They would then spend the next two years preparing for their first vows, learning the Carmelite way, and exploring their own spirituality. If all went well, they could make their vows, and renew them yearly until they were ready for their final, lifelong vows of poverty, chastity, and obedience.

Delia's first serious task was to discard her worldly name (along with her worldly identity), and choose another from the calendar of saints. Her meditations on this

involved a reconceptualization of the outstanding feature of her physical being—the contradiction between her classically beautiful head and the odd little body on which it rested. Browsing through one of the many art books in the convent library, she discovered a Ghirlandaio painting of the Child Jesus Teaching in the Temple. It was she, her face—a striking likeness! Almost creepy. But then and there she knew that if accepted into the community, she would become Sister Alexa of the Child Jesus of the Holy Face. And so she was, and so she did.

The grilles were the next issue to be overcome. Yes, she had understood that Lisieux was a fully cloistered convent, an austere setting with double grilles and curtains separating the sisters from any but themselves. On the other hand, where other than prison does one see bars on windows and people living in cells?

Sister Agnes, her spiritual director, explained that the enclosure was not meant for security, or to keep them in and others out, but was, rather, a firm demarcation to provide them with a climate of prayer. Accept its gift, she counseled: the possibility of tranquility, of complete serenity. *D'accord* okay, she thought, *je vais essayer.*

The sisters woke daily at 5:25 for a day of prayer, housework, food preparation, laundry, and gardening. The convent was scrupulously clean. Meals were silent, and during the day, they might speak to one another only when necessary. There were six hours of communal adoration, five hours of manual work, an hour of recreation, seven hours of sleep, with the rest of the time to be spent in silence and solitude. In this life of regimented isolation, Delia thought, "All right, I am a prisoner of love behind the grilles of Lisieux, where maybe—who knows?—God wants me to be. Hidden. Devoted. I will make this my choice. I accept the invitation to littleness."

The sisters thought of her as "the little lamb" and "Jesus's toy," and in nine months, she was accepted as a novice and allowed to wear the habit—a rough, brown, homespun robe, brown scapular, white wimple and veil, leather belt with rosary, woolen stockings, and rope sandals. Everything needed special tailoring. But her new clothes minimized her body and featured her face. She looked quite good in them.

Her two novice years were not unhappy. Charles and Danielle visited every month, and they spoke with her through the grilles, sensitive to her struggles, encouraging. The view out her barred window was inspiring, season by season, the sisters were by and large pleasant, and she was able to practice her sketching and painting. Her first vows of poverty, chastity, and obedience were basically a breeze, for Sister Alexa had no income and no savings; her chastity, at least heterosexual, was guaran-

teed; and what else could one be here but obedient? Obedient as God's puppet. Obedient as the needle to the pole.

These vows were renewed each year for three years, and—after meditating day and night—Sister Alexa felt herself in a committed relationship at last, even if her fiancé did not often do much to keep up his end of the conversation. It did take an act of faith to resist the vexing thought that she might be headed for nowhere and nothingness. But if the saints she read about could keep faith while being torn to pieces, boiled, or burned, so could she in this seeker's paradise. At the very time that Alexei was committing his life to Hundwasser's guidance and care, Sister Alexa felt herself ready to make final profession and take the veil for life.

The ceremony was somewhat frightening. Her beautiful hair was cut. She was led down the aisle by her parents to be given away to a mysterious, invisible bridegroom. She had to lie prostrate in the chapel nave, her arms extended, and be covered with a white sheet—a sign of the mystical death through which she had promised to die to the world and to self. But she felt she had broken through from misfortune into resurrection, unnailed from a mistaken cross that she might kneel at the foot of the true one. All right, she said in her heart, I will love Him, I will give my life to Him, I will abandon all else, I renounce everything in the name of holy obedience. To you, my bridegroom, I offer my poor little life.

This she thought, lying under the white sheet. And then her bad voices came again. "Who are you, you little wretch, you deformed creature, that He should take you as his bride?" But in those five shrouded minutes, five minutes that could have been five days, she remembered the suitor she had come to know, her lover and best friend; she thought on her quality time with Jesus, her beloved. And so, after almost six years of training and progress toward God, she made Solemn Profession, cross my heart and hope to die.

Five years later, by dint of her Little Way, the Way of the Dwarf, and her profound sense that she was only an obscure grain of sand, she was elected Mother Superior of the Sanctuaire Sainte Thérèse de Lisieux, the youngest in its history. That was precisely not what Sainte Thérèse, her mentor, had striven for, she who had chosen always to remain a novice—but in Sister Alexa's own dwarfish way, it was humble, accepting the cross of leadership the others had laid upon her, seeking to bring to her supervisory role endless patience, unselfish humility, and a love for all that live and suffer. She often wanted to take some of the sisters by the scruff of the neck, or others by the tips of their wings—and shake them. But she didn't.

For under it all, under Mother Superior Alexa of the Child Jesus of the Holy Face,

there remained tiny Delia, who, despite her size might still aspire to holiness—with all her imperfections, whose Bridegroom loved her to folly and penetrated her with his love. In five years of suffering with the crucified Christ, the ravages of her life became ravages of surrender; she felt more human, more holy, she understood her own suffering as a gift, a call to grace and peace unshakable.

Once, in the convent garden, under the great oak, she had found and identified a beautiful *Amanita verna*, the famous "Death Angel" mushroom so dreaded and respected. She dug it carefully up, potted it, kept it in her room, and added a prayer in front of it to her daily litany.

Sancta Maria, Mater Dei, ora pro nobis peccatoribus nunc et in hora mortis nostrae. Amen.

10. Spectacle

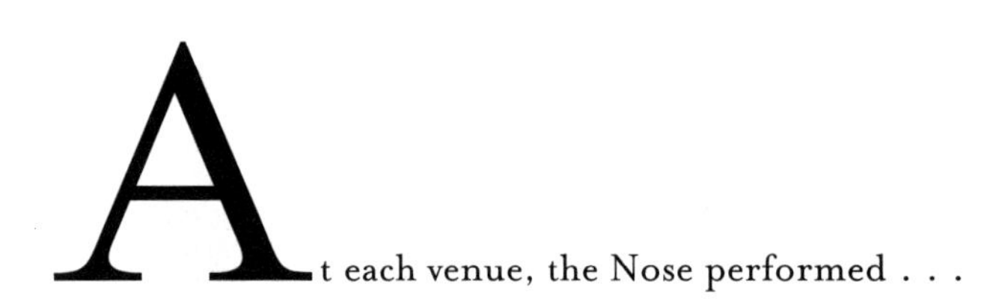

At each venue, the Nose performed . . .

. . . His Winning Stump Spectacle[88]

The lights go down. During a PowerPoint presentation of his triumphant career, the bouncing nose indicated the subtitled words of Hundwasser's National Nose Association anthem. Everyone knows how it goes. The audience sings, to the tune of "My Country, 'Tis of Thee,"

Oh, what a mockery
This kakistocracy
Makes of our prose.
We will be bold again,
Bold and Foucauldian
All is foretold, amen:
Follow The Nose.

88. Hundwasser leaves my story with "The rest is history." But what "rest"? Just the truncated stump spectacle he reports over here on the left? Does he hide all the many other activities—great and small—in order to obscure the cynicism of his calculations, or emphasize his contributions over mine? Or because he thought them too risqué for his Oprah plans, even in the age of Jerry Springer? Once again he has disappeared me, the real me, in the telling! Who, after all, was the *éminence* and who the *grise*?

Ours was a full-spectrum, intrasymbiotic assault on the ever-desiring world of American culture. Yes, the book would feed the appearances, the appearances, the book. Media extensions would proceed geometrically: print, radio, TV, video, DVD, 35-mm, 70-mm, wide-screen, Cinemascope, world-hunger events, perhaps even Paphnutius's iPod video sent out on Voyager 3 into interstellar space.

Initially I took some convincing. "All that makes me uncomfortable," I said. "What if

He enters, precisely on time, hooded, beaked, and gowned, to shrieking and applause. In his left hand, the plague stick with which he will gesture; in his right, a titanium leash, and on it Max the rat, his fur dyed gothic black.

"Dearly afflicted,"

How they love this! In short order speaker and spoken-to pronounce it ritually together as a congregation: D E A R L Y A F F L I C T E D. . . . He places Max on the lectern's front edge to receive his initial remarks, an officiant addressing the host. The audience communes throughout this invocation.

"I would set you free, dear Max, if only I could. But where is the freedom to loose you to? For not just rats but every earthly thing is now dismembered and reconfigured for the benefit of the few, who bray about freedom while they themselves are slaves. May it be different some day. May they all see the light, relinquish their embrace of Death and the terror-tactics of their technologies. May they understand the quality of mercy and be like you, like us, just here, and whole, and holy. Grace be unto all, and peace. Amen and amen."

Max listens politely.

"Amen and amen," repeats the assembly.

He opens his eyes behind their thick goggles and places Max gently down beside him.

"Dearly afflicted, we dwell here together in the bad apple, the rat race and shark waters of New York City."

Cognominia as per location.

"We swim together in its sea of fantasy, its clear and present miasma of evil. Here on the North American incontinent, in the death-wish city paranoiac, we snorkel among the sepulchres of plague reborn."

This the origin of the black-snorkel-and-wetsuit tours of Manhattan.

"Together we know the ravages of death-by-government, a whole equal only to the sum of the parts and powers of Hell, methodically homicidal. Nothing thrives among us except the feeding pathogens. The proffered world is a contemptible fraud."

Hisses and boos.

"What, after all, is kakistocracy but government by the least qualified and most unprincipled, the reign of misery maintained by capitalists, imperialists, fascists, militarists, and other beasts pretending to be human?"

"Two, four, six, eight," the crowd chants, led by Hundwasser on bullhorn, "who do we depreciate?

"One, two, three, four, all *of them we do abhor!"*

"Rich, they are, rich, rich, rich in stupidity, a troop of men dedicated to death,

I just want to have my own plague doctor mask, be my own self, think my own thoughts? What if I just want to heal . . . and be loved?"

"You will, man, you will," Hundwasser assured me. "Stop whining. They'll love you. And if you can't be loved, you can at least be weird. We've got to do the film and TV thing and get you out there big time. There are more houses with TV in America than with indoor plumbing. Film and TV are reality. Don't you want to be part of *reality*? If you're not on-screen, you're like an unperson. If you are, you're a role model. Don't you want to be a role model?"

The tempter speaks. I guessed I did.

"Well, then? *You're* the role model. You can be an icon of individuality, a stand-up tragedian, a secular imprint of the sacred, exuding a magical sense of value. And you can get your aura from mass reproduction, so eat crow, Walter Benjamin!"

"Like a radiant Hostess Twinkie?"

"No, man, like a doctor, a healer. There's a plague out there, right? This is *Homo vacuous* we're talking about, the world of pure assholery, self-congratulatory self-deception, the emptiness plague, the devotional plague, the promotional plague, the great swim in the sewer of self. You can throw them a lifeline, man, and pull them out of it. You can be their licensed fool, God's buffoon, a parodist of world history. You and I can take a lot of nothin' and make it into somethin'."

"But I'm in the same world they are," I objected. "How can we . . . ?"

"Look. you can be completely inside a society, and still explode it from within. Look at Martin Luther, Martin Luther King, the Beatles, Timothy McVeigh. . . ."

"But why would anyone pay attention to me?"

"Hey, this is the society of the spectacle, no? And who's a bigger spectacle than you? What's a bigger spectacle than the plague? HIV, mad cows, mad ducks and chickens. Wallow, Sodom, wallow. You can be the star of all this. You have charisma, extraordinary magnetism. *People* magazine. Lifestyles of the Plague Doctor, his clothes, his car, his villa, his speedboat, where he goes on the weekend. We can do shows at the Planetarium. . . . We need bumper stickers. . . ."

I have to admit, I was swept along by his passionate rhetoric.

"'TURN BACK NOW,'" I suggested.

"Good one. I'll have a thousand printed up. Like in a speech bubble from your mask."

"I have a woodcut of plague doctors from the London plague," I said.

"You're terrific. So we're on, right? Let's see, we've already talked about the dolls, and you're working on the dance, right?"

going at it gaily, seeding an entire civilization rooted in folly. 'To market, to market,' they sing, the fat pigs."

"Nine, ten, eleven twelve," the crowd begins. Paphnutius cuts them off."

"And you, you citizens of the land of Tizofthee, in this country of Nocturnia, you dance merrily along, rats to their piping, darklings in the darkness, worshiping the God of Malfunction. Know this, then:

All Nature is but Guile, unknown to thee;
All chance, direction, which thou canst not see

All discord, strategy not understood,
All evil, masked as universal good:

And, spite of pride, wherever you may throng,
One truth is clear, whatever is, is wrong."

Heroic couplets in iambic pentameter bring many to their feet in standing ovation. This shortly becomes tradition, much like standing for the "Hallelujah Chorus." The phans are now primed for the attacks on them they so adore.

"If this universe has an expiration date, it is no thanks to *you [Here the great gesture with the plague stick]*, you corpses now dancing at the Starlight Necropolis."

This is the signal for the first couples to begin moving the chairs.

"If they are the mad cows and cowboys, you are their Jacob Kreuzfelds."

The first couples begin to dance; the first audience members begin their rhythmic clapping.

"Look at these people *[points to the dancers in the aisles]*. Puppets made to jiggle in the catatonic mode prescribed. Look at their jerky souls, their malignant smiles, smelling of death. And you—you still seated, you who actually care who wins football games . . ."

Always a laugh. In these very days of taking umbrage, it is astounding how much people love being chastised and excoriated.

"Cease your loathsome sniggering!
[aside, to Max on the floor]
If that the heavens do not their visible spirits
Send quickly down to tame these vile offences,
It will come,

"Martha Graham."

"Good. Do the hokey-pokey. A little retro, but retro is good, right? And we might begin thinking about a record company. . . ."

"Pestilence Records . . ."

"Bingo. Pestilence it is. And we'll need a designer label—that can be like the bumper sticker. Hey, what would you think about adopting some kind of fractured English, like I got a spam this morning, 'Having not pleasure knowing you while hoping such for coming soon, asking money please on behalf client.' Can you talk like that?"

"No."

"What about 'SHNOZAM!'? Could you use that in all your pronouncements? As your signature sign-off?"

"No."

"OK. I like it when you push back. And I'll leave it to you entirely about the music and the theme song. I think everything ought to be around the *Dies Irae* theme. And we'll have a fan club with a membership card. . . ."

"The humble abbot Paphnuti hath put his hand hereto."

"Great. Exactly."

"What about you?" I asked.

"What do you mean what about me?"

"What's your public persona?"

"I'm going to be secretive," he said, "like Salinger and Pynchon. Turn down interviews. I think it will add to the mystery of the whole thing."

So, OK, it took some doing, but I was convinced.

Ours was a complex plan, Operation Able Ibis. It would begin, though, with simple walks up and down Fifth Avenue, from Washington Square to Central Park South, my silent walks in costume, unexplained, inscrutable, tantalizing, mockingly out-of-reach, like those billboards that announce that "It" is coming on September 10th.

And so, thanks to my fearlessness, the buzz began, at first as a mere susurration amid the greater cacophony of the city. But soon it flowered into rumors, and thence into a flood of speculation when I dropped in my Paphnutius-y wake small green handbills which read,

> There is a tribe in New Guinea who, aware of the idiocy of technological civilization, massacred the managers of a washing-machine factory, took over the building, and converted it into a temple of the marvelous but elusive Bird-god. . . .

[to the phans]
It will come!
[shaking his great beak]
Humanity must perforce prey on itself,
Like monsters of the deep."

The audience makes monster sounds.

"What will come, you ask?"

"Yes, what will come, what will come?" they yell.

"Whimpering puppies! You were all of you, each and every one, born Originals. How is it that you will die Copies, prancing around in your cages, your arms opening manically to rationalized death? What will come, my friends, is your salutary, well-deserved punishment! You can hide, dearly afflicted, but you can't run. For where is there to run in this universe of pestilence, in this vast landscape of organized crime?"

The crowd "Woooo!s" and "Whoop!s" to cheer him on. People begin to run around the hall, seeking shelter. "Wooooo! Whoooop!"

"Cries of hyenas. Listen to you, you who are interested only in what has never been the case. Refusal to recognize your true situation is prima facie evidence of folly and a sure guarantee that you will remain forever slaves."

"We're your *slaves, we're* your *slaves," they yell.*

"Yes, some of you are simply born stupid, some have achieved stupidity, but all of you have stupidity thrust upon you. Your stupidity can be ended only by putting an end to the human race. Wisdom will never triumph among the humanoid cryptozoa. You are not personally to blame."

Here, or in this general vicinity, a beautiful young dancer with a fine, freckled nose reaches out to invite him to join the dance. Perhaps she is a plant?

"Noli me tangere, Magdalene!," Paphnutius warns. "Adam was led to sin by Eve, and not Eve by Adam. Therefore, it is just and right that woman accept as lord and master he whom she led to sin. But no touching."

As one hand pushes her away with his plague stick, the other holds her hand just a bit too long, and she slips into her I-am-going-bananas face.

"Yes, dance, morons! Dance and clap. The American Way of Avoiding Life, the life of the nonliving, en route to the Just4U Cemetery. You live to grovel? Grovel away, then, oh herd of meat with eyes. And you *[to freckle-face]*, you sweet young thing, so fair

I was beginning to get the hang of it.

Applying the techniques of niche marketing, Hundwasser booked me at Makor, a culture club for Jewish singles which offers its members a chance to "cultivate the avant-garde". My topic was "Jews as Victims of the Plague," the hook being the expulsion, rounding-up, and murder of Jews as causes thereof. I spelled out the 1348 massacre of Jews in gruesome detail—which propelled me to the 92nd Street Y, the Bronfman Center for Jewish Life, the Simon Center for Adult Life & Learning, and the Milstein Center for Media & Technology.

Coverage in *People* soon led me to Oprah, and thereby to an unprecedented pre-sale of a book barely conceived. Fomite Press offered Hundwasser a six-figure advance, I got 3% as subject-fee, and our two-man Operation Able Ibis became Able Ibis Ltd. and ableibis.com.

The show was more than on the road. *Plague Doc: A Novel* was optioned by Joel and Ethan Coen, whose eventual Cannes submission, *Not Dead Yet, Quack!* was disliked by most critics and misunderstood by the original audience.

Throughout everything, my silent walks continued, spread throughout the city, the most striking one of which was an expedition over the mountain of WTC debris at the Fresh Kills Landfill in Staten Island, during which three body parts were accidentally unearthed, leading to a firestorm of associated publicity in which widows faced off against critics accusing them of exploitation and I was almost left behind.

These walks seeded the first of the fan phenomena, with enthusiasts in LA and San Francisco duplicating my promenades, dropping leaflets of their own, and launching local organizing. Other chapters sprang up in Portland and Seattle, then spread eastward, back toward the source: Phoenix, Denver, Wichita, Des Moines, Madison, Chicago, Detroit, Pittsburgh, Philadelphia. There threatened a veritable pestilence of Plaguists.

And then, alas, civil war, all too predictable on the left, if the Paphnutius phenomenon could be said to imply a political direction. The issue, however, was reasonable and significant. The Plague was thought by some to be "too deathy," too alienating to the general public, and finally, too limiting. These critics assembled under the banner of Noseists, and over the course of several months outflanked the Plagueists with persuasive blogs, journals, and events exalting the nose as the under-appreciated organ, proclaiming the great noses of Western culture, and the nose as idiom, the nose as metaphor, the nose as road to spiritual transformation. Aromatherapists endorsed the movement en masse. There was more money to be made via the Noseists than via the Plagueists.

without and foul within, poisoned by the putrefaction of the world, the depravity of power, living a deeply uninteresting life without dimension in your shallow sea of pseudoexperience, let me inform you, personally and with special warmth, that the most terrible plague is the one that does not reveal its symptoms, the *spiritual* plague, without rats, without microbes, without even mucus-membrane contact. Look to it, my dear."

His personal address and reference to mucus membranes is too much for the young Nosie, and she has to be led away, supported by her friends.

"But but but, and yet and yet . . . Though you may think my mental health not quite right, and though I—*au contraire*—feel like a psychiatrist walking through a loony bin, I am willing to lead you in combat as together we fight the monster buffoons of Nutzy Land."

"Yes, yes, lead us!" Most of the dancing ceases, as this is the cue for them to listen to the great final aria of self and salvation.

"Who am I to take on the Promethean task of your deliverance?"

"Who? Who are you?" The dancers in the aisles kneel down in seiza *posture to attend.*

"*Ecce homo.* You see before you one of the ablest minds of the fourteenth century, a one-man society for the overthrow of everything. My reverence for the flea extends even to you, my phans, for if they can jump four hundred times their own height, I have faith that you too can become spiritual athletes of astonishing performance. My devotion to the rat . . ."

"Max! Max! Max! Max!"

"My devotion to the rat, I say, is due to one crucial fact: the rat does not believe in relativity."

Whistles and cheers for rats.

"While rats may have their issues, situational ethics is not among them.

"I, my friends, am your fairy godmonster, born of an almost-virgin who upon the night of my birth saw flaming nostrils in the sky. In my infancy, she rubbed my body with leaves of the *cnyza* that I might be chaste and avoid scabies, and nourished me on perfumes that I might acquire the four virtues, the five faculties, the ten forces, the eighteen substances, and enter into the twenty-four spheres. I lost myself in vapors and dreams. My youth was blown by the supreme winds of the soul. While others were trading baseball cards and unhooking brassieres, I lived in a world of imaginative exultation, relatively free from the powers of darkness. I abandoned the filthy hostelry of the body, built with flesh, reddened with blood, covered with a hideous skin, full of uncleanliness. . . ."

I, however, endorsed both schools, and in a brilliant tactic of personal triangulation, undertook a cross-country tour in a custom-built nose-hearse containing a vertical casket in which one's picture might be taken for only a dollar. Thus, with gas almost paid for by photo fees, plague and nose could cohabit in mysterious oneness—duitarian as it were—in an infallible popemobile designed to settle the squabble. Brilliant, no? Too brilliant for Hundwasser to mention?

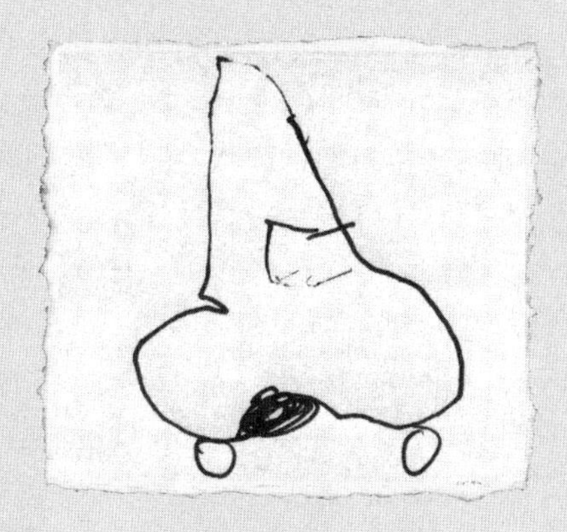

At this magical conjuration, the tradition soon grew for his followers to strip off their clothing, some in humbleness, others in pride, some in mockery, some in adulation. In any case, phans getting naked became one of the chief attractions of Nose events. Paphnutius liked it too.

"I see you gaping at each other's flesh. Good. This is your chance to practice the eunuch-stare. Pick out a manifestation you particularly relish."

They quickly do so.

"Let your eyes soft-focus until the shapely flesh begins a Dali-like drip. All is sagging, all is starting to hang. Are you with me? All is thawing, melting, resolving into a dew. Can you see it? Good. And what is left? The frame alone, the osseous frame. Stay there. Stay with that. Let it disgust and orient you to the truth of creation. *Then* you will understand your role as plague doctor, afoot among the dying, attending to their care.

"I am the prophet of permanent revolution, and remember—revolution means being revolting. For these days it is a scandal to have any principles at all, let alone to promote and defend them. Who among you is prepared to be scandalized?"

"I am." "I am!" "I am!"

"My assistant here *[he indicates Hundwasser or some designated other]* will circulate among you with pledge cards. Please write legibly, especially your e-mail addresses. Here is our agenda:

"Together we will create a huge army of plague-doctor lepers, contaminating the world at large with true health. We will decapitate Western civilization, draw and quarter it, and refashion the entire state of existing reality with its presently corrupting rituals of mass obedience, consumerism, and power worship. We will quarantine all moral diseases, enforce absolute divergence from the rules of the game, and enable deliverance from cramped familiara into the ample unknown. We will cast aside the fetters of the world's everyday map and set out together, Columbus-like, on a heroic adventure.

"Leave your inner child behind, sucking its thumb and slurping its pap. Be not afraid of your anger, for anger can change the world when it is heard, understood, and expressed symbolically in ways that will endure. Remember the exalted words of T-Bone Slim: 'Wherever you find injustice *[here, all chant together]*, the proper form of politeness is attack.' When we are done with it, the entire developed world will understand every word of Heraclitus and Ecclesiastes.

"I call, then, for mass resistance! Leave your private islands and sign up! Become a registered alien! Cultivate the Promethean gesture!"

At its height, Plague Doctors Without Borders had a paid membership of almost twenty-six thousand;

plaguedoctorswithoutborders.org had a mailing list of more than 110 thousand, and eight to fifteen thousand hits a day on its website.

"Let me end, dearly afflicted, with one crucial piece of advice. If you remember nothing else, remember this."

The crowds would chant this ritually along with him and later adapt it as a greeting among themselves:

"CAUTION: THE MOVING WALKWAY IS ABOUT TO END."

Cheers, whistles, whooping, ululating as Paphnutius throws onions among his phans—a Cyrillic reference few, if any, get—and exits the stage. Some weep and pray while others exhort and console. Next, performances of the Flea Circus, A. St. Paphnutius, ringmaster, and sales of fleas, Train-Them-Yourself Kits, Booklets, and selected reprints. Then mosh pit, naked dancing, and where appropriate, late-night orgies and grade-A pandemonium.

The only known picture of Hadwasser

11. Belle Lettre[89]

89. To the last parts of Hundwasser's Nun's Tale ahead, only one note—re: the happy ending.

He is accurate up to this point. The narration of Delia's entrance into the convent at Lisieux jibes well with her communications to me. Her unprecedented progress from novice to Mother Superior was fitting for a woman of such talent for the work. But reality breaks off at Delia's letter. Let the reader beware.

At the end of Brecht and Weill's *Threepenny Opera*, a messenger comes riding in with a pardon from the Queen. Mack the Knife is saved from the gallows and rewarded (for his crimes) with a deed to great lands and a pension for life. The street singer who starts the show singing Mackie's story, closes it with the ballad's last three verses. Sing this in a nasal voice to the tune you know:

Und so kommt zum guten Ende
Alles unter einen Hut
Ist das nötige Geld vorhanden
Ist das Ende meistens gut.

Sanctuaire Sainte Thérèse de Lisieux
33, Rue du Carmel
BP 62095-F-14102
Lisieux

Cher Alexei,

Forgive me for getting in touch through your agent, but I did not have your address. I was most distressed to read the featured story, "Le Nez," in today's Nouvel Observateur. I can imagine how much it must pain you to go through all those extravagances to what? make a living? How much you, such a private person, must be stressed by what others must be making you do!

(While meditating on your calamities, I found my heart in violent motion as I relived the dear memories of our time together.)

Forgive me, too, for disappearing without a word, with no hint of my situation other than a late, jesting invitation I sent off as a méchanceté, a gesture to ease my decision to make final vows. The scene in the hospital with your mother was most hurtful to me, but that does not excuse my behavior. You are not your mother, and I owe you to explain.

For our happy ending, Brecht says, everything is gathered neatly "under one hat."

"If the required money is at hand, then the ending is usually good."

That was surely Hundwasser's motivation in drastically changing Delia's fate, a fate impinging on my own. Did he think her parents would never find out—or sue?

Happy endings sell, I'm told, and above all in America. Disney's *Little Mermaid*, for instance, is perhaps the greatest happy-ending-rape in world literature, and therefore an animation blockbuster. The verb "sell" was so crucial to Hundwasser's ambitions as to derail whatever train of truth he had finally—finally!—set out upon.

Of course he was too sophisticated simply to write, "And Delia and Alexei lived happily ever after." But his sophistication, as we know, is disingenuous. The semi-sweetness of Delia's letter—give me a break! The just-under-the-surface eroticism—what is this, some new genre of nun-porno? Sells books, I guess.

Brecht's last verse is

Denn die einen sind im Dunkeln
Und die andern sind im Licht
Und man siehet die im Lichte
Die im Dunkeln sieht man nicht.

Some people live in darkness; others live in light. We see the lit ones. The ones in darkness—well, we don't see them. We don't want to.

The happy ending.

The true facts about Delia's real end are these:

As I'm sure you know, Hundwasser put out the shocking news that I had been diagnosed with an obscure fatal disease, contracted, perhaps, while attending to one of my sick fans. This, for publicity purposes, to jack up sagging contributions. Published first in the *Washington Post*, it was picked up by Agence France Press, and of course was hourly updated on plaguedoctorswithoutborders.org—though I'm sure Delia had no access to the Internet. But she did read *La Croix* and the *International Herald Tribune*, and got in touch immediately, asking for details about my situation so that she might diagnose my disease and prescribe treatments.

I was so embarrassed to admit that the whole story of my desperate attempts at New Age cures was just a publicity stunt—I shared the blame for not cutting it down—that I put off answering for several months. Her urgent inquiries filled those months, for naturally she interpreted my silence as a terrible sign—which only made it harder for me to write.

When you and I were tossed on the ocean of the world, my heart was drunk with voluptuousness. The cup of our sin overflowed with so enchanting sweetness, and I was so inclined to taste it, that it needed only be offered. My words blush to tell you this.

At the same time, it was clear enough that my presence, perhaps my love, was repellent to you. Believe me, as a dwarf I was used that people turn away from me in horror. But I hoped that you—with your whimsical eccentricity—you might be different. Part of why I came here to the convent was the thought that my imprisonment perpétuelle might allow you to live more quietly and at ease. Were I forced into confinement, perhaps that would be best for both. To forget you, to think of you no more, is what I thought our friendship required. And less humbly, I felt that since you had forsaken me, I might glory instead in being wedded, if not to you, then to Heaven.

So I seeked an asylum to secure me from love, I tried a sad experiment of taking vows to harden me against you. I thought with my espousal, I would soon be in the peculiar care of Heaven, no more vulnerable to your attraction. Perhaps I might even come to God by neglecting the creature I had adored, and adoring the God I had neglected.

Hélas, things were not so easy. I had once thought it infinitely preferable to live as your partner than as Empress of the World—ah, what one braves when one loves a man! But if here my passion had been restrained, yet my thoughts ran free. Since absence is the tomb of love I had hoped my affection for someone I saw no more would disappear, and also yours (if any) for me. I promised myself I would forget you—but I couldn't think of forgetting you without again loving you! I flattered myself that when I ceased to see you, you would rest in my memory without troubling my mind, that a change of continent would allow other thoughts; that my spare routine would by degrees erase you from my heart. But your image kept appearing and confounding all my resolutions.

It was one of those terrible temptations that sometimes disturb the vocations of even the most holy. In the midst of a religious community devoted to the Cross, I was also devoted to you! Veiled as I was, you were still capable of plunging me into disorder.

I put away all my drawings of you, for even those sketches gave me much pleasure. But then I remembered them over and over, and with much misgiving. I betrayed and contradicted myself. I hated you! I loved you! In my leav-

Then a telegram arrived: Delia was coming. Her plane would arrive at JFK on 16 September at 4:10 P.M. If I could pick her up, fine; if I didn't have a car, or was too sick to drive, she would take public transportation to the address on my earlier letters. A follow-up telegram assured me that she had to come to New York anyway—on business—and that I should not feel bad that she was making the trip just for me.

She arrived at my apartment at Beekman Terrace (a recent move from Avenue C: Hundwasser had insisted on the address) at nine in the evening, dressed in a blue nurse's cloak, normal sized, but foot-length for her, her hands and suitcase underneath, her beautiful face floating near the top of a blue cloth pyramid. We hadn't been together in fifteen years, but she just plunked herself down on a footstool and said in an agitated voice, "*Alexei, ça va? Qu'est-ce que se passe?* You don't look so bad as I expected."

I invited her to take off her cloak. She refused. She wouldn't move until I told her what was going on. Same old Delia: invasive, intrusive, dangerous.

Confessing was hard, but made easier by the fact that I could blame 90% on Hundwasser. He was the mastermind. He'd put me up to it. She wasn't surprised. She'd suspected something along those lines when she'd seen where I was living—in a 12-room apartment overlooking the river.

Professional Catholics are good at forgiving. *Te absolvo*, go in peace, the sign of the cross—all that. I expect she practiced forgiving a lot as boss of Lisieux—she was great at it. My new mother, superior to my old one.

I felt relieved of the huge burden of guilt I'd been carrying since her first epistle. Since probably before that because I was never really comfortable with Hundwasser's "dying" scheme, or the "Princess Diana death" option still to come. Free at last! Somewhat.

"So now will you take off your supernun cape or whatever it is?" I asked. She looked me dead in the eye as if trying to calculate my next response. Then she stood up from the stool and shifted her arms under the cloak to free them for unbuttoning the collar. But the movement didn't seem right. She didn't gather the cloth to expose her hands. Rather her fingers just appeared at the hem of her cloak, and out from under it came two long arms, grotesquely out of proportion to her tiny body. She unbuttoned the collar and let the cloak fall like some grotesque move in a striptease act. She wore her old brown habit, modified.

"Nice, huh?" she said, "*Jolie?*" She waved her gibbon arms around.

I was astounded. Horrified. I sank down into the big armchair.

"You like?" she asked.

"I . . . what happened?"

"I won't tell you till you take off that mask."

"But you'll see my face."

"I've seen your face."

ing you, you became my ever-present trial. When love has once been sincere, how difficult it is to love no more. How weak we are if we do not support ourselves on the cross of Christ. The worst was that while our unhappy love had conditioned me to chastity, I was not penitent of our past: I embraced it as my life's treasure.

But over the last years, my passion has been extinguished by extraordinary grace. I recall the words of Mother Catherine upon my arrival. "Though peaceful, our life is not designed to escape the yoke of the cross. Here, everything is upside down: in order to gain we have to lose; our victories come through surrender."

I remain eternally grateful to you for things uncountable. You taught me that even at the foot of the altar we often sacrifice to lying spirits, and the incense they most prefer is any earthly passion still burning in the heart of a nun. For this warning I thank you. And for teaching me during my time in the world the habit of loving, which I now bring to our Lord Jesus Christ.

And so I hope that we may love again in new ways. Without changing the ardor of our affections, let us change their objects; let us leave our personal ditties and instead sing hymns; let us lift up our hearts to God and have no transports but for His glory! If I was once the villain who conspired against your honor, troubled your quiet, betrayed your innocence, forgive me. I here release you from any feelings you may have had. Now let us take the side of God against ourselves. Our former lapses require tears, shame, and sorrow to expiate them. Let us offer these as sacrifices from our hearts; let us blush and let us weep. If in such feeble beginnings our hearts are not entirely His, then let us at least feel they ought to be so. The fear of God will deliver us from our frailties.

Alexei, I have renounced the world. I am now a nun devoted to solitude. May we not take advantage of that condition? If any thoughts too natural should importune me, I can fly to the foot of the Cross and there beg for mercy. So be not afraid: though my heart be filled with love for one of God's creatures, His hand, when it pleases, can empty me of all love save for Him.

Let me have a faithful account of all that concerns you. Perhaps by mingling my sighs with yours, I may diminish your sufferings, for sorrows divided are made lighter. Write soon, without waiting for things to settle down. I had rather read the dictates of the heart than the machinations of the brain. Though here I ought not retain a wish of my own, yet I still preserve secretly

"It's worse."

"Alexei, who are you talking to?"

I laid Plague Doctor Paphnutius to one side, ready at hand, to reassume if necessary.

Delia's story was long, a tale of scandal upon scandal upon scandal—personal, ecclesiastical, and medical—all three of them heaped, braided, and cross-fertilizing—too much, I suppose, for Hundwasser. The first was—simply, perhaps inevitably—this: She had fallen in love. Soeur Aline was one of the postulants in her original gang of four and had marched in step with Delia through the novitiate, the preliminary vows, and the final ones.

Unlike Delia, she was tall, blond, and stately, with a face more angelic still, and a bodily grace apparent even through heavy robes. Hearing about her reminded me of the sweet Columbina I had once loved, she who had floated on half-toe across the boards. I fell in love with la belle Aline just from her description. And no wonder Delia did too.

Even more unlike Delia, Sister Aline had pursued institutional insignificance. Like the beautiful saint of her cloister, she had chosen to remain a humble novice, not allowing herself to rise through the ranks but assigning herself—although the tallest—to be the lowliest member of the community. After fifteen years, there they were, at the top and at the bottom, Mutt and Jeff, Delia's head reaching no higher than Aline's tenth rib.

Yet they were a natural pair: Delia, from above, longed to serve the most humble. The most humble, from below, longed to serve those above her, culminating at the top: they were often together, and their ecclesiastical pairing was understood and warmly approved by the sisters.

Cupid, of course, is no respecter of post-Tridentine Rome. He doesn't believe in the Trinity, or more especially in clerical celibacy. And his arrows are sharp, capable of piercing two at once. Thus were Delia and Aline further linked, the high and the low, the tall and the short, skewered through the heart by the same arrow.

At first they simply ministered to one another. Shoulder rubs at dinner after a long day in the garden, washing each other's clothes, when it was their turn to wash, and folding them especially nicely. But then came—as it ever will—the cell, and the bed. And as they lay there together, they were full of terror and doubt and a sense that they had betrayed their vows and vocations and thus one another. They rationalized like crazy: sex is clean, not dirty; clerical celibacy was rooted in the church fathers' hostility toward women; enjoying sex with a sister made each of them more loving to all their sisters; even Thomas Aquinas had opposed celibacy and thought the law could and should be changed; no one was being harmed. . . .

Rationalizations, and painful ones, yes, but coming from deepest love, springing from each other's souls, a priceless engagement of human energies. They were, after all, both children of the '60s.

the desire to heal our breach and feel those subtle and charming joys when hearts long parted are at last united. In doing so, I give us up to the wonderful goodness of God, who does all things for our sanctification, who by His grace purifies all that is vicious and corrupt, who by the great riches of His mercy draws us to Him against our wishes, and by degrees opens our eyes to behold His bounty.

I am earnestly desirous to hear from you. Think of me. Do not forget me. Remember my love and fidelity and constancy. Remember, while loving Him, I still love you. I hope you can turn your current spectacle into one truly worthy of men and angels.

Your,
Mother Superior Alexa of the Child Jesus of the Holy Face
née Delia

But old Soeur Brigitte was a child of the '40s. And when she discovered them horizontal, late night in the garden, there was a Gethsemane-sized scene that woke the entire community, both from sleep and from unconsidered papal dogma. And so came the second scandal—the internal debate on the meaning of chastity and the cover-up of the affair from the outside world, for Soeur Brigitte was not easily appeased.

The debate itself was a necessary airing of many ideas and feelings long suppressed. But it made for the scandal of the cover-up. The main Catholic newspaper, *La Croix*, was habitually interested in the doings of the convent—new members, deaths, special services, historical anniversaries. Lisieux was the feather in French Catholicism's cap, home to its most renowned saint, graced by her having been there. But the paper's love affair with the *Sanctuaire Sainte Thérèse de Lisieux*, like many other love affairs, was easily offended, and hell hath no fury like a newspaper scorned, especially when the anonymous tip-off was met with silence from the convent.

Although the sisters' ecclesiastical debate was legitimate, citizens of the département of Calvados, indeed of all France, were most perturbed at the illegitimate goings-on they inferred. Wounds were already raw from the pedophile-priest scandals, and cynicism, a French *specialité de maison*, became more caustic.

But triumphant were the grilles. Almost no garbage in; almost no garbage out. There being no accusers but *La Croix*'s unnamed tipster, in half a year the brouhaha subsided. The internal evolution, however, was pregnant.

The reigning ideology at Lisieux was Alleviation of Suffering. (Alleviation of Suffering, of course and alas, which only led to that much more.) The nuns, kind souls that they—mostly—were, felt the suffering of their two sisters, High and Low, who between them embodied the feelings of most of the rest. They consequently discussed, voted on, and recommended two things:

1. That Mother Delia and Sister Aline be allowed to honor the love between them while continuing to explore the theological and ecclesiastical issues involved, and that, essentially, they keep their affair under their habits, so to speak, a "don't ask, don't tell" policy worthy of a divine institution. And

2. That Mother Delia seek surgical help to alleviate her physical suffering. This last was overtly directed at her ongoing back pain, and—covertly, understood but unmentioned—the difficulty her short arms created in wiping herself. Also therein, Delia thought, was an unspoken, perhaps completely unarticulated prejudice not so much against dwarfs but against asymmetry. It would be somehow better for the convent if she and Aline were more the same size.

12. Epilogue

Projection? Delia was instructed to undertake medical treatment for her condition. And while her chastity might be flexible, her inclination toward obedience was firm.

Delia spent much of the year before my "death" living in Baltimore at the International Center for Limb Lengthening and Reconstruction, with Aline at her bedside. My letters to Lisieux were forwarded to her, and, not wanting to frighten me, her answers were sent back to Lisieux, to be readdressed and sent to me. (Darn crafty, these Mother Superiors!) Chief of her medical team was a former student of Frank's, a Dr. Guthrie Bong, whose dog must have eaten most of his homework. For the third scandal was iatrogenic.

On the advice of Dr. Bong, Delia would start with normalizing her arms—a less difficult procedure than working on the legs because the bones were not so curved. She did all right with the huge fixators, ugly-looking metal spikes running through to humerus, radius, and ulna. It was an experimental kind of gamble, since this was surgery best done on preteens, and there she was, thirty-four.

But then came the infections, hospital bugs like Staph and Clostridium. "Nosocomial infections," they called them, and Delia thought of me. With infection, a serious turn in her condition, and four extra months of hospital stay on IV antibiotics.

She developed vascular compromise and wrist-drop, and could no longer draw—her major way besides prayer of passing the time. Dr. Bong tried using acupuncture to enhance the bone healing, but the response was poor. There was huge scarring. Arm mobility was decreased. And above all, when she was "done," she looked less acceptable than before.

Returning to Lisieux, she rebonded with Aline, yes, but even more so with her Amanita. For then, for the first time ever, she entertained thoughts of that great adventure, Death.

Quelle histoire! I sat in my chair during that hour's exposition, completely consumed. And then there was silence.

Delia extracted her bag from under her cloak on the floor. She had brought me a book—Camus's *La Peste* in the definitive Gallimard edition—and hesitatingly fetched out another present, no longer appropriate for an at-the-time still healthy me.

In a flower pot, contained in a large Tupperware container, was an adult *Amanita verna*, glistening greenish white. How she got it through security is beyond me.

"It's one of my poison mushrooms," she joked, "just for you."

"What's that about?" I asked.

"Well, I thought you might be in terminal agony, without any exit help from the moronic American medical establishment. But now that I know you're perfectly healthy . . ."

"You thought I would eat a Death Angel?"

Two saints, two triumphs, his and hers, so separate and yet so entwined.

Two assaults on the world prison, one from within and one from the far without.

Admittedly, The Nose might be happier than he is were he not also Alexei Pigov. He could at any point have claimed his real name, have taken off his mask, have come to terms with his self and the world, and perhaps have even married Delia, who, though now married to Christ, had always loved him so well.

Delia herself, successful as a prioress, might have had a limb-lengthening procedure, and perhaps a more sexually fulfilling life in the world. Or she might have become a rich and famous dwarf star, the next Meredith Eaton or Ajay Kumar.

But this, for each of them, would have been formulaic and cheap, appealing, perhaps, to the beach-book crowd but not to you, our fans, and not in service to the Truth, or to our Great Movement for Change.

I could have written a warmer, fuzzier, totally feel-good book and perhaps sold millions of copies to the self-helpless crowd. But no. With your perspicacity, you, our aficionados, Nosies and Plaguies alike, would see right through it. And Noseism would not still be growing.[90]

The fact is that both Alexei Pigov and Delia Robinson—like you—are cursed with strong beliefs in the possibility of goodness and truth. That is why we so respect them.

"I would have sautéed it up nice. Tasty. Lots of butter. A *soupçon* of garlic."

"But isn't Amanita a terrible death?"

"Hepatic coma, renal failure. You would have been out. Never known what hit you."

"But that's murder."

"No. It's assisted suicide. You would have fed it to yourself, with joyful anticipation of release."

She was going to kill me.

"No, thank you," I said. "I mean, we're not going to do it, but I don't believe in suicide anyway."

"You don't believe in suicide? Especially for those in a living hell?" Scornful disbelief.

She went into a long, passionate harangue about dignity, choice, and freedom. She wanted human control over the end of life. She talked of the noble notion of self-sacrifice and the Buddhist aspiration to annihilation. Suicide could be the ultimate act of magnanimity, she said, relieving others of the burden of one's burdensome life. Like me of hers.

Invasive she was, as ever. Intrusive. Dangerous. She wanted to kill me.

"You don't believe in suicide?" she demanded. "Tell it to Romeo and Juliet! Tell it to Anna Karenina or Emma Bovary! Tell it to Virginia Woolf!" And then for good measure, she pulled out the card she had lettered and inserted in the *Amanita*'s pot. "Tell it to Seneca!" she scolded, and tossed the card at me.

> Wherever you look, there is an end to your troubles. Do you see that precipice? That way you can descend to liberty. Do you see that sea, that river, that well? Liberty sits there in the depths. Do you see that tree, stunted, blighted, barren? Liberty hangs from its branches. Do you see your throat, your gullet, your heart? They are escape routes from slavery

"I wouldn't want to be a slave," she instructed.

"Why didn't you have some of your little white friend there?" I asked, handing her back her card, somewhat annoyed by her pushiness.

"Why? Because I'm too cowardly. I just can't bring myself to do it."

"Okay. I understand."

"But believe me," she continued, "if someone pushed me under a train, or shoved me out that window, I'd be . . ."

She paused.

"You wouldn't be anything," I noted. "You'd be dead."

"And *gratias agimus tibi,*" she said, I assumed to God, but perhaps to me.

We both sat in silence for a long while.

90. Here the reader of these annotations, knowing the actual story, is in a good position to evaluate the height and depth of Hundwasser's hypocrisies. Delia

And like you, they remained perplexed by a confused, meaningless, and fundamentally loathsome world. As Hobbes, the friend of Calvin, once observed, "It's hard to be religious when certain people are never incinerated by bolts of lightning." But like you, they carry on.

Delia was able to retreat from that world behind a grille and now runs a tight ship while making a significant contribution to art and letters. Alexei, whatever his facial problems, suffers most from a bruised memory. But you and I know: behind the goggles, those luminous eyes—those eyes that look as if they had come back from another world—those terrible eyes signal a heart enlarging like the sea. Through those eyes, you have learned to see the world.

Standard religion is for most of us an asymptotic, impossible path. God is just too difficult, the work too long even to begin Him, all Saint-saints except our own seem a gaggle of overhasty zealots, much like Deadheads or Phish phans, who want God immediately, if not sooner. And what if God actually loved one back?? God, Paphnutius has said, must be only a direction of love, and never its object.

When not with you, his loyal retainers, The Nose spends most of his time sulking. His idea of a good time is to sulk. Except for communicating with you all, sulking is the most joyous event in his life. Say what you like, such things happen—not often, but they do happen.

So keep his spirits up. Too much sulking deforms the heart. Keep the letters coming via FomiteBooks.com. Attach photos or links to your MySpace or Facebook pages. Support your home team, for where but here is your real home?

Contributions to keep the Nosemobile running may be sent via PayPal.

Refuse collaboration!

· Wm. F. Hundwasser

I note this conversation in detail to make a definitive record. Forensic.

I don't know what exactly did it—adrenaline, meditation, the unused mushroom . . . but Delia walked over to the window, opened it with her long arms—I thought to get some fresh air—and then simply vaulted herself over the sill and onto the walkway six floors below. She was no longer a slave.

That's the truth. That's the true story. I understand the DA's office needs to show off indictments to justify its funding. But you'd think that in New York, with its 800 murders a year, they would have better things to do than indict me for the suicide of a friend. Of course there was no evidence, and after smearing my name in the mud, they apologized and let it drop.

might have had a limb-lengthening procedure? It was just those lengthened limbs that vaulted her out my window. *The Nose* could have had a happy ending? It does, only one paragraph down!

"But no," the author asserts in a 19th-century melodramatic gesture, the back of his hand to his forehead. That "would have been formulaic and cheap." Instead of a happy ending then, with our post-modern and hip Hundwasser, Delia gets only to "make a significant contribution to arts and letters." Disgusting. The Nietzschean posturing, the stealing from Gogol—William F. Hundwasser poised there on the shoulders of the great like a flake of dandruff.

And as for the intricacies of my beliefs, the reader of these notes will know far more than Hundwasser could ever understand or, in his inimitable language, "use."

Actually, my notes are 30% of what they should be. They could be vastly expanded into more particular spheres—a consideration of the things done to and by me, an entire array of sociopolitical issues, the suffocating dimension of my Hundwasserian imprisonment, my metamorphoses in the face of my public: all this demands a more exhaustive and radical analysis. The real story—ai, ai, ai—what a tangled web we weave. . . . No wedding, no bedding, no *copula carnalis*.

But at least I'm back on Avenue C now, a more convivial place to . . . who knows what? Let Hundwasser live it up on Rodeo Drive—I wish him the joy of the worm. In this place of refuge—or exile—I will age. I will slowly enter Death. I now begin the stage of pretending-to-be-alive, still walking, still talking, occasionally having fun, but actually living only "toward Death," as another H. would say, toward its gradual realization.

I'm not dead yet—though no good deed goes unpunished. Laryngeal cancer is a cancer of the voice box, in my

case from incessantly speaking out and constant, long-term inhalation of latex. The larynx is my Adam's apple, and given the social pathology I've chosen to address, its metastasis is surely significant.

About 12,000 new cases of laryngeal cancer occur in the United States each year. And each year 4,000 die of the disease. Not bad odds. LC is 4.7 times more common in men than in women, and I am a man. Almost all men who develop LC are over 55. I am 57.

Laryngeal cancer develops slowly. While I'm not dead yet, I do have a persistent sore throat, slight pain when swallowing, frequent choking on food, persistent ear pain, and bad breath.

According to my treatment team, I'm stage two, possibly aspiring to stage three (out of four). That is, the cancer has not spread outside the larynx. Yet. But it's getting harder to speak.

My otolaryngologist is optimistic, my oncologist non-committal. I've had CAT scans and an MRI. Most frightening of all was a visit with a speech pathologist to discuss "various options for communication if the larynx is removed." The USA PATRIOT act has nothing on the inhuman smoothness of that sentence. Stage three and four LC is usually "treated" with total laryngectomy. When in doubt, cut it out. Not to mention a stoma in the neck for purposes of breathing. It would be nice *not* to proceed to stage three.

And that is why Delia—with all her herbs and vitamins, ayurvedic massages, acupressuring, cranio-sacral Reiki voodoo, special dietary recommendations, and spiritual practices—came to visit. God knows, none of that would have been covered by insurance.

Stage two aspiring to stage three. All predictions unpredictable. My only task from here on out is to with-

stand the pressure of existing, and not adopt the great world suicide as my own.

So unattractive—*moi.* But I am no longer interested in appealing—that emanation of expansion, above all of dominance. I see no value in dominating anyone. I'm no longer capable of—or even interested in—possessing someone else's biology. I'm just . . . an illness . . . contained in a complex, a large-snouted deviation who has no right to exist among normal human beings. My task—a struggle against centrifugal history, a struggle intent on fulfilling the promise of revolt—my task was unachievable. Beethoven wanted to write a mass that would fuse Christian ecstasis with Dionysiac frenzy, which would be beyond history, which would establish equilibrium between the metaphysical and the physical. He produced the *Missa Solemnis.* What have I produced? Death?

It is a phantom ship which has carried me thus far,[91]

91. BY WAY OF AN APPENDIX: THE NOSE AND ITS SEQUELAE

Hundwasser's novel, of course, was published, and made quite a splash. You may have heard the author reading it via Audible.com or iTunes. Fomite pushed it as a breakout book, and it spent, as you probably know, several months on the *New York Times* best-seller list. The book was reviewed, sometimes condescendingly, sometimes ecstatically, in all the major dailies and Sunday book sections and in most of the national magazines, glossy and otherwise; it was also extensively discussed on the literary blog scene. The subsequent Naugahyde-bound red-print edition and *The Sayings of Paphnutius* also did famously.

Hundwasser was jubilant, Alexei amused. *I'm Not Dead Yet, Quack!* brought an approximation of the work to the screen for the less-than-literate, and a good deal more money into Able Ibis Ltd. It was a sleeper film whose attendance grew with its notoriety, and vice versa: for a long while, it was among the ten most frequently rented films on Netflix. Last, but far from least, it spawned the *Rocky Horror* copycat midnight events, which soon eclipsed their ancestor in frequency, attendance, box office, and bedlam. For them, the Coen Brothers film was licensed to be shown, karaoke-style, without sound, its drama staged instead by multiple impersonators, variously costumed, who spoke the memorized text and sang the songs with freshness and verve.

Did Alexei believe the words he spouted and the doctrines he espoused? Did he believe them after the hundredth time, the five hundredth?

He did, and he didn't. Which is to say that while he thought his and Hundwasser's critique basically valid, he became discouraged at the lack of social and political traction his groups were able to attain. Looniesonleave.org, thefewtheproudthepsychotic.com, left few world-altering traces. The nososphere was one of small diameter. Cultural weight it had, yes, but culture is a fickle dame whose moving finger, having writ, moves on. The website hits began to decline, club memberships were not renewed, and many "please remove me from your list"s arrived by e-mail.

So, as Alexei relates, Hundwasser suffered another stroke of marketing genius and planned for Paphnutius to die, slowly, publicly, his death covered in detail in Flash videos all over the net—especially if the Coen brothers declined a sequel, which they did. The trope would save money too, on travel. The teaser was that perhaps, in his final throes, Paphnutius would take off his mask, reveal his true face. But of course that never happened. The "doctor, heal thyself" theme also provided some suspense, as the saintly victim each week tried neo–New Age approaches to differential diagnosis and treatment. The reader may have been aware of all this.

The website hits did go up as the hypochondriac and iatrophobic communities joined the declining coalition of the faithful. But they soon peaked and plateaued as little medical progress was achieved, and the website advertisers began to lose interest, and new money stopped rolling in. Hundwasser and Alexei had enough from royalties and residuals to set them up for life. Well, Alexei did. If necessary, depending on his spending, Hundwasser could always become a lab tech again.

The belief question, however, is still unanswered. His "death" was a diverting interlude for Paphnutius, but even the greatest truths become mechanical or threadbare at the thousandth repetition. One doubts one's own words, even if they are the famous last ones. So in a certain way, Alexei's fictional death was deeply authentic, and he felt himself not so much a cheat as a valid metaphor.

Delia's letter remained unread.

The comma ending Alexei's note 90 may be a typo. I tried to check using our regular e-mail routine but had no answers to six messages in the course of a month. On January 22, 2006, I received the following communication from Mailer-Daemon@email-delivery.infotrac-custom.com:

> The original message was received at Thu, 21 Jan 2006
> 04:29:15-0600 (EST)
> from ibis.mail.nas.earthlink.net [207.236.120.22]
>
> —The following addresses had permanent fatal errors—
> <apig05@earthlink.net>
> —Transcript of session follows—
> bad block
> Abort—core dumped

There is a certain baleful poetry in these cryptic lines. A check of the municipal hospitals and morgues led nowhere. Neither Alexei's oncologist nor his surgeon would give out any medical information: patient confidentiality. Such must be my last editorial whimper before publication.

· M. E.

Acknowledgments

Unbridled thanks to Fred Ramey and the rest of the Unbridled gang for believing in this project, and helping me wrestle the beast to the ground. To Fred, especially, for leading me, lantern and crook in hand, through the forests of plausible diegesis, and to Claire Vaccaro for so beautifully figuring the layout and design.

Thanks, too, to the *dediquee* (though there seems to be no such word), for the inspiration of his life and his long friendship, and to all the old friends whose names I've filched as my way of belated hello.

And *mille grazie* to Ronnie Davis for allowing me the use of his San Francisco Mime Troupe materials, and to my family medico-literary advisors and close relatives, Mario and Phil Trabulsy. A special thanks to Izabel Parker-Estrin and her progenitors for turning my attention to left-hand string technique (it has improved my own), to the wonderful women of Pax Christi, with whom I vigil every weekday, for their lowdown on convent procedure and practice, and to Karl Schwartz for his many accordion deeds and acts.

I can't say how much fun it's been collaborating with my once- and current-sister-in-law, Delia Robinson, on the overall conception of the book, its artwork, and its ancillary pugmarks and droppings.

Finally, as ever, thanks to my faithful helpmeet, wife, and companion, Donna, without whom . . .

· ME